A SHOP GIRL IN BATH

Hardworking and whip-smart, Elizabeth Pennington is the rightful heir of Bath's premier department store — but her father, Edward Pennington, believes his daughter lacks the business acumen to run his empire. He is resolute that a man will succeed him.

Determined to break from her father's hold and prove she is worthy of inheriting Pennington's, Elizabeth forms an unlikely alliance with ambitious and charismatic master glove-maker Joseph Carter. They have the same goal: bring Pennington's into a new decade while embracing woman's equality and progression. But, despite their best intentions, it is almost impossible not to mix business and pleasure . . .

Can the two thwart Edward Pennington's plans for the store? Or will Edward prove himself an unshakeable force who will ultimately ruin both Elizabeth and Joseph?

RACHEL BRIMBLE

◆

A
SHOP GIRL
IN BATH

Complete and Unabridged

MAGNA
Leicester

First published in Great Britain in 2018 by
Aria,
an imprint of Head of Zeus Ltd
London

First Ulverscroft Edition
published 2021
by arrangement with
Head of Zeus Ltd
London

A catalogue record for this book is available
from the British Library.

ISBN 978–0–7505–4893–9

Published by
Ulverscroft Limited
Anstey, Leicestershire

Printed and bound in Great Britain by
TJ Books Ltd., Padstow, Cornwall

This book is printed on acid-free paper

This book is dedicated to all the wonderful ladies of the Romantic Novelists Association's Bath and Wiltshire chapter for the amazing and endless support you gave me during the writing of *A Shop Girl in Bath* and beyond.

Every one of you is so important to me, and I'm sure I would've given up writing several times over without your endless encouragement, laughter and smiles. This one's for you!

1

City of Bath — January 1910

Elizabeth Pennington turned off the final light in the ladies' department of Pennington's Department Store and wandered through the semi-darkness to the window. She stared at Bath's premier shopping street below. Christmas had passed three weeks before, and all the excitement and possibilities of the New Year beckoned.

Nineteen ten.

Even the year held the ring of a new beginning. A new start for something bigger and better. Yet, how could she revel in any possible excitement when her plans to advance her position within the store were still halted by her father? She crossed her arms as, once again, her frustration mounted. Would this be yet another year where she remained static? Her father holding her caged and controlled?

As the only child born to Edward and Helena Pennington, Elizabeth had been a happy child under her mother's care, home-schooled by a governess, before being launched into society. Yet, the balls and teas, at home visits and theatre, had soon grown tiresome and she had longed to accompany her father on his days at work.

Edward Pennington, amused by his daughter's emerging passion for all things retail, had consented to her coming along whenever possible, teaching her the basics of merchandising and marketing, allowing

1

her to serve as a shop girl.

A role that had satisfied Elizabeth for a while . . .

Until, in 1906, her father had opened the largest department store fashionable Edwardian Bath had ever seen. From the moment she'd stepped into its sparkling, breath-taking foyer, Elizabeth would not be shaken from working as the head of the new ladies' department.

Having finally won her father's agreement two years ago, she'd launched herself into the role with determination and commitment, proving her worth through steadily increasing sales, footfall and morale amongst her staff.

Now, she wanted more . . . *deserved* more.

Elizabeth breathed in deeply as she stared at the hatted men and women who streamed back and forth on the busy street; the trams slowing to pick up or allow passengers to disembark. How many of these women had she dressed and accessorised? How many had she helped to spend their father's or husband's money? Did they, too, long to stand tall and proud and spend their own earnings, from their own success?

Although Bath was still only a small-scale industrial city, it was identified by its social elite. A city that was a bustling oasis of the firmly established upper class, but also a newly emerging middle class. It was these people that Elizabeth grew more and more determined to entice through Pennington's doors, thus demolishing its reputation of being a place where only the moneyed belonged.

She turned from the window. Twenty-four years old and still she had nothing to call her own, nothing to hold onto as evidence of her enthusiasm, vision and skill. If her father's belief stood that women had no true place in business, why introduce her to retail's excitement and possibility? Why pretend she was even needed at Pennington's?

The entire country hummed with the underlying fever of women's progression. The right to vote was on the minds and lips of the majority of women who frequented the store, teashops and boutiques. How could her father continue to ignore such impassioned determination? Women were finally making a stand and, sooner or later, Edward Pennington would have to admit defeat or risk losing the very gender that made up the bigger ratio of his profits.

Time and again, Elizabeth suspected his employment of her had been nothing more than a way to control her wilfulness. A calculated plan, allowing him to witness her predicted failure in order to be proved correct in his view that women were little more than vessels in which to bear children.

Tears of frustration pricked her eyes and Elizabeth swiped at the them as she strode from the department and into the main corridor, battling the debilitating fear that her father's treatment of her might one day force her to take her life . . . as it had her mother.

Helena Pennington had once been a beautiful, intelligent and gregarious socialite. A woman wanted by men and emulated by women. Her deep red hair and startling green eyes were revered throughout her social circles. The way Helena raised her only child, teaching Elizabeth about compassion, love and empathy, as well as enjoying her daughter's happiness to work beside her father, had been something admired, rather than frowned upon.

But as close as Elizabeth had thought she and her

mother were, Helena hadn't the strength to fight her husband's continuous disparagement, verbal torment and disdain.

Not even for her only child.

For a long time, Elizabeth had struggled to forgive her mother for leaving her alone with Edward but, four years on, she understood her mother's desperation and had entirely acquitted her. After all, her mother's death had given Elizabeth the resentment and passion needed to fight every inch of her father's dominance.

She walked to the gleaming white balustrade surrounding the circumference of the second floor and gripped its mahogany rail. Pennington's magnificence showed in every crystal chandelier, every glass cabinet and every luxury item on display. It was all there for the public to crave, aspire to own and want more than anything else.

The few remaining staff tidied and organised their stations before leaving for the day. No doubt going home to family, or maybe for a meal or drink with friends . . . maybe even lovers. Whereas she would remain here, waiting to be escorted home by her father.

The great Edward Pennington.

How much longer could she go on doing his bidding, adhering to his rules and expectations when deep in her heart she wanted so much to spread her wings? To show him who she was and what she could achieve for him and the store.

She had to speak to him. Had to make him listen.

Lifting her chin, Elizabeth headed for the grand staircase that spiralled from the lower to the upper floors of Pennington's breathtaking atrium. One by

4

one the dazzling lights were extinguished, the lit glass counters and extravagant displays of merchandise plunged into darkness. Pride swelled her chest as she climbed the stairs towards the top floor.

Before her father had opened this mammoth store, nobody had seen the likes of Pennington's outside of London, but Edward had successfully brought the glamour and enticement to Bath. Anyone who was anyone wanted to be seen here. Aristocrats and gentry, bankers and lawyers, actors and performers. They all came to Pennington's to shop. To depart with their purchases in the store's exclusive black and white bags. A rare idea of Elizabeth's that her father had taken onboard. A unified logo that worked as a walking advertisement as soon as paying customers left the store.

An idea he had eventually taken credit for himself.

She reached the upper floor and almost bumped into Mrs Chadwick, her father's ever-admiring secretary, at the top of the stairs. 'Good evening, Mrs Chadwick.'

'Ah, Miss Pennington.' Mrs Chadwick smoothed the grey curls from her brow and pushed up her spectacles. 'I believe your father is still in his office.'

'Thank you. You have a lovely evening.'

'I will. You too, Miss Pennington.'

Elizabeth continued her sure-footed journey to her father's closed office door. Tonight, he would listen to her. Tonight, he would not provoke her self-doubt. She was worth more than her singular role as head of the ladies' department. She wanted to shake up the men's department, too and inject a renewed energy into the toy department. To her mind, both current department heads had become stuck in their ways, in

5

much the same vein as her father. If Pennington's had any chance of remaining the consumers' number one choice of where to shop, the store had to move with the times and the demands of the people.

Inhaling a strengthening breath, she lifted her hand and knocked on the door.

'Come.'

Gripping the handle, Elizabeth entered the monster's lair.

Her father sat behind his huge walnut desk, his silver-haired head bowed over some papers, his usual early evening whisky within hand's reach.

Elizabeth crossed the plush sapphire-blue carpet and sat in one of the two chairs in front of his desk. 'Good evening, Papa.'

He raised his steely gaze to hers. 'Elizabeth. Did we not agree to meet at six thirty? I'm still finishing off a few things.'

'We did, but I was hoping . . . ' She briefly closed her eyes and straightened her spine. 'I want to speak to you about some new id — '

'Not again.' Her father slapped his pen to his desk and glared. 'My decision still stands. You made the trip to London and Selfridges against my wishes. Now you return with a plethora of new-fangled ideas. I will not stand for you — '

'Using my imagination?' Elizabeth glared, her frustration sparking her rare interruption. 'Wanting to make something more of myself than just being your daughter?'

He leaned back, the anger in his eyes cooling to malice. 'You are my daughter, Elizabeth. Lord knows, I wish you were my son, but there we have it. I have a daughter. A single daughter.'

'As you so often like to remind me.' Elizabeth ignored the tell-tale increase of her pulse. She would not falter. 'I want to push forward in the world. Prove to you and myself that I wasn't destined to spend my days overseeing the ladies' department while waiting for a rich gentleman to whisk me off my feet. I want — '

'More than I'm prepared to give you.'

'America is leading the way in retail and department stores. Their success is well ahead of Britain. We'd be foolish to stand by and allow that to continue without challenge.'

He huffed a laugh. 'And what would you know of America? You barely move from the house to the store. You refuse invitations to balls and soirees. You turn your back on potential suitors as though each of them is beneath you.'

'I do no such thing.'

'No?' He arched an eyebrow and put his forearms on the desk. 'Then when did you last attend any kind of social event? What is it you are so afraid of, my dear? Do you think a man might advance on you? Make you think about more than how you wish you could bury your father and take everything he's built. Is that it?'

Heat rose in Elizabeth's cheeks as her father's glare bore into her soul, making her tremble. Damn him and how inferior he could make her feel with a single look. Damn him for how he continually made her aware of her female status.

She leaned forward. 'Why would I want to be with a man when I have you and your senior staff as examples? I want more, Papa and, one way or another, I'll have it.'

7

'Is this where you tell me again we need to concentrate on the middle class? That they are the customers who could make up our primary market?'

'As a matter of fact, yes. More and more people are moving up in society through hard work, opportunity and determination. Pennington's needs to give them what they demand, or someone else will.'

'And you see their demands as what exactly? I refuse to have my store brought down to the level of the common herd. Pennington's caters to the carriage trade. What would you have me do, Elizabeth? Sell alcohol? Fish?' He huffed a derisory laugh. 'Heavens above, girl, what is wrong with you?'

Elizabeth inwardly cursed the shaking in her hands as she clasped them in her lap. 'Whether you like it or not, people are coming up in the world. Women are demanding more rights, a voice and equal respect that is given so freely to men. Do you not think there is potential in providing these women affordable merchandise? Harnessing their desires? Making Pennington's a place they come for their clothes, scent and jewellery will be a boon for us. Why are you being so short-sighted about this?'

'What absolute nonsense.'

Elizabeth leaned forward and glared. 'And what of the shop girls?'

'What about them?'

'They are dedicated, loyal and work extremely hard. We should implement a staff afternoon tea break. They work near ten-hour days. Would it be such a sacrifice to introduce a twenty-minute break in the afternoon?'

His eyes widened in disbelief. 'In addition to their lunch hour?'

8

'Yes. Looking after their welfare will benefit us in the long term.'

'Their welfare?' He picked up his drink and took a hefty gulp. 'Their welfare comes in the form of their wages. If they do not like working here, they're at liberty to leave. There are plenty of other young women who would be only too glad to work at Pennington's. Our reputation —'

'Is in dire risk of being tainted.'

His jaw tightened. 'I think it best we draw this conversation to a close, don't you? Why don't you take a carriage back to the house?' He put down his drink and pulled some papers towards him. 'I will see you at dinner with Mr Kelston and his parents this evening.'

'I assume this dinner is yet another ruse to convince me that the man whose marriage proposal you are so insistent I accept is worthy? That I should give up my work here, marry and stay at home like an obedient wife?'

'You are twenty-four, Elizabeth.' He raised his head. 'Your hair will not always be as red at it is, or your skin so unmarked. God knows, your mother's looks faded soon enough.'

Anger shot through her. 'Do not speak of Mama that way.'

He smiled. 'How much longer do you think a man will even consider you for his wife? Noel Kelston is a good man, a hard-working man. A man who —'

'Will inherit a railway fortune that his father worked for. I do not want such a man. I want a man who strives for his own living, his own ambitions and desires.'

'Yet, time and again you do your utmost to convince me to hand everything to you the minute I retire.'

'As you would have if I had been a son. How

9

hard do I have to work to prove myself to you? How long do I have to run the ladies' department before you see I am worthy of so much more? Sales, footfall and morale continue to rise under my management. Can you not see that I am more than capable of extending my skills through the store? I want more, Papa. You know I do.'

His cheeks mottled. 'And you think overseeing an additional department or implementation of your ideas will give you happiness?'

'I would at least like the opportunity to find out. What else can I believe? Mama's death showed me all too clearly that a woman's happiness cannot be found with a man, a home and marriage. To work and work hard is my only option for fulfilment. Anything else would either scar or kill me. Unfortunately for you, Papa, I'm not prepared to take that risk.'

His eyes narrowed. 'You are a woman with ideas above her station and I'll be damned if I'll have my peers joking and jeering behind my back that my daughter persuaded me to allow her to run this store. You will marry, Elizabeth. That is your role. If you are not careful, you won't work here at all.'

Frustration brought Elizabeth to her feet and she clutched her purse tightly. 'Do you not see it is your attitude that made me who I am today? Your insinuation that I'll never achieve what a man could has only driven me harder and harder into retail. Maybe if you had believed in my abilities years ago, I might have given up the idea of working here and gone on to become the wife you so desperately want me to be.' She shook her head, her heart beating fast. 'But not anymore, Papa. I've invested too much of myself into the store to ever let it go.'

'Fine.'

'Sorry?' The breath left her lungs. 'Did you say fine?'

A gleam came into his eyes and he sneered. 'Marry Noel and let him decide whether you continue to work. If you think my views antiquated, why not find out how a husband sees them?'

Sickness clutched her stomach as familiar hopelessness pressed down on her. 'Noel is fifteen years older than me. His views are not so different to yours and, as you've implied, our family business will be more his than mine, should we marry. Why would he not do exactly as you demand?'

He looked back to his work. 'I'm not listening to any more of this. I will see you at home shortly.'

Elizabeth glared at his bowed head. How could he continue to do this to her? How could she surrender to the life he'd given her mother — the death he'd given her? Suffocation squeezed at her throat and she stormed from his office.

Firmly closing the door behind her, she stood stock-still and concentrated on levelling her breathing. Was all she had to look forward to was living with a man who would eventually destroy her? Be that her husband or her father.

Their turbulent relationship weighed heavier and heavier.

He had recently turned sixty and embarked on a pastime of taking lovers thirty years his junior — an insult to Elizabeth and her beloved mother, barely four years dead. The women he paraded in front of Elizabeth, as though he did nothing wrong, varied in hair colour and wealth, but all were malleable and admiring, subservient to her father's every wish.

11

Not that their amicability kept them with him for more than a few weeks at a time.

Women, after all, were entirely dispensable according to Edward Pennington.

Stepping away from her father's office door, Elizabeth strode along the dark, wood-panelled corridor towards the lift; the lit ornate wall sconces flickering. She met the lift attendant's gaze. 'Ground floor please, Henry.'

'Yes, Miss Pennington.'

Elizabeth stepped inside. She refused to falter. Something would inspire her any day now. It *had* to.

2

Joseph Carter smoothed his tie, happy with his reflection in the spotted mirror at the rear of the family milliners and glove boutique. Smart. Professional. Confident.

He faced his father. 'What do you think?'

Robert Carter barely glanced from the felt on the workbench in front of him, his half-spectacles halfway down his nose. 'You'll do.'

Joseph smiled. 'If Pennington's agree to acquire my gloves, it will provide the extra income we need that will enable you to finally retire. I'm not doing this for Pennington's, as you seem to believe. I'm doing it for us. For you. You deserve to spend some time doing the things you enjoy, Pa. We can stop making hats and just concentrate on our gloves. If we have Pennington's backing, who knows how good our future could be.'

His father's blue gaze darkened with concern. 'That may be, but you shouldn't have to sell your soul to that place.'

'My soul will remain my own. Department stores are the future.' Joseph took his hat from the stand, struggling to not give in to his exasperation. 'It will benefit us if we get on board with them. Think of the exposure. The number of new customers who will discover the Carter & Son name.'

'But at what cost?' His father shook his head. 'Working yourself into the ground won't make you happy, Joseph. I curse the day you lost Lillian, but how much longer will you go on living alone? Working hour after hour?'

Pain struck at Joseph's chest and he glared. 'I didn't lose Lillian. My wife was murdered at the hand of the bastard who stabbed her.'

'If only you believed that.'

Joseph held his father's saddened gaze, his pulse thumping. 'I do.'

'You do not. You believe her death was your fault. That you deserve to live forever as a single man, to know no other happiness than monetary. Living this way cannot be all there is for you.'

'It's all I want.' Joseph tugged his lapels, straightening his suit jacket. 'If I had been with Lillian that night, she'd still be alive. I owe it to her to make a success of our business. To build the means to help others as she would have wanted. If Pennington's provides the source of that income, I'm going to accept it without apology.'

'Right, and she would've wanted you to devote your life only to the business? To live the rest of your life unmarried? Without the children you both wanted? Those wants and dreams don't disappear, Joseph. You're hurting and hiding behind your ambitions. You're not going to be happy until — '

'Her killer is found, I know. Don't you think that's something I pray for every damn day?'

His father held his gaze, his cheeks mottled. 'That wasn't what I was going to say.'

'No?' Anger swirled in Joseph's gut and he glared. 'Well, what else is there to say? All the time that low life's still out there, I won't be happy. While he walks free, Lillian's murder goes unpunished.'

'It's been two years, son. Two years. The chances

14

of finding him grow smaller every day. You've tried offering rewards, walked the streets and spoken with constabulary over and over again to no avail. What else can you do? You have to start filling your life with more than vengeance and hatred. Otherwise, it won't just be Lillian dead, it will be you, too. Inside.'

Joseph put on his hat, his hand shaking. He needed to change the subject before his temper rose any more. 'Look, men and women everywhere are looking for speed and convenience. They're looking to impress their friends and neighbours, without waiting for their wares to be made. That's what Pennington's is all about. Providing an instant service where their clientele can see and touch the products before they've parted with a penny. It's shopping genius, regardless of whether you agree with it or not. I have to be a part of it if I am going to implement Lillian's dreams of helping those less fortunate. That's all I'm concentrating on right now.'

His father lifted his hands from his worktop and held them aloft in a gesture of surrender. 'Fine. Do what you have to do but, mark my words, there is more out there for you than work, and it's no less than you deserve. Just go. I've got hats to make and it wouldn't do to keep the uppity lot at that department store waiting.'

Joseph stared at his father's silver hair and stooped shoulders, sadness squeezing his heart. 'I'll see you later.'

'That you will.'

Leaving the shop, Joseph breathed in the smoky air as he walked along Pulteney Bridge, passing the rows of shops either side. Clouds rolled in as the January sky above Bath darkened, threatening another

15

rainy afternoon. Picking up his pace, Joseph joined the people heading towards the city centre, the scent of rosewater and pomade infusing his nostrils.

He studied the suited men and women making their way back to offices and shops at the end of their lunch breaks. The timing of his visit to Pennington's was intentional. It was after the morning's shoppers had bought their daily wares, but before upper-class ladies emerged from their homes to take afternoon tea in the store's fancy restaurant. Joseph wanted as few people as possible to witness his potential snubbing. He took a risk by putting himself forward as a supplier to such an enormous store, but ambition had overridden any lingering doubts that he might not be taking the right course of action.

The Carter family business could no longer go on as it had. His father was tired and deserved to hang up his scissors and needle. Things needed to change, and Joseph was on the cusp of making those changes. *His* changes. His beloved wife had understood his need for more. Had understood his burning desire to take them from merely existing to thriving. He might have been born to working-class roots, but he refused to be permanently entangled in poverty's vines.

But Lillian was dead, and her loss haunted him. He would not stop until he'd achieved what they'd set out to do together. Success. The ability and funds to help others. To open the locked doors of opportunity to the poor.

He would make it happen. For him. And for her.

It had been soon into their brief and passionate courtship that Joseph had recognised Lillian's hunger to do more. Her kindness and empathy with those less fortunate as natural to her as her beautiful blonde tresses and pretty pink lips.

In the eighteen months they'd been married, he and Lillian had devised a plan for the business and a way to help those struggling. Through hard work, frequent laughter and individual sacrifice, they had worked with his father to produce hats and gloves that quickly became admired amongst the classes. Slowly, but surely, with the added bonus of Lillian's exemplary selling tactics and charm, profits had grown, giving them the extra money needed to provide food and blankets to the homeless and struggling. Living a better, more giving life, had been all they'd wanted.

And children.

Joseph clenched his jaw against the stinging in his eyes.

He was certain that they would've been blessed eventually. Regret clenched around his heart. Now, he'd never know . . .

Joseph slowed to a stop.

Pennington's stood in all its glory near the top of Milsom Street. A huge white stone building with twin entrance columns covering the width of what had once been four boutique shops. Pennington's now owned them all, and at its grand opening ceremony, a five-storey upwards extension was revealed, thus creating the largest and most prestigious store in the city.

It was where Joseph intended his designs to shine, where he dreamed his gloves would be displayed in a way that had been impossible before Pennington's arrival. Once the masses began to buy his designs, the Carter & Son income would soar, and Joseph would finally be able to make the tangible difference he and Lillian coveted.

Her death strengthened his determination that

today would go well. Despite his father's protestations, Joseph knew he deserved to live his life alone for failing to protect her. For choosing to solve a work problem on that fatal night, rather than accompanying her on their rounds as he usually had. Only belief that he had something of value to offer the world would go any way towards stemming the bleeding deep inside his heart.

Studying the displays in Pennington's large plate-glass windows, Joseph cast his gaze over the rolls of satin, silk, cotton and velvet. White, ivory and cream were interspersed with shots of dark, daring fuchsia artfully swathed over tables, dressers and boxes. Brooches and pearls, necklaces and cuffs flashed and sparkled amongst an abundance of hats and gloves he considered of a mediocre standard at best.

It was time to show Pennington's what affordable craftsmanship was all about.

Stepping back, Joseph touched the brim of his hat, allowing three giggling young ladies to enter the store ahead of him. They hesitated, their eyes brightening with interest and their cheeks colouring faintly as they studied him.

Joseph met their gazes with confidence and tipped his hat. 'Ladies.'

They emitted a trio of delicate sighs before dipping their heads and entering Pennington's fantastic foyer, their arms intertwined as they chattered to each other at a speed that would make a man's head spin.

He followed them inside and the smell of money mingled with expensive scent and sweetness from the abundance of flower displays. Tall white columns stood sentry on either side of the entrances to the various departments, while the central atrium was breathtaking in gold and marble.

It was vital to his success that he understood every part of what the store had to offer its customers. Pennington's was a rising commodity. One he didn't doubt had the potential to expand around the globe, and he would absorb its every lesson and merge them with his own until Carter & Son was the name on every woman's lips.

He fought to keep his face impassive and not let his awe show in his manner or expression. He could not afford to reveal how much Pennington's inspired and intimidated him in equal measure. He deserved to be here. He deserved to have the store consider his product.

For as far as the eye could see, marble shone and crystal sparkled. Glass-fronted counters displayed goods designed to entice and delight. Young, slender and impeccably uniformed shop girls stood at attention behind or in front of their counters, perfectly coiffed hair and delicately applied cosmetics enhancing their beauty and allure.

He approached a board in front of two handsome elevators, their doors painted gold and opulent enough to be at home in Buckingham Palace.

The ladies' department was on the second floor.

The elevator doors opened, and the young uniformed attendant nodded at Joseph. 'Going up, sir?'

'Indeed, I am, young man. The ladies' department, if you please.'

'Certainly, sir.'

Joseph stepped inside the lift, removed his hat and gripped it tightly in front of him. Rare nerves leapt in his stomach. He wanted Pennington's to commission him as soon as humanly possible. It was one thing that he'd managed to pull himself from the drink-induced, self-loathing gutter he'd wallowed in for a year after Lillian was killed, another if he slipped back into the abyss. Pennington's had the potential to inject fire in him for a future he never would have imagined before the store opened.

He exhaled a slow breath. He was the last of the Carter line and there was no chance of him departing this world without making his mark.

The lift pinged, the doors brushed open and Joseph stepped confidently onto the second floor.

3

Stepping from her office at the rear of the ladies' department, Elizabeth strode onto the floor and abruptly stopped. The gentleman stood with his back to her as he spoke with Aveline Woolden, the deputy head of the department.

Therefore, it could only be the breadth of his shoulders and his impressive height that caused her hesitation. Or perhaps it was the shine of his dark brown hair, curling over his snow-white collar beneath a suit of maybe not the best quality, but most certainly handsomely tailored.

Whatever it was, Elizabeth's feet refused to move.

'I've many designs I would like the opportunity to share with Miss Pennington. I truly believe they will be an asset for the department and Pennington's as a whole.' His voice was deep and unnervingly commanding. 'I am happy to wait if Miss Pennington is —'

'Good afternoon, sir.' Gathering her wits, Elizabeth stepped forward. 'You wish to speak with me?'

He turned. An immediate startle lit his bright blue eyes before they darkened with interest and then changed again with what looked to be sorrow. As though he constantly carried an invisible pain. Yet, despite her concern, something indiscernible struck Elizabeth about this man. She couldn't let him leave without finding out who he was and where he'd come from.

She held out her hand. 'Elizabeth Pennington.'

He blinked, as though collecting himself, before dipping his head. 'Miss Pennington.' He took her hand. 'A pleasure. Joseph Carter, at your service.'

A strange connection with this man bubbled inside her as Elizabeth eased her hand from his grasp and laced her fingers together in front of her. 'I couldn't help overhearing your conversation with Mrs Woolden. You are a designer?'

'I am.' He held her gaze, determination darkening his eyes as he stood a little taller. 'I would very much like the opportunity to share some of my gloves with you.'

'For?'

'For your possible consideration of adding them to your displays. I will take no more than a few minutes of your time.' His gaze softened. 'I assure you.'

Despite the interest this stranger ignited inside her, Elizabeth lifted her chin. The man clearly deemed himself as important to her success as every other male within Pennington's walls. Only this one wanted something from her, not the other way around.

She crossed her arms, enjoying the rare power. 'You have some designs with you?'

'I do.' He lifted a brown case from the floor beside him and tilted his head to the sketchpad beneath his arm. 'If we might move to the counter, I'll — '

'Have you supplied to a store of this size before, Mr Carter?'

'No, but — '

'Do you have a significant-size business?'

The gleam in his eyes vanished. 'We have a moderately-sized workroom in the back and the shop itself. Why do you ask?'

'Say I like your designs and decide to give them a

trial run, you'll be expected to supply quickly and in large numbers. If that's not possible, I'm afraid we are wasting our time.'

He held her gaze. 'I will meet any, and *all*, of your demands.'

Elizabeth's heart jolted. His quick response had sounded loaded with innuendo. Did he think he could mock her? She pulled back her shoulders. 'You are a man with ambition? Someone who wants to be a part of something new and revolutionary?'

'I am.'

Ignoring the flutter of the potential prospect she sensed in Joseph Carter, Elizabeth drew her gaze over his face. He really was extraordinarily handsome. She could not imagine anyone wouldn't be tempted to buy from this man — male or female. 'And do you enjoy the sales side of business?'

'Very much so, but it would be dishonest of me not to admit that designing and making gloves is my passion.'

There was a fine line between confidence and conceit, but the way Mr Carter described his ambition made it very hard to be certain whether or not he crossed that line. Her fascination and curiosity piqued, she turned to Mrs Woolden. 'Maybe you can check Mr Carter's testimonials and we will decide on a time and date for a meeting. My diary is on my desk.' She smiled at Mr Carter. 'I'll leave you with Mrs Woolden.' She offered her hand. 'It was nice to meet you.'

His eyes glittered with interest as he slowly enveloped her hand in fingers that were strong and slightly work-roughened. 'I look forward to meeting with you again soon.'

23

Elizabeth's heart quickened as her smile wavered. This man evoked an extremely unwelcome self-awareness. She slipped her hand from his and nodded, before exiting the department.

Stepping towards the staircase, she gripped the banister and descended the stairs. Anticipation fluttered in her stomach and her mouth itched to smile.

Joseph Carter had an aura of dangerous excitement that would be irresistible to men and women alike. His handsome face, extraordinary eyes and easy smile surely marked him out as the perfect salesman. His designs were something she was willing to consider, but her instinct told her Mr Carter would benefit Pennington's on the shop floor more than he would working at his own premises.

Glove maker he might be at present, but who knew what the future might hold for someone as charismatic, and clearly driven, as Mr Joseph Carter?

She pressed her hand to her stomach, more than happy to be the one to find out.

* * *

'I assume you have testimonials as per Miss Pennington's request?'

Joseph dragged his gaze from the archway through which Elizabeth Pennington had disappeared and faced Mrs Woolden.

The green of Elizabeth Pennington's eyes and the deep, dark red of her hair lingered in Joseph's mind and he swallowed against the undeniable stir of attraction. What in God's name just happened? He was here to push forth with his plans, but his sensibilities had been shot astray by a beautiful woman.

24

Something that hadn't happened since he'd last set eyes on Lillian.

'Indeed, I do.' Joseph pushed away his guilt and hastily drew some papers from his inside jacket pocket. He held them towards Mrs Woolden. 'I have produced work for many women of quality, who are willing to vouch for me. Not to mention one or two gentry.'

Mrs Woolden glanced at the papers, her brown eyes softening. 'That may well be so, Mr Carter, but Miss Pennington isn't the sort of woman to be unduly impressed by credentials . . . ' She raised her eyebrows. 'Or male charm.'

'Male charm?' Joseph huffed a laugh. 'I assure you I am here to propose a unity between myself and Miss Pennington that will be of benefit to us both.'

'I'm sure you are.' She folded the credentials. 'I see your address is clearly marked on the papers. Once myself and Miss Pennington have had a chance to consider your testimonials, and consulted our diaries, we'll be in touch regarding a meeting.'

Joseph tried to assess what Mrs Woolden needed to hear from him to muster a little more of her enthusiasm. He had sensed Miss Pennington's faith in her deputy and he didn't doubt that one wrong move and a meeting between them would never be scheduled. He couldn't allow that to happen.

However, for the time being, he had no choice but to bide his time. There was no way he would fail in having Pennington's buy his gloves.

He firmly clasped Mrs Woolden's hand. 'I thank you, ma'am.'

As he walked from the department, Joseph hesitated, reluctant to leave the store altogether. Ever since

Pennington's had opened, a strong sense of belonging overcame him each and every time he stepped inside. He'd be foolish to ignore or squander the chance to linger a while longer. Talk to the staff and have them remember his face and name.

His father might be reluctant to encourage his son's ambitions, but Joseph didn't need his father's approval to understand that, in this newly emerging world of consumption and greed, it was eat or be eaten. Customers wanted a different kind of shop and a different kind of shopkeeper. Pennington's, he was certain, was just the beginning of what would become a worldwide change.

If he could have his designs displayed and sold here, it would be the first step towards achieving his and Lillian's most ardent ambitions. Failure was simply not an option.

If he was granted a meeting with Miss Pennington, he needed to be ready and prepared with a deep knowledge and passion for the store. Not to mention the possibility his designs and vision might mean for Pennington's.

Moving from department to department, Joseph carefully watched the shop girls and the way they interacted with the clientele and, in turn, noted the customers' varying responses. The ladies and gentlemen who wandered the marbled floors and ran their hands over the luxurious and expensive merchandise were of a class he was used to serving at Carter & Son, yet the hunger in their movements and the almost manic gleam in their eyes was like nothing he'd ever seen before.

Money exchanged hands and order books were opened and written in at a mind-boggling speed as the gasps and squeals of delight from the ladies and the hearty laughter and good cheer of the gentlemen mingled with the soft, hushed voices of the cajoling staff as they charmed their way to selling item after item.

Joseph could barely contain a smile as the fire in his belly grew from a slow burn to an out-and-out inferno. Every hair on his body tingled with possibility.

Here, Lillian. Here is where I will atone for my neglect that night. Atone for the loss of you. One day, I promise, justice will be done and then maybe we'll both find peace.

How could his father not understand his son's vow to live his life alone while his wife's blood continued to stain his hands? What woman deserved to be with a man who couldn't protect her? A man like him did not deserve the love and care of a woman. His loneliness was just. His empty life warranted.

'Mr Carter, do you find yourself unable to leave us this afternoon?' Elizabeth Pennington's soft voice whispered like silk over his skin and Joseph turned, her green eyes hitching his heart a second time.

He swallowed and forced a slow smile. 'On the contrary. I wish to leave but find one thing after another captivating my attention.'

Satisfaction seeped into her eyes, a light flush darkening her cheeks. 'And what could it be in Haberdashery that so mesmerises you?'

'If you'll allow me to show you?'

Her gaze lit with curiosity and she nodded.

Joseph turned to the pretty shop girl standing behind the glass counter to the side of him. 'May I look at that tray of buttons?' He tapped his finger on the glass. 'The ones in differing shades of green?'

27

'Certainly, sir.' The girl extracted the tray and laid it on the counter.

Joseph tipped her a smile before plucking two different buttons, in two different shades, from the tray. He held them at Miss Pennington's temples, level with her eyes.

Surprise flashed in her gaze before she raised her eyebrows and her study returned to calm assessment. 'Can I ask what you're doing?'

He smiled. 'This button is in the shape of a flower and a deep brown-green, almost like moss dipped in soil. Whereas this triangular one is a startling emerald, bright and crisp as though kissed by sunlight.'

'And?'

'And both are colours I've seen in your eyes. So, was I to make you a pair of gloves, I would think of your eyes as I selected the kid, silk or satin with which to work. I would picture your eyes as I stitched the cloth and shaped the fingers. But when it came to the decoration, I would not think of your eyes.'

She carefully studied him before a soft smile lifted the corners of her mouth, her gaze holding just a hint of amusement. 'What would you think of?'

'I would think of exactly where I'd like you to wear them and with what dress. I'd think about the kind of woman you are and how I want you to feel when you are wearing my gloves.'

Her gaze slowly roamed over his face. 'You really do think highly of yourself, don't you, sir?'

'Nothing could be further from the truth.' He returned the buttons to the tray. 'But of my work? Yes, very much so.'

She studied him a moment longer before turning to the shop girl. 'Thank you, Flora.' She looked at

28

Joseph. 'Walk with me.'

Surprise rippled through him and Joseph fought to keep his face impassive as he dipped his head, extending his arm for her to lead the way. She strolled ahead, and he exhaled a shaky breath before following, wondering where this impromptu walk was headed and for what reason. Had he ruined his chances by being so forward with her? Had his picture-building failed with Elizabeth Pennington rather than succeeded as it had with others?

He studied the shine of her hair, the way her spine was so straight and her waist so small. The woman radiated purpose and clearly did not suffer fools lightly, yet she also had a quieter aura which he couldn't quite put his finger on. Something that interested and concerned him in equal measure.

Worse, he felt a kinship with the flashes of distrust he'd seen in her eyes. Understood the aloofness at the possibility he might intend to hoodwink her. He couldn't help but admire her integrity.

Joseph walked slightly behind her and waited for her to initiate further conversation.

'Do you live above your shop, Mr Carter? Might I ask where it is?'

'Pulteney Bridge.' Joseph turned his gaze from the shoppers around them to study the back of her elegant head. Why would she ask such a question? 'And yes, we live above the shop. My father and I have lived there since my mother died a few years ago.'

'You've lost your mother?' She stopped and turned to face him, her eyes softening.

'I have.'

'Would it be impertinent, or insensitive, of me to ask you how she died?'

Joseph frowned. 'A shadow on her lungs. It was a long death that I'd not wish on anyone.' Lillian's killer rose in his mind. 'At least, no one I've met yet.'

Her chest rose as she inhaled and looked past him. 'Then I hope you bear the loss better than I.'

His kinship with her uncomfortably deepened and he cleared his throat. 'You've lost your mother too?'

She nodded, a deep sadness in her eyes. 'Yes.'

'I'm sorry.' An inexplicable need to comfort her twisted inside him. 'They are always with us, you know. My mother was a formidable woman.'

'And a loving one?'

'She was. Very much so.'

The sense of loss emanating from her obvious wounds reopened those within himself. Those he had to believe were healing. The alternative would mean he would have to endure so much more than self-inflicted solitude. He could not allow his grief and anger to taint his passion for his work. Only success could bring his next breath, make him awaken and strike each new day as an opportunity to repent.

She nodded a greeting to two elderly women, wearing fox furs and elaborate hats, as they passed by, arm in arm. When Elizabeth Pennington faced him again, the coolness had returned to her eyes. 'And your father? Does he thrive without his wife's care or has he changed since her passing?'

Joseph struggled to decipher her thoughts, the intention behind her questions. People bustled and shouldered past them, the atmosphere fraught with eagerness for the next discovery, the next purchase. Was she so oblivious to the intoxicating power of her family's store that his personal life was of more interest? He had no desire to discuss his loved ones and could not understand why she would wish to either.

'These questions about my family are disconcerting. After all, I'm here as a supplier, nothing more.'

'You object to me asking about your family?'

Her curtly asked question stilled him. The last thing he wanted was to upset or irritate her and jeopardise his chances of working with Pennington's. 'It's not so much that I object — '

'I like to know my staff and business associates, Mr Carter. Contrary to what others might say about me, I don't manage my department like a machine.'

He followed her gaze to where two women harangued a salesman over the cost of a yard of satin. The bolts of colour piled alongside and on top one another gleamed like a bejewelled rainbow. Joseph's fingers itched to feel the lavishness of the cloth.

'I run the ladies' department with feeling, Mr Carter, and that feeling extends to my staff and their families. I want the people who work with me to be happy. I want to ensure they are not suffering unduly, and if there is anything I can do to help in their home lives, I will.'

Joseph studied her. She was most definitely not the stern, snooty-nosed ladies' department manageress he'd been prepared to barter with. In fact, not a single one of his imaginings had anticipated coming face-to-face with the future heiress of the store. Elizabeth Pennington was intelligent, kind and almost carefully distant . . . and one who unnervingly fascinated him.

It seemed her father's name might lay in the bronze plate above the store's grand double doors, but Miss Pennington had ambition and her own way of working. Could hers and Joseph's business association propel them both towards the places they wanted to be?

Her eyes darkened with curiosity or, possibly, suspicion. 'In return for my care, I expect honesty. Will you tell me why you look around the store and study the staff and customers with such intensity? It's as though you want to devour every part of Pennington's.'

Her choice of words and the undeniable pride in her tone was admirable, but Joseph also understood they implied provocation and challenge — one that stirred a raw and dangerous yearning to prove himself invaluable to both her and the store.

He looked at the elaborate stained-glass dome above them as he considered how best to reply.

Nothing came to mind but the truth.

He faced her. 'From the moment I walked into your store four years ago, Pennington's has been calling to me and I want to be a part of it.'

'So, your designs would be exclusive to Pennington's?'

'We could definitely agree on exclusivity for certain designs.'

'But not all?'

'No.' He shook his head. 'Not all.'

She studied him intently, her beautiful eyes revealing her consideration. 'Your protectiveness over your products is admirable.'

'I'm glad you think so.' He ran his gaze over her face, lingered a moment at her lips before meeting her eyes once more. 'Maybe it is meant that you and I work together. That I have a hand in Pennington's success, come to understand your vision and you do the same in return.'

She huffed a laugh. 'There might be others you need to convince of your skill before you get a glimpse of my vision, Mr Carter.'

Surprised, Joseph raised his eyebrows. 'Others? You're not solely in charge of the ladies' department? Is it not within your authority to decide what is bought and sold?'

Her gaze cooled. 'Rest assured, the ladies' department is mine to do with as I will.'

Joseph mentally kicked himself. Something in his question had prodded at a viper in her bosom. He'd be wise to tread carefully. 'Of course.'

'Myself or Mrs Woolden will be in touch.' She stepped away, stopped and then returned to him. 'Do you have dreams, Mr Carter? Dreams so fantastic they're in fact almost incredible?'

His heart quickened. Had she sensed his desperation? Did she think his ambition futile? He forced a smile. 'I do. My dreams are so incredible that I look forward to shocking you with each and every one of them.'

The longer she stared, the more the tension between them grew . . . as though a spark had been lit. Its heat licked and teased Joseph's chest as her smile spread to a grin before she turned and walked away.

4

Elizabeth closed her office door and strode to her desk. She surveyed its neat surface, everything in its place and ordered, unlike her galloping thoughts.

Almost from the moment she had seen Joseph Carter — and even more so after talking with him — her intuition bellowed that he could quite possibly be what she'd been waiting for.

She sat in her chair and gripped the edge of her desk before closing her eyes, waiting for her habitual distrust of men and their continued trampling of equality to re-emerge. Her premonition of possibility which surrounded Mr Carter made little sense. She'd even yet to see his designs. But something in the manner of his speech and address, to the impertinent glint in his eyes, spoke to her.

The pale grey shadows beneath his startling blue eyes and the roughness of his hand when he'd taken hers made her suspect him a working man. One who wasn't afraid of long hours and little sleep. Yet, still, he held himself with indelible authority and verve.

Excitement and undeniable attraction opened her eyes, her heart quickening.

To be drawn to such a man would be folly. Professional and personal ruin. She needed to exercise caution and not allow her imagination to run amok. Her father would never consider employing a lower-class man like Mr Carter anywhere but out of sight in the workroom. But what harm could Joseph do as a supplier? He clearly wished to escalate his prospects.

Had Mr Carter been right when he'd said that by working together they could meet their mutual aspirations?

The possibility stirred the drive Elizabeth had previously thought waning.

She had identified so much of herself in Joseph Carter. At first, the connection had been unnerving, but the longer she spoke with him, the more she felt his coming into the store had been fate.

God's deliverance of her next way forward.

She had a feeling that whatever Joseph Carter wanted, Joseph Carter got, and she would not allow a potential ally to slip through her fingers.

But she could not trust the man too easily.

She had first-hand experience of just how little male staff thought their female counterparts capable of. This infuriating and insulting mentality presented a battle she would fight to the end. As Edward Pennington's daughter — and the rightful heiress to his empire — passion burned inside of her to ensure the female staff would one day be as revered as the men. That the women who worked at Pennington's came forward with their ideas and innovations the same as any of their male colleagues. Equal opportunity had to be made possible, even if equal pay felt like an objective that would never be achieved.

If it wasn't for the forward thinking of Mrs Woolden, Esther Stanbury, their head window dresser, and the other women at the store, Elizabeth would feel she fought the fight entirely alone. Thankfully, she had friends at work and in her personal life who rallied for change as much as her.

She hadn't had an inkling of derogatory insinuation from Mr Carter. In fact, he'd looked at her with nothing but respect and interest . . . and it was the interest that had somehow sped her heart and heated her body in places that should not have been heating.

She rose from her desk and left the spacious back room she utilised as an office. Walking onto the department floor, Elizabeth studied the lady customers as Mrs Woolden and the other female staff served and showcased various scarves, hats and gloves. Elizabeth narrowed her gaze. The customers' eyes were not lit as brightly as she would've liked. Their expressions showing only mild interest as opposed to eagerness.

If Mr Carter's gloves could muster more enthusiasm than what she currently witnessed, all the better. She needed to devise a plan that would appeal and serve them both. He would have to be tested in the first instance and they could build from there. Her current suppliers were satisfactory enough, but they had offered nothing new or different for the last few seasons. The colours changed. The occasional adornment. But nothing astounding. Nothing that could be found nowhere else but Pennington's.

What if Mr Carter's designs trumped the store's current stock in ways she couldn't even imagine?

Mrs Woolden finished serving and approached Elizabeth. 'Is everything all right, Miss Pennington?'

'Absolutely. I wonder if you can spare me a moment at my desk? I'm eager for your opinion on Mr Carter.'

'Of course.'

Elizabeth waited as Mrs Woolden left instructions with the other staff before removing some papers from under the counter and following Elizabeth into her office.

Moving behind her desk, Elizabeth sat. 'Please, take a seat.'

36

As soon as Mrs Woolden was comfortably seated, the papers lying in her lap, Elizabeth cleared her throat. 'Mr Carter greatly impressed me during the brief time I spent with him and I'm curious of your first impressions.'

Mrs Woolden's gaze turned thoughtful. 'My first impressions were of a man most keen to work with us. In fact, I found his avidity quite inspiring. He seems very confident in his abilities, yet, from what I have read in his testimonials, he has no experience outside of his own shop, which I believe he runs with his father.'

'And you deem that a negative as far as him supplying Pennington's?'

'Not so much a negative. I just wonder if he fully appreciates the pride we take in delivery and service.'

Disappointment threatened that Mrs Woolden echoed Elizabeth's own reservations. 'You have doubts of his ability to keep up with demand should his gloves sell well?'

'I do.' Mrs Woolden lifted her shoulders. 'It's unfortunate, but I really can't see how he could supply as our bigger associates can. He freely admitted he only has a moderate workroom at his premises. Most of our suppliers have warehouses.'

'Hmm.' Elizabeth frowned. 'I could always suggest use of our workrooms should a trial run of his gloves prove fruitful.'

Mrs Woolden raised her eyebrows. 'Wouldn't that be highly irregular? I'm not sure your father would — '

'The ladies' department and its merchandise are under my control, Aveline. No one else's.' Elizabeth leaned back, concern dampening a little of her defensiveness. 'I am worried, if sales of his gloves exceed both ours and his expectations, he could well leave Pennington's high and dry at some point in the future.' Elizabeth picked up a pen and tapped it against the desktop. 'Of course, that could be quite some time from now.'

'Meaning?'

'If Mr Carter is as talented a designer and glove maker as he claims, then it will be up to Pennington's — up to me — to persuade him that his aspirations could be met here rather than going elsewhere.'

'The man seems extremely confident. I'm not sure he'd be satisfied as an employee.'

'I agree.' Disappointment threatened. So, it wasn't just her intuition that had been provoked by Mr Carter's unsettling good looks and clear desires. There seemed to be a depth to the man that Mrs Woolden had noticed too. A depth Elizabeth wanted to explore and expose. 'But that doesn't mean he wouldn't be open to a consultancy position sometime in the future, should I suggest a proportion of his gloves are produced exclusively for Pennington's.'

Mrs Woolden handed the papers across the desk. 'As impressive as the names are on his testimonials, at least three of the customers vouching for him also shop here for their gloves and hats. I'm concerned Mr Carter rates himself a little too highly.'

Elizabeth scanned the pages of testimonials, neither really reading nor caring about their content. For two years she had relied on her own instincts when deciding what was best for the ladies' department and, regardless of her father's refusal to extend her responsibilities, she had yet to make a bad decision when it came to her staff and suppliers.

'Would it really do us any harm to offer Mr Carter a trial?'

'That decision is yours. Should I have a message sent to Mr Carter inviting him to come in for a meeting on Thursday morning? We are both free from ten o'clock to eleven.'

'Yes. Thank you.' Elizabeth rose and walked round her desk as Mrs Woolden stood. They walked to the door. 'I'll join you in the department shortly.'

She closed the door behind Mrs Woolden and strolled to the bureau, where she kept detailed plans and sketches of her ideas. Selecting products for Pennington's required careful consideration. She wanted the department to be seen as a cut above their rivals; to continually astound and amaze each and every customer.

Her ideas to extend the number of toys in store and to integrate a collection of items to promote as suitable for both boys and girls had been immediately rejected by her father. He could not see that by reducing the gap between boys' and girls' playthings they would double sales. His stubborn blindness was infuriating.

She lifted a second sheet of paper and narrowed her gaze. There was also a possibility for a crossover between the men's and ladies' department by displaying gifts suitable for women in the men's department and vice versa. Pennington's was wasting endless opportunities of double-selling. Something Elizabeth thought imperative and her father deemed crass.

Frustrated, she laid down the papers and curled her fingers round the edges of the bureau.

Would she ever oversee more areas in the store? Ever persuade her father that the demand for better equality beat like a pulse amongst the masses and soon there would be a breakthrough? For Pennington's to be a forerunner in such a vision could be monumental.

How was she to convince her father of such a thing when he had recently insinuated that, in the absence of a male heir, he would ultimately pass the store over to corporate ownership, rather than pass it to a mere woman. Even though that woman was his own flesh and blood. His own daughter.

His desire to travel and see the world became ever more pressing and Elizabeth couldn't help but fear time was running out to convince him to name her as his successor. Again, and again, he insinuated her desire was grounded in greed and wealth, but she wanted the store because she couldn't imagine her life where she wasn't a part of its potential. Where she didn't come to work every day and revel in its wonderfully beating heart and play a part in its progression and growth.

Inhaling a shaky breath, her mind wandered to the previous evening's conversation with her father, Noel and his parents. Throughout the evening, Edward Pennington's round, reddened face had been eager with anticipation of his daughter's forthcoming engagement, an ever-present whisky glass swaying in his hand as his latest lover shamelessly wrapped herself around his bulk and words. The more her father pressed her into marriage, the more she resisted. Whether that be to a man she had yet to meet or Noel, who'd spent the entire evening boasting about his latest tour abroad or the amount of money he could spend at the card table in a single night.

The feeling of being entirely misunderstood bore

40

down on her and Elizabeth squeezed her eyes shut against the unexpected pricking of tears behind her eyes. 'Oh, Mama, how I miss you. Why didn't I see how desperate you'd become?'

Guilt writhed in Elizabeth's heart.

She had been twenty years old when her mother took her life, but Elizabeth's need to work with her father, to learn the retail trade and forge a position within the Pennington empire, had meant she'd missed the signs of her mother's depression that seemed so obvious in cruel hindsight.

A beautiful woman, her mother had always possessed an enviable figure, but in the months before her suicide, she had lost far too much weight. Her prominent cheekbones and shadowed eyes unacknowledged by Elizabeth and her mother's friends. Had they each chosen to look the other way? Believed her mother tired rather than soulfully unhappy?

Yes. Yes, they had.

Elizabeth snapped open her eyes and hastily swiped her fingers beneath them, her chin raised. Well, the subsequent hush-hush of her mother's health and state of mind had woken her daughter to her blindness with stark brutality. It had also ignited a passion to be more, do more than ever.

Her father would never reduce Elizabeth to the desperate, frustrated and overlooked existence he had her mother.

Never.

She would plan and live as she wanted, no matter how long her father held the reins of her existence. She would focus on generating maximum publicity and that all-important 'want' factor Pennington's needed to instil in its customers' minds and hearts.

The drive she recognised in Joseph Carter was what was completely lacking in the man her father wished her to marry. Noel was little more than a man waiting for his inheritance. A man who had no concept of changing what his family had done for years and years before him.

In contrast, Elizabeth wanted nothing more than to make Pennington's her own. Maybe, just maybe, Joseph's gloves would be the golden tip at the end of her striking arrow for the coming year.

Excitement burned in her soul. She could hardly wait to hear more of what he had in mind.

5

The bell above the door of Carter & Son announced the arrival of a customer and, for the third time that day, Joseph held his breath as he looked up from the glove he worked on.

He stared across the dimly lit room towards the doorway and strained his ears as his father greeted whoever it was who'd entered. Gripping the scissors in his hand, Joseph battled to not leap from his workbench as he'd done every time the shop bell had rang for the last two days.

His hope for some news from Pennington's grew pathetically desperate, and the continuous empty tidings only served to depress him further. Inhaling the musty scent of old wood and wax that was so vastly different to the sweetly perfumed corridors of Pennington's, Joseph fought his fear that it would only be his success, and the resources to finish what Lillian had started, that would stitch together the hole in his heart. He needed this contract. He needed Pennington's.

His father's voice filtered through the open door, followed by a reply, but the mumblings were too quiet for Joseph to make out the words. On and on they talked until at last his father bid the customer good day and the bell signalled the visitor's departure.

As his father's footsteps neared the back of the shop, Joseph stilled, praying his father carried a letter from Pennington's.

'Surprised you've given up striding into the front of the shop every time someone comes in.' Robert Carter appeared in the doorway, his spectacles pushed high on his head, his grey-speckled eyebrows sprouting in every direction. 'Thought it would be nightfall before you gave up peering through the window as though someone was on the street without any clothes on.' He tossed a sealed envelope onto the workbench. 'Think this might be what you've been waiting for.'

Joseph stared at the neat handwriting on the envelope and the Pennington's stamp in the left-hand corner. His mouth drained dry as all the bravado he had been rehearsing for the last forty-eight hours disappeared and turned into burning hope.

'Well, aren't you going to open it?' His father planted his hands on his hips. 'Don't keep me in suspense. Don't you want the infernal commission now?'

'Of course, I do. This could be the start of a new beginning for both of us.'

His father nodded towards the envelope, his jaw tight. 'Open it then.'

Inhaling, Joseph slit open the envelope as though tearing gauze from a wound. Quick and sharp. He scanned the writing. 'They want to see me tomorrow.'

'And does it say which of those bloodsuckers at Pennington's you'll be talking to?'

Joseph swallowed the temptation to tell him how far from a bloodsucker Miss Pennington seemed. Not to mention how the woman's beauty had stirred awake his desire . . . stirred and scared. He cleared his throat. 'Mrs Woolden, the deputy head of the ladies' department, and Miss Pennington herself. This is tremendous news.'

'You sound almost surprised. You're the finest glove maker in Bath. Why wouldn't they want to sell your gloves?'

Joseph stared at the note. Could this be the start of his redemption? The true path to appease the heavy guilt that badgered his mind and tore at his heart. Could he at last begin to think that one day he might forgive himself for failing Lillian?

He met his father's steady gaze. 'From now on, it's onwards and upwards for Carter & Son. Pennington's has the means to advertise and distribute in a way we can't. This is our true beginning. Can't you see that?'

Robert Carter sniffed. 'I see plenty.'

'Meaning?'

'Meaning you don't seem as proud anymore of our good shopkeeping. Knowing our customers. Pennington's is nothing more than an impersonal monstrosity that will never provide the one-to-one service we can.'

Frustrated, Joseph pushed back the dark hair at his brow and leaned his hands on the worktop. 'No, but it will provide the means for you to retire. That's what you want, isn't it?'

'Yes, but — '

'There you are, then. Plus, I'm not turning my back on what I've been taught and the legacy I've inherited. I'm building on it. I'm proud of Carter & Son. Proud to be a Carter. This isn't about me walking away or betraying the family name, it's about taking our name out into the world and making it bigger than ever.' Joseph stepped away from the bench and gripped his father's shoulder. 'Why won't you just look forward to living your life in comfort without worrying where your next meal is coming from? Let me make a success of this without feeling guilty about it, please. This commission will lead to bigger and better things.'

'And then what?'

Joseph released his father and stepped back.

Sometimes the ferocity of his father's tone made Joseph wonder if his passion was really about the shop, or something else entirely. He frowned. 'The world is changing. We need to change too. Move with the times or risk being left behind. We've done a grand job with the shop as Grandfather did before us, but it's time to inject something new into the Carter name. Make people really sit up and take notice of the kind of product we can provide.' Joseph stopped. 'You're still all right that it's just our gloves I'm taking forward, aren't you? I've never be the milliner you and Grandfather were, and I wouldn't be able to maintain the quality in our hats.'

'Of course, I am. I'm tired. It's time for me to pass the reins to you to run Carter & Son however you see fit. Pennington's or no Pennington's.' His father's eyes darkened from anger to sadness, and he slumped his shoulders. 'The thing worrying me is you, Joseph. I worry you think making sackloads of money will make you happy.'

Hope, or maybe shame, warmed Joseph's cheeks, and he dropped his gaze to the gloves on the bench. 'It will.'

'With no one to share it with?'

He snapped his gaze to his father's. 'That's just it. We will share it. I won't forget what Lillian stood for, Pa. What she wanted.'

'And that will be enough, will it?'

'Yes.'

The wall clock ticked out the passing seconds, the usual creaking of the floorboards and the continuous clip-clop of passing horses outside strangely mute.

Joseph lifted Pennington's letter, determination burning inside him. 'This isn't sending me to the

46

firing squad. You — '

'It might be that yet.' His father turned and walked towards the door.

Joseph stared after him. Something was amiss. Something his father felt he couldn't share. Clutching the letter, Joseph followed him through to the front of the shop.

Robert Carter stood behind the counter and hauled a bolt of satin from one of the cubbyholes behind him. 'People need people, Joseph. You need a family around you. Lillian's gone. Don't you think it's about time you thought about a bit of love? Some romance? Finding a woman to live with and share your life?'

Fear to love again spread through Joseph's chest, squeezing painfully around his heart. His mother had passed years before and not once had his father shown an iota of interest in taking a second wife. Why think Joseph would feel any differently? 'We were both married to phenomenal women, Pa. We're good enough on our own now they've gone.'

His father lifted the cloth onto the counter, his eyes sombre. 'Yes, we were, but I won't be here forever, you know.'

'I know that.' Joseph swallowed. 'But while you are, it's going to be just you and me.'

'And after I've gone?'

'I'll work it out.'

'Do you know something?'

'What?'

His father hesitated and then shook his head. 'Forget it. Just do what you have to do. You're your own man. The days when I could tell you what to do are long gone. It's up to you to live your own life. No matter how much I might fret about your decisions.'

The initial euphoria of reading the letter disappeared as Joseph studied his father's defeated expression. 'How am I to go to Pennington's tomorrow knowing you hate the idea of me working with them? I have to do this. I have to prove to myself that my life, our lives, were always destined for bigger and better things. It's what Lillian and I wanted. What was destroyed when she was killed. She wanted us to succeed and be charitable with that success. Provide opportunities to others so that they might have a chance in this world. I have to show her I'm still trying to pursue her dream.'

'By not loving another soul for the rest of your life? You think that's what she'd want for you?'

Joseph clenched his jaw, nausea coating his dry throat.

'Well?'

Joseph glared. 'She's not here to ask, is she? So, I guess we'll never know.' He walked to the counter, tossed the letter onto the cloth and summoned up every ounce of enthusiasm that had sent him to Pennington's in the first place. 'The invitation for a meeting is the possibility of a life we've never known. This could be my chance to introduce colour, vitality and new ideas to hundreds of people.'

'That's what you believe, is it?'

'Yes.' Joseph tilted his chin. 'It would be good for you to meet Miss Pennington if I get the commission.'

Robert huffed a laugh. 'And why on God's earth would I want to do that?'

'Because the way she sees things, her values and her measure of people, aren't too far away from yours.'

'Bah. That woman was born into money, born into her position at that monstrosity of a place. What would

48

she know about people and their problems?'

'A lot, from what I gathered in the short time I spent talking with her. Within minutes of meeting her, she'd found out I lived above the shop, where it is, and that we'd lost Ma. She's a canny woman. A smart woman. She struck me as fair and kind. Not bad attributes in a potential associate.'

'Fair and kind, eh?' His father exchanged scissors for a measuring tape and pencil from the box at his side. 'And I don't suppose she's too bad to look at either.'

Joseph bit his teeth together against his father's astuteness. Elizabeth Pennington was phenomenal to look at. Not that her beauty had anything to do with Joseph's respect for her. Not at all. She had earned that by her questions, her responses and her careful, steady way of looking straight into his eyes as she spoke with him.

His father raised his head. 'That commission will be yours the minute you walk into that meeting.' He rounded the counter and gripped Joseph's shoulders. 'I only want the best for you. I'm being a thorn in your side because it isn't easy watching you work yourself into the ground under a cloud of sorrow. You're my boy. My son. My right-hand man.'

'I'll be all right.'

'That you will.' His father pulled him into his embrace and squeezed. 'That you will.'

He slapped his hand to Joseph's back, released him and returned to his work.

Joseph exhaled a shaky breath as he studied his father's turned back. Concern whispered through him, quashing his euphoria of re-entering Pennington's . . . of seeing Elizabeth Pennington again.

Was his plan the wrong one? Was his father right that Pennington's could be Joseph's downfall rather than the promise of a better future?

There was only one sure way he'd find out.

6

Over the rim of her wine glass, Elizabeth eyed her father's latest lover, thankful dinner was almost over. The light from the chandelier and the candles on the table flickered and danced across her eyes, adding strain to the headache threatening at her temples. No matter that the table had been dressed to the house-keeper's exemplary standards, no amount of crystal or bone china could conjure away Elizabeth's resent-ment towards her father.

She lowered her glass and lifted her fingers to her temples. Closing her eyes, she attempted to rub away her headache.

'Are you unwell, Elizabeth?'

She slowly opened her eyes. 'Just a headache, Papa.'

'I see. You've barely touched any of the four courses Mrs Wainwright so carefully prepared.' His tone accu-satory rather than sympathetic as her father raised his hand to Cole, their loyal butler since Elizabeth was a little girl. 'More wine, please, Cole.'

He topped up her father's glass, as Elizabeth shifted in her chair, irritated and uncomfortable. She could scarcely remember a day since her mother's passing that she and her father had not had a confrontation of one sort or another. Their disharmony was infuriating at best, tiring at worst.

She turned her attention to Miss Rebecca Long-bourne, her father's latest companion in a succession of much younger women. 'How did you enjoy Christ-mas in Bath, Miss Longbourne? Does your family not take umbrage with you spending this time with my father rather than at home?'

Miss Longbourne's cold gaze held Elizabeth's stare, her pretty face turning ugly in Elizabeth's eyes. 'Not at all. My family are very forward-thinking and at my age —'

Elizabeth raised her eyebrows. 'Which is?'

Two spots of colour appeared on Miss Longbourne's cheeks. 'Twenty-nine.'

Elizabeth laughed inwardly. At twenty-four herself, she had guessed Rebecca to be at least ten years her senior.

Miss Longbourne coughed delicately. 'As I was saying, at my age, my family is more than happy for me to spend my time anywhere, and with whomever, I choose.'

'Well then, you must lead quite the life. I must admit, I am a little envious. My father tends to have a say in almost every part of my life.'

Miss Longbourne smiled and picked up her water. 'You father can be extremely wise to the wants and needs of women. Don't you agree?'

Elizabeth glared at her. The woman was little more than a harlot. A harlot intent on ensnaring her father. 'Well, I'm glad your family is so forward-thinking. My father is clearly thrilled you are available to him whenever, or for however long, he wishes for your company.' Elizabeth rose to her feet just as her father spoke.

'Clearly, you are keen to dash away from us, Elizabeth.' Her father studied her intently, his gaze steely. 'But I'd like to discuss matters at the store.'

Reluctantly, Elizabeth sat back down to avoid a scene. She glanced towards Miss Longbourne. 'Now?

When you have company?'

Her father nodded, his jaw tight. 'Yes, when we have company.'

Annoyed, Elizabeth reached for her glass and drained the remainder of her wine. What was her father thinking by discussing business in front of someone as indiscreet as his latest lover? Rebecca Longbourne would undoubtedly think it most advantageous to share inside information about the store with whomever would listen. She faced her father. 'What is it you wish to discuss?'

Trepidation knotted her stomach. Did he know about her meeting tomorrow with Joseph Carter? If he did, why choose to debate it now? All day she'd been relishing the prospect of seeing Joseph Carter the following morning, and now the man who had the power to strip Joseph from her in one fell swoop, regardless of her wishes to work with him, sat opposite. Well, whether her father accepted Joseph as a new supplier or not, he would have a fight on his hands.

He slowly leaned back. 'How are things in the ladies' department, my dear? Everything ticking along nicely?'

She cleared her throat, suspicion writhing in her mind. 'Very well. Profits are up and preparations for the spring displays are in full swing. I've spoken with Miss Stanbury and we agree it would be beneficial to have an entire window dressed for the ladies' department. I thought we could —'

'And what of suppliers?'

Elizabeth froze, the sudden silence in the room oppressing. She darted her gaze between her father and Miss Longbourne. So, he knew of Mr Carter. No doubt the intelligence had somehow come from the head of the men's department. George Weir was her father's eyes and ears. Her heart beat a little faster. 'If you know we've received interest from Mr Carter, why not just say so?'

Her father's eyes glinted with spiteful satisfaction and Elizabeth's temper flared. It took all her willpower not to kick back her chair and march from the room before she committed assault.

She held his gaze. 'Mrs Woolden and I will be meeting Mr Carter tomorrow. I really don't understand why such a routine conference should concern you.'

'I'm concerned because I've been told your keenness to work with him was immediate. Not to mention unwarranted. There could be a hundred and one men out there with the same credentials. So, what is it about this Carter fellow that has struck you exactly?'

How was she to explain the overwhelming, yet unproven, potential she sensed in Joseph Carter? Should she lie? Incite a distraction? She closed her eyes and took a deep breath. No, she would not let her father undermine her integrity as he had everything else.

She opened her eyes. 'Whoever passed on that information was right in one respect, but wholly inaccurate in another. My interest in Mr Carter was immediate, but as for there being a hundred and one men out there like him, I wholeheartedly disagree.'

Much to her satisfaction, her father shook Miss Longbourne's claws from his forearm and leaned forward on the table, mirroring Elizabeth's posture. 'Then, pray tell me, what it is about this stranger that so impressed you?'

'Well, for one, he is incredibly attractive.'

Her father's eyes narrowed. 'What?'

She lifted her shoulders in a gesture of nonchalance, her tone even. 'I'm only following your example and considering working closely with someone based on their looks. Isn't that what you've always used as a deciding factor with the shop girls?'

His cheeks mottled, a sure sign of his rising temper. 'The man is a glove maker. A supplier. He could resemble a gargoyle and it would make no difference.'

'For now.'

'What do you mean?'

'Mr Carter is bursting with ambition.' She glanced again at Miss Longbourne, whose eyes were now alight with avid interest. Elizabeth longed to demand she leave her and her father to talk alone. However, to do so would be a sign of weakness. She faced her father and pulled back her shoulders. 'I see a fire in his eyes, the like of which I haven't seen in anyone for a long time. He's passionate about designing and making gloves. He exudes enthusiasm and vision. I believe Mr Carter could bring something truly unique to the store.'

Her father's eyes turned cold. 'You've clearly been blinded by this man. What do you really know of him? Has he worked in retail for very long?'

'I suspect he's been a part of the industry for most of his life. He owns a small shop on Pulteney Bridge.'

Her father stilled. 'Pulteney Bridge?'

'Yes.' Elizabeth frowned. 'What of it?'

His eyes glazed as though momentarily lost in thought, a muscle flickering in his tightened jaw. 'Well, that is interesting.'

Unease raised the hairs on her arms. 'Why?'

He smiled. 'So, the man has ambition. What else?'

She swallowed and forced a shrug, wanting her

father to believe the sudden glint in his eyes wasn't bothering her. 'That's a part of his intrigue. I have no idea. Yet.'

Her father emitted a burst of dry laughter and picked up his glass. He raised it in an ironic toast and drank deeply before returning the glass so abruptly to the table, splashes of claret spilled onto the white tablecloth. 'As I suspected, you know nothing about him. You, my dear, are clearly thinking with your body rather than your mind.'

She flinched at the insult. 'My body has nothing to do with it. Joseph Carter — '

'Is undoubtedly taking full advantage of your obvious infatuation. You are a fool to display such eagerness towards anyone, but especially towards a supplier. Will you be able to control your feminine desires long enough to wrangle a profitable deal for the store? Or will you split the revenue however he sees fit?'

She clenched her teeth behind her closed lips and fought to keep hold of her temper and decorum. It was bad enough her father had goaded her into mentioning Joseph's looks and caused her to fall headlong into another of his carefully laid traps, but to do so in front of the gloating Miss Longbourne was out-and-out torture. For so long she'd tried to defy her father's gender bias and now he would think her responses entirely female.

Elizabeth glared. 'Once again, you doubt my business acumen, and once again, I shall undoubtedly prove my competence.'

The seconds ticked by on the mantel clock before his smile dissolved and his gaze bored into hers. 'You want complete control of Pennington's, yet you continue to make decisions that astound me. That, my dear girl, is why women do not lead in business.'

The statement finally snapped her careful control and she glowered. 'You're wrong.'

He sipped his wine. 'I am never wrong.'

'Women do not yet lead in business because men like you do not allow it.' Elizabeth snapped. 'That will change, whether it be next year or a hundred years from now. Either way, I'm determined not to give up on my success happening sooner rather than later. You treat the shop girls as though they are your possessions. You've no interest in them or their lives. They visibly tremble when you appear and, to your discredit, you positively enjoy that reaction.

'If they were happy, they would flourish. They would work harder, do more to please and assist our customers. They would become as important a part of Pennington's as our products and service. Yet, you see nothing more than females doing your bidding. It will be the ruin of the store if that doesn't change.'

His livid gaze locked on hers and Miss Longbourne shifted in her chair beside him, her face pale.

He shook his head. 'Your ideals are laughable.'

'Yet, I do not see you laughing.' Elizabeth pushed back her seat and stood. 'What have I ever done to deserve your bitterness and disdain? Ever since you first took me into one of our shops, I have learned and worked hard. Is it because I remind you of Mama? Am I too intelligent and strong? Just as she once was before your treatment of her destroyed every ounce of her self-worth and confidence.' She snatched her glare to Miss Longbourne. 'Is that the sort of man you want to be with, Miss Longbourne? I would think a woman as independent as you would abhor such a man. However, I find myself not surprised by your wishing to keep my father's company, only deeply disappointed.'

'Sit down, Elizabeth.' Her father growled. 'Right now.'

She snatched her gaze to his. 'I think not. I've played an important part in running the store for two years. If you disagree with that, then please present me with evidence to the contrary. In the meantime, I will continue to manage the ladies' department and employ whomever I see fit. With or without your approval.'

Trembling with the effort it took to control her rage, Elizabeth exited the room and strode into the hallway. Time and again she felt so alone in the world — and she had no idea when that would change.

She walked upstairs and into her bedroom, pushing the door firmly closed and sliding the bolt. Plucking the pins from her hair, she dropped them onto her side dresser and shook out her hair, fury thundering through her.

Sitting on the bed, she opened the drawer of her bedside table and drew out a small floral box. Battling the stinging in her eyes, she withdrew a folded letter, creased and worn with wear.

My dear Elizabeth,

There is not a day goes by that I am not inspired by your care, love and attention to not just me, but the servants, too. You are a kind woman, an intelligent woman and one I know, deep down, your father recognises as being everything a son could have been.

He would never admit this, of course, which is why I beg of you to keep faith that one day you will be all you want to be and have everything you have ever dreamed of.

Don't let your father bully you as he has me, my love. Stay strong and choose your battles wisely. I fear he will never value your voice, my voice or, indeed, any female voice, but you have a will I could only have wished for in myself.

Go forth and conquer the world, Elizabeth. Go forth and conquer your father.

I love you,
Mama xx

Elizabeth pressed the letter to her bosom, her tears damp on her cheeks. 'I miss you, Mama. I miss you so very much.'

The letter had been left by her mother in Elizabeth's bureau the day Helena Pennington had decided to walk away, never to return. She was found miles away in a hotel room in Bristol. Hung from a ceiling beam, one of her husband's belts around her neck.

Refolding the letter with trembling hands, Elizabeth returned it to the box and slipped it into the drawer. She lay back on her bed and closed her eyes.

Her father might control her working life, but his time of controlling her personally was over. She'd prefer to spend her life a spinster rather than marry a man of her father's choosing. Railway heir or no railway heir.

One day she would know freedom. Of that much she was certain.

59

7

Joseph stepped from the lift and walked into Pennington's ladies' department. Once again, the astounding opulence and grandeur of the vast space surrounded and strengthened him. Never before had he felt he was taking the right path to a better future. A richer future, most certainly, but most of all, a future where he could start to make amends for his miscarriage to Lillian.

The anniversary of her death loomed in his mind.

In just two weeks' time, she would have been dead two years and, still, he continued to fail her. He visited her grave once a month and imparted his news, tidings of the business and reports on the occasional visits he'd made to the slums lining the river in an attempt to carry on his wife's good work.

Time constraints meant his commitment to those less fortunate fell woefully short of Lillian's, yet she'd always, somehow, *made* time. Even working side by side with him and his father, checking and packing gloves and hats, taking them to be delivered and collecting anything needing adjustment, she never faltered.

He had to do better. *Be* better.

His mouth dry and adrenaline pumping, Joseph concentrated on keeping up the outward appearance of someone used to treading upon a carpet so plush, the soles of his shoes had all but disappeared. He could not afford for Miss Pennington to see his inner faults and struggles. He sensed she sought an associate

60

who possessed drive and ambition.

Anything less would not suffice.

'Ah, Mr Carter. Good morning.'

Joseph started as Mrs Woolden came towards him, her eyes kind and her smile wide.

She waved towards a chair to the side of the department. 'Can I ask that you wait here for just a moment? I'll just let Miss Pennington know you're here.'

'Of course.'

He glanced at the bustling activity around him before sitting on a pale green upholstered seat and placing his case of samples at his feet. Taking the opportunity to study some of the female customers, he noticed that the interest in the gloves and hats was good, but not as fervent as he would have expected.

Possibility hummed through him. Would his gloves add the zest needed to get Miss Pennington's department truly animated? Somehow, it had come to matter deeply to him that his gloves and their popularity benefited her as well as Carter & Son. He sensed her need for something more. Something he hoped he could provide.

Fighting the urge to tap his foot on the floor, he slowly exhaled, in a bid to calm his breathing. Yesterday, he'd convinced himself that if their meeting concluded without offer of a commission, it wouldn't be the end of the world. The desire to gain recognition for his work had taken hold so fervently, he was confident that sooner or later he'd find a good retailer elsewhere. Pennington's was not the be all and end all of his ambitions.

But sat here now, as he glanced at the closed door at the back of the room once more, it felt in that moment as if it was. That, and working closely with Elizabeth

Pennington. She intrigued him. Excited him. How and why, he didn't know — didn't want to contemplate too deeply — but the feelings were there, all the same.

And considering just how much pain he'd endure if he were to ever give into his emotional desires again, the invisible threat Elizabeth Pennington posed was a dangerous one. One that held the power to make him doubt his presence here. Provoke a fear about what a positive outcome of today's meeting could mean to his future well-being.

The door opened, and Joseph rose to his feet. Well, it was too late to beat a hasty retreat now. It was time to concentrate on why he was here and ensure he impressed Elizabeth Pennington enough for her to give him the opportunity to demonstrate his skills and talent.

She walked confidently towards him, her deep red hair and startling green eyes striking him anew.

'Mr Carter, it's a pleasure to see you again.'

He cleared his throat and shook her proffered hand. 'Miss Pennington.'

The woman radiated a confidence that he silently wished he could find within himself. He wore his façade well, but it stubbornly remained so very fragile.

She gestured toward what he presumed to be her office. 'Please, won't you come in?'

He followed her into the room and tried not to stare in awe at the grandeur around him. Vast and flamboyant floral displays stood on two handsome plinths either side of a beautifully carved desk. Two armchairs, tastefully upholstered in pale pink velvet, were placed in front of a low table in the far corner. The windows were draped with great swathes of white satin edged with gold. A feminine room, but the message given by the stacked papers, a simple glass lamp on her desk and the two bookshelves jammed with leather-bound books gave a straightforward air of professionalism.

Elizabeth Pennington was a pleasant blend of strong and soft that dangerously deepened his attraction.

'Mr Carter? Won't you take a seat?'

He blinked. 'Of course. Thank you. Your desk is quite a wonder.'

'It was my grandfather's. He bequeathed it to me after he died.' She smiled wryly as she sat in the high-backed leather chair behind it. 'It seems he had no doubts I would need it one day.'

Unsure how to respond to her unexpectedly dry response, Joseph sat next to Mrs Woolden in one of the two chairs in front of the desk. Smoothing his trousers against his thighs, he crossed his legs at the ankle in the hope he projected an air of relaxation and confidence.

'So . . . ' Elizabeth Pennington's voice broke the silence, and any trace of affability vanished as her expression sobered. 'Your passion for your work impressed both Mrs Woolden and myself, but Pennington's isn't just about artisans showing off their skills. It is a prerequisite that all staff and suppliers are open to new challenges, changes and suggestions. The fact that you have worked nowhere other than your own shop concerns me. Working with a department store like Pennington's might prove to be far from what you are accustomed to.'

Joseph uncrossed his ankles and sat forward. This was it. This was his chance to voice ideas he had hardly dared to broach with his father. 'I might have only worked in a boutique, but I have big ambitions for my designs. My father will soon be retiring, which gives me free rein to embrace the changing times. For a while now, I have seen that bespoke manufacturing will soon have a very limited place in the market. My mission is to provide affordable luxury for the majority of people who, before now, could only dream of such things.'

She remained silent, her gaze on his and her expression unreadable.

'Pennington's won't be the first store to offer a wide range of products that are affordable to all classes, but it could be the first in Bath. Yes, I want to see my gloves worn by as many men and women as possible, but . . . ' He drew in a long breath as her continuing silence began to unnerve him. He needed to lay his aspirations on the table. Her unwavering study and confident posture denoted a woman who had no patience with flannel and wanted only facts.

'I want to help make fashion affordable to the masses without cutting on quality.' He held her gaze. 'Pennington's can still cater to the wealthy with high-end silks and satins, but let us have the hard-working men and women who help run this wonderful city experience what it feels like to wear reasonably priced kid and leather, ribbons and pins, too. It's said that British fashion lags behind Paris. I believe this is because the Parisians have made fashion as delectable as their food. Elegant, delicious, a sensory delight. We must follow suit if Bath is ever to become as much a centre of fashion as London or Paris. Let us make it that a housewife can afford an elegant pair of gloves, a decorative fan, and exquisite parasol. Let us give the working masses more to live for than their day-to-day existence. Let us give them something to aspire to and dream of.'

Joseph fell silent, his body rigid and his hands tightly clasped in front of him. He looked at Mrs Woolden. She stared blandly back, her gaze unreadable.

Joseph turned to Miss Pennington. 'I truly believe — '

She lifted her hand and he snapped his mouth closed. Her gaze lingered on his before she turned to Mrs Woolden. 'What do you think of Mr Carter's impassioned speech, Aveline?'

No clue to Elizabeth Pennington's reaction to his words showed in her expression or tone and Joseph's innate fear of failure hit him like a sharp punch to his gut. Would she dismiss his dreams — his need for professional happiness — out of hand?

'Well . . .' Mrs Woolden turned to him, her gaze bordering on suspicious. 'You are quite the visionary, Mr Carter. As much as I applaud your aspirations, you're here as a potential supplier only. It concerns me that you might not take kindly to any suggestions from myself or Miss Pennington.

You do not strike me as the sort of man who takes well to authority. Let alone from a woman.'

'You couldn't be more mistaken.' Joseph sat forward. 'I'd be a fool not to listen to the suggestions of women. Any woman. Is it not them I wish to dress? To see looking beautiful, confident and able to achieve anything they wish? I love women, Mrs Woolden. Truly.'

'All women?'

'I mean . . .' He turned to Miss Pennington. Her eyes shone with amusement, her pretty lips pressed together. She raised her eyebrows and, much to his shame, Joseph's cheeks heated. He laughed and relaxed into his chair, encouraged by her increasingly insouciant demeanour 'I mean to say, women are my business. They are all that matter to me. In fact, I thought I'd be working side by side for the rest of my life with a woman I loved deeply. Unfortunately, that was not to be, but that doesn't mean I'm willing to turn my back on everything she envisioned.'

The amusement disappeared from Miss Pennington's eyes as she studied him. Her stare bored into his as though trying to understand him, to see deep inside his heart and mind. Joseph quickly turned away lest she see too much.

The seconds ticked by until Elizabeth Pennington leaned her elbows on her desk and laced her fingers. 'It's all very well to have grand imaginings, Mr Carter, but are you prepared for the challenges you will face working with Pennington's?'

'I don't shy away from challenges.'

'May I ask what you do shy away from?'

He nodded, his response instinctive. 'I shy away from failure.'

'We all fail. It's, more often than not, the best way to learn.'

'Maybe, but for me failure is when a person gives up completely. Decides they no longer wish to push forward for what they want. I believe Pennington's has the potential to be the most successful store in Bath. I want to be a part of that. To help you make that happen.'

Mrs Woolden cleared her throat. 'That's all very noble, but Miss Pennington doesn't own the store, her father does. It seems to me these are fine words, but you have no knowledge of Pennington's as a whole.'

Before Joseph could respond, Elizabeth Pennington spoke. 'That's something I believe Mr Carter will take no time at all to learn.' She faced Joseph. 'As much as I appreciate your enthusiasm for change and modernisation, things move slowly in retail and I'm not sure you'll accept that the best things come to those who wait. What is it you want from me, exactly?'

'Well, firstly . . . ' Joseph stood and opened his case of samples and lifted them out to spread along the desk. 'I'd like to offer these and, possibly, two more to sell exclusively at Pennington's. If they sell well, which I know they will, we can review my contract and take our arrangements forward from there.'

Her gaze wandered over his gloves, her brow creased as she inspected and lifted each pair. 'I would insist on a month's trial.' She smoothed her thumb over the leather in her hands, her gaze brightening with clear interest. 'But these are impressive. Very impressive, in fact.'

Joseph's heart quickened. 'A trial would be acceptable.'

She slowly laid down the gloves and faced him, her gaze lingering on his before she gave a curt nod. 'Good. Then I suggest you leave these samples with me to consider. I'll send message to you tomorrow. In the meantime, I would like your commitment to understanding what mass production of your gloves would entail and, in turn, come up with a plan for the sort of numbers you're imagining.'

She stood and held out her hand.

Euphoric, Joseph shook her hand, suddenly impatient to leave the office so he could get outside and yell his triumph from the rooftops. 'Thank you.' He turned and offered his hand to Mrs Woolden. 'And thank you, too, Mrs Woolden.'

She smiled, her kindly eyes shining once more. 'You're more than welcome.'

Snapping his case closed, Joseph flashed another smile at Miss Pennington before walking to the door, feeling as though the carpet beneath his feet was made of clouds.

8

Elizabeth laughed as Esther Stanbury, Pennington's head window dresser, snatched a glass of champagne from the tray carried by one of the Cavendish Club waiters, before the poor man even had time to put it down on the circular table in front of them.

'You seem decidedly thirsty tonight.' Elizabeth nodded her thanks to the waiter as he passed her a glass.

'I am. One thing after another went wrong today.' Esther sipped her drink. 'I'm thoroughly exhausted after a day of convincing your father's favourite employee that the men's department will not collapse if I add a riding hat and crop as props in the new window.'

Elizabeth rolled her eyes, sympathy blooming for her friend and colleague. 'George Weir is a thorn in every female employee's side. In my opinion, you should override his every instruction.'

'And I'd lose my position in a heartbeat.' Esther stared towards the bar. 'A position I need and love.'

Elizabeth sat back to survey the scene around them. Candles flickered on the dozens of intimate tables and lights glittered from the stage where the four-piece band played. Men in evening dress and women in all their bejewelled finery swayed to the music or laughed uproariously as they clinked glasses. Despite the Cavendish's slightly risqué reputation, a large number of people were packed into it tonight.

It neared ten o'clock, but no one seemed in a hurry to leave — and that suited Elizabeth splendidly. She was far too energised by the day's events to consider leaving just yet. 'I met with a potential new supplier today.'

Esther raised her eyebrows. 'Well, he must be someone exceptional to set your eyes glittering the way they are.'

Elizabeth turned away. 'He's . . . interesting.'

'Interesting?'

'Yes.'

'Really?' Esther glanced at the wall clock beside them and grimaced. 'I really should get home to my aunt, but . . . ' She nudged Elizabeth's shoulder.

'You can't just say someone is interesting like that and then button your lips.'

Elizabeth tried and failed to stop her smile. 'His name —'

'Elizabeth, come and dance with us!'

Elizabeth turned to face Charlotte, one of her closest and dearest friends, only recently married. 'You look more than happy with Stephen. Why don't you lovebirds dance while I talk with Esther?'

Her friend pouted, her arm clumsily wrapped around her new husband's shoulders. 'Spoilsport.'

Elizabeth smiled as Stephen practically carried Charlotte towards the dance floor. 'She's far too much fun to be a married woman.'

'More about this *interesting* man, please,' Esther prompted.

Joseph's face filled Elizabeth's mind's eye as she sipped her champagne. 'He's different. Good, different.'

'How?'

Elizabeth put her glass on the table as she struggled to find the right words to describe just how much

70

Joseph Carter had struck her. 'Well, for one, he's passionate about women.'

'Women?'

She nodded. 'He said something about working side by side with a woman whom he loved. His eyes lit with a passion I've never seen before in anyone who spoke of a lover. It was . . . enchanting. It was as though this woman, maybe his wife, inspired him, drove him, rather than the other way around. As though, for the first time in my life, I watched a man who truly believed women to be equal to men.' She shook her head, excitement whispering through her. 'Can you imagine what it would be like to work with someone like that every day? What I could do in store for women and our much-sought equality?'

Suspicion clouded Esther's eyes. 'He seems a little too good to be true.'

'He should, yes, but you didn't see him, Esther. You didn't listen to him.' Elizabeth exhaled a shaky breath. 'There's something special about him. Mark by words.'

'A something your father would embrace, too?'

Elizabeth slumped back into her seat. 'Therein lies the biggest problem, I fear.'

Since meeting with Joseph Carter, she'd struggled to keep her euphoria under control. She could not risk her father witnessing her enthusiasm for a man who was not only working class, but also attracted her. Such an associate, when her father believed himself close to sealing her engagement with Noel Kelston, would most likely miraculously disappear from the store before he'd barely started working there.

She put down her drink and sighed heavily. 'I have to find a way to convince my father that providing

71

reduced-price lines throughout the clothing departments will be profitable. He refuses to embrace any
sort of diversity which, I fear, will be Pennington's
undoing.'

'And you think this new supplier could be the person to convince your father otherwise?'

'Maybe together we could, yes.'

'What is his name? This supplier. Had you known
of him before?'

'No. His name is Joseph Carter. I truly believe him
to be visionary. All he wants is to offer more affordable merchandise to our customers. To sell to patrons
of lesser means than the wealthy customers my father
holds in such high esteem.'

'Well, that is most refreshing.' Esther's hazel eyes
shadowed. 'Having money, privilege . . . it can't be
relied upon. Things change. Sometimes circumstances
can be completely beyond a person's control. If Pennington's can be a store where everyone is welcome,
regardless of their means . . . ' She abruptly stopped
and huffed a laugh, her cheeks lightly flushing.

Elizabeth stared at her friend. 'Are you all right?'

'Of course.'

Concerned, Elizabeth picked up her glass. Esther
had joined Pennington's just a year before, her exceptional talent, eye for detail and phenomenal window
displays had propelled her to head dresser in a matter
of months. As for her personal life, Elizabeth had yet
to persuade her friend to share more than the most
basic of details. Sometimes Esther's eyes flashed with
sadness, others with a fire that was inspiring.

Despite getting along from the very first day Esther
had started working as a shop girl at the store, Elizabeth sometimes felt her friend held back from further

72

deepening their friendship. Why, she had no idea. They often saw one another away from the store for after-work drinks or maybe tea at the weekend. Surely, Esther trusted that Elizabeth saw her as more than an employee?

With the gathering tension for women to be more and do more, Elizabeth firmly believed the more female friends a woman had, the better.

If they couldn't support each other in their lives and endeavours, who would?

She sipped her drink. 'If anything is bothering you — '

'It isn't.' Esther smiled. 'Truly.'

Knowing it would do no good to provoke Esther's protection of her private life, Elizabeth exhaled. 'Well, Mr Carter's wish for a range of moderately-priced goods has occurred to me in the past, but I've always hesitated in bringing up the possibility with my father.' She smiled. 'That changed with Mr Carter's confidence. He has the presence, personality and skill to help me make such an expansion successful. I'm sure of it.' She glanced around the room. 'Look at this place. The young working-class people stare at the wealthy patrons with mixed expressions of envy and adulation, but they are here. Amongst them. Drinking, relaxing. Seeing that just reinforces my instinct that such a venture could have a huge impact on sales.'

'Maybe, but I wouldn't think Mr Pennington will agree. He'll not like altering anything so drastically.'

'Do you know, his latest rantings often consist of his ridiculous opinions about the women's vote.'

'The Cause?'

'Yes. All he can talk about is the effect their campaigning might have on the store. On women in general. His fury at the sight of seeing upper-class women campaigning alongside working-class women is laughable. The man is living in a changing world and doesn't see that, somehow, that world will change regardless of his disapproval of it.'

'Indeed, it will.'

Esther's quiet tone turned Elizabeth to face her. 'Are you working for the Cause?'

'Yes, and the longer time goes on, the more I want to get further involved. The more support we have, the sooner things will change.'

'I'm glad, but just be careful how much you say when my father is around. He's vehemently against women's progression. I would hate for your job to be put in jeopardy.' Elizabeth pulled back her shoulders. 'Although, I'd promise he'd have to get through me first for that to happen.' She drained her glass and replaced it on the table. 'I have to find a way of doing something big that will make him accept a woman can manage a project, an exciting change, and Pennington's won't fall to pieces. You're the only female he gives the mildest appreciation of. You should be proud of yourself.'

'Oh, I am.' Esther glanced at the clock again. 'I should really get going.'

'Of course.' Elizabeth passed Esther her purse from the table and shook her head, her thoughts still impossibly shrouded in frustration. 'My father is little more than an old-fashioned snob who has the power to bring Pennington's to a grinding halt. If Mr Carter proves himself capable of creating a range of affordable, ready-to-wear gloves in a short time frame, I hope my father will find the idea impossible to veto.'

'Hmm, I'll need convincing of that, but for the time

being . . . ' Esther stood and wiggled her eyebrows. 'I do believe you are a little smitten with Mr Carter.'

Elizabeth's cheeks heated. 'Don't be absurd.'

Her friend's eyes widened knowingly.

Elizabeth laughed. 'Fine. I find him fascinating, but I wouldn't dare let him know just how taken I am with him.'

'Taken with *him*? Or his ideas?'

'His ideas, of course. It will be good to have someone inject some fresh ideas into the ladies' department. I wouldn't be surprised if Mr Carter proves his worth quicker than even I can predict.' She frowned. 'Why are you looking at me like that?'

'I'm probably overstepping the mark by saying this . . .'

'But?'

'But I deal with a lot of suppliers, and there are many trusted ones who'd love for us to expand our orders with them. Don't you think your enthusiasm for Mr Carter, a man you don't know, could mean opening yourself up to the risk of some serious backbiting?'

Elizabeth stared. Esther was right. Never before had she risked upsetting existing suppliers. They were the department's backbone. The people she relied on to deliver the merchandise in the correct number and on time. If Joseph Carter were to let her down, her father would use the incident as a way to further undermine her.

She shook her head, ignoring the trepidation unfurling inside her. 'No, I have to follow my instincts. My father won't be running Pennington's forever and I want to be the one to take the reins. Unless I prove myself capable of innovation, of plausible and profitable ideas and working relations, he'll never give me that chance. How else are women ever going to progress unless we take risks?'

Esther studied her, before she slowly smiled. 'We're the future whether men like it or not. We will not be silenced. Not anymore. I'll see you in the morning.'

Elizabeth watched her friend walk towards the cloakroom.

I'm good enough. Have always been good enough. No more will I bow down to Papa and let him destroy my spirit like he so devastatingly did Mama's.

Two lovers gently swayed on the dance floor, their eyes locked and their embraces tight about each other's bodies. She had sacrificed love; her fear of what it could provoke, and her mother's death, making it impossible to expose an inch of her heart, let alone give it. She'd come to accept a life alone yet couldn't help wondering what Joseph Carter would have to sacrifice for his ambition.

Success at Pennington's always came at a high personal cost. Always.

9

Joseph laid the glove he'd been stitching on his workbench and picked up the second letter he'd received from the ladies' department at Pennington's. Satisfaction warmed him as he re-read Mrs Woolden's words.

Dear Mr Carter,

After much consideration, myself and Miss Pennington would very much like for you to come into the store tomorrow at 2 p.m. so we might further discuss a trial commission.

We were very impressed with the samples you provided, and Miss Pennington has asked that you bring along any further design ideas you might have. We are keen to hear your suggested numbers and delivery time estimations during a trial period of one month.

If your gloves prove popular, Miss Pennington will, of course, very much welcome a new and continuing working relationship with you.

Yours sincerely,
Aveline Woolden (Mrs)
Deputy Head (Ladies' department)

Joseph glanced at the wall clock. He needed to get ready.

Putting away his work, he drew in a deep breath. A trial was by no means a guarantee, but the need to work with Pennington's continued to consume him.

A working relationship with the store would mean an income that would set his and Lillian's dreams in motion. He would not give up looking for her killer and bringing the bastard to justice. Nor would he falter on earning enough money to provide employment and help to those who needed it. This second meeting with Elizabeth Pennington had to go well.

Closing the workshop door, Joseph walked through the silent shop.

With his father out searching for new felt and cloth, Joseph turned the door sign to closed and looked around the darkened space. The difference between the striking, glamourous interior of Pennington's plunged Carter & Son into something dark and unappealing.

A notion that Joseph had been daft to ignore for so long.

The common men and women of this new era wanted more, demanded more, just as Joseph did himself. He slowly walked towards the back stairs that led to the upper living quarters.

Lillian had been a woman with a heart as big as the world. Her only want in life was her husband's happiness, children of their own one day and to help those in dire need. A need so strong that her charity had led her ever closer to the river at the edge of Bath. The river whose banks were resided by desperate, hungry and angry men, women and children.

Blighted by starvation and misery, crime was not a sin to these people but a necessity. A necessity that Lillian had seen past and acknowledged their suffering. Using whatever money she and Joseph could spare, she would diligently pack baskets with food, knitted blankets, socks and mittens and give them to the needy at least two nights each week.

Since her passing, Joseph had only managed the

food and the odd bit of cash, but once he had the means, he hoped to be in a position to offer work to some of these people. Or at least suggestions of how and where it could be secured for those willing to do whatever they could to escape their squalid surroundings. There had to be a happier life for the working men and women of the city.

Frustration coursed through him as Joseph mounted the steps. He would bring hope to these people and he would find Lillian's killer.

He blinked back his tears as his fury rose.

* * *

An hour later, Joseph followed Elizabeth Pennington around the ladies' department, energised and keen to get to work. He concentrated on everything she said in an effort to remember every tiny detail. Only a small number of women browsed the merchandise, three shop girls following them, offering suggestions and encouraging the customers' interest.

The department was separated from the main walkway by two alabaster columns, identical to those near the entrances of the other departments. Jewel-coloured velvet curtains divided one shopping area from the next; otherwise, the departments kept to a clear arrangement of counters and furniture, racks and shelving.

Despite the attractiveness of the displays, the subdued lighting and the pleasing scent of perfume and fresh flowers drifting through the department, Joseph itched to make some alterations.

Situated far in the back, the dresses, skirts and jackets could only be selected by a salesperson and

79

handed to the customer. Surely it would be a far better sales technique to allow the customers access to the clothes and have the opportunity to feel their weight and texture? The boundaries between the sales staff and customers needed to be reduced.

Furthermore, the limited selection of hats was placed on two stands on the serving counter, the gloves on three shelves to the side, more or less obscured by a huge potted palm. Lord only knew how he'd find the opportunity to suggest any changes to Elizabeth Pennington, but eventually he would.

'Mr Carter?'

He blinked and faced Elizabeth Pennington.

She raised her eyebrows. 'You were miles away. Is everything all right?'

'Of course.'

'Only you were not wearing the expression of a man eager to work with us. Quite the opposite. Is there something in the department you don't like?'

Joseph weighed up his options. Miss Pennington's demeanour towards him hadn't strayed from the professional for the entire time he'd been there and her assertion of one month's trial had been reiterated several times.

He cleared his throat. 'Can I be candid?'

Her dark green gaze wandered over his face before she nodded.

Walking past her, Joseph inhaled the soft scent of her perfume before he could consider the impairment of its effect. Flowers in springtime. Soft summer days and heady, tempting evenings. He swallowed hard and laid his hand upon the glass-topped counter. *Concentrate, you fool.*

'Your gloves and hats are displayed way back

here. Might you consider setting up a display at the entrance? Position them close enough that customers might touch them? Try them on? Maybe add a full-length mirror to the side here.' He gestured with his hand, visions forming in his mind. 'That way, the women could see how they look and the shop girls and Mrs Woolden could suggest colours and materials.'

Her brow creased as she considered him, the dark green of her tailored jacket emphasising the beautiful hue of her eyes. 'That's quite a suggestion, Mr Carter. But one I like very much.'

Encouraged by her confidence in his proposals, Joseph stood a little taller and smiled. 'I'm glad.'

'But before we make any changes to the layout of the department, we need to concentrate on your designs. Won't you join me in my office?'

He followed her through the department and into her office, his optimism heightened, and any previous nervousness quashed. If she was prepared to listen to his ideas at such an early stage in their association, who knew what she might agree to with regards to his products in the future?

She walked behind her desk. 'Take a seat.'

Joseph sat as she pulled a thin sheaf of papers towards her.

Casting her gaze over them, she looked up. 'I have given your month's trial some thought and wondered if you would be agreeable to producing ten pairs of gloves each week. If they sell, we can then think about increasing production, but I'm not willing to commit to any more than that in the first instance.'

Joseph nodded. The number would be a stretch considering the existing orders he had to honour through Carter & Son, but he would work day and night to deliver. Better still, over-deliver. 'I think that will be a good position to start. Did you want specific gloves made from the samples you've seen?'

'I've chosen my four favourites for now.' She passed him the papers. 'You'll see I have written the design number and amount to be produced for each pair. What do you think?'

He took the papers and read her notes, slowly nodding. Two designs were fairly straightforward and two were a little more complex but nothing he couldn't manage. He raised his eyes to hers. 'Perfect and my cut of the profits?'

She held his gaze. 'Seventy-thirty to Pennington's.'

He smiled. 'Sixty-forty.'

Her eyes lingered on his. Slowly, a brightness lit the startling green and she smiled. 'Sixty-forty, it is. For the trial. We'll renegotiate when we've seen how well and how fast they sell. Agreed?'

Triumphant that his targeted split had been established with such quick arbitration, Joseph inhaled the welcome feeling that he and Elizabeth Pennington just might work together exceedingly well. He nodded.

'Agreed.'

'Good. Then if you'd like to sign the contract, I'll do the same.'

She plucked a gold pen from her desk and handed it to him.

Dragging his gaze from hers, Joseph signed the paper, his heart thundering. This was the first step on what he hoped to be an entirely fruitful road.

He passed her the papers and she scribbled her signature beside his. 'I'll have a copy made for you to collect when we return.'

'When we return?' he asked, confused.

'Yes. I thought you might like a peek into our work-room.'

Joseph frowned. 'Why?'

'Because, Mr Carter, if we intend to sell in numbers that will make us both money, it's inevitable your designs will be made here. If you are uncomfortable with that, then — '

'No. Not at all.' Excitement unfurled in the pit of his stomach. The numbers of gloves that could be produced by a permanent, working staff was mind-boggling. Although, Lord only knew how his father would react to Pennington's staff knowing the ins and outs of Carter & Son's design and production processes. 'I hadn't even contemplated that you might provide me with manufacturing staff.'

'But of course. Why don't we head downstairs?'

She brushed past him and exited the office, leaving him to follow. This investment in his gloves — in him — most certainly meant Elizabeth Pennington believed a joint venture between them could indeed make money . . . lots of money.

Enough money that he could one day soon offer employment to others.

They walked through the department into the corridor.

The powerful kinship he felt with Elizabeth Pennington surprised him over and over again. Her ability to knock him off balance when he least expected it only made her more and more intriguing. She walked ahead of him and Joseph roamed his gaze over the back of her head, lower to her small waist and skirted backside.

In two long years, he'd thought of nothing but work,

money, success, but now he found his libido awakened. It was madness.

Briefly closing his eyes, he fought to realign his equilibrium. To falter in his focus now would mean certain disaster. His growing attraction to this woman — this upper-class woman — had to be quashed and quickly.

As they descended the stairs, Joseph swept his study over the glittering extravagance of the store. Expensively dressed people bustled back and forth, women's faces alight with excitement and delight. There was a certain magic to Pennington's. An enchantment that hovered over the customers, tempting and enticing. Making them purchase that scent, that fan, that stole . . . become the people they longed and aspired to be.

Elizabeth Pennington led him along a darkened corridor in the basement of the store.

They'd only walked a short distance when she abruptly stopped and faced him. 'I very rarely come down here, so some workers may be surprised to see me, but I wanted you to see how and where we produce our merchandise. Most small suppliers are happy for our staff to produce their products once they are satisfied with the quality. Fingers crossed, you'll assume that same trust to us, as well.'

'I'm sure I will. Business is business. Profit is profit.'

Turning, she opened a door to the side of her and stepped inside.

The unmistakable smell of scorched textiles and glue immediately assaulted his nostrils. As the familiar smell grew stronger, Joseph breathed deep. It was like coming home.

He looked around the room, noting the hat blocks in the far corner, their blue flames flickering, and a row of six wooden benches, each with three men working on either side. A quick summary indicated four benches were for the production of hats and two for gloves.

Bright fabrics, feathers and netting were piled in cubbyholes along one wall. Another table held boxes marked with different-sized templates, needles, tape and pins.

As Joseph studied the men toiling away at various stages of construction, his eagerness to see his gloves produced and placed on the shelves of the ladies' department burned ever hotter.

'Let me introduce you to our most experienced glove maker.' Elizabeth Pennington strode towards the other side of the room, her heels clicking on the stone floor. 'Mr Griggs? Might I interrupt you for a moment?'

Mr Griggs started as he turned, his eyes widening for a second before he whipped off his spectacles and stood. 'Miss Pennington. This is a surprise.'

She gently touched the older man's elbow and smiled. 'You know I like to pop in and see everyone from time to time.' She turned to Joseph. 'This is Mr Carter. He's a designer and glove maker and we will be giving a selection of his gloves a month's trial. I thought it a nice touch if he saw where they could be made en masse if the trial is successful.'

Mr Griggs stuck out his hand to Joseph. 'Albert Griggs, sir. Nice to meet you.'

'Pleasure is mine, Mr Griggs.' Joseph firmly grasped the other man's hand and immediately recognised the calloused, toughened skin of a man used to working with his hands day after day. 'You have quite the busy team here.'

'We do, sir.' Albert wiped his forearm across his brow, leaving a grey streak in its path. 'Orders come in thick and fast but, between us, we keep on top of things.'

Elizabeth Pennington smiled. 'Mr Griggs is being modest, Mr Carter. Pennington's would be lost without him and his staff.'

Her eyes gleamed with admiration and sincerity. The way she'd gently touched the man's elbow spoke volumes about the kind of woman who lay beneath her professional persona. A woman who respected. Who cared. Attributes that only served to worry Joseph further. She was fast becoming a woman he wanted to know better.

She faced him. 'Well, why don't I leave you to look around? If you return to my office once you're done, we can discuss when you estimate to have your first batch of gloves ready.'

With a final nod to Albert, Elizabeth Pennington walked to the door, stopping to exchange a few words with different people before she disappeared into the corridor.

Joseph turned to Albert, who visibly slumped the minute the workroom door closed. 'Thank the Lord Miss Pennington is nothing like her old man.' He turned to Joseph. 'So, what would you like to see first?'

Intrigued how different the owner of Pennington's was compared with his daughter, Joseph frowned. 'What's he like? Mr Pennington.'

Albert shrugged. 'We never see him down here and I haven't even spoken to him. All I know is, he keeps Miss Pennington on a very tight leash.'

A tight leash? Joseph frowned. He couldn't imagine anyone achieving such a thing with regards to

Elizabeth Pennington. 'Meaning?'

'Meaning, if she was running this place, things would be different. She has vision, kindness, a sense of who we are, listens to what we have to say.

Her old man cares for nothing but the moneyed folk who grace the floors upstairs.' He sighed. 'Unfortunately, while Pennington remains in charge, there's very little his daughter can do to change things. Anyway, why don't I show you around?'

As Albert walked ahead, Joseph slowly followed, his mind lingering on Miss Pennington and her father. He looked at the grim concentration etched on the employees' faces. All the workers were male which surprised Joseph considering Miss Pennington's obvious care and respect for Mrs Woolden and the other female staff. Was the lack of women stitchers employed in the workroom her father's doing?

Joseph instinctively felt it must be.

The distinct lack of conversation and the way the men shot morose looks at one another's work, illustrated a clear lack of morale — not to mention what he suspected to be a very unhealthy and misplaced sense of rivalry. 'Is this how it usually is, day to day?'

'How what is?'

'Cutting and stitching. On to the next one. Is there nothing creative in between?'

'Creative?' Albert chuckled as they walked. 'We're stitchers, cutters and finishers. There's no in-between. The sooner a worker accepts that, the better.'

Joseph stared at the men's bowed heads as Albert pointed out their various jobs and positions. These men worked with gloves and hats every day. Had anyone ever asked them whether they had an interest in design or ideas for speedier manufacturing?

He thought not.

Impatient to pick up a pencil and paper, to do something towards cooling the fire inside him to do better — be better — Joseph flexed and relaxed his fingers. He might be inside Pennington's doors, but he had a tough journey ahead to make his mark. Frustration unfurled as his objective to get his gloves to the masses suddenly felt uncomfortably distant.

Would it benefit his goal if he laboured in the workroom for a time? Side by side with these men and learned about Pennington's from the lower rungs through to the top. The strange sensation of belonging in this room only grew stronger with each step.

What if he could find a way to allow these men to produce gloves more quickly and in greater volume than ever before? Right now, he sensed only tedium, laced with a resigned acceptance of little more. If he could provide the inspiration to help these workers enjoy their endeavours until they took immense pride in their occupation, wouldn't that go some way to giving Joseph the closure he sought? The self-satisfaction that he couldn't seem to find within himself anymore, no matter how hard he tried.

He had sufficient workspace at the family shop but needed to be seen by Miss Pennington. Gain her trust and belief in him. She'd already procured both from him. Her kindness to her staff, the way she held their gazes when she spoke with them and the soft smile at her pretty lips, all went a long way to securing his trust in her . . . his like of her.

Beginning to care for her was undoubtedly foolhardy considering his unworthiness of any relationship with a woman, but he couldn't worry about that right now. There was work to be done.

10

'Wait, so if the trial goes well, Elizabeth Pennington will consider giving you a manufacturing team? On her premises?'

Joseph lowered his newspaper and met his father's disbelieving stare. 'I wouldn't have thought she'd give me a team. I'll still continue to work at Carter & Son, Pa, if that's what you're worrying about. If the trial is a success, I'll offer my services as a short-term consultant.'

'There's got to be more to it as far as Miss Pennington is concerned.'

Bracing himself for yet another onslaught of negativity, Joseph put his paper to the side and reached for his brandy. 'Pennington's production staff manufacture goods for other suppliers. Why not us? The output will be something we could only dream of and that would be with me working night and day.'

'I understand that.' His father narrowed his eyes. 'What I don't understand is why you need to be there.'

'Look, let's wait to see if I pass the trial first, but I need to be at Pennington's as much as possible in order to secure Miss Pennington's belief in me. I've already identified possible flaws in their production system and if I can show her ways things can be improved, all the better for our future.'

'So you think she'll just give you free rein to implement changes in a store that she'll most likely own one day?' His father huffed a laugh. 'I think she's setting you up for a fall. No woman of that class is going to give a damn what the likes of us think or say. They never have, and they never will.'

Defence for Elizabeth Pennington rose. 'She's not like that.'

His father raised his eyebrows, his gaze sceptical as he eyed Joseph over the rim of his glasses. 'If you believe that, I think you'll be better off staying far away from the place. Clearly, when you're with this woman, you're not thinking straight.'

Joseph feigned intense interest in the flickering flames in the hearth. 'If I can make improvements to the production of merchandise within my month's trial, I can ensure a more profitable cut of revenue for us. This is as much about providing you with a comfortable retirement than it is about anything else.'

Joseph sipped his drink, the warm liquor welcome against the chill permeating the room despite the fire and drawn curtains. 'My plan is to become important to Miss Pennington. Have her need me like we need her. Pennington's workers are tired, unmotivated and bored. I'm convinced I cannot only inject some enthusiasm into them, but also gain their trust.'

'To what end?'

'To the end that they'll have pride in their work and thus work better, harder and faster. The entire foundation of approaching Pennington's was to get my gloves in their store and selling by the hundreds. If their manufacturing team are motivated, they'll work harder and, in turn, that will impress Miss Pennington. Which, fingers crossed, will lead to higher wages, promotion and other things for these men. Hopefully, women, too. I felt the monotony, lack of hope and ambition.' Joseph took a gulp of his brandy. 'Doing this will be no less than what Lillian would've

90

expected from me.'

'If you manage to make those men happier in their work, that will only benefit Pennington's, not us.'

Maybe his father spoke the truth, but Joseph had to help the workers at Pennington's. Doing something good would hopefully help soothe a little of his pain. Give him another reason to keep going, keep believing that in time he wouldn't feel as unworthy as he had every day for the last two years.

He swirled his brandy and took a hefty gulp, fighting his demons as they sat heavy on his shoulders. 'Helping, inspiring, producing and selling, that's all I have to offer the world, so why not use it any way I can?'

'I'm not stupid, son.'

'What does that mean?'

'It means this has got nothing to do with helping those men. Working at Pennington's, having your face seen by the moneyed there, is helping you, not them.'

Joseph clenched his jaw, silently cursing his father's continued negativity and wondering when he would ever feel as free and happy as he once had. He glared. 'What will it take to convince you having ambition does not equate to being selfish? I love my work. Why not use that passion to inspire others?'

'You're not Lillian. That was her job, her heart, not yours.'

Tears burned painfully behind Joseph's eyes and he steadfastly blinked them back. 'No, I'm not her.' He stood, his body trembling. 'But I was her husband. I was the man she loved, and God knows, since she died, every lesson, every part of her that was good, has seeped inside me. Deep inside, where I know she'll live for the rest of my days. So maybe it's that making

91

me reach out to people. Making me want to help them. Why not think on that for a while?'

Slamming his glass on the table, Joseph stormed from the room and along the landing to his bedroom. Closing the door, he walked to the window and planted his hands on his hips as he stared at the moonlit water running beneath Pulteney Bridge.

He would see his plan through no matter what his father said. Changing that workroom, encouraging those men, had now merged with Joseph's plan to be more than successful in business. He wanted to be a success in life, too.

He stared at a courting couple as they walked arm in arm along the river.

Love.

Something everyone wanted, but not everyone deserved. He'd been blessed with a taste of its paradise and would never ask for it again. Love hurt. Love broke hearts.

He would always be better off alone.

11

Elizabeth threw her head back and laughed. 'Charlotte, you are incorrigible. How can you ask Stephen to whisk you away on holiday when you have barely been back from your honeymoon a month?'

Her best friend grinned. 'Because, my darling Elizabeth, he loves me even more when I'm relaxed and enjoying myself.' She wiggled her eyebrows. 'Believe me, it benefits him much more than me in the long run.'

Shaking her head, Elizabeth lifted her teacup and stared around the small tearoom situated on Gay Street. Cosy and sweetly decorated in soft pastel shades of pink and blue, the tearoom was a simplistic escape from the glamour of the store that Elizabeth occasionally craved. She and Charlotte liked to frequent Mrs Mackle's Tearoom as much as possible when they could find time to spend a couple of hours together.

'You know,' Elizabeth sighed, knowing her friend wanted to learn more about Joseph Carter than anybody else in the whole of Bath. 'You haven't even asked me if Mr Carter passed his trial.'

'Has he?' Charlotte's eyes widened, and she grinned. 'I knew it. The man sounds absolutely wonderful and very talented.' She reached into her purse and revealed a pair of kid gloves. 'These are his. Look at them.'

Elizabeth laughed. 'There is no need for me to look at them, I'm almost as familiar with Joseph's work as he is. Not only have his gloves sold phenomenally well, he's met every delivery deadline, no matter how tight I set it and continues to offer new designs. In fact, the man is so driven, so exceptionally talented and affable, I am in a state of nervousness that he might well seek association with a competitor at some time in the future.'

'Surely not? If you are getting along as splendidly as you seem to be. Why would he seek an alternative buyer?'

'True, but . . . ' Elizabeth exhaled. 'I need to ensure his excitement to work with us doesn't falter. He might be working as a consultant in the workroom for now, but I really want to offer him something permanent. How can I do that when he has premises of his own?'

'But if his gloves continue to sell as they have been, and he earns more money, he could well come to be in a position that he no longer needs his shop. It is only a small establishment, you know.'

Surprised that Charlotte would know such a thing, Elizabeth lowered her voice. 'You've seen his shop? Carter & Son?'

Charlotte raised her eyebrows. 'Haven't you?'

'No. No, I haven't.'

'Why not? Aren't you curious?'

Elizabeth lifted her cup. Curious was an understatement of how she was growing to feel about Joseph. It seemed the man intruded her thoughts more and more often, as well as making her ever more determined to make Pennington's hers so she was free to make and implement every decision and idea that came to her. 'I am curious, and time and again, I've considered venturing past his shop but thought it far too risky to be caught looking. I want to exude the same confidence Joseph seems to have. Something tells me he belongs at Pennington's and always will.'

'But you suspect you might have trouble convincing Mr Carter of that?'

'Yes, but little by little, he's spending more and more time at the store. Fingers crossed, something will work out that suits us both. I've agreed to a fair wage on top of his profit cut on the gloves. We're producing four times as many per week, already.'

'Well, that's wonderful.' Charlotte squeezed Elizabeth's fingers where they lay on the table. 'I'm thrilled for you.' She grimaced. 'But I have to get moving, I'm afraid. We're having Stephen's parents for dinner and he'll never forgive me if I'm not there to supervise the staff.'

Elizabeth smiled. 'Of course.'

They left some money on the table and gathered their things.

Once on the street, Elizabeth kissed her friend's cheeks and began making her way back to the store.

When she arrived, Pennington's foyer was thinning in the mid-afternoon lull and Elizabeth slowed her usually hurried steps. It was nearing the end of February and footfall had steadily increased over the last two weeks. It pleased her to see the smiling faces of the shop girls behind the counters, their uniforms and hair pristine, their faces open and friendly.

Her concerns about lack of morale wavered as the employees nodded and smiled in her direction, their hands busy boxing products and writing receipts to be taken to the cash desks. Was her father right? Could her concerns for the younger men and women who worked at Pennington's be purely emotional?

The insecurity that she might not possess what was

needed to run the store in an entirely businesslike manner struck ice in her heart once more, reminding her of every one of the derogatory comments her father had thrown at her over the years.

Again, and again, he told her she would never be capable of managing his empire. Never be good enough to not only run the store but make it even better that it was today.

She *had* to be good enough. Becoming the mistress of Pennington's had consumed her since her mother's death. Overtaking her heart and mind, until there was no room for anything else. Everything inside her fought to be more than a woman who married a man and bore him children, only to have him chip away every ounce of her self-confidence until death seemed the only avenue to liberty.

She breathed deep.

The store might look as sparklingly efficient as it always had, but something inside Elizabeth had changed. 'As it always had' screamed of stagnancy and immobility and, with that, her father's grip clasped around her like the devil's claws. She had to make her mark in some way, so Pennington's felt like hers, even if it remained her father's for years to come.

Resentment inched into her blood and she cursed her inability to fight back, hating the ugly stain her frustration left on her soul. Constantly striving to prove her worth and persuade her father she was capable of making every decision, not just the ones he deigned to allow her, was as tiring as it was depressing.

As she ascended the stairs to the second floor, Joseph came into her mind once again.

They had sold out of every pair of his gloves in the first two weeks of his trial, and he'd quickly volunteered to make double the agreed amount for weeks three and four. Elizabeth smiled. He really had a force all of his own. A force that had not only exceeded her expectations, but those of Mrs Woolden, too.

Not to mention the extremely stony-faced Mr Weir, the head of the men's department, who had begun to ask more and more questions about Joseph. So far, her father had remained suspiciously distant about Joseph's trial and his instalment in the workroom. Something that caused a deep protectiveness of him to stir in Elizabeth. She didn't doubt for a moment her father would have something up his sleeve ready to use to his advantage, and her humiliation, whenever he felt cause to utilise it.

She had to be on her guard at all times, otherwise her father would succeed in taking Joseph away from her.

His performance and work ethic had convinced Elizabeth wholeheartedly to persuade him to oversee the manufacturing of his gloves in-store. She had barely been able to contain her elation when he'd agreed — albeit with the clear conditions that he would return to his own shop as and when he was needed and would not linger at Pennington's without a wage.

She'd contracted everything he'd asked for, and for not a single day in the last two weeks Joseph had been working at the store had she had cause to regret her decision.

She longed to speak with him again, but how could she enquire after him without raising suspicion about her over interest?

Taking a deep breath, she pulled back her shoulders and shook off her self-doubt. If she wanted to speak with Joseph, she had every right to do so.

He'd had time to get a feel for the store by now and she was keen to know his thoughts. And there would be thoughts. His blue eyes were a window to a quick and intelligent brain. A brain she suspected never stilled.

Once again, her heart gave an unfamiliar blip. A little shock to her system, reminding her that she had not felt as drawn to a man as she was to Joseph in her entire life. Men were usually a nemesis. A gender to watch and be wary of. Yet, with Joseph, the opposite in her was evoked. She wanted to be closer to him . . . have him watch her as she watched him.

Shame and fear burned her face and neck as she continued to walk.

Her gaze fell on a board beside her indicating the various floors of the store. Notification of the elegant Butterfly restaurant on the fourth floor struck an idea.

An after-hours drinks party for the men's and ladies' department staff.

A genial gathering that provided the perfect opportunity to talk to Joseph in a relaxed and easy environment. Not only with Joseph, but the rest of the workforce, too.

She walked into the ladies' department, excitement quickening her steps. What better environment in which to listen to what her staff had in mind for the coming months or garner any dissatisfaction?

She approached Mrs Woolden as she was quietly reprimanding Millicent, one of Elizabeth's favourite shop girls. She bit back her smile. Millicent wore the same carefree expression she always did, her gaze darting from Mrs Woolden to the customer waiting at the counter.

Elizabeth delicately coughed. 'Mrs Woolden, could you spare a moment?'

The older woman turned, her frown vanishing under a smile. 'Miss Pennington. Of course.' She turned to Millicent. 'Let that be a lesson to you. Now, please see to the lady waiting.'

'Yes, Mrs Woolden.'

Millicent made her escape and Mrs. Woolden shook her head. 'I wonder how the girl manages to charm so many customers. Her head is so rarely in the here and now, I cannot think how she secures so many purchases.'

'I detect a certain ambition in Millicent. She's an asset to the department.' Elizabeth touched her hand to Mrs Woolden's elbow and steered her towards a corner of the room. 'I would like to host a small drinks party for the ladies' and men's departments this evening. Could you let the staff know? I'll be heading to the men's department shortly to inform Mr Weir. The manufacturing staff will also be included. Six o'clock. Top floor.'

'I'm sure the girls will be delighted.'

'Then I'll see everyone shortly.'

Elizabeth left the department and strode along the main area of the second floor towards the men's department, optimism flowing through her. There was something about Joseph that instilled hope and possibility in her. His love of his vocation and tenacity to reach his objectives matched her own, making her certain they could work side by side to achieve both their goals.

He looked and spoke to her like an equal. He respected her opinions. Wanted to hear her input. That alone stirred her deepest, most untapped, feelings. Feelings that scared and excited her in equal measure.

Considering her tentative happiness could be quashed within moments of her father and Joseph meeting, if he should suspect her overfondness, she prayed she could keep Joseph far from her father for as long as possible — preferably forever. At least Joseph was placed in the workroom. The one area of the store in which her father would never set foot.

The floor was thick with activity as she neared the men's department. Smartly dressed men and women, some with children, strolled around the store, their gazes equally as admiring of the glittering, perfumed decor as the merchandise itself. Anyone could see her father's strategy of appealing to the carriage trade brought customers through the door, but Joseph's prediction of increased profits through providing the middle class a chance to own beautiful things fuelled Elizabeth's imagination.

Pennington's glittered with a promise of affluence, achievement and prosperity. Everyone deserved a slice of that beguiling aspiration. Everyone.

Something had to change.

Her gaze fell on her father as he spoke with a well-dressed lady and gentleman farther along the main walk of the second floor and dread immediately knotted Elizabeth's stomach. She had no choice but to inform him about tonight's gathering. If he were to discover the meeting halfway through, he would have no qualms about publicly reprimanding her, thus destroying any progress she might have made with the staff.

Her father's gaze caught hers and she nodded, offering him a tight smile as she approached him.

Taking a deep breath, she held fast to the inspiration and energy Joseph evoked in her.

Edward Pennington bid good day to the couple and faced Elizabeth, slowly drawing off his spectacles and studying her with his sharp, grey eyes. 'Elizabeth, my dear, I was just about to ask Mrs Chadwick to summon you. Your timing is perfect.'

Curiosity mixed with caution as Elizabeth clasped her hands in front of her. 'There's something you wish to discuss?'

'Many things, but the first is the latest memorandum you left on my desk regarding the toy department.'

She straightened her spine, summoning every ounce of her fortitude. 'I think I could be an asset to the department, Papa. You know children interest me. My suggestions are valid and — '

'Frankly impossible.'

She curled her hands into fists at her sides, her nails pinching her palms. 'How so?'

'For one, you have grand plans of spending and stocking the department to capacity all year round.'

'Do children not play all year round? Why limit ourselves to Christmas? You have promised me you will consider my idea of reflecting the seasons in the store's décor, why could we not reflect the seasons in the toy department, too? Bats and balls, dolls and prams in the spring. Kites and boats, soft bears and picnic baskets for the summer.' Encouraged by the tiniest flicker of interest in his eyes, Elizabeth continued. 'We need ways of appealing to our existing customers, as well as drawing in the new. We have to keep stretching our imaginations.' She took a breath. 'Which is why I have invited the ladies' departments for drinks in the restaurant this evening. I was just on my way to speak to George about the men's department staff joining us, too.'

'What?' Spittle dashed Edward Pennington's lips as he quickly looked about him, before gripping her arm and forcing her to the edge of the corridor. 'Floor staff enjoying drinks in my store after-hours? Have you lost your mind?'

'My mind is exactly what I'm using. We need to understand the staff who deal with the customers every day. What can we really learn from our floor walks? We might share the odd pleasantry or two with our customers, but rarely are either of us on the receiving end of complaints or dissatisfaction.' She lowered her tense shoulders and dropped her voice. 'Please, Papa, let me have this drinks party. If it proves fruitless, then I'll not suggest such a thing again.'

He pulled back his shoulders, his jaw tight. 'No.'

Frustration mounted, and Elizabeth glared. 'I'm the head of the ladies' department. Let me make the department more profitable and, God willing, the same will be reflected in menswear. This gathering is a sound business strategy.'

Their gazes locked, and Elizabeth cursed the way her heart beat a little faster under his scrutiny. It was time she used every bit of ammunition she had. Her most prominent advantage over her father would always be her mutually respectful relationship with the floor staff — something her father would never achieve because of his antiquated opinions on how to treat their employees.

Suddenly, something flickered and changed in his gaze. A soft smile playing at his lips, he stepped back. 'Fine.'

She baulked. 'Fine?'

102

'Yes.' His eyes gleamed with inexplicable glee. 'Why not? I, too, shall attend. I will mix and smile with my staff and watch how your latest madness unfolds.'

'So, you're coming to mock me?'

'Of course not. I'm giving you what you want. The rest is up to you.'

12

Joseph stood alone as he studied the scene in front of him.

There was no denying the opulence of Pennington's Butterfly restaurant. Crystal chandeliers lit the room, a long table bearing sherry, wine, water and pink lemonade lined one pale green and cream wall. Along another, a table offered tiny sandwiches and canapes. Each table was scattered with delicate pieces of coloured paper.

Everything seemed just a little too flamboyant for the staff. So why were they here? He understood from Albert Griggs that this gathering was the first of its kind as far as he knew. Was it Elizabeth Pennington's doing? Or her father's? And what were either of them expecting to happen?

'Mr Carter. Good evening.'

Joseph turned, hoping his expression did not betray his surprise — and pleasure — that Elizabeth Pennington should choose to seek him out.

'Miss Pennington.'

'Are you enjoying yourself?'

He lifted his glass. 'Absolutely.'

'Good.' She glanced about the room. 'And what are your impressions of Pennington's so far?'

'I'm working with some decent chaps. They've made me very welcome.' Now he had her undivided attention, it would be foolish to squander it. He coughed. 'But . . .'

Her eyes glinted with undisguised curiosity. 'Yes?'

He hesitated. One wrong move and his plans could come to an abrupt halt at the end of the month. Obviously still a little cautious about their agreement, she'd written into his contract that his consultancy position would be reviewed on a monthly basis.

'Mr Carter?' She frowned. 'Please, what else is it you wish to say? I cannot help but wonder if I, my father, and the rest of the department heads have failed to explore whether your enthusiasm can be found in other members of staff. There could be untapped ideas simmering in their minds and we've extended no invitation to share them. That's what I wanted this evening to be about. Allowing *all* the clothing staff to speak openly with me.'

Joseph studied her. She appeared to be genuine enough. He exhaled. 'The men in the workroom are bored . . . and painfully uninspired. They come into work knowing today will be the same as yesterday. This week the same as the last. They're neither challenged, nor excited about what they do, or why they are doing it. Their skills — and they have many — are not being used in a way that could be outstanding for Pennington's.'

'I see.'

'There are many extremely skilled glove makers and milliners in that workroom, who are proud to work here, and that pride shows itself in them working hard and taking their wages home without complaint.'

'Then I'm not sure I entirely understand what you're trying to tell me.'

He looked at Albert Griggs who stood talking with some other manufacturing staff. The split between them and the sales staff was laughingly evident by the breadth of tiled floor separating them as they socialised on opposite sides of the room.

Turning, he faced Elizabeth Pennington. 'But are they thanked for their work in the same way as the sales staff? Probably not. They feel undervalued. Unimportant.' He nodded towards the space in front of them. 'Look at the segregation between the manufacturers and the sales staff. Does that seem right to you?' He faced her. 'Although they probably wouldn't thank me for pointing that out to you.'

She studied her staff, her brow furrowed.

The murmur of conversation, clinking glasses and occasional laughter seemed to grow in volume as her silence continued.

Abruptly, she faced him, her gaze intense and her colour high. 'Why wouldn't they thank you if you have their best interests at heart?'

'Because their jobs mean food on the table and a roof over their families' heads.' He sipped his drink. 'I'm not a man without money, Miss Pennington, but the fact remains that I don't have a family to feed as many of these men and women do. I'm not even sure I ever will, but that doesn't mean I'm oblivious to the struggles of those who do. If Pennington's wants to stand out amongst the competition, we need to get the men and women who work here excited about their work, rather than merely grateful.'

She lifted her eyebrows, her green gaze almost teasing. 'We?'

He smiled. 'We.'

Her eyes burned with interest, although what interested her the most, Joseph couldn't determine. The financial bondage he'd described affected at least three-quarters of the city. He understood she had a professionalism to uphold, but time and again, Joseph sensed her deep care for her staff's personal circumstances, and if that virtue helped his cause, all the better.

She sipped her drink. 'Does this mean you could be willing to spend more of your working day at Pennington's? Maybe lessen your load at your own premises?'

Joseph frowned. What was she inferring? Did she mean for him to give up Carter & Son in favour of Pennington's? Good God, his father would have a heart attack if he heard her suggest such a thing. He coughed. 'I think that's a slight presumption, Miss Pennington.'

A light flush coloured her cheeks and she dipped her gaze, before meeting his eyes once more. 'It's just you seem wholly invested in my staff. I can't help wondering if you have other plans you've yet to share with me.'

She certainly had him there. He drew in a long breath and released it. 'Maybe it's because I don't just want the chance to excel myself but help others to have their chance too.' His passion stirred awake as he felt Lillian beside him, encouraging his boldness. 'Why shouldn't these men become a part of the bigger picture? I have many changes and innovations I think will benefit your staff as well as your customers and, in turn, add to your personal success, too.'

'Why would you so generously offer your ideas to me rather than keep them for yourself?'

'Because I haven't the means to help others at the moment. You do. One day, I hope to employ those desperate to work but have no idea where to start. Give others the opportunity to move forward.'

'And is that why you came to Pennington's? To move forward?'

'Yes.'

Joseph hesitated. What choice did he have but to reveal more of himself if he stood any chance of gaining an offer of a permanent contract? The more he thought about the prospect of that, the more it made sense for him to have a guaranteed income in order to finance his plans. But Elizabeth Pennington was shrewd, and well within her rights to challenge him should he push too hard.

He pulled back his shoulders. 'Progression is threatening to put an end to the small shopkeeper. I want to be on solid ground before the ship sinks. I refuse to see my grandfather's, my father's and my successes tossed aside as though they are worthless. I want to walk away with money in my pocket and my head held high, and that's exactly what I'll make happen.'

Her green gaze lingered on his and Joseph was certain he saw a spark of admiration in their depths. 'You are very proud of your family's achievements, aren't you?'

'Yes.'

'But, clearly, you still want more.'

Joseph's heart quickened. 'For my family and others, too.'

She softly smiled. 'I understand. In many ways, I wish I didn't, but I do. My father owns a house on one of the most prestigious streets in Bath. He owns another in Surrey and another in Brighton.'

Joseph frowned. Why was she telling him this?

'But . . . ' She sighed. 'I want nothing of his money. Nothing of his property.'

'What do you want?' But he already knew the answer.

'I want this store.' She roamed her gaze over his

108

face, hesitating at his mouth. 'Do you know why?'

Joseph smiled, attraction spreading through him. 'Because it's here you can make a difference.'

She grinned, her beautiful eyes shining with an intoxicating blend of relief and pleasure. 'Exactly.'

Their gazes locked, and Joseph stood stock-still as an almost overwhelming need to press his lips to hers simmered inside him.

Abruptly, she turned away, her cheeks flushed. Her gaze landed on something, or someone, across the room and her smile immediately vanished and her body stiffened.

Joseph followed the direction of her gaze. Edward Pennington. The man's face had graced enough newspapers over the years that Joseph immediately recognised him. Tall, robust, and considerably over-weight, Pennington strode through the remaining staff towards them, his focus on Joseph.

He slid his gaze from Edward Pennington to his daughter. 'Is he the type of father to stop you from leading your own life?'

She flinched as though he'd unwittingly stabbed her with his words, but before he could say something, apologise or ask her what it was he had said that so clearly affected her, Edward Pennington drew to their side.

'Elizabeth, my dear, people are leaving, yet you stand here alone with this gentleman as though he is the only person of interest in the room.' He held his hand out to Joseph. 'Edward Pennington. And you are?'

Joseph stared at Elizabeth Pennington's father. How was it possible that this man, with a pockmarked, red-veined face and grey hair oiled to within an inch of its life, could have sired a woman as astoundingly beautiful as his daughter?

He forced a smile, taking Pennington's hand firmly. 'Joseph Carter, sir. At your service.'

An unfathomable satisfaction flitted through Edward Pennington's gaze as he shook and released Joseph's hand. 'Carter, you say. Well, my daughter seems very taken with you, sir.'

'Papa —'

Pennington sharply raised his hand, cutting off Elizabeth's words. He held Joseph's gaze. 'You are a glove maker, are you not?'

'I am, sir.' Joseph stole a glance at Elizabeth. She looked away into the distance, her jaw tight. 'One I hope will benefit your fine store.'

'And your father is a glove maker, too?'

'A milliner, sir.'

'Indeed. And you are a product of your parents, not the other way around, correct?'

Joseph looked again at Elizabeth who regarded her father with undisguised suspicion. Which was exactly what filled Joseph. Where was the man going with this? He faced Pennington. 'I am, yes.'

'Then do you not agree it makes a child full of their own self-importance if they feel they are in the position to save a parent or, indeed, attempt to undermine them?'

'That depends, sir.'

Pennington arched an eyebrow. 'Oh? On what, exactly?'

'I am working hard to do the best I can by my father, by a man I not only admire and respect but love deeply. However, I agree no one has the right to steer other people's lives. Not sons or daughters, nor parents. We're all on borrowed time. How we spend that time should be up to the individual. Whoever they are. I hope my father can comfortably retire and have time to do other things with his life other than work.'

Edward Pennington laughed. 'And that's your decision to make for him, is it?'

Joseph's irritation hitched higher. 'No, it's his, but —'

'Then you are talking nonsense.'

Elizabeth stepped between them, her eyes burning with anger as she glared at Joseph. 'Mr Carter, I would really like to speak with my father alone. If you will excuse us?'

Joseph stared into her eyes, certainty burning inside him that she possessed the same wish for self-achievement and the achievement of others as he did. Yet, he saw something more now she was side by side with her father. Could it be that her need to stretch her imagination and ambition battled with the love and loyalty for her father, no matter how much her eyes revealed her clear resentment towards him?

Joseph put his glass on a table beside him and dipped his head in Edward Pennington's direction. 'It was a pleasure to meet you, sir. If you'll excuse —'

'Stay where you are, Carter.' Edward Pennington tossed back the remainder of his brandy. 'I'll leave you with my daughter. Elizabeth and I will have plenty of time to speak alone when we return home.' He nodded at Elizabeth, his stare icy-cold. 'Elizabeth.'

As soon as her father was out of earshot, Elizabeth faced Joseph, her green eyes bright with anger. 'What were you thinking by speaking that way to my father? If he doesn't see to it that your contract is terminated —'

'I just . . .' Joseph shook his head. What was it about this woman that made his mind whirl and his mouth spew words of its own accord? They could work together in harmony, if only she'd allow it. Every instinct in his body screamed of their professional compatibility. 'I just sense your ambition and frustration and I'll bet a hundred guineas you sense mine. I feel strangely bound to you and Pennington's, but I'm yet to decide whether that is a good thing or very, very bad.'

Her cheeks reddened. 'You should leave, Mr Carter.'

'The store or the party?'

'The party.'

'As you wish.' He stared at Edward Pennington as their gazes met. 'Knowing you feel as duty-bound to your father as I do mine only strengthens my wish to work here.'

The skin at her throat shifted as she swallowed.

Joseph brushed past her and paused. 'That isn't to say I am any less sorry for your entrapment.' He dipped his head. 'The evening is young, Miss Pennington. There's work I need to finish downstairs. I bid you a pleasant evening.'

He walked to the lift at the end of the long, wood-panelled corridor, stopping to pat Albert Griggs' shoulder before he nodded to Henry and entered the lift.

As he turned, he held Miss Pennington's stare until the doors whispered closed . . . and only then did he release his held breath.

★ ★ ★

With his pencil between his teeth, Joseph held his sketchbook out in front of him and closed one eye

112

as he critically assessed his latest design. He'd drawn the gloves with Elizabeth Pennington in mind and, because of that, the drawing failed to meet his high standards.

A glove should reflect the wearer. Unadorned silk denoted simplicity; a woman who didn't need embellishment but, at the same time, acknowledged the finer things in life. Kid was perfect for a woman full of maternal instinct and love, regardless of whether or not she would one day have children of her own. Someone who cared, nurtured and looked out for her fellow human beings. Leather suited a woman intent on her destiny. Whether that might be running the biggest department store in Bath or raising ten children amid a life that was as joyous as it was fragile.

For him, Elizabeth Pennington was a complex combination of all three, and to come up with the right design, using the right material was driving him dangerously close to caring rather than creating.

He dropped the pad to the workbench and leaned back, lacing his hands behind his head. The woman should appear to him as untouchable. Someone out of reach. Yet, she struck him as a woman waiting for something — for what, he couldn't be certain, but the way she looked at her father had intrigued him. It was as though Edward Pennington held an invisible and potent power over her.

What had happened between them to create such palpable animosity? She worked here in a position of authority, at least in the ladies' department, so Pennington must believe in her abilities on some level. Maybe he undermined her at home as well as work? Saw her as his property to do with and treat her in any manner he'd like. Just like so many other fathers and husbands tended to their daughters and wives. The implication that a woman like Elizabeth should be anything but free to live as she wished drew a dangerous feeling of protection to spread through Joseph.

He clenched his jaw, trying to fight his attraction to Elizabeth Pennington that stubbornly continued to simmer raw and undeniably deep inside him. He had to fight back his yearning to mean something to her. Lillian's death had paralysed his heart. Locked and bound his emotions . . . or at least, he thought it had. Surely, it would take more than an intelligent, ambitious and beautiful woman to ease back the hinges and expose him to unbearable loss a second time?

His words to Elizabeth about her staff and their lack of motivation had been spoken with the absolute intention of telling her the truth, but his provocation of her temper by sparring with her father had been a mistake.

Joseph cursed into the darkened room, his breath causing the candle on his table to flicker. What right did he have to test the boundaries of her personal life? What was it about her that made him want to know her beyond her work?

Soft footsteps approached the workroom door and Joseph strained his hearing towards the corridor beyond.

A gentle knock ensued.

Elizabeth Pennington stood on the other side of the door. He was certain of it.

Every muscle in his body tensed.

He quickly shoved his sketchbook beneath a pile of wrapped and ready gloves before drawing an unstitched pair towards him. Plucking a needle from a nearby box, he bent his head over the bench, suddenly

114

aware of the silence, the darkness and lack of other people. 'Come in.'

The door brushed open.

His heart picked up speed and Joseph pressed his fingertips harder on the needle as the soft scent of floral perfume preceded her.

'Mr Carter? Might I interrupt you?'

To his shame, his entire body trembled, aware of her close proximity and the fact she had closed the door with a soft, yet firm click. They were alone, with only the faint glow of his candle and the dormant machinery standing guard. He wasn't stupid enough to think this situation anything but wholly unusual. Unease rang alarm bells loud and clear.

He raised his head. Her eyes shone like emeralds in the subdued light, shooting two dangerous and unwanted arrows straight to his groin. 'Is there something I can help you with, Miss Pennington?'

'There is.' Her gaze lingered on his before she looked at the gloves on the workbench and lightly fingered them. 'I thought our conversation upstairs unfinished.'

Surprised but cautious, Joseph leaned back. 'And here I was thinking we both might have said too much.'

'On the contrary.'

He raised an eyebrow at her challenging tone. Was she nothing more than a rich girl rebelling against her father? Or was she the epitome of a woman who knew her own mind and to hell with anyone else? His attraction to her heightened.

'My father interrupted us earlier. I wanted to talk with you further.' A flash of doubt, or maybe insecurity, flickered in her eyes before she blinked and dropped her gaze to the workbench. She smiled. 'Tell

115

me more about your gloves. When you explained how you work with women in mind as you create, it interested me.'

She had asked him about his work, but the hushed hitch of her words made him suspect she had yet to dismiss their conversation about their personal situations too. He couldn't help wondering what their relationship would be if they'd met on the street, rather than being thrust together as supplier and buyer.

The tension in the room was tangible, simmering dangerously between them as though one foolish movement on his part and his arms would be around her, his lips on hers. Would she want that? Slap him? Demand he leave and never come back? Or would she hold him closer? Kiss him deeper?

He cleared his throat and concentrated on the glove in his hands. 'I imagine my gloves on the hands of every woman in the city. Every woman is beautiful in her own right. Beautiful, powerful . . .' He lifted his gaze to hers, his heart giving another infernal blip at the unmistakable passion in her eyes. 'Intelligent and caring. If my gloves make them prouder, stand taller, I can think of no better calling.'

She held his gaze. 'And what of love, Mr Carter?'

Joseph stilled. 'Love?'

She tilted her head, her gaze soft. 'Is love not a calling?'

He swallowed, looked to his work once more. 'To some, maybe.'

'But not you?'

'No. Not me.'

The strength of her study bored into his temple and Joseph's heart thundered. Why did he suddenly feel the need to tell her of Lillian? To warn her that his drive and ambition held the power to make him forget his role as a protector, as a man a woman could rely on?

'Mr Carter?'

Slowly, Joseph raised his eyes to hers.

Her gentle study drifted to his mouth and back again. 'Did you love her? The woman you once worked with?'

Joseph stared, as disquiet whispered through him. 'Why do you ask?'

'I find it implausible that a man who holds women in such high regard has not known what it means to love one. You have been in love. I see it in your eyes. Unfortunately for you, they're very revealing.'

He ran his gaze over her face and hair. Every sound muted. The amber glow of the few lit candles danced over her skin, turning it pearlescent. 'I was married. To a wonderful, caring woman. A woman who worked beside my father and I every day after we were married.'

Her voice softened. 'What happened to her?'

'She died.' He would tell her no more, the shame of his failure burned like acid in his chest and he quickly stood, wanting the intensity to ease, her justified scrutiny to end. 'Will you try on a pair of gloves?'

He brushed past her and breathed deep as he approached a box of his finished gloves. Lifting a pair of soft kid, perfectly stitched and the exact green of her eyes, the pale cream stitching the colour of her skin.

When he turned and walked back to his bench, she had sat in his seat. She carefully watched his approach, her eyes unreadable.

'Put your hand out like this.' He held his hand out,

117

palm down and leaned closer. For just a second, he lingered his gaze on the soft curve of her bosom before flitting his study to her fingers. 'I want you to tell me how they feel, what the material makes you think of.'

'How do you know they will fit?'

'They will.' How could they not when this was a pair he'd made himself? While stitching them, he'd been forced to acknowledge how closely he'd been watching her, studying her, admiring her. All subconsciously, as though somehow, she'd burrowed into his mind, into his care when he hadn't taken the precaution to ensure that did not happen. He smoothed the glove onto her hand and her breath whispered over his face. Joseph resisted the urge to close his eyes against such a welcome sensation. 'How do they feel?'

'Wonderful.'

She stared at him, her cheeks lightly flushed and her smile wide. 'How did you — '

'Because I watch you.' *For the love of God, man . . .*

'You watch me?'

Their eyes locked, and Joseph slowly straightened. 'I watch you.'

The need to touch her, hold her, swept through his body, but instead of desire, it was guilt that pressed down on him. Guilt that he would even dare to talk to her this way, dare to allow her to guess at his inner thoughts, his sexual yearning.

'I watch you, too.'

He froze, as panic swept over him. To have her care for him as he cared for her was terrifying. Something impossible. Something most assuredly doomed.

She shook her head and huffed a laugh. 'But don't worry, I will only ever allow myself to look at you as an associate. To do more would undo all I strive to

118

achieve.' She stood and slowly slipped the glove from her hand, dropped it to the workbench. 'We have both known deep pain, it seems. Why would either of us step close to the fire only to be burned again?'

A hard knot formed deep in his stomach.

She walked a few steps towards the door before turning, her skirt sweeping over the floorboards. 'How do you envisage making your ambitions come true? What are your stepping stones? Dreams are challenged, tossed aside and often destroyed by someone else's hands. Do you really have what it takes to carry out what you hope to become a reality?'

The abrupt change in subject and the hardness of her voice that, for just a few blessed moments, had been so very soft, it had torn at his heart, caught him out. He fought the exposure her pain caused in him. 'I do.'

Joseph studied her. What did he have to lose by showing her more of his designs? She could hardly commit them to memory before she kicked him out the door. Neither would she ever have cause to know each pair had been, in one way or another, inspired by her and only her. Never in a thousand years could he have imagined having such a connection with the future heiress of Pennington's, but he did. In his brief time here, Elizabeth Pennington had surprised, impressed and surpassed his expectations in so many ways. He owed it to her to be entirely honest. Lay his cards on the table.

'Would you spare me another minute of your time?'

She frowned and slowly approached him.

Leaning forwards, Joseph drew his sketchbook from its hiding place and held it out to her.

She glanced at the book. 'What's this?'

'Take a look.'

She took the sketchbook and turned to the first page. The line between her perfect brows deepened as she turned to the next page and the next, until she flipped over each page quickly as though eager to see the next.

She lifted her eyes, her cheeks faintly flushed. 'These are extraordinary.'

Satisfaction swirled inside him. 'These are just a few examples. I have sketchbooks fit to bursting in my bureau at home. Since the first day I stepped into Pennington's, I've wanted my gloves on your shelves, and now, I want nothing more than to come up with the perfect manufacturing solution.'

She dropped her gaze to his sketchbook and resumed turning the pages back and forth. 'These are wonderful. Surely each pair would take several days to make?'

'But that's the beauty of my idea.' He stood and leaned over her shoulder, briefly closing his eyes as her scent teased his nostrils. He glanced at her turned cheek before pointing at the pad. 'This one here would be made from leather. The glove itself is basic and could be made quickly. It is the adornment, the additional trinkets and such, that may take a little more time, but as the men get used to working with the materials, their speed will increase.' He sat down and leaned back. 'Until the production staff have an incentive, a reason to work like they never have before, it would be foolish for me to imagine production of the quantity I dream of.'

She closed the sketchbook and laid it in front of him. 'You have thought of an incentive?'

'Yes.' Taking a deep breath, he exhaled. 'You pay

them commission.'

Surprise flashed in her eyes. 'Commission?'

'Why not? The production staff are salaried, whereas the shop floor staff are salaried and commissioned. Commission would build a healthy competition and provide a way to earn sums of money that, up until now, these glove makers and milliners would have thought impossible. The majority are the sole breadwinners. What would it do for their morale and confidence to go home with a wage packet to be proud of every week or month? Almost every man I've worked with so far has told me he feels privileged to work here. Privileged.' He shook his head. 'I never thought I would hear such a claim from any man stuck nine or ten hours a day in such a small room. What a foundation to build upon. You're in charge of the department. Is it not up to you what they earn?'

Something indiscernible flashed in her eyes before she blinked and intense concentration burned instead. 'It should be my decision, yes.'

Should be? Edward Pennington seeped into Joseph's mind. Clearly, he was the one with his hands on the reins. If Joseph had Elizabeth Pennington's belief, maybe they could convince her father of the feasibility of their plans together.

Joseph frowned. 'Do you have ambitions that stretch further than the ladies' department?'

'I have many.'

'But they are thwarted?'

'Some. Yes.'

'And you think the idea of commission for the workroom staff would be thwarted too?'

'I'm not sure.'

Hope simmered inside him and Joseph pushed

121

on. 'If a man considers himself privileged, he's being treated well and respectfully by his employer. Whatever Pennington's has done for their staff so far, these men aren't unhappy, but they also behave as though there is no point in hoping for more.'

As the seconds ticked by, the working cogs of her brain were revealed through her phenomenal eyes. He yearned to say more to convince her that his idea for commission was a viable one, but the worst thing he could do was interrupt her thoughts at a crucial moment and risk her dismissing his suggestion out of hand.

'I think it best we discuss this further.' She walked towards the door. 'Blow out the candles, Mr Carter. I'd like you to escort me safely home.'

The moisture drained from his mouth. Had the woman lost her mind? Was she suggesting . . . ?

She smiled softly. 'Oh, don't look so horrified. I promise you will be quite safe. You have a lot to learn about me. The foremost being, I despise conventionality. I'll just collect my hat and coat. Meet me by the staff entrance.'

Opening the door, she left the workroom and Joseph quickly snuffed the candles. Whatever happened next, there could be no turning back. One way or another, Elizabeth Pennington had completely, entirely, ensnared him.

13

Bath's streets were dark and almost deserted by the time Elizabeth walked beside Joseph towards her home on Royal Crescent. The street lamps flickered, but their soft glow didn't prevent the clear, star-studded sky from seeming close enough to touch. She glanced at Joseph as he stared straight ahead, his strong jaw tight and his shoulders high.

Every part of her yearned to ask what he was thinking.

She had never met a man who made her feel that if a person became his focus, he would find a way to make them reveal their soul. She had never met a man with whom she didn't immediately feel his agenda included taking advantage of her, using her for his own gains.

There was an honesty in Joseph that poked and prodded at her to lower her determination to succeed without need of a man. She respected him, understood him, wanted to know more about him.

Which was exactly why she should put as much distance between them as possible. Yet, the possibility of him truly knowing her, of her being able to talk to him openly, appealed to her beyond reason.

Considering their shared time and candour this evening, she wanted to rewrite his contract and ask if he would consider a permanent arrangement with Pennington's. How could she let him go at some point in the future when she knew he had so much more to offer? So far, he had exceeded all her expectations.

Proven to her he worked extraordinarily well under pressure, and delivered.

On top of that, customers were beginning to ask his name. Who was the designer behind the new range of gloves and what had he planned for the spring? Everything suddenly felt so much more exciting than it had before Joseph walked through Pennington's doors.

Her fervour faltered.

But what if he was little more than a chameleon? A man capable of slipping beneath the iron defences around her heart and burrowing deep inside until she lost control, lost what she'd built so far?

To have someone at Pennington's, though, who shared her passion to take the store into the new decade would be a dream come true. Joseph could be the ally she'd been looking for, and she couldn't banish the feeling they'd grow to trust and support one another — that he might stand beside her and fight her father on the many issues they continued to disagree upon.

He'd proven that by standing up to him at the drinks party . . . even though the place, time and his ferocity had initially angered and shocked her, she now realised seeing Joseph that way had only further intensified her certainty he should be by her side permanently.

She tucked a fallen curl behind her ear and drew as much authority into her voice as she could muster. 'I think your idea of commission for the workroom staff is inspiring, Mr Carter. Truly.'

He turned, his slow smile hitching something in her chest.

'I'm glad.'

Struggling to level the accelerated beat of her traitorous heart, Elizabeth cleared her throat. 'Furthermore, I believe that once the workers know it was you who suggested the change, they'll see I'm more than willing to listen to their ideas. I want my staff to believe I'm open to hearing from everyone. Not just the senior staff.'

'Equality.'

'Pardon?'

'Equality. Whether male, female. Middle or working class. That's what I want, too.' He smiled wryly. 'Through every avenue of life, I hope. Maybe. One day.'

She smiled. 'Another dream we have in common.'

They stood looking at one another until Elizabeth glanced along the street, lest the amusement shining in his eyes made her forget what she wanted — no, *needed* — to say to him. 'So, the quick sale of your gloves and your enthusiasm for my department has made me want to offer you a proposal.'

He abruptly stopped, his gaze wary. 'A proposal?'

'Yes. I'd like to offer to carry your gloves for the foreseeable future. We will, of course, need to sit down to agree a new revenue split.' She faced him, his smile was wide, and she cursed the tightening in her stomach as she fought to keep her defences in place. 'But we need to discuss the feasibility of the changes you suggest first.'

Insecurity whirled deep in her stomach. Her inability to fully trust men lay at her father's doing, but she had to be sure Joseph wouldn't betray her faith in him further down the line. No matter her pull to him, he was still a man capable of hurting her.

Carefully, she studied him, her every instinct on

high alert for a sign of any insincerity in his response. 'So far, my other suppliers have not said too much about our receiving your gloves, but if yours continue to sell as they have, that may well change. I'm happy to defend my decision and let other suppliers go, if needs be. Having said that, I've dealt with many innovators, investors and so on, and when their own desires are the sole driving force, people become greedy, impatient and demanding. I'm afraid I won't be able to work with you if that is true of you.'

He looked at her for so long, Elizabeth struggled to keep her gaze level with his. His eyes burned with annoyance, a muscle clenching and relaxing in his jaw.

'So, in your experience, selfishness is usually the basis of all motivation?' His gaze flashed with insult. 'And that's what you suspect of me, too? Even after I confessed to you how much I wish to help others?'

An alien guilt wound through her and she fought to retain her authority. Did the man think her a doormat? Someone without a right to question him when he wanted something from her, too? Her naive hope that she'd found a kindred spirit wavered. His anger was palpable. His words spoken as sharply as knife blades. She would not be intimidated. She crossed her arms. 'You ask for my support of your ideas, and I have also offered to carry your gloves on a permanent basis, I think that gives me the right to question you.'

His jaw tightened.

She held his glare. 'All I'm asking for is your honesty. Lord knows, I have my own, deeply rooted reasons for working and pushing forward. Are yours all about others? Is there nothing in your motivations entirely for yourself?'

The night seemed to close in the longer she looked

126

into his eyes and recognised his defensiveness, his passion. Nerves mixed with pride that she'd had the courage to challenge a man as her father so often challenged her.

As much as being in any way similar to her father sickened her, she had come to understand the importance of being in control, of being brave and forthright in order to gain respect. It just rankled that she needed to be so harsh with Joseph. A man she truly liked.

He slumped his shoulders and a little of the animosity seeped from his gaze. 'Why is it so important to know what's going on inside me? I'm nothing more to you than a supplier, after all.'

Discomfort niggled inside her. Weren't her questions built somewhat on her need to know Joseph, the man, as much as Joseph, the associate? She gripped her purse tighter. 'I've made it my business to know the people I work with. To help them as and when I can. You entered the store with an extraordinary talent and a plan in place. You came to me to see that plan through. If you want my help, I need your openness. In everything. I will not be taken for a fool and I won't be pulled in a direction not to my liking. Not by you or anyone else.'

His eyes darkened before he looked away, his brow deeply furrowed.

Elizabeth willed herself not to fidget. She couldn't show an ounce of weakness, no matter how much the insult in his eyes made her want to retract her questioning. This was business, and any faltering on her part would mean certain loss of Joseph's respect.

Yet, she feared seeing disappointment in his eyes as much as she did in her father's.

Swiping his hand over his face, he blew out a breath.

127

'Passion for equal, working freedom lies behind my motivations for wanting to work with Pennington's, but you weren't wrong about selfishness having a part in that, too. Through hard work and perseverance, I want to earn enough money to enable my father to see there are options for his retirement. Having said that, I've also experienced heartbreak which I believe was caused by my neglect and selfish focus on what I want. My distraction meant pain for others. I want to find a balance. Happiness as well as work. That, Miss Pennington, is my truth. If you cannot accept my sincerity, then maybe I shouldn't be working with you after all.'

Elizabeth searched his eyes looking for any indication he played her, but nothing but a deep, heart-rending sadness burned in his beautiful eyes. Her heart thumped wildly, and her hands turned clammy inside her gloves. Everything Joseph said moved her. Everything he wanted she understood. And because of that, she should ask him to leave the store. She could not afford to feel anything other than professional respect for him.

She drew in a long breath. 'Since my father made me head of the ladies' department, I've been brought almost to my knees in my quest to prove to him a woman can be of the same substance as any man. I need to be certain I have that belief from you.'

His gaze slowly softened, and he lifted his hand as if to touch her arm before he lowered it into his trouser pocket. 'You do have my belief and I don't understand how your father cannot see what he has in you.'

She could not let him go, no matter how much her head screamed at her to do so. She sighed. 'The longer you remain working with Pennington's, the more you'll come to understand my father is a man unto himself.' Hope for change whispered through her and she smiled. 'Your dreams aren't over, Mr Carter. And neither are mine.'

They continued to walk as the depth of Joseph's morality and determination seared her deep inside. Part of her longed to applaud such undisguised zeal, yet another part longed to run into the safety of her home, firmly locking the door behind her.

Joseph's verve mixed with hers had the potential to explode, thus obliterating them both in its smoking path. Over and over, she'd had to shout to make herself heard, been regarded by male associates as though she had two heads or should be locked away where she could cause no further mischief.

In Joseph's eyes and words, she saw no such judgement. Instead, she saw a man with a deep longing to fulfil his ambitions while helping others and supporting hers.

The sheer humanity of him made her fearful of making rash, dangerous decisions. What if she agreed to everything he desired, and her father stripped her authority further down the line? She could not allow that to happen, knowing Joseph's ambitions were honourable.

She came to a stop outside the house beside her home, knowing if her father should see her, the evening would not end as she wanted it; with her and Joseph tentatively satisfied, if not happy.

Glancing towards her front door, she reached into her purse and drew out her house key. 'So, you will consider a permanent position?'

He looked at her house. 'That is your home? You live on the Crescent?'

'Yes.' She studied him. His expression had softened, a slight smile playing at his lips. 'Is that . . . a problem?'

'No, not at all.'

'But it is something?'

He faced her and shook his head, his gaze amused. 'You live a life I can only dream of. A beautiful home. An amazing job. I envy and admire you in equal measure, Miss Pennington.' He glanced towards her house again. 'And hope your respect for me doesn't change should you ever visit my shop and home.'

Elizabeth stilled. How could he possibly think such a thing of her? Did he not understand by now that she wanted equality for everyone in the same way he did? 'Pulteney Bridge isn't a million miles from here. I could see your shop anytime.' She stared at her front door. 'Don't be fooled by opulence and brass. Whitewash and glistening paint. It's what is inside a house that makes a home a haven. My fancy address on Royal Crescent is just bricks and mortar. I fear, that's all it ever will be to me.' She forced a smile. 'I'll bid you goodnight, then.'

He stared at her for a long moment before dipping his head. 'Thank you.'

'For?'

'Seeing me. Believing in me.'

Elizabeth's heart kicked to see such genuine gratitude in his eyes. It was clear he'd experienced repeated rebuttal of his ideas and wants, just as she had. He also believed in his dreams and was equally tired of waiting for others to acknowledge his passions.

She stepped towards the short pathway leading to her front door. 'We will speak again soon. Goodnight.'

Without waiting for his response, she opened the

door and entered the house, closing and locking the door behind her. She paused in the hallway as though waiting for his knock.

She couldn't be sure if she was relieved or disappointed when it didn't come.

* * *

The raucous laughter of passers-by and the clip-clop of horses' hooves that filtered along Pulteney Bridge slowly died away as Joseph closed the door to Carter & Son and walked up the back stairs. Throughout his return journey from Elizabeth Pennington's house on Royal Crescent, Joseph's mind had raced with everything he and Elizabeth had discussed. Her questions and comments had been laced with the hint of what Joseph suspected was a deep fear, an embedded distrust of those around her that occasionally flashed in her otherwise kind eyes. No doubt the fault of her insecurity lay in her father's past words and deeds.

Before Joseph had met her, he'd imagined the manageress of Pennington's ladies' department to be a hard-hearted businesswoman with the power to accelerate or halt his goals, but the conflicting emotions in Elizabeth Pennington's eyes had knocked him off-kilter. There was so much more to her than business. So much more to her than being Edward Pennington, millionaire retail tycoon's daughter.

Joseph exhaled a slow breath. He'd been arrogant in his presumptions about her. He had only been working with her for six weeks, for crying out loud. Why on earth would a sophisticated, educated and successful woman take him at face value? He was an artisan. A man born into daily struggle, moderately educated and of adequate means, but by no stretch of the imagination was he wealthy.

Why shouldn't he have to prove himself to her? Especially as she was being made by her father to prove herself.

'Joseph? Is that you, son?'

He walked into the parlour. His father sat in front of the fire with a newspaper open on his lap, looking all of his fifty-eight years as shadows from the fire flickered across his tired features. Joseph slowly removed his hat and placed it on the sideboard. No matter Elizabeth Pennington's fragile trust, he would not fail in his endeavours to ensure his father a comfortable retirement.

'How are you, Pa?'

'Good.' His father dropped his gaze to the newspaper. 'Business wasn't too bad today at all.'

Joseph didn't need to see his father's eyes to know he lied. The stiff set of his shoulders and the rigidness of his jaw spoke that business had been far from good. Why couldn't his father understand why Joseph had so ardently sought Pennington's as a buyer of his gloves? Couldn't he see what mass production would mean for them?

He walked farther into the room and cleared his throat. 'I'm glad to hear it. Sorry I'm back so late.'

'That place is certainly putting you through your paces.' His father looked up, his eyes glittering with annoyance. 'As I warned you it would.'

'Elizabeth Pennington has offered me a permanent commission.'

His father's eyes widened, clearly surprised. 'She's done what?'

'This is good news, Pa.' Joseph forced a grin in an

132

effort to calm the risk of an outburst from his father. 'My gloves have sold above and beyond, and at a faster rate than Elizabeth Pennington imagined. She wants more, and so do the public.'

Seemingly struck between pride and caution, his father frowned. 'So, what, you've already accepted her offer?'

'No, not yet. I intend to sleep on it and give her an answer tomorrow.'

His father swiped his hand over his face, his shoulders slumping. 'And that answer will be yes.'

Confused by his father continuing lack of enthusiasm about Pennington's, Joseph lowered into the armchair opposite and sighed. 'Pa, listen to me. This isn't just about sales anymore. It's not just about the money we'll make. It's about the manufacturing staff, too.'

'What about them?'

'I suggested commission for them. On top of their wages. She's seriously considering the possibility.'

His father sniffed. 'That isn't a yes though, is it?'

'Maybe not, but it's a move in the right direction. With me spending time there, overseeing the production of Carter & Son gloves, I can push the commission through. I can help these people.'

His father stared at him, his gaze concerned. 'As Lillian would've wanted you to, right?'

'Right. Can't you at least *pretend* to be glad for me?'

His father mutely returned his stare and Joseph sighed.

'When I walked Miss Pennington home — '

'*What?* You walked her home?' His father's eyebrows shot to his hairline. 'Why in God's name would you do that?'

Feigning nonchalance, Joseph shrugged. 'She asked me to. What else could I do?'

'What did she want with you? If someone saw you with her in the dead of night, it will surely lead to your downfall, rather than hers. Good God, boy, haven't you got the sense you were born with?'

Joseph stood and walked to the bureau to pour himself a snifter of brandy, the liquid trembled as he raised it to his lips. 'Elizabeth Pennington isn't like that. I keep telling you.'

His father moved his newspaper to the small table beside him and studied Joseph through narrowed eyes. 'Does her father ever show his face?'

'Her father?' Joseph frowned, thrown by the sudden and bluntly delivered question. 'I've seen him a couple of times. Why?'

'Hmm.'

'What does that mean?'

'Nothing.'

'The look on your face tells me differently. What do you know about Edward Pennington?'

'Forget I mentioned him.' His father stared towards the fire. 'I can't help wondering what your mother would have made of you working for that man, that's all.'

'I'm not working for him. I'll be working *with* his daughter.' Joseph pushed the hair back from his brow, concerned by his father mentioning his mother. He only usually spoke of her when something seriously bothered him. As though he needed her support or counsel. 'Besides, if I knew Ma at all, she'd be happy for me. Proud I'm getting on with my life and doing all I can to persuade you to slow down.'

His father snatched his gaze from the fire and glared.

134

'I do not need to slow down. I'm happy as I am.'

'Pa — '

'Edward Pennington has always thought he was a cut above the rest of us and I don't want you turning out the same way. Some of us are proud of our backgrounds. Not ashamed we've known poverty and hard times. Our shop might be nothing to the likes of him, but for my father and me, it was the proudest moment of our lives when our names went above the door. He can't take that away from me, no matter what he might think.'

Joseph stared, the only sounds in the room the crack and spit of the fire and his father's heavy breathing. 'Why would Edward Pennington want to take anything from you? The man has everything he could possibly want.'

'Is that so?'

'What's going on, Pa? Has your path crossed with Edward Pennington's at some time?'

His father snapped his gaze to Joseph's, his eyes blazing with anger. 'It doesn't matter. Not anymore.'

'Of course, it does. If something has gone on in the past — '

'I said it doesn't matter.' His father stood. 'Let that be an end to it.'

Brushing roughly past Joseph, his father stalked from the room into the small kitchen. A resounding banging and clattering of crockery and cutlery ensued, illustrating his father's rage with every clink and thud.

Joseph stared towards the open door, his mind whirling with what ifs and maybes. His father's animosity toward Edward Pennington was clear in the bulge of his usually kind eyes, the dark mottling on his cheeks. What the hell had happened between them?

Was Elizabeth Pennington any more aware of their association than Joseph?

He stood and walked to the bureau to replenish his glass. He picked up the remaining glass and sniffed it. His father had already had a drink, which was completely out of character. Pouring himself a measure, Joseph tossed it to the back of his throat and grimaced against its heat. He had never known his father to drink alone. Was the reason he had Joseph's doing?

He lowered his glass to the bureau, holding it tightly. Despite knowing how reluctant his father had been about his son pursuing Pennington's like a man scouring for gold, Joseph had always assumed his father's averseness about the assumed faceless façade of Pennington's was founded in professional reasons. Could his father's reservations have a more personal origin?

Well, whatever they were, his father could not give preamble to some kind of revelation and then fling it back into its darkened space to be forgotten. One way or another, Joseph would uncover the truth. Pouring another measure, he took the drink with him and entered the kitchen.

His father put the kettle on the stovetop to boil and turned. 'Shouldn't you get yourself off to bed so you can be at your best in the morning?'

'I want an explanation.' Joseph walked to the scratched and marked wooden table in the far corner of the small kitchen and sat. 'How do you know Edward Pennington?'

The seconds ticked by, but Joseph kept his mouth firmly closed, despite the horrible trepidation working its way through his gut. There was every chance that once his father spoke, Joseph would wish he hadn't.

136

His father extinguished the flame beneath the kettle and stilled, his turned back rigid with tension.

The silence pressed down on Joseph, the heat in the kitchen suddenly more oppressive than before.

Finally, his father turned and exhaled heavily. 'None of it matters anymore.'

'None of what? If there is a reason other than pride that I shouldn't be relying on Pennington's to improve our future, I have the right to know.'

His father strode by him into the parlour, returning a moment later carrying a glass and the bottle of brandy. He sat down, the ticking of the clock on the kitchen mantel echoing through the otherwise silent room. Joseph could not remember seeing his father so riled. Anger etched his reddened face, his eyes staring blindly from his son to the brandy bottle as though he fought an internal battle, uncertain how to rid himself of a weight that had finally worn him down.

Joseph sat straighter and braced for whatever came next.

Slowly, his father filled his glass before pushing the bottle aside. He took a hefty slug, placed the glass on the table and locked his gaze on Joseph. 'All I've ever wanted for you is happiness. You found it in your work and you found it with Lillian.'

Joseph nodded, uncertainty twisting inside him. 'And?'

'And if Pennington's is where you'll find happiness again, so be it, but what I really want for you is to see you deserve more in life than money. You're a good man, Joseph. A man with heart and dedication. A man who has a lot to share with the world. If Elizabeth Pennington can provide something that will bring a stop your infernal belief that there's nothing left for you to do other than carrying on as Lillian would have, I won't stop you working there.'

'So, you do want me to work there? Your doubt of whether being in Pennington's is a good thing has nothing to do with Edward Pennington?'

Two spots of colour appeared high on his father's cheeks and he drew his gaze from Joseph's to stare into the dark depths of his glass. 'When are you at your best? When you work alone? Or were you better when you worked with Lillian?'

A slow ache seeped into Joseph's chest. 'With Lillian.'

'Good, because you need people, Joseph. More people than just me.'

'The men in the workroom — '

'A woman, Joseph. I want you to be with a good woman.'

Elizabeth Pennington came into his mind and Joseph drank deep. 'That might happen one day, but I definitely won't go looking for it.'

His father's eyes darkened with clear frustration. 'You were always stubborn, but the way you are now is slowly killing you, boy. You need to move past Lillian's death. You need to pursue your dreams with the belief you deserve them and a whole lot more. Until you see that, you're never going to fill that void inside you. Not ever.'

Joseph squeezed his eyes shut. He refused to go over this ground again. Talking about his loneliness only left him feeling more wretched and less determined. He opened his eyes and abruptly stood. 'If you're not willing to talk about Edward Pennington, I'm going to bed. I'll see you in the morning.'

'What about your supper?'

'I've no appetite. Not anymore.'

'Son — '

'Maybe you'll be ready to talk some more over breakfast.'

Joseph left the room and walked along the corridor to his bedroom. Closing the door behind him, he dropped backwards onto the bed and glared at the ceiling as pain, loss and fear cut through his chest. No matter his fears, his obsession to do more and be more were wearing him down. He might want to scoff at his father's concerns, prove his worry for his son's loneliness was without merit, but the fact was, Joseph was lonely.

Lonely and, when he thought of Elizabeth Pennington, afraid.

Very, very afraid.

From the day Lillian had died, taken far too early by the knife of a suspected drunkard, Joseph's belief in people and God had wavered. He might feel something tangible and extraordinary could happen between him and Elizabeth if they were to work together, but it was far too soon for either of them to freely give their trust. Who was to say she wasn't cut from the same dark and menacing cloth his father seemed determined to drape over Pennington's?

The resentment in his father's eyes when he'd spoken of Edward Pennington had shaken Joseph to his core. Never before had he seen such unadulterated anger from a man known throughout town as kind, forgiving and humble.

Joseph swiped his hand over his face. Could it be that once a person's trust in humanity was broken, it would never be restored?

And where did Edward Pennington come into it all?

14

Elizabeth left her bedroom and fought her nerves as she descended the stairs. When she'd arrived home last night, Cole had told her, while she'd removed her coat, that her father had waited up for her until finally giving up and retiring with a headache.

Which meant he would know she'd come home late and want to know who, if anyone, had chaperoned her. Either way, he would undoubtedly be in a foul mood at breakfast.

Gripping the handle on the dining room door, Elizabeth took a deep breath, forced a smile and entered.

Her father sat in his usual place at the head of the long dining table, the sideboard behind him filled with covered dishes and platters of bacon, eggs and toasted bread. She headed straight for the buffet.

'Morning, Father. How are you feeling? Cole mentioned you had a headache yesterday evening.'

'Is it any wonder?'

Picking up a plate, Elizabeth helped herself to some food, determined to do all she could to avoid them having cross words. It would be preferable to them both if they started their day amicably. She walked to the table and sat beside him. 'You've been working very hard, lately. It's no surprise that — '

'My headache had nothing to do with my workload, and well you know it.' His angry gaze bored into hers. 'You left the store with Carter.'

Elizabeth stilled, her knife and fork in hand. 'You're having me watched?'

'Don't be absurd. George saw you leave and rightly told me. What on earth possessed you to — '

'We had business to discuss and I asked him to escort me home. I thought that preferable than making the journey alone. Mr Carter is a gentleman, Papa. You have nothing to worry about.'

'Nothing to worry about?' His cheeks mottled. 'You barely know the man.'

'I know enough to feel safe in his company.' Elizabeth sipped at her water, dread unfurling in her stomach at what she needed to say next. 'I intend carrying his gloves on a more permanent basis once we've agreed a satisfactory revenue split, numbers and delivery times.'

Her father slowly put down his coffee cup, his gaze cold. 'I see.'

Encouraged that he hadn't immediately demanded she cancel the agreement, or worse, told her she had no right to make such a decision, Elizabeth lowered her shoulders and cut into her bacon. 'Joseph — Mr Carter shows a real care for his work and by working with the manufacturing staff in the workroom I think he will — '

'He's still there?' Her father's eyes darkened. 'I thought that a temporary arrangement. Since when have suppliers seen fit to oversee the workroom?'

'He's not overseeing per se. He's simply acting as a consultant. The staff there respond well to him. He has some truly worthwhile ideas regarding manufacturing speed and output. We'd be foolish to not utilise his processes and experience for as long as possible.'

His silence forced her gaze to his.

He watched her with what looked to be barely contained fury. 'This man has well and truly bowled you

141

over, Elizabeth. Did you not stop to think why he so easily convinced you that rather than a mere supplier, he should actually be working at my store? As far as you know, he could have an entirely different agenda than the one you're imagining. The man is either a glove maker or a businessman. How can he possibly be both? He needs to be kept in his place.'

'In his place?' She slowly put down her cutlery. 'His place, just like anyone else's, can be wherever he strives for it to be. I don't want the people I work with to be put into boxes like our merchandise. Mr Carter is passionate, ambitious and talented. I suspect he is equally as capable as I am of running his own empire one day. Isn't it better to have such a person working with us rather than a competitor?'

'His own empire?' Her father's gaze changed to clear amusement, his lips twitching with a smile. 'I think not.'

'Why? Because he hasn't our education or means, he'll never have the opportunity to better or elevate himself?'

'The man has been working with you for how long, exactly?'

'Almost two months.'

'Then how on earth can you show so much confidence in him?'

'Because I can. Why can't you ever trust my instincts? My integrity? I work hard, yet you refuse to accept or compliment my efforts. Why?'

His gaze held hers for a long moment, before it softened and his shoulders lowered. 'Fine. You have something I don't often see in the fairer sex, but that does not mean I'll give you free rein over everything. Having said that . . . '

Elizabeth held her breath. Was he finally going to give her further responsibility? 'Yes?'

He put down his knife and fork and reached for his coffee. 'I've decided to give you the position as head of the toy department as well as the ladies'.'

Jubilation coursed through her as she struggled to retain a business-like expression, her heart nearly bursting from her chest. 'That makes me immensely happy, Papa. Thank you.'

He sipped his coffee and then lowered the cup to its saucer. 'I've not taken the decision lightly, Elizabeth. Running two departments will stretch you, but the ideas you've had regarding seasonal changes seem to have merit. You've proven yourself steadfast and reliable.'

'Thank you.'

'But to have your head turned by — '

'My head turned?' Elizabeth tried not to let his brief, yet significant acknowledgement that she was worth something to him, something to Pennington's, diminish her happiness or her determination to continue to work with Joseph. 'Are you referring to Joseph?'

'Who else?' He shook his head. 'My instinct tells me that man arrived at the store with an ulterior motive. You'd be foolish to trust him prematurely.'

'I know and intend to work closely with him to ensure all continues in the same vein as it has been. Joseph has impressed me with his work and his work ethic. He is proving his worth over and over. You have to trust me, Papa.'

'I *have* to do no such thing. Pennington's is mine to do with as I will.'

Frustrated they had returned to locked horns once again, Elizabeth folded her hands in her lap. 'How

143

much longer can this go on, Papa? How much longer can you continue to see me and other women as little more than what you want them to be? Did you ever respect, Mama? Ever care for her interests or passions?'

'She had neither interests nor passions . . . ' He glared. 'Apart from you, of course.'

Elizabeth stiffened from the spite in his voice. 'Were you jealous of me? Was that why you treated her as you did? Because of me?'

He sneered and picked up his coffee. 'Why else, my dear?'

Loathing burned bitterly in her throat. 'You're lying.'

'Am I?'

'Yes. The truth is, you weren't enough for her, were you? She wanted more in her life. *Needed* more. So, you put her in her place. Well, I want more. I need more. What do you have planned for me, Papa?'

He continued to glare at her, his cheeks dark with anger.

She abruptly stood, nervousness that he might take the toy department away from her as quickly as he'd given it whirling through her. Well, it was a risk she had to take if she was to continue to stand up to him. 'Well, I imagine I'll have to wait and see.'

Storming towards the door, Elizabeth's legs trembled. No, she would not leave like this. She turned. 'If Joseph were a salesperson or a member of the upper class or, indeed, the prime minister, his opinions would matter to you. As he's not, they don't.'

Caution whispered through her. She didn't want her father knowing too much about Joseph. In fact, she didn't want him knowing Joseph at all. The moment her father showed more than a passing interest would be the moment she lost her slowly rising control. Every time her mother had showed excitement or interest in a person, a pastime, a play or even a book, her father found a way to disparage her, take away any independent thought or action.

Something she couldn't name glowed in her father's eyes. She couldn't believe it to be so, but he suddenly looked on edge. Maybe even a trifle anxious.

Disconcerted, Elizabeth fought against any weakness. 'All the while I've been trying to impress you, I haven't considered the ideas that might be bubbling away in the workrooms, in the minds of the serving staff in the restaurant or even the delivery men in the loading bays. We could be sitting on a mountain of originality.'

'What is Carter's father's Christian name?'

'Pardon?'

'I said, what is — '

'I have absolutely no idea. Why do you ask?'

He continued to stare at her, before he gave a dismissive wave. 'It doesn't matter. What matters is you do not give the man more than you would any other supplier.' He regarded her carefully. 'Do what you will, but bear in mind you have no idea of the man's background. No idea what has instilled the passion you talk so freely of that made him walk through our doors looking for an association. People are not all they seem. You should know that by now.'

Elizabeth hesitated. He was right, of course. And why would he understand what she saw in Joseph Carter? She wasn't entirely sure she understood it herself. His looks, charm and intelligence had certainly evoked an attraction that frightened her, but it was more than that. The fact he'd not shown his designs to anyone but her meant he trusted her to keep her council until his say-so. That was as humbling as it was flattering. She would not betray his confidence in her.

She opened the door. 'Just trust that what I see in him is deserved. Do I at least have that much support from you? I need some semblance of control if I'm ever going to persuade you I could run the store as well as any son might have.'

'In this moment, I'd rather see my company split ten different ways, to ten different men, rather than be a laughing stock. How can I bestow such a fortune on a woman happy to trust a complete stranger? You have to decide who you are, Elizabeth. A business woman or a mere female.'

Elizabeth trembled with frustration as their dance of one step forward, two steps back resumed. 'I've proven who I am over and over again. Pennington's means everything to me. You know it does.'

'That maybe so, but do you know how often I hear your mother's admonishments over and over in my ears?' He squeezed his eyes shut, before opening them again, his gaze defeated. 'But I'm struggling, Elizabeth. I'm struggling to be the man she and you want me to be.'

Elizabeth stared, uncertain whether she witnessed her father's genuine regret. The anger had vanished from his tone, his gaze sad. She swallowed. 'Papa, I —'

'I want you to marry Noel Kelston.' Her father's eyes turned cold once more. 'The man comes from an exemplary family. He's primed to inherit a fortune and, combined with Pennington's, your sons would

146

be among the wealthiest in the country. Yet, still you refuse him.' He shot his hand towards the window. 'And instead, choose to walk out with a man not fit to wipe your shoes. Do you really believe I'll just sit by and let things progress between you?'

'I wish for nothing to progress other than the business.' Elizabeth pulled back her shoulders, hardening her heart against anything but her need to achieve what her mother never had. Respect from her father. Respect from every man who worked for a company that would one day be hers. 'Joseph Carter has ambition. True ambition, and I *will* work with him.'

He studied her through narrowed eyes before standing. 'I have made numerous enemies in the past and enemies have a way of reappearing at the most unexpected moments. You'd do well to utilise caution.'

Trepidation skittered over her skin. 'What do you mean?'

He came forward and placed his hand upon her shoulder. 'You're my daughter and I love you. You might not think it so, but I do. Carter has shown a personal interest in you, has he not?'

'Of course not.'

'Maybe, maybe not. But since when has someone had such an effect on you that you'd willingly walk through the darkened streets as though you were lovers?'

Heat leapt into her cheeks. 'We hardly — '

'Trust me. There's more to Carter than we know about.'

Before Elizabeth could respond, her father walked past her into the hallway and she stared at his retreating back as he headed upstairs. Despite his insinuation that there might be more to Joseph than met the eye, and his conceding to give her the toy department, the only thing that shook her was her father's claim he loved her. She could not recall the last time he had said those words to her. What had stirred him enough that he might soften? Even for just a few, brief moments.

She glanced towards the top of the stairs before pushing away her concern. If her focus slipped or lessened into care rather than business, Pennington's would never be hers.

One day she would be the store's sole proprietor. She had to be, or forever feel she'd failed her beloved mother. Yet, guilt that she so often thought ill of her father whispered through her. No matter how badly he might speak to her, or not believe her capable, she found it impossible to entirely stem her love for him.

Couldn't he understand she wanted his unconditional love and approval?

Couldn't he understand she wanted him to have pride in her? She straightened her spine, left the dining room and walked upstairs. One way or another, she would prove herself. Whether today, tomorrow or a year from now, Edward Pennington would admit she'd succeeded and be proud of his daughter and only child.

15

Joseph wandered around a medium-sized store situated across town that, although somewhat larger than Carter & Son, was nowhere near the size of Pennington's. The decor was an inviting mix of cream and pale blue, the wooden flooring shone under the soft lighting and the staff were amicable. Yet, the sombre atmosphere lacked the temptation and excitement of Pennington's on an almost crippling scale.

He'd spent the morning working at Carter & Son, eventually making his way through a small back log of glove orders. Throughout breakfast and the rest of the morning, neither Joseph, nor his father, had mentioned the previous night's conversation. The silence had been self-preservation on Joseph's part, not wanting anything to destroy the new path he'd found. He could only put it down to regret on his father's part that he'd mentioned Edward Pennington at all.

Business was definitely slowing for Carter & Son whether his father wanted to accept that or not. The time for the small shopkeeper was coming to an end and, no matter the concern his father had planted in Joseph's head about Edward Pennington, Joseph knew with absolute conviction he had to keep his foot in the door, or else lose his rightful place at the forefront of retail.

Although juggling his time between Carter & Son and Pennington's was manageable at the moment, Joseph feared when his father retired, Pennington's would call to him with even deeper vigour and the decision to close the family shop would become inevitable. Guilt whispered through him and Joseph firmly buried it. By furthering his prospects, he was furthering the Carter name. He wasn't abandoning all his grandfather and father achieved, but merely building on it.

He roamed the quiet walkways as his father's warnings of a life alone gathered volume in Joseph's head and threatened to further weaken his broken heart.

How was he to contemplate a romance or come to love another woman when he had so much else to do? He had to build a future that would help others. He had to find the man who'd so brutally murdered his wife.

He had no time for love. His loyalty and commitment were meant for Lillian from the day they married . . . from the day they'd met. Yet, time and again, his thoughts now drifted to Elizabeth Pennington. Her beauty had caught his attention, but it was her intellect, care and kindness that had kept her firmly in his consciousness. Or maybe conscience.

Shame clawed at him. Two years Lillian had been dead.

Two years.

How could he be thinking — desiring — another woman so soon? What sort of a man did that make him?

Nodding to two young women as they emerged from the ladies' department, Joseph stepped into the area and looked around, desperately trying to focus on business, rather than his disloyal heart.

He slowly walked the floor. The clothes and hats were displayed in a more artistic way than they were at Pennington's, but not to the standard he envisioned.

Ideas and sales techniques grew ever stronger in his mind. How much longer would he have to wait until the imagined canvas in his head become a full and living painting?

He reached out to touch the display cabinet of gloves and stilled.

The soft, floral scent of Elizabeth Pennington's perfume tormented his nostrils and he inhaled, his heart picking up speed as he slowly turned.

Her beautiful, emerald eyes glistened with amusement as she smiled. 'Mr Carter. This is a surprise.'

Joseph stared, unsure what to say or do. Why did it suddenly feel as though he deceived her by being here in this store? Why did explanations and excuses dance on his tongue? He cleared his throat and forced a smile. 'As it is to see you. Are you looking for anything in particular? I would've thought Pennington's has everything a woman could want.'

Her gaze held his, her cheeks lightly flushing. 'Not quite.'

The softness of her voice gave breath to insinuation and desire traitorously stirred in his groin. Damn his maleness. Damn her ability to make him think of more than work.

Feigning nonchalance, he raised his eyebrows. 'Care to elaborate?'

'I think you know.' She drew her gaze around the department before facing him. 'What are *you* looking for that you can't find in Pennington's?'

'On the contrary, I find all I want is in Pennington's.' He stilled. Was he flirting with her?

Time stood still as she languidly drew her gaze over his face, lingered a moment at his lips. 'Then why are you here?'

151

His bravado deserted him under the intensity of her blatant study. How much did he want her to know of his thoughts and dreams? Would she think him overly ambitious? Scoff at his naivety? Yet, if he was to become valuable to her, he had to take a risk. Had to see if she was all he suspected her to be. 'I'm exploring how I want to run Carter & Son and how I *don't* want to run it.'

Her eyes brightened with pleasure. 'I'm here for the exact same thing. There's something missing at Pennington's, isn't there? Something, I suspect, neither of us can quite put our fingers on.'

Excitement churned inside him. 'Yet.'

Her gaze dropped to his mouth again. 'Yet.'

Their eyes met once more and the need to keep her to himself awhile longer gripped him. To have her here, talking alone with him without the workings of Pennington's going on around them, suddenly felt as vital as every one of his aspirations.

He glanced toward the department exit. 'Do you have time to take tea with me?'

Her smile vanished, and her eyes widened. 'Now?'

'Why not?' He lifted his shoulders.

Indecision showed in her eyes.

Joseph's heart beat hard, as alien apprehension hummed inside him. It took every ounce of self-control not to take her hand and ask that she not disappear as quickly as she'd appeared. He wanted her close. Probably too close, considering the speed in which his sanity had vanished.

'Yes.'

Satisfaction unfurled inside him. 'Yes?'

She smiled softly. 'I'd like to have tea with you, Mr Carter. Shall we go to the restaurant upstairs?'

He pointed his hand out, gesturing for her to lead the way. As she walked ahead of him, Joseph absorbed every inch of her from head to heel. Her softly painted rose-coloured lips matched her dusky pink suit to perfection. Her red hair should've clashed with the colouring, but curled and pinned as it was beneath a small black hat, she looked perfect. She was an astoundingly beautiful woman, but when he looked into her eyes, he saw her softness, too. God, he wanted so much to make her laugh. Smile. Dance and sing.

If there ever came a time when he could forgive himself for Lillian's death, allow himself the pleasure of a woman again, Elizabeth Pennington would be just the type of female to make him feel again. Of that much, he was certain.

His desire cooled to its usual numbness. He was pretty sure that day would never — ever — materialise. Or that, he'd ever have the courage to allow it.

As they rode the lift to the restaurant, mere inches separated them. Joseph glanced at her. She stared ahead, her exquisite profile turned to the closed doors, her hands tightly clutching her purse in front of her. Tension permeated the small space and Joseph looked away, inching to the side as culpability admonished and shamed him. He should not be feeling this way about her and the last thing he wanted was for her to feel pressurised to spend time with him away from the store. Yet, it wasn't fear on her face. It looked to be anticipation. Curiosity. Maybe even delight. He longed to know what she thought and felt about their proximity, about the two of them playing truant together.

The lift pinged, and they stepped into the corridor leading to the restaurant's bevelled-glass doors. She glanced at him. 'I have ideas for the store that stretch beyond the ladies' department. Beyond the men's department. I'd like to share one in particular with you.'

Pleased that her need to disclose her thoughts could be an indication of her growing trust of him, Joseph smiled. 'Of course, I'd love to hear them.'

Her shoulders lowered as though relieved that he wanted to listen to her. 'Let's get seated, shall we?'

She walked into the restaurant as Joseph followed. Why had she looked so reassured by his compliance? Had no one agreed so readily to hear her talk before? He frowned, unable to process the suggestion that anyone would ignore her. He'd seen how Mrs Woolden intently listened to her. Had observed the shop girls and Esther Stanbury, the window dresser, laughing and smiling as they chatted and joked with her. Everyone seemed to be fond of Elizabeth Pennington, so what was the reason for her insecurity? Was it him? Her father? Joseph frowned. All men?

Was the general feeling of inequality that steadily deepened throughout the city, equally prevalent in Pennington's? So much so, that even its heiress doubted her opinions would be respected and absorbed by a man? Joseph narrowed his eyes. If he learned that was indeed the case, he'd have yet another item on his agenda he'd work with her to change.

He entered the restaurant as she briefly spoke with the suited maître d' before he led them deeper into the room. Infuriation simmered inside Joseph. He'd only ever viewed Lillian as his equal and she had told him, time and again, it was because of his confidence and belief in her that she had so enjoyed life.

If a woman of Elizabeth's calibre struggled to have

154

her voice heard, he suddenly understood completely why women all over the city so vehemently battled the same injustice. Her disregard towards her father must be the root of the anger in her eyes when she'd looked at him during the drinks' party. Was Edward Pennington so blind, so archaic in his views — so bloody arrogant — that his daughter *and* his store suffered for it?

Conflicting emotions warred inside Joseph. If he'd guessed the truth of her existence, getting involved would mean combining the personal with the professional. He couldn't do that . . . the possible outcome had the potential to be painful for them both.

Yet, as he slid onto the chair beside her and looked into her eyes, the challenge gripped him.

16

Elizabeth glanced at Joseph from beneath lowered lashes. Their earlier conversation should have been simple but, for her at least, it had been anything but. The way he'd watched her, listened to her, smiled at her. The seconds and minutes had felt suspended in time. As though no one else stood in the department store but her and Joseph. Completely alone and entirely cocooned in an unspoken, mutual understanding that had quickened her heart like never before.

Something had shifted inside her and, now, he was no longer Joseph the glove maker, but Joseph the man, the confidante.

The notion was insane, but she felt empowered to embrace, rather than fight, whatever it was that burned so intensely between them.

Quickly reaching for the glass of water on the table, she drank delicately, resisting the urge to swallow the water rapidly to ease the sudden dryness in her throat. She smiled and put down the glass. 'It is most fortunate that we met today.'

He drew his gaze over her face. 'It is?'

'Yes.' Elizabeth inhaled a long breath, slowly released it. 'I wanted to ask you if you'd consider joining me in thinking of ideas which will enhance the ladies' department.'

He raised his eyebrows. 'You want me to extend my role past the workroom and my glove design?'

Nervousness swirled through her stomach as she

fought to hold his gaze and maintain an aura of business only. 'Yes. I think you're enjoying your time at Pennington's as much as I'm enjoying having you work with us. You've told me your aspirations come with the need to earn enough money to help others. Why not work with me so we can see that aspiration come alive in Pennington's?'

He leaned back, his brilliant blue eyes intense on hers. 'You're considering the employment of others as well as innovation?'

'I am. You're right that Pennington's should open opportunities to one and all. My father has given me the added position as head of the toy department. I want to start thinking bigger, Joseph. More encapsulation of everyone who wishes to work. Involvement of everyone who dreams big and wants more.'

She battled to form the right words, the right enticement, for him to work more closely with her. 'Is there any harm in me asking your thoughts? Any harm in us helping each other?'

There. She'd said aloud what she had been thinking for the last few days and nights. Unsure of why or how, but Joseph had crept deep inside her and her instinct now screamed he was the person — the man — she'd been waiting for to propel her position forward within Pennington's. Maybe even in her personal life if the strange trust she felt growing toward him was anything to hold measure by.

Fighting her habitual vulnerability, she cleared her throat. 'You see, you've already recognised I want more than I currently have at the store, but I'm struggling to find an idea to make the senior staff sit up and take notice. Your enthusiasm and intuitive eye is what I need. To ask a man . . . ' She exhaled a shaky breath.

157

'To help me is difficult to say the least but, with you, I'm prepared to swallow my pride. I think . . . '

Her courage wavered, and she picked up her water glass again. Would he make her finish her pathetic entreaty? Make her admit her daily humiliation under her father's tightened reins?

He gently touched her hand, easing the glass to the table.

Elizabeth's eyes prickled with shameful tears as he studied her intently, his gaze dark with understanding and what she perceived to be anger on her behalf.

'You think I understand your frustration,' he said, quietly. 'You think I look at you and see something of myself. You think that maybe I, even though a man, might work with you equally. Am I right?'

Her stomach knotted. 'Yes. But — '

'Elizabeth? Oh, and Mr Carter, too.'

Elizabeth looked to Joseph's side as he turned in his chair.

Esther.

Heat seared Elizabeth's cheeks. Her friend's eyes positively glowed with satisfaction.

'Esther.' Elizabeth laughed. 'How lovely to see you here. And you know Mr Carter, of course.'

He nodded. 'Miss Stanbury.'

Esther smiled. 'It's my day off so I am having a wander about town. The last place I would've thought to see you both is in a competitor's restaurant in the middle of the afternoon.'

Elizabeth struggled to engage her brain. Would Esther tell everyone at the store she'd seen her taking tea alone with Joseph? No, she wouldn't. Of course, she wouldn't.

'Would you like to join us?' Elizabeth waved towards

the chair beside Joseph. 'You're more than welcome.'

Esther grinned, her hazel eyes shining. 'Oh, no. I'll leave you to your . . . conversation.'

Joseph abruptly stood and pulled out the chair. 'Stay. I insist.'

The window dresser's smile faltered as she looked from him to Elizabeth and back again. Elizabeth inwardly smiled. Joseph had called her friend's bluff, his raised eyebrows and sparkling gaze confirming his canny intention entirely. Maybe having Esther as part of this conversation would be a positive addition. Her friendship with Esther had deepened from mere employee-employer status through their mutual want of female equality and progression. Surely, Esther would be as enthusiastic about opening opportunities to everyone as Elizabeth and Joseph.

Elizabeth smiled. 'Yes, please do.'

'Well . . . ' Esther slowly lowered onto the seat. 'If you're quite sure.'

'We are. In fact, I think it will be beneficial for you to be a part of our conversation.' She looked at Joseph. 'Don't you?'

He studied her as though trying to work out what she thought and then he slowly smiled. 'Three heads are always better than two.'

They looked at Esther who frowned. 'What's going on? You're both acting very strangely.'

The waiter approached and filled Esther's water glass. Elizabeth ordered afternoon tea and when the waiter had departed, she leaned forward and clasped her hands. 'After a recent conversation with my father, I'm beginning to hope his confidence in me is slowly increasing . . . albeit reluctantly. As he's now given me the toy department to run as I see fit as well as the

159

ladies' department, I —'

'That's wonderful.' Esther squeezed Elizabeth's arm. 'You must be thrilled.'

Elizabeth grinned. 'I am. Things are slowly starting to turn in the right direction, but I still feel the need to implement something drastic. What, I don't know. But I do know, with your help . . .' She smiled at Joseph. 'And the help of Mr Carter, we can come up with something.' She took Esther's hand. 'You and I have become good friends over the last two years and I know you feel as strongly as I about change. Female change. My father's views are, frankly, ludicrous and entirely outdated. It's time we did something about it.'

'Well, I'm not one for bad-mouthing the hand that feeds me, but Mr Pennington can be stubborn, unmoving and entirely demeaning to his female staff at times.'

'And that must change. If I was in charge —'

'When.' Joseph stared at her, his jaw tight. '*When* you are in charge. You have to believe in yourself, first and foremost. Anything less and he'll win. Every time.'

Elizabeth held his gaze as she slipped her hand from Esther's. He was right. Of course, he was right. She gave a firm nod. 'When.'

Esther smiled. 'Hear, hear.'

'So, what can we do?' Elizabeth looked at them in turn. 'If you're both willing to help me, of course.'

'Well, I am,' Esther said, firmly. 'Absolutely. My work with the suffragists had shown me all too clearly that in order to get things done, we have to fight for what is right.'

'Exactly.' Elizabeth sighed. 'I admire the campaigners hugely, and wish I could be involved, but my

160

position at the store means I need to remain neutral in anything remotely political. My father rants and raves about the Cause, the newspaper coverage and how their words will be effecting his female staff.' She smiled. 'It's actually absurdly satisfying to watch him squirm under the pressure of what I suspect he knows will be inevitable. My father knows change is coming, but it's how long he can hold it at bay that keeps him awake at night. It's time to bring that sense of fighting for what is fair into Pennington's.'

Joseph crossed his arms, his brow furrowed. 'So, your father is clearly against equality. What do you want to happen? More promotion for your employees? More responsibility? Whether male or female.'

'Yes. I want him to see that men and women have equal capability and skill.'

'But, if he's yet to accept skill and talent in his own daughter, how will he see the same in other women who work for him?'

'I don't know, but there has to be some belief in him. Otherwise, why allow me to come to work with him day after day? Why bring me into the business if not to train me and pass the store to me one day? The man is either a complete contradiction or, deep down, he knows I can run Pennington's but is terrified to admit it to himself or publicly.'

'So, you stand firm.' Esther's hazel eyes lit with vigour. 'You stand firm until your time presents itself, which I'm confident it will. It's all any of us can do. Fight and wait. Fight and progress.'

'I agree, but . . .'

Joseph leaned forward. 'But?'

'I just can't seem to discard my instincts that men will almost certainly override my wishes in the end. I suppose that means I need to grow to trust myself.' She held his gaze, conflict warring inside her. 'Trust you.'

His eyes clouded, and he looked away across the room. 'You're not alone thinking some things impossible. We've all got our beliefs borne from broken promises . . . sometimes broken hearts, but I'm willing to reach out a tentative hand for the greater good of my goals.' He glanced between her and Esther. 'If you'll both do the same, who knows what we could achieve?'

The waiter approached, and they sat back in the seats as he placed the tea and two filled stands with sandwiches, scones, and delicate petits fours on the table. Elizabeth continued to study Joseph, uncertainty and her infernal distrust of men and their motivations twisting inside her. Was she a fool to ask for his help?

He lifted his gaze to hers and winked. Shock gave way to a flurry of attraction that rolled over her, inflaming her skin with a heat that spoke of danger. She quickly snapped her gaze to Esther, whose grin told Elizabeth she'd witnessed the intimate gesture.

Elizabeth smiled at the waiter, her cheeks burning. 'Thank you.'

'Miss.' He dipped his head and left the table.

Joseph leaned his elbows on the table, his eyes on hers. 'You have an idea, do you not?'

Disconcerting nerves continued to leap in Elizabeth's stomach. Unused to feeling anything but relaxed around her staff, her awareness of Joseph as a man, rather than an associate, only perpetuated the possibility that her father was right, and it was feminine weakness that drew her so wretchedly to Joseph.

162

Dressed in a well-cut suit, and collared white shirt, an aura of confidence surrounded him, and she couldn't help but wonder if anything ruffled him.

Lifting a sandwich onto her plate, she embraced her determination to make progress at the store. 'I thought to ask each member of the ladies' and men's department to come up with a new initiative. Turn it into an informal contest where the winner gets to share their idea and its implementation with me, Mrs Woolden and Mr Weir. That way, it will convince everyone they have a voice and the department heads will seriously consider their views. I hope the process will be seen as fair and make everyone feel valued. Including the production staff.'

Joseph's brow furrowed as he studied her face before he leaned back. 'It's a good idea in theory.'

'In theory?' Esther raised her eyebrows and turned to smile at Elizabeth. 'I think it's a wonderful idea. There is one woman, in particular, in my department who shows great promise but seems a little timid in coming forward. If she could write her ideas down, perhaps that will give her the confidence she needs.'

Elizabeth turned to Joseph. 'Joseph?'

He grimaced, his gaze almost apologetic. 'It could have the opposite effect to the one you're hoping for.'

'How?'

'It will undoubtedly create competition between the staff. Between sales and the workrooms.' He raised his eyebrows, his gaze burning with challenge. 'Are you willing to expose yourself to new, possibly emotive, problems?'

Elizabeth studied him, before lifting her chin and nodding curtly. 'Of course. I will deal with anything like that, as and when it may happen.'

He smiled and reached for a sandwich. 'That's all I wanted to hear.'

It pleased her that her words were enough for him to trust her in their endeavours. 'It was actually your idea of commission that inspired the idea. Why not make the staff excited for the future? Why not strive for independent thought? They need incentive and encouragement, not silence and ungratefulness. I know you understand what I'm saying.'

'I do.'

She looked at Esther. 'It does us all good to be kept on our toes. It is how a person deals with the changes that matters.'

She nodded. 'Absolutely.'

'Wonderful.' Elizabeth smiled, eager to get started. 'Then I'll arrange for a memorandum to be sent to Mr Weir and Mrs Woolden telling them about the contest. I'll choose a winner next week and that person will have a lunch meeting with us where we can further discuss their idea.'

Elizabeth's mind raced with possibilities of the deluge of ideas that might soon emerge from her staff, and a power swept through her that was exciting and challenging.

17

Another week had passed when Joseph walked up the stairs leading to the living quarters above Carter & Son, his satisfaction far from concealed as he entered the living room. 'Good evening, Pa.'

His father turned from the kitchen table, where he laid a second plate, his eyebrows raised. 'Well, someone looks happier than I've seen him in a while. Things went well in the dungeon today, did they?'

Joseph grinned. 'How could Pennington's ever be a dungeon? The place is bigger and brighter than anywhere else in Bath.' He tossed his hat onto the dresser. 'I've had a good day. A really good day. My sixth batch of gloves has sold out, with more orders waiting. Even Mr Pennington had no choice but to shake my hand today.' He laughed. 'Well, maybe his daughter might have forced his hand a little, but still.'

'And shaking that man's hand means something to you, does it?'

Joseph's smile dissolved as his father's icy-cold tone and pessimism tainted the room once again. 'Not this again, Pa. What is it about Edward Pennington that riles you? As you've not mentioned him again, I thought no more about him and you knowing one another.' He crossed his arms. 'I think it's about time you told me what's gone on between you. Miss Pennington is keen to keep me working on the premises. It's hardly going to be the start of a good working relationship if my father can't stand the sight of hers.'

'It doesn't concern your work, so forget about it.'

His father moved from the table and took some cutlery from the sideboard, laying the knives and forks
beside the plates. 'If you're getting along with his
daughter, Edward Pennington has to like or lump it.
Not that I give a damn what the man thinks.'

Joseph frowned. The tea, that had turned into a
business meeting, he'd shared with Elizabeth and
Esther the week before entered his mind, causing a
barrage of uncertainty about what continuing to work
so closely with them could mean in the long-term. He
liked Elizabeth. Probably too much. The more they
talked, shared in the success of his gloves and her new
initiatives and ideas for the department, the more his
keenness to work permanently at Pennington's grew.
If he was to continue down the Pennington's route, he
had to get to the bottom of whatever gripe his father
had.

'Sit down a minute, Pa.'

'Can't. Dinner's on the stove. We don't want it to
ruin.'

'Then I'll turn off the burner. I want to know what
happened between you and Edward Pennington. I
mean it this time.'

Irritation burned inside him as Joseph extinguished
the burner beneath the boiling pot of soup and turned
off the oven, the smell of baking bread making his
mouth water.

'Let's go into the living room.'

Leaving his father to follow, Joseph sat in one of the
wing-backed chairs in front of the fire and stared into
the flames. Unease rippled through him as his father
took a seat beside him.

Joseph looked at him. 'Well?'

'I want you to let me tell you the entire sorry story

166

before you utter a word. Are we clear?'

Apprehension swirled in Joseph's gut. His father's eyes were dark and sombre, his jaw tight. Joseph nodded. 'Clear.'

His father exhaled a long breath. 'William Pennington, Edward Pennington's father, was good friends with your grandfather. They worked together at the local drapery as delivery boys, before going on to learn the trade. Eventually, they saved up enough money to buy a small shop.' He leaned back and exhaled heavily. 'Within two years, it was clear they had different ideas about how the business should run. Their animosity became too much, and they agreed to go their separate ways. The partner who kept the shop was decided by a game of cards.'

'Cards?' Joseph stared. 'They bet the ownership of a shop on cards?'

His father's gaze sharpened. 'I asked that you not interrupt me.'

Joseph clenched his jaw. 'Sorry.'

'Pride and anger causes the best of us to act without thinking. Your grandfather lost, but a deal was a deal.'

Joseph shook his head, a bad taste coating his mouth. His father had taught him the importance of working hard for a living, of saving to get the things a person wanted in life. To wager so much on the turn of a card went against everything Joseph believed in and the revelation stung. Who could say if his grandfather would've won that shop, the Carters wouldn't be where Edward Pennington was now?

His father blew out a breath. 'Your grandfather went on to work for a milliner, eventually opening a place of his own. As time went on, Pennington's business

167

went from strength to strength until he moved into bigger premises.'

Disgust twisted Joseph's stomach. William Pennington had clearly been a man on a mission, regardless of who he hurt, forgot or trampled on along the way. Was that the sort of man Edward Pennington was?

'The two friends were rivals, and very soon folks around town enjoyed the spectacle whenever William and your grandfather crossed paths. The friction grew, and by the time their respective businesses were passed to Edward and me, the rivalry had become too ingrained to be undone. Neither Edward nor I sought reconciliation.

'You were born, and your mother and I were delighted.' He smiled softly, his gaze glinting with pride. 'A boy. A son. I was fit to burst the day your mother put you in my arms. The love I felt . . .' He shook his head, his smile dissolving. ' . . . Well, that spurred me on to build something you'd be proud to take over one day.'

Shame and guilt mixed as a horrible realisation seeped like poison into Joseph's gut. After everything his grandfather and father had endured in the rivalry with the Pennington's, Joseph had just sauntered across town and offered himself as a supplier to his family's nemesis, intent on making his name.

'Pa, if you'd told me — '

'I haven't finished.'

Joseph scowled, unable to keep quiet any longer 'Isn't it enough I walked into the Pennington's store as though it was the answer to our prayers?'

'It *is* the answer.'

Joseph flinched and widened his eyes. 'How can you say that? Now I know what happened, there's no way I'm — '

'You're not leaving there, son.' His father glared. 'I had my reservations when you approached that place but, over the last few weeks, you've proven you can work there and here. You're driven, son and your abilities are strengthening every day, I'm an adequate milliner, but you have a talent like I've never seen. If you can find a way for your gloves to grace the hands of as many men and women as possible, then you damn well grab it.'

Humbled by his father's change in attitude and belief in him, Joseph sank back in his chair, uncertain of what to do. 'I can't believe you mean that. You're as angry with Edward Pennington now as when I first approached his store. I can see it in your eyes and hear it in your voice whenever his name is mentioned.'

Joseph's gut clenched with fury. He could have sworn there were tears in his father's eyes.

'You're right, but my anger isn't about you, is it? It's about Edward Pennington.' His father lifted the brandy bottle from the table beside him and poured a hefty measure into a glass. 'Edward Pennington . . . ' His father took a gulp of brandy. 'Wasn't satisfied with his business exceeding mine. He wanted more . . . ' He locked his gaze on Joseph's. 'He wanted my sister. Your Aunt Clara.'

Joseph stilled. 'What?'

'He came after her. With all the grace and charm of a man arrogant enough to believe everything he sets his sights on is his for the taking. He spoke of marrying her. Taking her away and giving her a life her family never could.'

'When was this? Didn't Aunt Clara — '

His father's jaw tightened. 'Take her own life, yes.

169

She was twenty.' He took a drink, wiping the back of his trembling hand across his mouth. 'She would have been forty-one now. That bastard Pennington is the reason Clara is dead.'

'How could Pennington have married her? His daughter must be twenty-three or twenty-four. He was married to Elizabeth's mother, wasn't he?'

'Yes, but once Elizabeth was born, something happened to Pennington. He went from being a greedy, grasping man in business to a greedy, grasping man in his personal life too. He wanted women. I would wager my last crown our Clara wasn't the only young woman he got in the family way. He was a hawk seeking out his prey.'

Fury bubbled inside Joseph. 'She was pregnant? With Pennington's child?'

'Yes, but I'm pretty sure he never knew. I suspect the bastard had most likely already cast her aside by the time she found out. He ruined her and left her. Clara told no one she was pregnant and hanged herself. The doctor at the morgue told our mother about the baby.' He squeezed his eyes closed. 'And that knowledge damn near killed her, too.'

Joseph shook his head, struggling to process what his father told him. 'Did your parents know about the affair?'

His father huffed a laugh, took a gulp of his brandy. 'Of course. Our Clara was spirited, Joseph. Spirited and, some would say, wayward.' His eyes burned with protectiveness. 'But she had a good heart. A romantic heart and that's what Pennington took full advantage of. Make no mistake.'

Rage welled dangerously behind Joseph's ribcage. Whether his aunt's behaviour was right or wrong, his grandparents had lost a child, his father a sister and he an aunt. And the fault lay at Edward Pennington's hands. 'I'm severing my agreement with Pennington's first thing in the morning.'

'You'll do no such thing.'

'How can I work there knowing Pennington was the reason your sister, my aunt, chose to end her life? I have to leave. I've no choice.'

'Of course, you have a choice. Don't let him ruin your life, too. I'm telling you this so you understand my anger, not so you throw away what might be the opportunity of a lifetime. You're staying.'

Joseph gripped his hand tight to his thigh, his heart pounding. 'How am I to look at his daughter knowing what kind of man her father is?'

'I suspect the poor girl already knows and that won't be an easy thing for her to carry around. I'd love to walk into that store and tell all his fancy customers what sort of a man he is, but I promised my parents I'd not say a word to him for fear of our Clara's memory being tainted even more than it was by her suicide. You staying at the store and making a success of yourself is all the retribution I need. Do you hear me?'

Joseph stared, as rage mixed with cold determination to avenge his Aunt Clara. How was he to keep his anger from spilling over whenever he laid eyes on Edward Pennington?

His father drained his glass. 'He's not a man to lock horns with, Joseph. I'm warning you.'

Joseph glared. Pennington's actions had affected the Carters' past and now he threatened their future. 'What about Elizabeth?'

'What about her?'

'Do you think she knows about Aunt Clara?'

171

'I doubt it. Pennington is unlikely to brag to his daughter about his fondness for young women, but I wouldn't doubt she is all too aware of how much he likes them. You only have to see the way he looks at the young women coming and going from his store.' He held his glass towards Joseph. 'No good will come of telling her. It's ancient history. Your aunt's dead and she deserves to rest in peace. You just prove yourself to Pennington. Work hard and show him what kind of a son I've raised. Work side by side with his daughter and bring an end to a feud that could've destroyed the Carters and the Penningtons.'

Thoughts and possibilities of what might have happened between his aunt and Edward Pennington whirled in Joseph's mind. Had they been lovers before Elizabeth was born? Did Pennington have illegitimate children scattered throughout Bath? What if Elizabeth was not an only child?

'Joseph?'

He met his father's fiery gaze.

'Promise me you'll show that man you can work alongside his daughter, but also pave your own path to success. Promise me you won't let my grievances and painful memories, taint what could be a fine future for you. No good will come from letting the animosity contaminate another generation.'

'I'm supposed to smile and shake the man's hand if confronted with him again? If the business was Miss Pennington's to do with as she pleased, things might be different, but —'

'It will be hers one day. Don't you see? The empire will pass to her and the feud will be over. Finally. I want that, son, I really do. I couldn't do that for your aunt because my hatred of Pennington was so raw, but now you're working with his daughter, I sense things coming to an end. You can ensure both Clara and I rest in peace when, at long last, we're together again. Can you do that for me?'

Joseph held his father's suddenly tired gaze. Every part of him wanted to agree. Wanted to put his father's mind at rest that the past would not jeopardise the future, but if he agreed now, it would mean lying. Something he had never done to his father and would not start now. 'I can't promise you that. Not yet.'

18

'Joseph? Everything all right?'

Blinking out of his sickening thoughts about Edward Pennington that had consumed him since his father's revelations the night before, Joseph lifted his gaze to Albert's as they sat opposite one another in the work-room. 'Yes, just tired.'

'You have the look of murder on your face. Woe betide whoever it was you were thinking about.' Albert chuckled and smoothed out the fingers of the glove he worked on.

Joseph tried and failed to concentrate on his work as he gripped his pencil so tightly between his fingertips, his pulse throbbed beneath it. Would the link between his and Elizabeth's families make them unavoidable rivals too? It seemed impossible she could be any more aware of their shared parental history than he had been. The quiet interest in her eyes when she listened to him seemed too genuine to doubt. Yet, her challenge of his motivation and aspirations showed all too clearly in her inability to fully trust him. He was now entirely convinced it would've been Edward Pennington's influence that had ingrained that wariness.

He had to be certain of Elizabeth's intentions about their association before he shared any more hopes and dreams with her.

The slow thump of a developing headache knocked at Joseph's temples. He wanted to work with her so damn much, but now knew something so horrible, the right thing to do would be to walk out of Penning-ton's and never look back. Yet, how could he do that, knowing, with the utmost certainty, that it was Pen-nington's that would provide the money he needed to finally start realising his ambitions and a future that wasn't shrouded in guilt and failure?

'Joseph? Are you listening to me?'

He snapped his gaze to Albert's. 'Sorry. What did you say?'

'I said, what do you think about this contest Miss Pennington put to the staff? Since the day you walked in here, you've talked about the changes that need to be made. This is your chance to put your money where your mouth is.'

'Any other day it might have been, but not today.'

Joseph remained focused on his work, but the weight of Albert's stare bore into the top of Joseph's head. It was nobody's business what had put him in such a bad mood. He couldn't care less if Albert and the other workmen speculated all day and night. He owed no explanation to anyone. Elizabeth was per-fectly in her rights to dismiss him or any other of her minions. What were they but the mere working class who worked their fingers to the bone all to the benefit of Pennington's and their bloody fortune?

Albert cleared his throat. 'You're a good worker and good company. Why not take the chance to show Miss Pennington there's more to you than glove mak-ing? I sense a fire in you that ought to make Miss Pennington sit up and take notice.'

Joseph looked to his work and made another few marks on his sketchpad. Annoyance buzzed like the drone of bees in his ears and his fingers refused to hold the damn pencil steady. He put it down and narrowed his eyes. 'I'm no longer sure I want her to take notice. How much do any of us really know about the Penningtons?'

His anger gathered strength. Could Elizabeth be as underhand as her father? What if this contest was little more than a ruse to wheedle out easy pickings for dismissal?

Joseph scowled, hating that, deep in his heart, he had begun to trust her. He hadn't seen a single drop of malice in her beautiful green eyes. Every time they spoke, she'd held his gaze directly, her expression open and curious, making him feel she cared about what he had to say.

Making him feel like a good and worthy man again.

Could he have been so blind to miss an undercurrent of mockery? Did she feel sorry for him? Or worse, had his father been wrong and Elizabeth knew about the rivalry between the families and decided to strike back at Joseph's father by giving his son hope for the future he yearned for?

He took a deep breath. He needed to talk to her; have her answer his questions.

Albert let out a low whistle and shook his head. 'Imagine winning the opportunity to lunch with a woman like that? A man would feel like a millionaire.'

Joseph stilled. If he won the contest, could he find a way to be alone with her after the lunch? Maybe imply there was a workroom concern he wanted to share with her that did not need Mrs Woolden's or Mr Weir's involvement? Yet, did he really want to share any more of his ideas with Elizabeth without being certain of her? He cleared his throat. 'I can't help thinking it's too risky to share my innovations with Pennington's powers to be. I've barely been here more than a couple of months and already have the feeling some people aren't to be trusted.'

'Miss Pennington's all right.'

Joseph sniffed. 'Only time will tell.'

Yet, his mind whirled as he sought the perfect idea to beat any competition and secure lunch with Elizabeth. Did she know what kind of man her father really was? Was that why blatant animosity dripped from her tongue whenever she spoke of him? Or was it all a smokescreen and the opposite of what she actually felt?

How was he to forget that tears of grief — or possibly anger — had welled in his father's eyes when he'd shared what Edward Pennington had done to their family, and then continue to forge onward with the career Joseph so desperately wanted? Pennington's actions were the cause of his father's pain, and Joseph would not rest until that pain had been avenged.

Day and night, ideas tossed and turned in his mind. To come up with an innovative idea for the clothing departments would be no challenge at all. He would put forward a single idea to secure lunch with Elizabeth, but over his dead body would she get any more until she had shared with him what she knew of their families.

Maybe it had been a mistake coming to this godforsaken place, but he would not leave until the Penningtons understood just how successful, how influential, the Carters could be.

19

Elizabeth gathered up the bundle of staff ideas that had been submitted and stood from behind her desk. She believed Joseph's idea to be the clear winner, but she had to tread carefully in case anyone accused her of favouritism. Or worse, her father came to the conclusion that by choosing Joseph as her first contest winner, her emotions were being publicly displayed, thus deeming her unfit for business.

She had to continue in her mission to achieve equality throughout Pennington's, Joseph's support had further stimulated her intention to help him in his goals, too. Her ambitions were no longer solely about proving herself to her father, but proving Joseph's and her other staff's talents, too.

Excitement and energy whispered through her. She had not felt this powerful, this strong, in months . . . maybe forever.

She picked up the sepia photograph of her mother from its permanent place on her desk. It had been taken when Helena Pennington was around the same age Elizabeth was now. Beautiful and serene, her mother looked the epitome of Victorian conformity, but if the viewer looked closer, there could be no mistaking the fire and mischief in her mother's eyes.

The confident lift of her chin said it all and Elizabeth smiled as she contemplated how quickly her mother's smile would have slid into place once the picture had been taken. She didn't doubt it had been immediate.

Yet, her father had slowly destroyed her mother's love of life through the years of their undoubtedly unhappy marriage.

She returned the picture to its place and pushed her saddening thoughts aside.

Scanning Joseph's idea that if a customer spent a minimum on hats, they would receive an easily produced pair of matching leather gloves was unprecedented . . . and so simple. Yet she hadn't thought of it. She couldn't help but worry that her mind didn't work in the way needed to succeed her father, but she refused to yield and if Joseph helped her perfect her own ideas, the more excited she became about him.

She glanced at the ornate wall clock.

It was time.

With her head held high, Elizabeth left her office and walked into the ladies' department. Pleased to see the men and women of the clothing departments already assembled, she glanced around. There were many women, as well as men, who surely wanted Pennington's to provide a gateway to a better future. She was confident people came here to work with their own ambitions. It was time for her father to realise the folly in dismissing such enthusiasm. Time and again, he overlooked people in favour of his own wants and desires. She had to be the one in charge. She had to become more than her mother could have ever dreamed for her.

It was after closing and the night was dark outside, an early April shower pattering against the windows. Anticipation for the forthcoming summer lightened Elizabeth's mood and buoyed her spirit.

She sought Joseph amongst the crowd and found him standing slightly to the back. His gaze met hers

179

and she stilled. His expression was blank, his body seemingly rigid with tension. Unease whispered through her and she quickly snatched her focus to the rest of the staff.

Forcing a smile, she fought to keep her composure. Joseph's usually affable demeanour had caused a worrying hitch in her chest, and she longed to approach him and soothe whatever it was that had brought such distrust to his gaze.

She raised the sheaf of papers clutched in her hand. 'Ladies and gentlemen . . .'

The chatter dissolved as all eyes turned to her.

'Thank you so much to those of you who took part in my contest and gave your ideas to Mr Weir and Mrs Woolden. Both department heads and myself have studied each one carefully, taking into account the feasibility and merit of each suggestion.

'Due to the high level of innovation amongst the entries, I've decided that despite there being only one winner announced today, we will be taking several other ideas forward, as and when we can. Those people whose ideas we intend to implement will be contacted in due course to discuss them further. On top of that, I've decided to regularly hold these contests with a different prize each time. So please don't be disheartened if yours isn't the winning idea today. There will be plenty of other opportunities.' She took a deep breath. 'So, without further ado, I'll announce the winner. Congratulations, Mr Evans. Please come and join me at the front.'

The staff broke into applause and most, if not all, of the faces lit with smiles, happy for William Evans as he came forward. Elizabeth glanced in Joseph's direction. He clapped along with the others, but his jaw was tight and his smile weak.

Elizabeth turned to William and shook his hand. 'Congratulations, Mr Evans. I was very impressed with your idea of having the clothes displayed in both the men's and ladies' departments so customers can inspect and touch the materials.' She faced the men and women around her. 'Once more, please offer your congratulations to Mr Evans with another round of applause. I wish you all a good evening.'

As the applause died down, Elizabeth moved amongst the staff as they slowly drifted towards the department exit, chattering and laughing. The mood was buoyant, and when she heard Albert Griggs suggesting a drink at the local tavern, she suddenly yearned to be included in the camaraderie of Pennington's workers, to peek into their leisure time and share in their stories. Elizabeth watched Joseph from the corner of her eye as he agreed a drink sounded like a fine idea. It was obvious to her that although he had done his best to muster enthusiasm into his voice, his usual cheerfulness was absent. Elizabeth frowned. Was he angry that she hadn't selected his far better idea? Surely, he understood her motivation behind bringing an alternative employee forward for new opportunity.

Well, whatever it was affecting Joseph, she sensed it was serious.

A sudden longing to observe him interact with his colleagues without the pressure of their daily work and quotas, swept through her. Although she played with fire by showing such interest in Joseph, her intuition burned strong that he was what she'd been waiting for to make her happy.

'He is but one man, Elizabeth.'

181

She started and turned. 'Esther, will you stop? I'm merely enjoying the staff's happiness.'

'You are merely wishing you could join Mr Carter for a drink.'

Heat warmed Elizabeth's cheeks as she slid her hand into the crook of Esther's elbow. 'Why would I do that when I have you to join me at the Cavendish?'

Esther's pretty hazel eyes glinted with teasing. 'You know, it does my self-confidence no good to know I'm second choice.'

'You, my sweet, reliable friend, will never be second choice.'

'Hmm. Only time will tell.'

Elizabeth laughed as they walked from the department, but her laughter did nothing to quash the worry that Joseph's obvious unhappiness had nothing to do with the contest and everything to do with something else entirely.

20

Pennington's production staff regularly drank at a pub on the other side of the city centre, nowhere near Joseph's usual drinking den. Yet, as he shook the rain from his hat and pushed the damp hair from his brow, the familiar sights and sounds that greeted him as he entered The Star Inn were as comforting as a warm blanket on a dank and dreary night.

The arguments Joseph remembered between his parents when he'd been a young boy, the late nights his father returned home and the occasional meal when nobody spoke all ran together in his mind. These memories must have been around the time of Pennington's seduction of Aunt Clara, or maybe even around the time of her subsequent death. He would have been about five or six. Elizabeth, he guessed, would have been three or four years younger.

There must have been some substance to his aunt's relationship with Pennington, no matter his father's insistence to the contrary. Had Pennington told her he would leave Elizabeth's mother? That he truly loved Aunt Clara above any other woman? Pennington had either been mercilessly convincing, or her history with him must have at least gone back further than his father had said or even knew.

Shouldering his way to the bar, Joseph passed men who jested and flirted with the brashly dressed prostitutes sitting on high bar stools, the ale flowing from the pumps as an old man tickled the ivories somewhere beyond the sheet of grey smoke that curled around the patrons.

Taverns like this made a hard day's graft worth every scratch of the pencil and every prick of the needle. A man could forget his need to succeed and, most of all, he could forget how his past and future were so cruelly linked.

Tension seeped slowly from Joseph's shoulders, even as the concern in Elizabeth's eyes and the momentary stillness of her expression at the contest presentation rose in his mind's eye. He hated that she'd been so obviously affected by his cold stares but had been unable to hide his suspicion that she might be aware of their fathers' history.

There was every possibility she had mistakenly blamed his moroseness on him not winning the contest. She would undoubtedly think him petty yet securing a private meeting with her had been the next vital step in his quest to speak with her.

He would now have to find another excuse for them to be alone and away from prying eyes and eavesdropping ears.

Inwardly cursing the scuppering of his strategy, Joseph tried to maintain his defences by imagining her to be like her father but couldn't banish his admiration and respect for her.

The energy between them each time they spoke was almost addictive. Even though her magnetic green eyes drew him in and her beautiful auburn hair taunted his fingers with the urge to reach out and grip the strands, it was the way their enthusiasm and passion tripped over each other's that truly gripped him.

Which meant he was most likely headed towards a whole lot of trouble.

He took a cash note from his back pocket and waved

it at the six foot tall and wide man standing behind the bar. 'A pint of ale when you're ready, landlord.'

He lumbered towards Joseph, his eyebrows as grey as the tufts sprouting from his ears, the rest of his head as bald as a baby's backside. 'Coming right up.'

The landlord pulled on the pump nearest Joseph and filled a tankard with dark brown ale, before putting it down on the surface of the stained and scarred bar.

Joseph passed over the cash. 'Keep the change.'

'Thank you kindly, sir.'

Taking a hefty slug of ale, Joseph joined Albert and the other workers where they sat on a long, battered and bruised seat facing three small tables. The second his backside touched the chair opposite them, Albert spoke. 'So, out with it then, Carter.'

Joseph stilled, his tankard poised at his lips. 'Out with what?'

Albert tipped a lewd wink around the table. 'We're not blind, you know. Everyone saw the way Miss Pennington looked your way earlier. Reckon the lady's got her eye on you. Now, why would that be?'

Joseph shrugged, hoping to God they didn't sense how much he'd come to welcome and enjoy Elizabeth's attention. 'She's a woman, isn't she? Why shouldn't she look?'

Albert shoved Joseph's shoulder. 'As if you could get the likes of her.' He laughed. 'She no doubt wants your brain more than your brawn.'

Trying to maintain his valiant act of bravado, Joseph puffed out his chest. 'Well, there is plenty of brawn as well as brains.'

Albert laughed. 'Aye, but she's never likely to add you to her list of suitors, is she? The woman is high

185

class. She'll be wanting a man with money and that puts her way out of your league.'

Joseph fought to keep his face impassive as a stab of what felt far too much like jealousy assaulted his gut. 'Maybe, but I'm not looking at Elizabeth Pennington that way so it makes no difference to me.'

'No? Then how are you looking at her?'

He shrugged. 'She's interesting. Seems to want to make Pennington's a darn sight more modern than it is right now.'

Albert took a sip of his ale. 'Well, she definitely knows her mind. That's true enough.'

Joseph couldn't have agreed more. But all that concerned him right then was exploring the question of Elizabeth's suitors . . . and ignoring the reason he cared. He cleared his throat. 'Who's the chap at the top of her list then?'

Albert took a sip from his tankard before placing it on the table and crossing his arms. 'Haven't a clue, my friend. I sometimes see this dandy of a bloke meandering around the store with her or her father, but I haven't a clue if he's in the running. All I know is, she might be educated and wealthy, but Miss Pennington's a good woman. One I like to think doesn't care much for society. I don't ever get any snobbishness from her. Whoever wins her hand will have to accept her love along with her dedication to Pennington's, that's for sure.'

Joseph frowned. 'Why do you say that?'

Albert raised his eyebrows. 'It's obvious, isn't it? She wants to be in charge. Seems to me her father is growing too old to run the store the way it should be. The world's changing and it's about time the old man accepted that and passed the baton onto his daughter.'

Joseph's heart picked up speed with hope Albert might say something that would help Joseph identify the root of Elizabeth's animosity towards her father. 'Can you really see him passing it on to her? I mean, they must be close working side by side and all that, but —'

'I don't get the impression they're close. The complete opposite, in fact. Nope, I can't see her father passing her anything without a husband by her side. Damn shame.' Albert shook his head and lifted his ale. 'She lives in a man's world and does a fine job without losing her femininity. That's no easy feat with a tyrant for a father.' He took a gulp of his pint, licking the froth from his upper lip. 'Well, maybe less tyrant, more predator.'

Joseph's stomach tightened, and he gripped his glass. 'He likes the ladies, does he?'

Albert looked around the table and Joseph followed his gaze. The men looked back at him, their eyes full of disgust and disdain.

He met Albert's gaze. 'Am I missing something?'

Albert inhaled a shaky breath. 'He likes the girls more than the ladies. If he ever came near one of my daughters . . . ' He shook his head. 'I have no idea how Miss Pennington puts up with it. Anyway, she certainly isn't the type of woman who will be tied to the kitchen sink with a brood of kiddies hanging off her. Her eye is on business and making the store hers. I don't doubt she'll make proper use of every person who can help her make that happen.'

Unease prickled through Joseph as thoughts of his meeting with Elizabeth and Esther surged into his mind once more. Had Elizabeth been using them? Had the shine in her eyes been founded in ambition rather than the prospect of change as he'd hoped? Could he have revealed too much of himself to her? Too many of his designs? Who was to say she wouldn't turn a profit and claim the success as her own? He had money, but not compared to her family's fortune. There would be no prizes for guessing who would win in a legal dispute.

Joseph picked up his drink, cursing the sickness knotting his chest that he was a fool to think he could come to know Elizabeth . . . come to care for her without consequence.

A man Joseph had barely spoken to during his time in the workroom, looked up and sniffed. 'Miss Pennington's new contests are all well and good, but it will take more than that to convince me she'll listen to what we have to say as much as she listens to the department heads.'

The rest of the men nodded their agreement. Joseph glanced at each of them in turn, suddenly understanding a little more clearly what Elizabeth was up against. 'How many of you put forward an idea?'

They gazed blankly at him or turned to look around the bar.

He raised his eyebrows. 'The opportunities are there. It's not Miss Pennington's fault if the staff doesn't take them.'

Albert leaned back and crossed his arms. 'Don't go judging us, son. You've barely been at the store five minutes.'

Joseph cursed the defensiveness that Elizabeth's possible manipulation stirred in him. He could not allow his anger to loosen his tongue and cause him to lash out at the wrong people. He stared across the pub, trying to get a handle on his irritation.

Every part of him had come to want more for these men, more for everyone looking for a chance to shine and get on at the store.

'All I'm saying is, why not put her to the test? Think of some changes and improvements to the working conditions and processes.'

Albert huffed a laugh. 'I don't know what you're used to, and, don't get me wrong, I like Miss Pennington, but the rest of us don't expect more than what our employers can get out of us.'

Joseph sat forward, desperate to ignite some passion into the men he respected and had enjoyed working with these past months. 'I'm used to working hard and expecting to reap the rewards. Why should it be any different for the rest of you?' Joseph swiped his hand over his face, feeling like a fool on more levels than he'd like to admit. 'Don't we all want a better way of life? To enjoy it a little more?'

A few nods and murmurs of agreement ensued.

'Then let Pennington's foot the bill and increase our pay.'

Albert picked up his tankard. 'I'm all for that, Joseph, but you'd be wise to not get above yourself. Make hay while Miss Pennington's listening to you. Don't go doing something stupid to rock the boat and have us all falling head first into the water. If you have her ear, that should be enough for any man.'

Joseph drained his tankard and stared towards the prostitutes and their prey at the bar.

His newly emerging doubts about Elizabeth whispered through him, a horrible disappointment lingering like a lump of lead in his chest. He had no one else to blame for his familiarity with her. No one to blame for thinking, in time, they would come to work more closely with one another. That was his misjudgement, his blindness.

But now his eyes were wide open, and he wanted the truth of their families' past out in the open to see where that left him as far as a woman who had come so very close, very quickly, to thawing a little of the ice around his heart.

21

Pleased that after two weeks of discussions between herself and the department heads the implementation of Mr Evans' idea was ready to go ahead, Elizabeth strode through the opulent Butterfly restaurant on the store's fourth floor, leaving Mr Weir and Mrs Woolden to finalise the details.

Even her father hadn't vetoed the idea and had left Elizabeth to oversee things as she saw fit. Ever since she'd asked him about the foundation of his distain towards her and accused him of being jealous over her relationship with her mother, her father had taken a step back — albeit a small one. She'd already sat down with the senior member of the toy department and plans for the summer season had been decided. As soon as Esther was available, they could start thinking about promotion and displays.

Her father's slowly loosening restrictions were a small, yet significant, victory.

Although always decidedly horrible to her mother, her father's demeanour had grown ever harder and more self-centred the more time that had passed since she died. Hence, his lust for younger and younger women and his disregard for Elizabeth's feelings. Could it be that he was finally softening? That her tenacity would pay off and eventually he would come to see her as a worthy successor?

Elizabeth silently admonished herself. It was far too soon to hope for such a turnaround.

Edward Pennington had proven how quickly he

could change, she just prayed his next metamorphosis would be in her favour, once more.

She nodded at customers, clearly enthralled by the restaurant's glinting chandeliers as they shone above them, prisms of light bouncing from the mirrors interspersed in the panels of the golden, intricately engraved walls.

Joseph drifted into her thoughts. Maybe she should invite him to her office to discuss his idea for the complimentary gloves? She wanted to see him again. Alone.

They'd barely exchanged more than two or three hours of businesslike talk for days and his distance bothered her more than she wanted to admit.

'Elizabeth.'

As she turned into the main corridor, her father's commanding tone behind her drew Elizabeth to a halt. She briefly closed her eyes before turning. 'Papa.'

'Have you just come from your meeting with George and this Mr . . .'

'Evans. Yes, I have.'

'And it went well?'

'It did. We will be restructuring the layouts of both the ladies' and men's departments this week.'

'Very good.' He gave a small smile. 'I concede your little contests are, in fact, a very commendable idea. I've looked through the staff suggestions, and I think you might be right. There are some untapped ideas we could expand upon.'

Elizabeth fought to keep her expression businesslike. 'It pleases me to hear you say so.'

He looked at the crowds around them, the atmosphere charged with the usual palpable excitement that was highly coveted by father and daughter alike. 'I would like you to be in charge of overseeing the staff ideas. I think, as far as staff innovation is concerned, you might be better at it than me.' He faced her, his gaze seemingly blasé and calm.

They both knew this was yet another substantial moment. Never before had her father admitted she might be better than him at something.

She swallowed as her pride rose, threatening to spill into joyful laughter. 'Thank you.'

He walked away, briefly stopping to exchange pleasantries with the lucky few he deemed worthy of his attention, before heading towards the lifts.

Purposely turning in the opposite direction, Elizabeth walked to the grand staircase. She needed some air. A few minutes alone to get her scrambled thoughts and feelings under control.

Descending the stairs, she approached the store's gilded double doors and nodded to the doorman as he held one of them open. The bright April sun glinted on the store's enormous plate-glass windows, adding an illustrious spark of glamour to the sumptuous dressing beyond.

She walked past a young news seller as he shouted out, *'Read all about it! Halley's Comet seen above England. Read all about it!'*

Elizabeth smiled and shook her head. All morning she'd heard excited and hurried conversations about the sight of Halley's Comet. It was such a momentous occurrence and she was disappointed not to have seen it. She could only imagine what such a thing must have looked like.

She breathed in fresh air as exquisitely and expensively dressed women entered the store around her, their wide-brimmed, flamboyantly decorated hats trembling with their chatter and laughter. Turning, she splayed her hands on her hips as she stared at Esther Stanbury's grand window designs and wondered if Esther had in mind to capitalise on the frenzied excitement about the Comet. Elizabeth smiled. She didn't doubt for a moment her friend was in the basement right now, working on a design and wondering what products she could use in the display.

She and her father had everything to be proud of in their store and staff, yet still an ultimate sense of achievement continuously eluded her, as if what she sought did not exist.

Her wants were many, but none impossible: To be given carte blanche to run the store as she wished. To have her father's respect and be his absolute heir. To one day be able to freely marry a man of her own choosing . . . she grimaced as Joseph entered her thoughts *again*.

Was all of that really too much to ask?

She could not have said what drew her gaze to Joseph as he stepped from the alley leading from the back of the store into the street, but his gaze immediately met hers.

Her heart beat a little faster as he stared at her, his jaw tight and his face completely absent of its infectious smile. Traffic streamed by and walkers brushed past her, but Elizabeth's feet refused to move. His face was a frozen mask. Not even a single strand of his dark hair lifted in the breeze.

She tightened her fingers on her hips and raised her voice. 'Mr Carter, it is barely two o'clock and you're leaving?'

He looked along the street in the opposite direction, as though desperate to walk away from her, to go about his business.

Elizabeth waited. *Don't go. Stay here and talk with me.*

Her impossible pull to the man shamed her and her cheeks burned.

At last he faced her, only to briefly close his eyes and then, as though yielding to the inevitable, slowly walked forwards.

The closer he came, the harder Elizabeth fought the urge to step back, knowing once he stood in front of her, his imposing height and build would succeed in shrinking her to an uncomfortable size.

He stopped and nodded. 'Miss Pennington.'

She tipped her head back to meet his eyes. 'Is anything wrong?'

His bright blue gaze held hers before he turned to the window in front of them. 'My father has been taken ill. I need to go home and tend to him.'

Concern immediately swept through her and Elizabeth reached out to comfort him before sanity dropped her hand to her side. 'Is there anything I can do to help?'

Suspicion clouded his gaze. 'Like what?'

'Well, I don't know. I just — '

'He'll be fine.' He glanced along the street again, before returning his steady gaze to hers. 'I really should go.'

Each word was clipped, his jaw tight. His stand-offish attitude sparked a slow simmer of annoyance inside her.

'Has something happened that you might want to share with me?'

The tension strained between them and the air crackled with unspoken words . . . with a dangerous attraction she wished to both embrace and deflect.

Joseph was a challenge. A man who knew his own mind. The dangerous, inexplicable yearning to work with him, her admiration for his intelligence and skill, needed to be controlled. Yet, his good looks made it harder and harder to resist him.

Hating her vulnerability, Elizabeth scrambled for something to say. Something to make him believe she thought them nothing more than business associates. It was a lie, of course. Joseph already felt strangely like her equal, a potential partner. Which made no sense whatsoever.

His chest rose as he inhaled. 'My father's name is Robert Carter.'

The change of subject startled her.

His gaze had turned carefully guarded as though gauging her reaction to his revelation.

What he wanted from her, she had no idea. 'Yes?'

'Does that name mean anything to you?'

She shook her head, confusion and wariness rippling through her. Hadn't her father asked if she knew Joseph's father's name? 'No. Should it?'

He frowned. 'So, my family business, Carter & Son, holds no significance to you?'

'It does not.'

'What about my aunt? Clara Carter? Has her name ever been mentioned to you?'

'No, I can't say it has.' She drew her gaze over his face, shamefully drawn to his mouth for a brief moment before meeting his eyes. 'Should your family be known to me?'

He studied her a moment longer before he looked along the street. 'I should go.'

'But —'

'My father needs me, Elizabeth — Miss Pennington. Please excuse me.'

He moved to walk away, and she reached for his arm before she could think just how dangerous such contact could be. He halted, and even when he looked at her fingers clutched on his forearm, she did not remove them. It suddenly felt important she touch him; that he understood she had care for what he said or asked her.

Even though the physical contact set her heart racing, she held her grasp. 'Why do you ask me about your family?'

He closed his eyes and dropped his chin to his chest.

Disquiet whispered through her. What had caused such uncharacteristic hesitation in him?

'Joseph . . . ' She slid her hand from his arm, ignoring the pang of loss that the break of contact brought. 'If there's something bothering you, please, share it with me.'

He slowly raised his head, his blue eyes full of irritation once more. 'I will, but not here. Not on the street. I'd prefer to come to your office tomorrow.'

How was she supposed to wait until tomorrow? Her curiosity was rife. It was clear something had changed between them. Something, it seemed, of which she was the cause.

She nodded. 'I'll send a message to you first thing in the morning.'

'Thank you. Until then, I bid you good day.'

He walked away, leaving Elizabeth with questions and words flailing on her tongue. She stared after him, fearful of the pull deep in her chest that Joseph's concerns had somehow become hers. No good could come of such caring. Her only goal should be proving her worth and capability in Pennington's and beyond. She could not allow one man, any man, to have such an effect on her.

She inhaled a long breath and walked towards Pennington's doors.

Her father stood on the street watching her, his eyes narrowed.

Her steps faltered, but she pushed forward, her shoulders pulled back. Once she was in front of him, she nodded, 'Papa.' And walked inside the store without uttering another word. All the while pretending she was as in control of her feelings for Joseph as she was about Pennington's future and her father's incessant hold over her.

22

As Joseph marched along Bath's bustling streets, the spring air did little to staunch the stench rising from the River Avon as he walked along the sloping, cobbled streets and deeper into the city centre. Here, the moneyed mixed with the desperate. Colourful, beautifully made clothes blended with the ragged, shoeless grey and brown of poverty. Bath might well be a playground for the rich, but it was also a place of pitiful desperation for the poor.

Elegant, honey-coloured town houses stood in rows on the upper streets, just as squalid slums formed communities closer to the water. As much as Joseph's ambition raced through his blood, so too did the innate wish to make a difference. He approached a flower seller and bought some lilies for Lillian's grave. He'd visited her grave on the anniversary of her death, the same as he did every month and as he would today.

At first, he'd visited daily, then weekly, now monthly.

Not that his memories of her faded, but he found enforcing some distance made it easier to work, easier not to drink himself into oblivion as he had for so many weeks after she'd been killed. This way of loving her was much better and one she would've approved of.

Because he'd lied to Elizabeth about his father being ill in order to escape the suffocation of the workroom, a tangled knot of thoughts and possible scenarios scrambled through his brain, along with the recurrent guilt that he should only be thinking of Lillian.

His father's disclosure about Edward Pennington, and Joseph's growing doubts and attraction towards Elizabeth, became more and more difficult to face. A confrontation with her was inevitable.

As usual, he purposely walked to the cemetery via the place Lillian had brutally lost her life, killed by a man Joseph was yet to find. He needed the punishment of the dirty, festering alleyway to regulate his confused head and weakening heart into regimented order. Tears burned behind his eyes as he stopped, his gaze on the spot where his wife had been struck down.

The habitual nausea rose bitter in his throat and a painful jolt slashed deep in his chest. He gripped the lilies tighter and embraced the poisonous fury that surfaced, hot and dangerous, every time he thought about his absence and what had happened as a result of his neglect that fatal night.

There to deliver bread and partially bruised fruit to the needy, Lillian had walked out of Carter & Son, leaving Joseph to finish whatever job he'd deemed so important. A selfless and wonderful woman, she had refused to miss a single night of her rounds, always wishing for Joseph to find whatever he needed to bring peace to his restless soul.

He'd once believed Lillian had provided everything he desired, but, in hindsight, he realised her protestations that he'd always want more had been true.

Still, he wanted more. Still, he couldn't stop running at full speed.

Lillian's death had only served to perpetuate his disquiet . . . until now.

Now, he'd become more energised, more enthralled with the world around him, only to slow down to an almost hypnotic standstill when in front of Elizabeth.

Running into her outside the store earlier had made it clear God himself taunted him. Every time he looked into her extraordinary eyes, or laid his sight upon her flaming curls, his fingers itched to touch her.

Then she'd touched *him* . . . and the contact had ignited a bolt of desire that shot through his entire body. It had taken every ounce of self-control not to pull her into his arms and kiss her.

Betrayal to Lillian twisted like a jagged knife in his gut.

Turning away from the alley, Joseph strode to the cemetery, entering through the black, wrought-iron gates and along the narrow pathway to her grave.

Dropping to his knees on the grass, he plucked the wilted flowers he'd left at his previous visit and straightened the bunch of carnations his father had leaned against the headstone a few days before.

'Hello, my love.' He placed the lilies atop her grave and kissed his fingers before pressing them to the cold stone. 'I'm back. It's been a different few weeks. I thought I'd found my place, Lillian. Thought I'd found the answer to settling my soul and finish our work helping others, but . . . ' He sat back on his legs, tears burning his eyes. 'I'm so very scared I'll get it wrong again. That I'll make a huge mistake with Carter & Son, with Pa, with . . . ' He inhaled a shuddering breath, released it. 'I've met a woman. A wonderful woman. I think you'd like her.' He swallowed the lump that rose in his throat. 'Her name's Elizabeth. Elizabeth Pennington and I have no idea what I'm doing, how I feel . . . or how you'd feel if you knew. Or do you know? Do you watch me? Judge me?

Help me?' Dropping his chin, he blew out a breath. 'God, I don't know what I'm doing now any more than I did when you were here beside me.'

He closed his eyes and let his wife's spirit wash through him as he remembered her scent, her smile and soft laughter. Slowly, the tension in his shoulders eased and his heart slowed as he felt Lillian inside him, whispering her encouragement and sending her love.

Joseph opened his eyes and stared at the inscription on her headstone.

LILLIAN LOUISE CARTER. WIFE. DAUGHTER. FRIEND. MAY YOU REST IN PEACE. WE WILL NEVER FORGET YOU.

'I never will, my love. Never. And one day . . . ' He clenched his jaw, his body trembling. 'I will find him. I will find him, and he will pay. I promise.'

Pressing his hand to her grave, Joseph inhaled a strengthening breath and rose.

He walked from the cemetery, hastening his pace as he returned towards the town centre. His strides were long and determined until he stood in front of the Abbey, allowing its magnificence to wash over him as though the divinity inside might cleanse him of the torture his self-loathing brought.

Was it so impossible that he might one day flourish at creating beautiful, sought-after gloves and the bitter loss of his personal happiness would cease to hurt as deeply? As much as he wanted to walk away from Pennington's, Elizabeth's influence on his professional and personal dreams proved difficult to ignore. He could not allow the past to poison his future. He had to find a way to make what happened between his aunt and Edward Pennington strengthen his decisions, not weaken them.

Turning away from the Abbey, Joseph neared the rows of shops along Pulteney Bridge as the River Avon gushed and burst in frothy waves beneath. Indecision about whether to tell Elizabeth about their families' histories continued to badger him. Only confusion and concern had clouded her eyes when he asked her if she recognised his father's and aunt's names.

He hated doubting her sincerity, but until he was certain she was as much in the dark as he had been, his distrust would linger, preventing him — them — from moving forward with their plans.

Walking to the end of the bridge, the street ahead opened into Laura Place. In the centre, an intricately carved fountain provided a picturesque backdrop to the small gathering of women holding placards and shouting towards a semicircle of spectators.

Joseph wandered closer and immediately recognised Esther Stanbury as she stood on an upturned crate rousing the crowds for support of the women's right to vote. It must be her day off, the same as when they'd shared tea with Elizabeth.

He smiled.

The woman was a force to be reckoned with, that was for sure. The women's movement continued to gather momentum and hope or horror for its outcome burned like wildfire all over the country. Yet, as Joseph watched Esther and the women surrounding her, he was awed by the proud and handsome scene. Their hair and dress were impeccable, their faces determined and their voices loud and clear, carrying across the masses and making people stop to listen.

Admiration rose inside him.

Couldn't the government see they fought a losing battle? That these women, and thousands like them, would join the fight and eventually win what they so rightly deserved? Reports had filtered through from London that some of the campaigners for women's suffrage had become so enraged, so frustrated by the lack of success, that militants now clashed with peaceful petitioners.

From the look of pure, unadulterated passion etched on Esther's face, he was convinced she would strive to be at the forefront of the campaign. He applauded her . . . as well as worried what Pennington's view would be on her making such a public stand. Elizabeth had shared with him and Esther how Edward Pennington felt about the Cause and the campaigning. If he were to discover Esther so publicly protesting, Joseph wasn't sure what the man would feel compelled to do about it.

Inspiration gripped Joseph's imagination as four or five of the women, ranging in ages from their early twenties to late fifties, shouted their protests and rallied supporters. Around them, at least twenty other women handed out fliers or stopped to respond to questions.

He noted the disapproval of a few small clusters of men and women, their fear of change clear in their eyes and hostile demeanour. These petitioners, and many more like them, projected fearlessness, strength and united determination, and he knew enough about the Women's Suffrage Bill to be confident these women and their supporters edged ever closer to success.

His focus sharpened on Esther once again and passion rolled through him as Joseph stepped away from the crowd.

Instead of being merely decorative, clothes, hats, gloves, perfume and jewellery could help these modern women show their strength. What they wore could contribute to their success. They should be supplied with whatever they needed to aid their plight, to help them stand out, be heard and respected. Bold, bright colours, big hats and spectacular gloves covering the hands of women working to make the government see sense.

Joseph hurried towards Carter & Son. People, shops and houses passed by in a blur as his imagination ran wild. He had no doubt that if he presented his ideas to Elizabeth, she would want to help him dress her fellow females for battle and their ultimate victory, even if Pennington's couldn't be seen to show blatant support to the Cause.

Could he forgo his doubts and offer the ideas rushing through his mind to Elizabeth? Relinquish his impatient need for personal success and merge his desires with hers? Working together, side by side, for something astounding.

He would see her tomorrow armed with designs, but first, he would tell her of their horrible historic connection. She deserved to know the truth and he cared for her too much to let her linger alone in the dark.

23

Elizabeth stared toward the Pump Room's gilt-edged doors and wondered how soon she could leave her father's and Noel's company.

Noel Kelston turned to her and smiled, his gaze so full of admiration, guilt pressed down on her. Her resentment towards her father's superiority had nothing to do with Noel. He'd been nothing but attentive towards her for the past ten months . . . which she'd found excruciatingly boring. He had no passion in his conversation, seemingly no interest past socialising, horse racing and the railways.

As for his interest in her? The man did little more than play the marriage game. Yet, was she not also playing? Albeit an entirely different way. Having her father on her side as far as Noel's courtship was concerned, rather than against her, only aided her limited liberty at the store, so she continued to see Noel — despite having no intention of marrying him. Her lack of integrity was horrible and shameful.

'Elizabeth? Are you not eating?'

She blinked and faced her father. 'Of course. Sorry, I was admiring that lady's outfit.' She nodded towards the table a distance away. 'I thought we might provide something similar at the store.'

'Do you see my frustration, Noel?' Her father smiled. 'The girl never ceases to work.'

'I do indeed, sir.' Noel smiled at her, his gaze soft. 'You love your work very much, don't you?'

'More than anything.'

Her father coughed. 'That isn't to say she loves it more than *anyone*. Am I right, Elizabeth?'

She forced a smile. 'Tell me more about your weekend plans, Papa. You said you might visit Aunt Margaret in the country?'

Her father grimaced. '*Might* being the operative word. Even though I continue to offer my sister money and elevation, she prefers to live with her farmer husband and their four children in a residence that resembles a falling-down outhouse.'

Elizabeth clenched her fork tighter. 'They live in a beautiful farmhouse on many acres of land. Aunt Margaret is happy. Should you not feel the same for her? After all, isn't a quiet life away from the store what you want for me?'

He grunted and speared some meat and potatoes. 'I see you more in a town house or on a country estate, such as the Kelstons enjoy. What do you say about that, Noel? Would Elizabeth not fit round the table quite nicely?'

Elizabeth glared. 'Fit round the table? Heaven's above, I have no intention — '

'Elizabeth is a strong woman, sir.' Noel smiled at her, his eyes warm. 'I'm not convinced she'd enjoy the life my mother and sister find so satisfying.'

Elizabeth lowered her tense shoulders. At least Noel knew that much about her, if little else.

'There's no need to look so self-satisfied, Elizabeth.' Her father snapped. 'Noel only wishes for your happiness. Once you're his wife — '

'And you do not, Papa?'

'I beg your pardon?'

'You do not only wish for my happiness?' Elizabeth laid down her fork and picked up her wine. 'I hope you feel as much affection for me as Noel does, if not more.'

Her father's cheeks reddened. 'You can be so maddening at times, my dear.'

Tension stretched between them, the knock of cutlery on crockery interspersed by the conversation and bursts of laughter around them. Staring at the string quartet playing on a small dais at the end of the room, Elizabeth breathed deep. She would not lower herself to making a scene in front of Noel, but she wished her father would leave her to make her own decision of a husband — if she chose to marry at all.

'Why not tell me more about Mr Carter if you'd prefer to talk of work?' Her father dabbed his mouth with his napkin. 'Is he still proving himself the current star of the store?'

Elizabeth's heart began beating a little faster. She glanced at Noel before meeting her father's challenging gaze. 'As you pointed out, Papa, is it fair to discuss the store now when Noel, I'm sure, would much rather speak of something that also involves him?' She smiled at Noel. 'How are your parents? Are they well?'

'Very well. In fact, they — '

'It was you who raised the subject of the store, Elizabeth. I suspect Noel will have just as much interest in Mr Carter as I do,' her father interrupted. 'After all, should you marry, the store and its staff will be something Noel will want to be involved with more and more. Isn't that so, son?'

Elizabeth flinched. Son? Icy-cold fingers tip-tapped up her spine as claustrophobia threatened. She had to stop this charade continuing before her relationship with Noel become out of her control.

'What is it about Mr Carter you'd like to know, Papa?' Elizabeth asked as the questions Joseph had asked about his family came into her mind once again. 'I can't remember when you have taken such interest in a male employee.'

He smiled. 'I take an interest in all my employees, my dear. I pay their wages, not you, remember? It is in my interest to pay attention.'

'Well, then, to answer your question, Mr Carter is still very much the current star of the store. As well as enthusiastic and hard-working, he's also made a number of suggestions I'm considering implementing and glove sales continue to grow.'

'Suggestions? Isn't the man merely a supplier?' Her father's eyes darkened with suspicion. 'Or have you given him further rope within the ladies' department? The man seems to have quite the control over you.'

Because he knew full well the words 'man' and 'control' in the same sentence would provoke a reaction from her, Elizabeth kept her expression impassive. She would not take the bait. Instead, she'd do whatever it took to put space between her father and Joseph. She couldn't believe for one moment that Joseph would remain working at the store if her father became part of the arrangement. Joseph was a man of integrity, a man determined to do all he could to improve the lives of others and having her father's poison infuse Joseph's goodness was something Elizabeth would not allow.

She held her father's malicious stare. 'Some of his ideas are quite ingenious.'

'Oh?'

'In fact, I'd like to implement his suggestion of increasing in-house morale by offering commission

209

to the production staff.'

'Commission? In the workrooms?' Her father's dropped knife clattered onto his plate and his eyes bulged. 'It's one thing to allow staff an opinion on department layout, Elizabeth. Quite another to allow a supplier to think himself important enough to have an opinion on how we pay staff wages.'

'All Mr Carter wants is to find a way to increase production and reward the staff accordingly. Which, in the long run, will benefit Pennington's.'

'You really imagine his ideas are for our benefit rather than his own? He has his own business. Sooner or later, he'll leave us. Then what?' He picked up his knife. 'You are a woman with fanciful ideals, Elizabeth. If I was to consider further expanding your position, as you'd like, you'd need to start living in the real world. I worry you are woefully unprepared for such a thing.'

Anger burned inside her, and Elizabeth set down her glass before her father noticed how the wine trembled. 'How could I not be prepared when I am forced to know how hard things can be? How staunchly people must fight for what they want? For what makes them happy. Joseph's agenda is admirable and — '

'Admirable?' Her father threw a snide look at Noel who shook his head and smiled in response. 'Since when has admirability had a place in business?'

Frustration burned inside her as Elizabeth's cheeks heated. 'It is not my place to tell you his plans, but if Pennington's sell his gloves en masse, Mr Carter will earn more money and realise his dreams all the quicker. Why not have the store benefit while we can? If, or when, he leaves . . . ' She swallowed, the loss of Joseph already making her weakening heart ache.

'There will be nothing stopping us continuing with his processes if they work well.'

Her father looked again at Noel and sneered. 'Can you believe this? Have you ever seen a woman so animated about business?' He faced Elizabeth and laughed. 'The next thing I know, you'll be banging your drum for the women's vote like the rest of those idiot females currently appearing on our streets.'

Noel grinned. 'They look quite the picture, do they not, sir? All dressed up with nowhere to go. I find the whole carry-on quite amusing.'

Elizabeth curled her hands in her lap. 'These women will be heard eventually, you know. You and my father can hide away in your gentlemen's clubs, smoking your cigars and sipping your port, but one day you'll find yourself sitting right beside a woman while you do.'

Noel glanced at her father and smiled. 'Maybe we will, eh, sir?'

Her father laughed and looked at Elizabeth. 'I apologise, my dear.' His tone dripped with mockery. 'Do continue telling me about Mr Carter's current innovation.'

Pushing their derogatory slights to the back of her mind, Elizabeth mustered every ounce of her determination that her father would come to respect Joseph as she did. 'He's confident that if we have an array of basic gloves in every fabric, the staff could be trained in stitching, creating and applying different adornments. Varying from the very expensive to the very affordable, thus implementing faster manufacturing and providing products for people of all classes.'

Her father stilled, his fork hovering at his mouth. 'All classes?'

'Yes. It's detrimental to favour one set of people over another. The days of catering to only the carriage trade are over. Grandfather was a man of humble beginnings who built the Pennington name from next to nothing. Who's to say the people with so much less than us will not be inspired to reach for greater heights when they come into the store and can afford something that makes them feel better about themselves? Pennington's could really help people realise their dreams. Doesn't that excite you?'

He watched her carefully, his gaze sceptical but also interested. 'Hmm . . . ' He turned to Noel. 'Your thoughts?'

He looked between her and her father before placing his napkin on the table and leaning back, his expression guarded. 'I think what this Carter says has merit, but Pennington's is a huge corporation, Elizabeth. You have many aspects to consider if you wish to venture into the wider market. You might well inspire, but you could also annoy. Who's to say the upper-class people who spend a lot of money in the store will not boycott it entirely if faced with a lesser breed of person?'

Elizabeth glared, her nails pinching her palms. 'A lesser breed?'

'Maybe breed is too strong of a word. I am merely saying — '

'I think you've said enough,' Elizabeth snapped. 'I understand your feelings without further explanation.'

Her father cleared his throat, the sound laced with warning. 'Elizabeth — '

'Mr Carter is an asset to the store. Instead of spurning his ideas without trial, I intend listening more to what he has to say.'

Silence fell and everything from the clothes she wore, to the expensive food she ate and the company which currently held her captive, coated her throat with the bitter taste of elitism.

Her father pushed his plate aside and leaned his elbows on the table, linking his fingers. 'Your obvious attraction toward Carter's ideas concerns me. What is his background?'

'His background?'

'I know many glove makers, Elizabeth. It might be that my path has crossed with the Carters in the past.'

Could it be true? Did her father know Joseph's family? What did she really know of Joseph's past except for what he'd told her?

Her father raised his eyebrows. 'For all you know, the man could be a charlatan masquerading as a successful businessman.'

'Your father's right, Elizabeth.' Noel picked up his wine and drank deeply, before slowly returning the glass to the table. 'This Carter fellow sounds as if he is doing all he can, and playing on your weaknesses into the bargain, to get his feet firmly under the Pennington table. You are wealthy, my love. Very wealthy. There are many wolves in sheep's clothing about town, you know.'

Incensed, Elizabeth's heart thundered. How dare he be so condescending? What did Noel know of weakness versus strength, honesty versus dishonesty? The man relied solely on his ancestors' successes. He'd barely added a penny to his family's wealth since the day he was born.

She pulled back her shoulders. 'Mr Carter's gloves are far too good for him to be masquerading. He is supremely talented, and I believe he'll succeed even

213

beyond his own expectations.' Pride and passion echoed in her voice and Elizabeth inhaled. Why was she risking her father sensing her feelings for Joseph ran deeper than mere association? Did she want these recent months of tentative happiness and possibility to be destroyed in a single night?

She turned to Noel, his patronising speech teamed with her growing feelings for Joseph making her decide to draw a line, then and there, through any prospect of marrying the man her father had chosen for her without a modicum of consultation. 'I'm disappointed by your need to show your disapproval, Noel. Mr Carter and his status at the store are none of your concern. You don't know him and, considering your views, I will ensure it remains so. In fact, as our views on industry and people differ so much, I feel it best that we no longer — '

'I love you, Elizabeth.' Noel's jaw tightened, and his eyes flashed with irritation. 'How can I not be hurt when I see your eyes gleam so brightly when you talk of a man who isn't me? I, like your father, dislike your admiration for this man.'

Her cheeks heated. 'I have admiration for his work. Nothing else.'

'Then I'll ask you this, do you ever intend leaving the store? Or do I waste my time courting you?'

'Are you saying if I agree to marry you, you would expect me to leave?' Her disbelief rose and she huffed a laugh. 'Then yes, I believe you're wasting your time.'

'Elizabeth,' her father growled, 'you take that back this instant.'

Noel held her gaze, a muscle flexing in his jaw. 'Well then, I have more self-worth than to play second fiddle to a working-class man who captures your attention so much more than I.' He rose and held out his hand to her father. 'Sir, thank you for such an informative evening. I'll settle the bill on my way out.'

Her father stood, throwing her a livid glance before turning to Noel and clasping his hand firmly. 'I can only apologise for Elizabeth's attitude this evening. Please, come by the house tomorrow.'

'Thank you, but I think we'd all benefit from some time apart for a few days.' He turned to Elizabeth and nodded. 'Elizabeth.'

She swallowed against the dryness in her throat and looked to the table as Noel walked away. Sooner or later, he would see their courtship had always been doomed to fail. She felt no guilt for shunning him. In fact, she felt a weight had been irrevocably lifted.

Her father resumed his seat and Elizabeth's heart sank. Clearly, Noel's abrupt departure had not brought the evening to an end. She raised her eyes.

His cold gaze burned with anger, his cheeks red. 'What is it about Carter that has you ruining your chances of such a wonderful match?' His voice was almost a growl. 'It must be more than the man's *talent*.'

'It *is* more.' Elizabeth glared, her body tense with the depth of her protection over Joseph. 'It's his intelligence, intuition and passion. All the things that are vital to the future success of the store.'

Her father studied her, his eyes mere slits, and Elizabeth struggled not to fidget as the seconds passed.

'You see clear potential in this man?' he snapped.

'I do.'

'Then I think it only right I meet him properly.'

Panic rolled through her. Every part of her wanted to shut his request down with a firm refusal, but to do so would only inflame her father's interest in Joseph.

Satisfaction came from her father in waves as he reached for his wine glass. 'It seems the cat has got your tongue, my dear. Why would I not want to talk further with the only man who seems to have broken through your iron-plated veneer?'

'Fine. I'll arrange a meeting with Joseph in due course, but not yet. Having you single him out now could result in staff asking questions. I don't want anything to deter Mr Carter from continuing to work with us for as long as possible.'

'As you wish, but I will not wait forever to speak with him.' He raised his glass, triumph burning in his dark eyes. 'Let us toast. To the store and the intriguing Mr Carter.'

Elizabeth glared. She would do all she could to keep her father away from Joseph for as long as possible. Her distrust of her father injected an ugly poison into her blood. A poison she fought against every day and yet still failed to find an antidote.

She reluctantly touched her glass to her father's.

24

Joseph glanced across the workroom just as Mrs Woolden finished talking with the supervisor and approached the bench where he and Albert worked. 'Good morning, gentlemen.'

'Morning, Mrs Woolden.' Joseph's greeting joined Albert's.

'I've come to collect you for a meeting with Miss Pennington, Mr Carter. Have you time now?'

Relieved Elizabeth hadn't gone back on her word yesterday to meet with him, Joseph stood. 'Of course.' He grabbed his sketchbook from under the table and held his hand out. 'After you.'

Following Mrs Woolden from the room, he ignored the blatant stares of the workmen as anticipation beat with every thump of his heart. He walked confidently towards the lift and, once they were inside and the doors had brushed closed, he took a moment to prepare himself for whatever came next. He had ten designs of hats and gloves and two of jackets. Even though clothing wasn't his specialty, the inspiration the women campaigners provided meant Joseph had worked feverishly through the night, drawing whatever came to mind.

Not that his work had altered his jumbled conscience.

Could he really take this opportunity to speak with Elizabeth about their shared history? Even though it was his father's wish that Joseph continued to work with Elizabeth, he could not banish the betrayal of his aunt's trust, or maybe even her love, of Edward Pennington. Joseph was now convinced continuing to work with Pennington's daughter could only lead to certain hurt for one — or both — of them.

The lift doors opened on the second floor and Joseph stepped out. Following behind Mrs Woolden, he straightened his spine as they walked through the bustling ladies' department to Elizabeth's closed office door.

Mrs Woolden knocked and entered. 'Miss Pennington, I have Mr Carter to see you.'

'Thank you, Aveline. Would you arrange for some tea, please?'

'Of course.'

With a brief smile to Joseph, Mrs Woolden ushered him inside and closed the door. He met Elizabeth's soft gaze, where she sat behind her mammoth desk and his heart kicked. Damn, she looked beautiful. Dressed in a light grey suit, her auburn hair was twisted and decorated with pearl-tipped pins, her pretty lips glistening a delicate pink. 'Good morning, Miss Pennington.'

'Good morning.' She smiled. 'Come and have a seat.'

Joseph walked forward, trying and failing to draw his gaze from her hair. The notion of how all that thick, luscious hair would look loose and tumbling over her bare shoulders whispered through Joseph's mind.

Blinking, he cleared his throat and sat.

'Your father is feeling better today, I hope?'

Guilt slithered into his stomach. 'Yes, much. He thinks it might have been something he ate.'

'Ah, I see. Well, I'm glad to hear he's on the mend.'

She continued to watch him, and Joseph shifted in

218

his seat under the weight of her scrutiny. She seemed to be looking for something in his eyes or manner. Not that he could blame her for any suspicion, after the way he'd behaved when talking with her yesterday.

'Miss Pennington, I'm sorry for —'

The door opened behind him and Joseph turned as a shop girl entered carrying a tea tray. She walked to a small seating area at the side of the office. 'Would you like me to set the tea out here, Miss Pennington? Or shall I pour a cup for you and Mr Carter to have at your desk?'

'Leave the tea there, if you will, please, Alice. I can serve Mr Carter.'

Serve Mr Carter . . . He couldn't imagine Elizabeth Pennington having to serve anyone.

Nervous anticipation rippled through him as they waited for Alice to leave the room. The moment the door clicked shut, Elizabeth rose from her desk.

'Come and sit over here. We'll be more comfortable.'

Joseph stood. He wouldn't be comfortable around her until he'd asked about her father and what she knew of the cad's history. Which meant his dilemma, of whether to withhold his father's revelation from her, was decided.

She walked ahead of him across the wood-panelled room, the scent of fresh flowers from the displays beside her desk sweetening the air. The tea had been laid on a table in front of a plush, expensively uphol-stered settee and two matching armchairs.

As Elizabeth sat on the settee, she was the picture of businesslike elegance and Joseph ran his gaze over her hair once more as she leaned over to pick up the teapot. Attraction shot through him and he trembled

219

from its intensity. He studied her hands and the inch or two of her revealed wrists. Her skin was unblemished and looked creamy smooth. He sat and briefly closed his eyes. His increasing attraction towards her was growing into a dangerous problem.

'Milk and sugar?'

'Just milk, please.' Joseph slid his sketchbook into the space between the arm of his chair and his thigh, forcing himself to sit back and relax. 'I want to apologise for my mood yesterday. I had no right to be so abrupt with you.'

Her focus remained on pouring the tea. 'Thank you, but there's no need to apologise. In the few months we've been acquainted, I'm already becoming accustomed to your candour.' She handed him a cup and saucer and smiled. 'I find it most refreshing.' She lifted her cup and shifted back on the settee. 'Far too many of my employees and associates watch every word they say to me. You don't, and I like that. I think you incapable of lying and that's something I highly value.'

Shame warmed his face and Joseph sipped his tea to ease his suddenly arid throat. Considering the gargantuan revelation he was about to disclose to her about their families, he owed her his absolute honesty. In everything. He coughed. 'But I did lie to you.'

Her eyes widened with surprise before she blinked, and they clouded with what looked far too much like disappointment. 'Oh?'

He put his cup and saucer on the table. 'I lied about my father. He wasn't ill yesterday, but I needed to leave the store. I'm sorry.'

'You're employed as a consultant. You're free to leave during the day whenever you have reason to do so.' She studied him, her spine rigid and the cup in her hand seemingly forgotten. 'Did something happen yesterday that you felt you couldn't be honest with me?'

Sickness gripped him. What to tell her? The whole truth? Or should he ask her some questions in order to ascertain how much she knew about their shared histories? Cowardice threatened, and Joseph drew in a strengthening breath.

'Something's happened that I need to share with you, but first I'd like to show you some designs I spent almost all of last night working on.'

Her eyes lingered on his awhile longer, their depths shrouded with a sombre intensity he had no idea how to interpret. Finally, she sipped her tea and slid the cup onto the table. 'Then don't keep me in suspense.'

Joseph drew out his sketchbook and turned to the first page. 'When I was walking around town yesterday —'

'When your father was not really ill . . . ' She raised her eyebrows, teasing sparkling in her dark green gaze.

Joseph grimaced, although pleased his dishonesty hadn't obliterated her humour. 'When my father was not really ill.'

She smiled. 'I interrupted you, please, continue.'

He coughed. 'I came upon some members of the women's suffrage movement demonstrating in Laura Place. They held me entranced. I was inspired by their spirit and determination. These women stood tall and proud, not at all deterred by the heckling.' His enthusiasm banished his previous trepidation. 'They're fighting a battle none of them is sure they'll win, yet they fight on regardless.'

She frowned, her gaze now filled with intense interest.

221

'And that inspired you to design more gloves?'

'Yes, and hats. And for the first time ever, I drew clothes too. Here.' He passed her the sketchbook. 'I've used a military influence. I think the wider shoulders and glinting buttons speak of soldiering, of fighting for good over evil. The gloves will be made of strong leather, yet feminine and soft to the touch. The hats are big and bold, maybe in grey, black, deep green or purple, but with accentuating flashes of pink, blue or white on the wide lapels of the jackets, corsages and the cinched waistbands. These are clothes that will demand to be seen amongst a sea of others. I think they'd appeal to these women and the growing number of others like them. I'm certain they'd sell well.'

She slowly flipped through his designs, turning back to look again at pages already turned, her brow furrowed. 'And how do you envisage promoting such a line?' She looked at him. 'It wouldn't be a good idea for Pennington's to be involved in the politics of the Cause. At least, not yet. It would be detrimental for us to be seen choosing a side. There's no way of knowing who we'd alienate.' She shook her head. 'And I know for certain that my father would be vehemently against any such support.'

He clasped his hands together. 'I understand. The Cause is merely what inspired my thoughts of strong women and dressing them for success.' Passion burned inside him as their gazes locked, the familiar excitement hovering silently between them. 'Women have voices, strengths and weaknesses, just the same as men. Why shouldn't they be dressed equally as smartly? Equally as notably?'

'I agree.'

'My designs speak of unity, purpose and women

222

making a stand in a man's world, without losing any of their femininity. Do you not carefully select what you wear to the store? Conscious of the presence you need to maintain and uphold.'

'Yes, I suppose I do.' She looked again to his sketchbook. 'These designs have real possibility. Maybe creating a line for women forging towards something new and courageous is just what's needed to bring some new energy to the Pennington name.'

Relieved, Joseph leaned back. 'I'm glad to hear you say so.'

She raised her eyebrows. 'Did you think I might reject your ideas?'

'Part of me worried that my confession of lying to you would push you in that direction, yes.'

She smiled softly, her gaze amused. 'I have a little more integrity than that, but you did still lie.' She put the sketchbook on the settee beside her. 'I'll arrange a meeting for us to sit down with Mrs Woolden sometime tomorrow and we can discuss your designs further but, in the meantime, would you please explain why you asked me yesterday if I knew your father's and aunt's names?'

He stilled. Why had he not considered she would raise the subject first? 'Pardon?'

'Yesterday, Joseph. Why did you ask me if I know your father's and aunt's names?' Her jaw tightened. 'I'd appreciate the truth this time.'

His heart hammered. Her use of his Christian name, whether intentionally or not, affected him more than he could stand. The intimacy between them intensified, making him want to take her hand, inch closer, so he could steal a comforting arm around her should she need it after his revelation.

'Mr Carter?' She stared at him expectantly, her body rigid.

Joseph leaned his forearms on his knees as he grappled with how to begin the conversation. He liked and respected Elizabeth too much to keep such an enormous and tawdry secret from her. He wanted them to work together without a ticking explosive between them that was certain to detonate sooner or later, destroying whatever they had built.

Exhaling, he held her gaze. 'Our fathers know one another, as did our grandfathers before them.'

★ ★ ★

Elizabeth froze. 'Pardon?'

He shook his head. 'I'm sorry.'

She swallowed, her mouth dry. 'You're sorry?'

'Yes.' He swiped his hand over his face, closed his eyes as though unable to look at her. 'Their relations were completely unamicable.'

'Unamicable?' What on earth was she about to learn that could have Joseph reluctant to face her. 'Joseph, what is this about?'

He opened his eyes. 'The most important thing is that neither of us is used as a pawn in some sort of plan your father might have.'

'Pawns?' She frowned. 'What are you talking about?'

He exhaled and clasped his hands to his thighs, his gaze steady on hers. 'It seems I am the son of a past rival of your father's.' He clenched his jaw. 'But the fact is, whatever has happened between them in the past, I won't be used by anyone; including your father.'

Dread lifted the hairs at the back of her neck. Once

224

more her father's ever-lingering shadow threatened to darken another good thing, another good person, who'd come so unexpectedly into her life.

Fighting for control, she cleared her throat and folded her hands in her lap. 'Our fathers know one another? And our grandfathers before them?'

His eyes shadowed with what looked like sympathy. 'Part of me hoped my revelation wouldn't be a surprise to you. Does my surname not mean anything to you at all?'

Her mind raced for recollection — recognition — yet nothing but confusion scrambled her brain, along with the horrible suspicion her father might know more about Joseph than she did. The interest he'd shown. The questions.

Sickness churned inside her. 'No. Nothing.'

His gaze travelled over her face before he drifted his focus towards the window. 'Then I am indeed sorry to surprise you with this.'

The way he looked away, as though unable to face her, tore a pathetic fear of loss through her chest. 'Why are you sorry? Why does it matter what has gone on before? It only matters that we respect and appreciate each other now.' Seconds passed as he continued to stare towards the window, a muscle flexing in his jaw. 'Joseph?'

He turned, his lips pursed and his blue eyes dark.

She took a long, steadying breath. 'Whatever has happened between our families, you must tell me. I have a right to know.'

For a long moment, his gaze locked on hers before he closed his eyes and took a deep breath. Slowly, he opened his eyes and looked directly at her. 'Our grandfathers once worked together at a small drapery in town. They were friends and partners until the animosity between them grew to such an extent it became impossible for them to continue.' He exhaled. 'Your grandfather won the drapery in a game of cards.'

Elizabeth's mind darted from Joseph's words to her father. Did he already know that Joseph was from a once-rival family? Could Joseph's suspicion they were being used as pawns be accurate? She wouldn't put the prospect past her father.

Her anger rose. 'Again, whatever has happened before has no bearing on the fut — '

'Your father has never mentioned mine? Never said a single word to you about the rivalry between Pennington and Carter?'

'No.' What if her father had somehow lured Joseph to the store under false pretences and his appearance had been staged rather than destiny as she had so fervently hoped?

He shook his head. 'I'm sorry, but I find that very hard to believe.'

'It's the truth.'

'You have no memories of a Carter family being talked about in your home?'

'No, and it seems neither did you about my family.' Defensiveness stole over her as yet another man seemingly thought her blind, deaf and dumb. 'I've no reason to lie to you. Anyway, if the feud is in the past I see no reason why my father should talk of it now.'

'But is it in the past?'

Caution tiptoed over the surface of her skin. 'Yes, unless you wish to confess yourself an adversary to me? To Pennington's?'

'That's the last thing I am.'

She held his gaze. Did he mean to harm the store?

Harm her? 'Did you know about this feud when you came to work here? Are you here to right a wrong?'

'You really think me capable of such a thing? I'm the least underhanded man you're likely to meet. I came to Pennington's in good faith to earn the money I need to help others. I've told you this.'

She studied him before gently nodding. 'And I believe you.'

'Good, because I was as unaware as you of this friction between our families. My father told me just days ago. He also told me to stay here, work with you to bring an end to the feud.'

'And you wish to end it how exactly?'

'By working with you and making my gloves sell well so that we might both profit. I want to believe we can continue to work together despite the past . . . and your father's presence here. I've jumped from wanting to run a hundred miles in the opposite direction to Pennington's, to out and out determination that whatever has happened before will not steal what I see as an amazing opportunity. But, if you feel you cannot work with me — '

'I'll need to speak of this with my father.' Unease continued to badger her. How was she to know Joseph spoke the truth? As much as she liked and longed to trust him, she could not risk anything happening to the store and ruining the chance it would one day be entirely hers.

She could not afford to trust Joseph in that moment any more than she could her father.

Joseph's pained expression and soft gaze threatened to weaken the anger she needed to hold onto if she was to confront her father.

'You should've come to me with this the moment

you learned of it.'

'Maybe, I should have.' He exhaled, pushing away the soft dark hair that had fallen over his brow, his eyes glazed with regret. 'But I was reluctant for fear of what it might mean for both of our futures. The last thing . . . ' He stared into her eyes. 'The last I want is for you to be hurt by any of this.'

The deep care in his gaze twisted her heart and she lowered her gaze. The sudden urge to stand and ease him to his feet shot through her. She trembled with the fantasy of what it might feel like to be held by him. Have him show her comfort and reassurance when she'd only received ridicule and hilarity from her father.

'You need to leave this revelation with me for the time being.' She lifted her gaze to his. 'I'm stronger than you realise.'

'You're wrong.'

She stilled. 'Pardon?'

His gaze burned into hers. 'I know just how strong you are. How fair and considerate.' His jaw tightened. 'What I don't know is what your father thinks and feels. He could be playing us, Elizabeth, and enjoying every minute.'

Despite the knowledge of just how ruthless and uncaring her father was, Elizabeth's innate need to defend him to anyone outside of the family rose. 'Business is business. If your family has not managed to achieve the same success as mine, that does not mean — '

'This is about more than business.'

The clipped anger in his tone warned of further revelations and Elizabeth braced for whatever came next. 'Meaning?'

228

He swiped his hand over his face and slumped his shoulders. 'Your father seduced my aunt. He cast her aside while she carried his baby.'

Elizabeth's pulse beat hard as nausea rose bitter in her throat.

'If this was just about business, I would have kept my counsel, but it is about so much more than that. As far as either of us knows, your father could have been considering leaving his wife, your mother . . . you.'

Sickness rolled through her. Deep down she knew her father capable of what Joseph claimed and more. She swallowed. 'And what of your aunt? Did she have the baby?'

He leaned back, his shoulders low. 'My aunt is dead. She took her own life.'

Shock swept over her and Elizabeth clasped her hand to her throat. 'And the baby?'

'Died with her.'

'My God.' Guilt pressed down on her as though it was her that caused the poor woman's death. 'And she took her own life and that of her baby because of my father?'

Joseph's face was pale with fury. 'Yes.'

Elizabeth's heart hurt, and her mind raced. He was lying. He had to be . . .

'You cannot expect me to accept you speak the truth when I barely know you. When did this happen? Was I born? Were you born?'

'I think you would've been an infant. Myself a little older. You *do* know me, Elizabeth. You knew me from the moment I walked into the store as I knew you. You and I . . . ' He snatched his gaze towards the window once more. 'Have an unspoken understanding. I know you feel it too.'

229

Whenever she looked into Joseph's eyes, all she saw was his sincerity, his integrity. How could it be that she instinctively trusted him when she'd barely known him more than a few months when she'd known her father her entire life?

Cruel longing wound through her, making Elizabeth hold her breath. She yearned to touch her fingers to his hard jaw, soften the rigid muscles in his neck and shoulders. Tears burned, and she quickly blinked them back. Was her father's and Noel's reservations about her unquestioning faith in Joseph justified? Had she been too quick to relish his ambition and embrace the excitement and pleasure of his company?

Yet, he'd not asked anything of her but for her belief and support.

There were questions to ask her father before she became any more embroiled in the future possibility of standing with Joseph.

Unsteadily, she stood. 'I think you should leave.'

'Elizabeth . . . ' He turned, his gaze shadowed with a soft pleading as he lowered his voice. 'Please listen to me.'

She stepped away from him. 'I must speak with my father.'

'Do you think him incapable of what I accuse? Do you think me a liar?'

'Have you not already apologised for being just that?' Her heart hammered painfully against her chest.

He shook his head, his gaze sad. 'And I would've been happier if I was right in my suspicion that you already knew about our fathers, but you didn't and now I feel your pain with the same intensity I feel my own.'

Confusion and hurt tumbled inside her. 'Why

230

would my knowing have been better?'

'Because then I could see you in the same light as your father.'

'Which is?'

'Ruthless. Dangerously ambitious. Someone capable of taking what they want regardless of whom they hurt in the process. Someone capable of keeping secrets and living their life without conscience.'

Her father was everything Joseph accused him of being and more. He was capable of luring Joseph into Pennington's just to give him hope and, at the same time, setting up a test to see what Elizabeth would do in her ignorance of Joseph's significance in her history. 'You need to leave.'

He stood and whipped his sketchbook from the settee, before stepping towards her. 'I would not lie about something like this. What would I gain by doing so? I wanted you to know so that . . . '

'So that what?' Her gaze locked with his, her body rigid.

'So that you and I can go forward on an even keel. So that if we can ignore the past, we'll create something amazing together. Something that will show our fathers the past is over and we, you and I, are the future.'

Her gaze fell to his mouth as her heart beat for everything he described. Her words came out in a whisper as she slowly lifted her eyes to his. 'I will speak with him.'

He stepped back, determination burning bright in his beautiful eyes. 'I'll go, but be sure in the knowledge that if it comes to light your father knew me to be Robert Carter's son, I'll walk out of your store, taking my designs with me. My success might take longer

231

than it would working with you, but I don't need to be here. I want to be here. I shared what I knew with you as soon as my temper had cooled enough to form the words. I hope that means something to you.'

Words flailed on her tongue. Her heart believed him, but her brain screamed at her to take care. The only man she should be able to trust had betrayed her mother — effectively killed her — and now Joseph asked that she trust him when she barely knew him. He'd told her that her father had a history with his aunt, had seduced and impregnated her. The pain of his revelations, or maybe it was her ease to believe them true, was terrifying.

Joseph walked to the door and grasped the handle, before facing her once more. 'I believe us to be fighters. Two people who won't allow the past to influence our future. I assumed you would be of the same mind and that's why I showed you my designs first. Maybe I was wrong, and your father's say-so will always remain the right one as far as you're concerned. I like you, Elizabeth. Probably too much, but God help you if you allow what your father has done to affect what we could do, what we could be, together.'

She opened her mouth to respond, but he stormed through the door, leaving it wide open as he marched through the ladies' department.

Her legs trembling, Elizabeth walked to the door and firmly closed it. She leaned her back against it and closed her eyes as contempt for her father ignited. His malicious satisfaction at taking the son of a rival family under his wing would be unprecedented.

Snapping her eyes open, she pressed her hand to her stomach. Anger surged through her and she embraced every dangerous drop as she pushed away from the door. If her father had been stupid enough to underestimate the integrity of a man like Joseph, she would relish delivering Edward Pennington's mistake to him on a plate.

He was out of the store at a business meeting all day. One he deemed too important to include his daughter.

Revulsion gripped her as she glared blindly ahead. She would speak to her father tonight. By the time they were both home, her anger would have festered and worsened to a dangerous degree. Just as she needed it to be.

25

Elizabeth stared at her father's bowed head as he shovelled the last morsels of what had been an enormous dinner into his mouth. Her stomach convulsed, and she quickly looked towards the dining room's drawn curtains, the frozen expression she'd purposely worn throughout the meal still firmly in place.

The business meeting he'd attended predictably ran to drinks at a nearby hotel until after six. By the time he'd ambled into the house, her nerves were stretched to breaking and her temper boiling.

She turned as he pushed his plate aside and Cole immediately came forward. 'Are you and Miss Elizabeth finished, sir? Shall I clear?'

Her father met her gaze. 'Elizabeth?'

She quickly focused her attention to their faithful butler and smiled. 'Yes, thank you, Cole. We'll retire to the drawing room. Could you ensure my father and I are left alone unless we ring for you?' She faced her father, her jaw aching with tension. 'Papa? Would you like brandy? A cigar maybe?'

He frowned, his wily gaze locked on hers. The seconds ticked by and the tension in the room grew. Slowly, he drew his napkin from his collar and set it on the table. 'Yes. That would be most welcome.'

As the plates were cleared, Elizabeth briefly closed her eyes and inhaled a strengthening breath before she stood and brushed past her father to the door. From the way he glared at her, her demeanour tonight had already riled him, which was precisely her intention.

He was unused to her holding her tongue, and her continuing frostiness would only anger him further.

For once, she did not care.

All her care was for Joseph, for the lost lives of his aunt and her baby, for the very real possibility her father had not just duped her, but duped Joseph, too. Fury whirled inside her, her hands trembling. No matter what her father thought he would achieve by playing with her and Joseph's lives, he would not succeed.

She no longer wished to fight her attraction to Joseph. She no longer wanted to be afraid of the tragedy she'd always believed would befall her if she ever succumbed to a man. With Joseph, she felt it wouldn't be succumbing but joining. A heart-racing possibility her father would not prevent her from exploring.

He followed her into the drawing room and slammed the door.

Elizabeth flinched and snapped her gaze to his. His satisfactory smile knotted her stomach, but she held his gaze. He would not get the better of her this time.

He walked to the drinks cabinet. 'So, what is it troubling you, my dear?' He pulled the stopper from a crystal brandy decanter and poured a large measure. 'Your expression has been most disapproving all evening. If I have done something, or maybe even *another* thing, to annoy you I'd prefer you say so.'

She walked to the settee in front of the fire and sat. 'I'll speak once you're seated.'

He took a mouthful of brandy and Elizabeth stared blindly ahead, the flames in the hearth dancing before her eyes as her father took a seat in his wing-backed chair. She took a long breath and faced him. The flicker of concern in his eyes surprised her and she forced her anger to the surface once more. Any care on his part would be for himself, rather than her.

She pulled back her shoulders. 'There's something I need to discuss with you.'

'Then whatever it is, please tell me. Your silence through dinner was trying at best, annoying at worst. I have little patience for histrionics from anyone, but especially from my own child.'

'Your own child . . . ' She raised her eyebrows. 'Am I your only child, Papa?'

He stilled, his raised glass at his lips. 'What?'

Elizabeth leaned back. 'Considering your numerous affairs during your marriage, has the possibility you could have other children never crossed your mind? Who knows if I have half-brothers and sisters throughout the city. Maybe even abroad if we take into account the number of times you've *had* to travel overseas.'

He took a drink, his gaze burning with fury. 'What on earth has caused this latest nonsense?'

'It's a valid question. I've also wondered why you and Mama did not have more children. Especially considering your passion for a son.'

'Unfortunately, your mother failed to be with child again.'

'*Mama failed*? It was entirely her fault?' Elizabeth smiled wryly. 'But, of course, it was. How could the failure ever fall to the great Edward Pennington?'

'Exactly.' He sipped his drink. 'My relationship with your mother grew distant. You know this.'

'Yes, but how soon after you married? Did it change after I was born?'

He clenched his jaw, his gaze steely. 'Yes.'

'Why?'

'Because she wanted no more children after you.'

236

'Mama was loving, attentive and proud of me. Why wouldn't she have wanted more children? She had so much love to give. Could it be that she wanted no more children with *you*? Was the marriage arranged? Forced?'

He glared. 'What is the cause of all these questions? Who have you been speaking with?'

'Was it your treatment of Mama that drove the distance between you? That drove her to end her life?'

He stared at her for a long moment before he nodded. What looked to be sincere regret lingered in his gaze as he sighed. 'Yes. Yes, I believe it was.'

Her heart kicked. Was he finally acknowledging the blame that her mother's death lay with him, and him alone? Shifting back in her seat, she narrowed her eyes. 'What does the name Carter really mean to you, Papa?'

The colour drained from his face and his knuckles strained around his glass. 'It means nothing more than Mr Carter has somehow become your new muse.'

'I don't mean Joseph. I mean Carter. Any Carter.'

He looked towards the window and Elizabeth watched a pulse beat in his temple.

'Well?'

He turned and scowled. 'Is the glove maker the reason for your ridiculous questions?'

'It's not so much Joseph himself, but more something he told me.'

'Really? Then, please, my dear, enlighten me.'

The sanctimonious tone of voice hitched Elizabeth's irritation higher. 'He told me you know his father, Robert Carter, and Grandfather knew his grandfather.'

His glass trembled, the silence of the room contrasting against the blood roaring in Elizabeth's ears.

237

Her father knew of Robert Carter. Of that she was now sure.

Everything Joseph had told her was true.

'You know who Joseph is, don't you?' Her heart thundered. 'Did you entice him to the store? Are you using him in some way?'

He put his glass on the small table beside him and leaned back. 'I suspected he might be Robert's son, but I didn't know for certain. He has his father's eyes. He has his infernal optimism, too, it seems.'

Elizabeth glared. 'Do not disparage him. Joseph doesn't deserve your scorn in any degree. He's made me excited to be working at the store again. Made me believe myself possible of anything. Something you have endlessly failed to do, just as you did with Mama.' Elizabeth's breaths turned harried as her disgust of him grew. 'Did you really ever love her? Or was all your love for another woman? A woman who happens to be Joseph's aunt?'

'What?'

'Yes, Papa. I know.'

His gaze bored into hers. 'You know what?'

'I know you had an affair with Clara Carter. Joseph's aunt.'

He abruptly stood and walked to the fire. He gripped the mantle and stared into the flames before meeting her gaze, his hands clasped behind his back. 'I might have fallen foul to many affairs over the years, but it is only Clara Carter who comes into my mind. Try as I might to forget her, our separation wasn't amicable, and I hurt her. Possibly deeply.'

The pain in her father's eyes threatened to steal Elizabeth's determination to know the truth of his actions towards members of Joseph's family. She'd

238

expected her father to deny any association. Blame his actions on anyone, anything, but himself. She fought to keep her face impassive and her emotions under control.

'If you cared for Clara, why cast her off? Why not divorce Mama and spare her all the anguish you continually bestowed on her? Why did you not leave and allow me the chance to believe in myself? To not live with years of believing myself unworthy.'

His face had paled, his gaze almost defeated. 'Because divorce is not allowed in the Pennington family. The same will apply to you.'

'Of course, divorce can sometimes be disapproved of, but your marriage with Mama was hardly — '

'It was what it was. You know nothing of a real relationship. Absolutely nothing.'

'Yet, you continue to force me to accept Noel when you know I do not love him. You looked pained when I mentioned Clara Carter. It's as though, for the first time in my life, I might believe you actually capable of loving someone.'

He exhaled, his shoulders dropping. 'When Clara mentioned marriage between us, I had to end our relationship quickly and with force if I was to save her from a broken heart. I cast her aside, Elizabeth, but I did so with love.'

'Love? What would you know of love?'

'I loved her, but when she threatened to speak to your mother of the affair and cause a fuss, I had no choice but to leave Clara and never see her again.'

He doesn't know about the baby. He doesn't know Clara killed herself and a baby that could have been his unborn son.

She swallowed against the dryness in her throat,

fearful of what telling him about the baby might do to him. No matter how much of a monster he could be, Edward Pennington was her father. She closed her eyes. He deserved to know the truth.

'There's something you need to know.'

His eyes were almost deadened, as though he had shut down, shut her and her words out so they couldn't affect him.

Elizabeth's heart ached. 'Clara Carter was pregnant.'

Her father's sharp intake of breath sounded above the crack and spit of the fire and Elizabeth held her breath.

His cheeks flushed. 'She had a baby . . . *my* baby?'

His quietly whispered question sounded as though he spoke from behind a sad and lonely veneer.

'No, Papa.' Elizabeth's eyes burned with suppressed tears. 'The shame of the pregnancy, of her affair with you and your subsequent rejection was too much. She took her own life and that of her . . . *your* . . . unborn child.'

His mouth drew into a line so tight, his lips trembled. His eyes turned glassy.

'Papa . . . '

'Enough.' The dark command of his voice sliced through her, reminding her of his unpredictable temper. 'It was Joseph Carter who told you this? He knows for certain Clara was with child? Or could he be fabricating this story as a way of sticking a knife into me as he no doubt has longed to for years.'

Elizabeth's sympathy vanished under the malice in her father's eyes, the way he spat the Carter name as though it was dirt. 'He wouldn't do that. Joseph is a good man. Honest and hard-working. He only discovered the truth a few days ago and told me so I wasn't in the dark. So I knew the truth about the Penningtons and Carters. I believe him and I think, in time, you will too.'

'I should thrash him to within an inch — '

'Is that so? Well, he also told me because he suspects you could be setting a trap for him. Planning something to further humiliate his family. Is that true, Papa? Is that what you planned the moment you met Joseph and realised who he is?'

'Of course not.'

'I'm loathe to believe or trust you. Your actions have already caused unhappiness everywhere, yet, your expression tells me you still can only think of yourself. Despite your love and loss of Clara, you went on to have more affairs. You still pursue women with a seemingly insatiable lust.'

He glared. 'What does any of this matter anymore? Clara went away, and I never saw her again. The affair is little more than ancient history.'

'She did not move away. She died. Maybe that wouldn't have mattered to you if Joseph hadn't arrived at the store, but he did, and I want to continue working with him. I *have* to. He's giving me hope and passion for my work and that makes him special to me whether you accept that or not. I am proud of his work. The difference he's made to morale and sales is like nothing I've seen before. I'm prepared to do whatever I have to in order to keep him.'

'Keep him?' Her father's smile was wolverine. 'Is that so? My God, do you have feelings for him?'

No matter how much she wanted her feelings about Joseph to be strictly professional, she cared for him . . . deeply. She lifted her chin. 'Joseph has dreams

241

and ideas that are new and exciting. I refuse to lose him because of something he and I had no part of. Clara killed herself, Papa, as well as a child who could have been a son.'

His eyes bulged as he shot forward, grasping her hands in his and pulling her roughly to her feet. Her breath caught as he brought his face inches from hers.

Elizabeth stared at him, revulsion, disappointment and hurt colliding. She snatched her hands from his vice-like grip. 'How will you sleep at night with two women's and a child's death on your conscience?'

She whirled away from him and crossed her arms in a bid to stop the trembling. The blinds around her eyes had been lifted. From now on, she would not fight for her father's approval or for release from the bonds of his control.

She would break every one of them herself.

She turned. 'I'm sorry for your loss, Papa. I'm sorry that a woman you supposedly loved lost her life, a family their sister and aunt. I'm sorry for you, full stop.'

'I want to meet with Carter.'

'No.'

'I have every right — '

'What do you want to say to the man your actions so bitterly hurt when he was just a boy? I won't allow it. Through telling me about our shared history, Joseph has proven himself honest and trustworthy. Not only will we continue to work together, I'll see to it that his work is produced and promoted with everything Pennington's has. Joseph is an outstanding designer and he will be deservedly rewarded for it. And you . . .' She inhaled a long breath, her heart slowing to a steady and calm rhythm. 'You will apologise to Joseph and his father for all the pain you have caused them.'

He stared at her, before walking to his chair and picking up his brandy as he sat. 'I'll do no such thing.'

Elizabeth drew her gaze over his face, her fists clenched. 'You betrayed Mama and ultimately caused her death. Now I learn of another woman who took her life and that of her child because of you. You will come to accept your role in this tragedy. Otherwise, you and I are over, Papa. I will no longer be your daughter.'

She strode from the room, drawing the door sharply closed behind her. Anger, shame and regret burned deep in her stomach. How dare her father play with people's lives? From this day forward, it would be Joseph and her side by side. She would prove to herself and her father that the Pennington/Carter feud was over for good. No matter what he might do or say.

She took a long, steadying breath. And if that meant she buried her personal feelings for Joseph, so be it. The business had to come first for them both. Anything else was shrouded in danger and possible heartbreak. She had to be strong.

To be anything else was terrifying and always would be.

26

The workroom door opened and Joseph turned as Elizabeth entered. Struck once more by her beauty and poise, he tried to fathom what might have happened in the two days since he'd told her something that must have deeply upset her. With work still coming in at Carter & Son, Joseph had spent those two days working alongside his father, mentioning nothing of his sharing the past with Elizabeth.

It suddenly felt that he kept things from a father to whom Joseph owed his total honesty, but worry about further upsetting him had kept Joseph tight-lipped. How much longer could he go on juggling things at Carter & Son as well as giving everything he could to Pennington's? A deep sense that the mammoth store was the right place for him continued to relentlessly burn in Joseph's gut.

Whatever happened next with Elizabeth would be the deciding factor of where he would work in the future. His father had to accept the prospects at Pennington's would always outweigh those of Carter & Son. Did they really have any reason, other than family tradition, to not close up shop and reach for pastures new? He thought not.

Elizabeth slowly made her way towards him as she stopped to exchange a few words with some of the men, nodding hello to others. Joseph's desire for her stirred. He was hurtling towards something he wouldn't — couldn't — name lest he made it real. Made it tangible. Powerful.

Her green eyes glittered with determination and her spine was ramrod straight as she came to an abrupt halt at his side. 'Mr Carter.'

He nodded. 'Miss Pennington.'

'I wonder if you can spare Mrs Woolden and myself some time?'

'Of course.' Joseph stared deep into her eyes trying to ascertain her temperament, but her expression was unreadable. 'What time and where?'

'As soon as business finishes for the day?'

He glanced at the wall clock. Quarter to six. Fifteen minutes. He met her expectant gaze. 'Of course.'

Her gaze lingered on his before she gave a curt nod. 'Wonderful. Then we'll speak again shortly.'

She turned away and once she'd left the workroom, a rare silence descended. His colleagues' stares burned into Joseph from every direction.

He cleared his throat and faced Albert, raising his voice to be heard around the small room. 'Well, I guess she's interested in my designs, if nothing else. That can only mean more work and pay for all of us if things go ahead.'

'More pay?'

'God willing. I've suggested the idea of being paid commission if we exceed our daily quotas. There's no saying Miss Pennington will go for it, mind you.'

Muttering and whispering broke throughout the workroom.

Joseph waited for any hostility. His revelation could be misinterpreted as audacity, but he had no choice but to reveal some incentive in order to instil enthusiasm and keep the men onside. Talented and skilled, he needed their support, or else the plans he had to manufacture new gloves, hats and clothes would fail.

'It might be best if you reel your neck in a bit, Joseph.' Albert frowned. 'Miss Pennington might like your fancy drawings, but I can't see she'll like the idea of increasing our wages.'

'You don't know that any more than I do.' Joseph looked around the room, catching the gazes of as many of his colleagues as possible. 'None of us do. I'm pushing for something that could benefit us all. If Miss Pennington wants my designs, she knows I also want commission paid. Why bother asking to see me if she's not willing to at least consider everything I've asked for?'

There were a few nods before the men turned back to their work, looking mildly more hopeful and enthusiastic than they had before.

Relief whispered through Joseph's gut and he looked to Albert. 'It's got to be worth a try, right?'

The older man stared at him before his face broke into a smile. 'Yeah, I reckon it has.'

Joseph grinned. 'Good man.'

Picking up his pencil, he pondered what he'd say and do when confronted with not only Elizabeth but Mrs Woolden, too. How were he and Elizabeth to talk about their fathers with the department's deputy present? If their familial history was left to fester between them, it would only corrode any trust he and Elizabeth had built. Surely, she had spoken to her father by now? Could it be that inviting Joseph to her office to talk about his designs was just a ruse to be followed by him being formally asked to leave?

He tightened his fingers on his pencil as the opportunity to atone for his part in Lillian's death wavered. He could not let this chance slip through his fingers. Guilt gripped hard in his chest and a familiar sickness rolled through him.

Elizabeth might not yet have spoken to her father, but she knew Joseph would take his designs with him and leave if he was to be a pawn in the continuing feud between their families. Did he remain replaceable to her? Entirely unimportant?

He glanced at the wall clock and stood.

She wanted to speak with him and the outcome would reveal itself soon enough. He drew his sketchbook from atop the desk and took his coat from the back of his chair, before forcing a smile at Albert. 'Right, I'm going upstairs. I'll see you tomorrow.'

'Good luck.'

Joseph nodded and walked to the door, taking his hat from the stand before he left the workroom and headed for the lift. The past that linked him and Elizabeth was a terrible one, but they could do their best to erase it through unity and determination if only she gave them the chance. There was nothing but themselves that could prevent them from working together to build a new harmony between the Penningtons and Carters that their future generations could be proud of.

The lift drew to a halt on the second floor and Joseph nodded at the young attendant, before striding towards the ladies' department. He tightened his fingers on his sketchbook, willing every ounce of his faltering belief in righting past wrongs to the surface.

Once he entered the department, he glanced around the near-empty space looking for Elizabeth or Mrs Woolden. Neither were there. The last of the shop girls flashed him a shy smile as she left the department and Joseph approached Esther Stanbury where she stood at the counter, her brow furrowed. Large sheets of paper were spread over the countertop, and when Joseph neared, he peered over her shoulder at the pencilled design of what looked to be a future window display.

He smiled. 'Gosh, that looks pretty impressive.'

She turned. 'Thank you. I've been working with Miss Pennington on it for a while. We're hoping we can pull it all together for next week.' Her eyes glinted with satisfaction. 'Do you recognise anything?'

Joseph cast his gaze over the paper once more and when he saw his gloves in prominent position at the forefront of the window, elation swept through him. 'All that space? For my gloves?'

'Yes.' Esther grinned. 'I'm so excited about the coming month and you should be, too.'

Hope burned in his chest and he nodded. 'I am.'

Soft footsteps sounded behind him and he turned.

'Ah, Mrs Woolden. I apologise for my delay, I was just talking with Miss Stanbury.'

'I can see that, Mr Carter, but it won't do to keep Miss Pennington waiting.' She waved towards Elizabeth's open office door. 'If you please.'

Feeling suitably chastised, Joseph walked ahead of her into the office and met Elizabeth's gaze. 'Apologies, Miss Pennington.'

'No need, you're here now.' She tilted her head towards the two empty chairs in front of her desk. 'If you'd like to take a seat.'

Her demeanour, although not entirely frosty, certainly lacked its usual warmth. Uncertainty knotted Joseph's stomach as the idea he might be here to be fired rose once more. Slowly, he laid his hat on the floor and his coat on the back of the chair before sitting. Mrs Woolden took the seat beside him.

248

Elizabeth leaned forward and laced her fingers on top of the desk. 'Now we're all here, I would like to propose something to you both.' She looked at Joseph. 'Have you brought your sketchbook?'

He passed it to her, trying to gauge her mood, or even what came next.

'Thank you.'

She quickly dropped her focus to the book as though reluctant to look at him for too long. His unease grew.

She flipped to the first design and showed Mrs Woolden. 'My plan is as follows.' She put her finger to the drawing. 'These gloves . . . .' She flipped a few more pages, 'These hats . . .' A few more pages. 'And these jackets, will all be produced and put on display in the ladies' department. Joseph — Mr Carter, will oversee the manufacturing and work with Miss Stanbury on a front window display as well as displays in the department. I am excited by Mr Carter's inspired idea to design a new line of ladies' wear which encapsulates the spirit of the modern, progressive woman and I want you to fully support this project and do all you can to ensure its quick implementation.'

Joseph glanced at Mrs Woolden. Her expression was interested, but he recognised the caution in her eyes, too. 'Might I have a closer look at the designs?'

'Of course.' Elizabeth passed over the sketchbook.

As Mrs Woolden studied the pages, pausing at some, quickly passing over others, Joseph turned his focus to Elizabeth. Her green gaze met his and a tentative smile lifted her lips so quickly if he'd blinked, he would've miss it. Relief and anticipation twisted pleasantly in his chest.

Mrs Woolden delicately coughed and Joseph quickly faced her.

'These are good. Very good. But I have to say, I think it's a huge risk to take on the designs of some-one in-house. We have a range of tried-and.tested designers, Elizabeth. Designers who have consistently offered exclusivity to Pennington's every season since we opened.'

'I agree, but it's on my authority whose designs we manufacture and supply in the department. Why not try something new? Be the first to supply something that will undoubtedly come to be in demand.'

Mrs Woolden turned her kindly eyes to Joseph. 'I mean no offence, Mr Carter, but your designs, as splendid as they are, may be a little too avant garde for our customers.'

Joseph cleared his throat and straightened, his passion for the new line providing the conviction he needed to tackle Mrs Woolden's, and anyone else's, doubts. 'I have every confidence these designs will sell and sell well. The progressive energy around women right now is tangible. We have to embrace it. Of course, to manufacture hundreds of gloves, hats and jackets without at first gauging the response would be foolhardy, but, if we start with a small range, I'm confident the store will soon see a profit.'

Mrs Woolden frowned, before looking to Elizabeth. 'And this will happen how and when?'

'We'll start immediately. I've considered what we have to manufacture in the coming weeks and as I've decided to pay commission to the workroom staff, I'm sure their output will increase along with our profit.' She looked at Joseph, her eyes revealing her excitement. 'Do you not agree?'

Joseph inhaled and slowly released his breath, elation rippling through him. 'I do.'

Whether or not she'd spoken with her father, Elizabeth's gaze told him, all too clearly, that their future of working together was far from over. Relief wound through him. The notion of not seeing her every day bothered him as much as losing his position.

He quickly looked to Mrs Woolden. 'Are you on board, Mrs Woolden? I'll really need your help and that of your staff if we're to go ahead with this.'

The silence in the room was accentuated by the noise of the passing traffic and chattering pedestrians outside the open window. He might have Elizabeth's backing, but he wanted the staff's, too. He wanted everyone to benefit from this new venture. Everyone to have a chance to prove their worth and gain Elizabeth's and her father's belief in them as well as appreciate their value.

Mrs Woolden smiled. 'I work every day with women much younger than myself, Mr Carter, and judging from their conversations, it makes for a brighter, more exciting future. I'm confident my ladies will welcome these designs.'

Joseph smiled. 'Thank you, Mrs Woolden.'

Elizabeth handed him his sketchbook and exhaled a shaky breath, her pretty green gaze darkening. 'Then I'll run the project past my father and we'll take it from there.'

Joseph's stomach plummeted. If she'd shared with Edward Pennington what she now knew about his past, there was every chance her father would not only veto their plans, but shove Joseph out the door with a sharp kick to his backside.

But what else could he do but wait for Elizabeth's report back?

He carefully watched her as a wisp of a smile played

at her mouth. She looked different. Stronger. More beautiful. Attraction simmered deep inside him as the urge to stand, walk around the desk and kiss her gathered strength.

He quickly blinked, praying his eyes had not betrayed his thoughts.

She pushed to her feet and offered him her hand. 'Congratulations are in order, Mr Carter. Well done.'

He stood and dipped his head as took her hand, the skin to skin contact heating his desires to touch her, discover her, in places he should not be contemplating. 'It will be a pleasure and an honour to work with you . . .' He turned to Mrs Woolden. 'And you.'

Elizabeth eased her hand from his and hesitated, her gaze on his mouth before she quickly looked to Mrs Woolden. 'You're free to leave for the day, Aveline. I'd just like to keep Mr Carter awhile longer to further discuss the details of his designs. Could you tell Esther to leave, too? The woman never stops working until I push her out the door.'

Mrs Woolden flitted her gaze between him and Elizabeth before a knowing smile curved her lips. 'Of course.' She nodded to Joseph. 'Mr Carter.'

The moment the office door closed behind her, Joseph looked at Elizabeth, concern for what might have happened between her and her father quashing any semblance of his patience. He frowned. 'Are you all right?'

'Absolutely.' Her smile was too wide. 'Now, let us put our heads together, shall we?'

'Elizabeth — '

'Work first, Joseph . . .' She sat behind her desk. 'We can talk about my father and everything he's done to your family once I have convinced you to stay with

252

me . . . with Pennington's, for a while longer.'

He stared deep into her eyes. 'No persuasion required. I want to be here. Probably more than I should.'

27

Probably more than he should . . .

Elizabeth tensed as every part of her leapt with the possible underlying meaning of his words. She had seen him watching her. Heard the occasional flirtation in his words. The connection between them was real and, at times, even intense. No man had ever affected her this way, made her feel like an equal or excited her with his vision.

She swallowed against her suddenly dry throat, her gaze on his as he intensely watched her. 'Joseph.'

He came closer. 'Elizabeth.'

She could see or hear nothing but him. Everything faded away until the rest of the world seemed distant, unable to touch or influence them. Fear danced through her heart along with a deep longing that she had never felt, or even wanted to feel before. Her self-imposed defences weakened with each passing second.

Slowly, she stood and came towards him. 'I . . . we . . . '

He lowered his gaze to her hand and gently took it. 'Your support of my work must mean you believe what I told you about our families. You haven't sent me away but made it possible to work even more closely together. It's futile to deny how much I enjoy being with you. I know our classes are — '

'No.' She gently shook her head. 'Don't say another word. This can only be a working relationship.' Her heart beat fast as her deep-rooted anxiety that she

254

would only become a shadow of her poor mama if she should fall in love, loomed like a dark phantom around her. She eased her hand from his. 'Anything more is impossible.'

But another look into his beautiful blue eyes, so full of soft admiration and, dare she imagine it, desire, made her long to retract her words. Joseph was nothing like her father. He respected her ambitions. Positively encouraged them. How could she ignore that?

Abruptly, she headed for her office door, swiping at a traitorous tear as it slipped over her cheek. 'Walk with me.'

'Wait.'

She halted, her feelings burning and growing at such a terrifying speed, she had no idea how to resist if Joseph should say another affectionate word or touch her again. Swallowing hard, she turned.

He slowly walked forwards. 'We need to talk.' His gaze settled on her mouth and her yearning intensified. 'I cannot remain silent any longer.'

'What do you want to discuss?'

'I want to ask you a question. Something personal.'

Fear swirled through her that her answer might alter the tenderness in his eyes. 'You can ask, but I cannot promise to provide an answer.'

'Why haven't you married?'

Surprised, she lifted her hand to her throat. 'What does that have to do with our fathers?'

'Nothing, but I'd like to know, if you'll tell me.'

'But why?'

He looked to the floor before meeting her eyes once more. His gaze bore a shadowed sadness that brought an ache to her heart.

'Joseph?'

'Don't you want a family of your own one day? I do, more than anything, but I believe I don't deserve such happiness. Such an abundance of love. I have made dire mistakes, Elizabeth, and for my sins I must live a life alone. But you?' His gaze ran over her lips and hair. 'Even in the brief time I've known you, I truly believe you deserve all that love and more. Yet, here you are, living and breathing the store as though nothing else will fulfil you. Why?'

Words and wishes caught like talons in her throat, scratching and scraping. Why had he mentioned having a family? Something that she'd thought of time and again. Could his admission he didn't deserve such a thing be true? She couldn't believe anything so evil of him that he should strike from his future the family his eyes told her he ardently yearned for.

If his lonely future was merited, then surely that would quash her increasingly forceful want of him and bring an end to what felt like a very dangerous road. Mustering every ounce of the strength that had enabled her to face her father's scorn time and again, Elizabeth held Joseph's soft gaze. 'Why do you say you don't deserve such happiness?'

He looked into her eyes before stepping back, opening the space between them as he pushed his hand into his hair. 'I . . . My wife was murdered. I am yet to find her killer. I deserve nothing until he is found and I've fulfilled her legacy by finding every way I can to help those who deserve it. Everything I do, everything I am, should be fuelled by that desire, nothing else.'

'But I see those desires in everything you do.' She paused, suddenly desperate to comfort him and alleviate a little of the heavy burden he carried. 'I can help you, if you'd let me.'

He frowned. 'How?'

She took a deep breath, knowing she was taking another perilous step towards the personal, towards intimacy, but longed to bring him peace. 'If you stay here, at the store, and work with me, I will do all I can to help you find your wife's killer. I have contacts in both the press and the constabulary. I give you my solemn vow I will work with you to ensure justice is done for both you and your wife. You deserve that, Joseph, as does she,'

His gaze locked on hers, his eyes slightly narrowed as though he scrutinised her sincerity. At last, he stood back and nodded. 'Thank you. It's been a hard road. A lonely road. Doors seemingly closed to me as I get no further towards finding the man who hurt her. Your help would make a difference.'

'Good.' Admiration swelled inside her along with a deep sadness. 'Joseph, you deserve a happy life as much as anyone else. Surely you know that? The man who killed your wife . . . ' She took a deep breath unable to stand that he must shoulder a pain deeper than she could ever know. 'Will one day be punished for what he did to your wife. What he's done to you. Until that day, you must live to make yourself happy, as I'm sure your wife would've wanted you to.'

'Lillian.' He dropped his hand from his hair. 'Her name was Lillian.'

Elizabeth softly smiled. 'A beautiful name for an undoubtedly beautiful woman.'

His eyes darkened with deep pain, his jaw tight. 'I have to atone for my part in her death, Elizabeth. I have to.'

'Then atone by leading a good life. A happy life.' She longed to pull him into her arms and hold him, but how could she when they were employer and employee? Buyer and seller. Nothing more. Nothing less. She swallowed past the lump in her throat. 'I would like to meet your father. Shake the hand of the man who raised such a wonderful son.'

He studied her. 'You want to meet my father?'

'Yes. I believe there are things I need to say to him. My father needs to say to him. But first, I want to show both you and him that I am not a cold-hearted spinster any more than you are a cold-hearted widower. We both have room in our hearts for others, do we not?'

A modicum of hope returned to his beautiful eyes. 'Maybe we do.' He moved to touch her, but then dropped his outstretched hand to his side. 'Your reaction to the hurt your father caused mine is testament to your heart. The way you've embraced my ideas and excitement another. You're a beautiful woman. One making her way in what, sadly, is still considered a predominantly male domain. Why a gentleman has not asked for your hand — '

'Oh, they've asked.' Heat warmed her cheeks that she should blurt such a thing. 'But I've yet to be asked by anyone I can imagine happily spending my life with.'

'I see.'

Feeling foolish that she should have such fanciful longings about Joseph when experience had taught her well with regards to the fidelity of men, Elizabeth crossed her arms. 'There's every possibility our union will be a temporary one. Your own plans are at the forefront of your mind with every decision you make. It would be foolish for either of us to edge into our intimate yearnings.'

258

'Then why, in this moment, all I can think of is you and I.'

The silence stretched as uncertainty wound through her. Just how much could she say to him? Admit to him? Without risking not only his respect, but her heart, too.

'You intrigue me, Elizabeth. I find myself wanting to know everything about you.'

She walked to the door. 'And I thoroughly like that you do. Now, I think we need to start working on our plans, don't you?'

Ignoring the knot of attraction wound tight in her stomach, Elizabeth waited for Joseph to follow her into the ladies' department.

As they walked around, the store closed for the night, Elizabeth's heart hammered. Silent in their thoughts, the atmosphere shifted to something new and tangible. Something exciting and forbidden. As though their short conversation had held so much more than she could determine.

Her pull to Joseph might be foolish, but it pleased her that there had been more than business on his mind. He'd spoken of mistakes and, Lord knew, she didn't want to be his next, or he hers, but the prospect of more than work between them thrilled her. Made her happy.

Of course, it would be wiser to look at him as her new weapon, in an armoury she felt necessary to keep close, now she'd learned of her father's connection to Joseph's family. But to do so, when she'd seen flirtation in his eyes, would be a difficult challenge.

She flicked on the lights from a concealed switch behind the velvet entrance curtain.

Joseph walked to one of the counters and

smoothed his hand over the solid wood top. 'Customers want . . . need . . . to picture an entire outfit.' Excitement burned in his gaze as he looked at her. 'Mannequins are in the store windows, but we should install them in the department, too. Have them fully dressed and accessorised as women preparing to enter a male-dominated world, while maintaining their femininity. Better still . . . ' He brushed past her to the centre of the room and held out his arms, his blue eyes bright with eagerness. 'Why don't we launch the new line with a live mannequin show?'

She laughed. 'A live mannequin show? Are you mad?'

He strode towards her and took her hands, seemingly unaffected by their touch, whereas her stomach emitted a loop the loop.

'I'm confident you could persuade at least one or two of the shop girls, if not more, to model for us.' He grinned. 'Our first production can be the range of clothing and accessories just needed for the show.'

Forcing her mind to the thrill of this new and exhilarating idea rather than the delicious, sensuality of his warm, slightly work-roughened skin on hers, Elizabeth tore her gaze from his and looked around the department, enthusiasm gathering inside. 'We could issue invitations to a select few and then leave news of the evening to spread by word of mouth. By the end of the evening, we'll have an idea of the demand. If it proves profitable — '

'We host another show to even more people.' He smiled. 'A show like that would create just the stir we want.'

She eased her hands from his as the dark cloud of her father loomed over her once more. 'It would also likely be the cause of my father having a heart attack. He'll never agree to it.'

'Why not?'

She sighed. 'My father sees the girls in this store as his personal property, and as wrong as that is, he'll never agree to them modelling for the public.'

'We'd be doing everything wrong if the customers looked at the models instead of the clothes. Convince him of the possible revenue if we cast the evening out to a wide range of people, from different walks of life. We could price the clothes and accessories from the very accessible to the very expensive, but everything will be well made and reflect the spirit of Pennington's. How could he say no?'

Elizabeth's heart quickened. Why did it seem anything was possible when she was with him? He looked at her with such belief, she'd become convinced of winning this battle, and more, with her father. 'We could put on a show like no store in Bath has ever before.'

'It will be fantastic. I promise.'

The moment stretched, and Elizabeth's awareness grew of how close they stood, how the subtle spice of his cologne teased her nostrils. A voice in her head screamed at her to step away, but still she didn't move.

'Elizabeth . . .'

Just the sound of her name on his whispered breath was all it took to chase sanity from her mind, and when he slowly leaned closer, she didn't move. When he tentatively touched his mouth to hers, she surrendered.

★ ★ ★

261

Joseph stepped back, his body heated from their kiss. Had he lost his damn mind? Why in heaven's name had he kissed her?

Heat continued to simmer between them and she was yet to step away or admonish him. Her green eyes were wide and her mouth slight agape. He searched her gaze for a clue of what she felt. Their invisible, yet tangible, connection was confusing when they knew so much, yet so little, of one another. Ever since Lillian's passing, his heart had been firmly under lock and key, but with Elizabeth, his attraction and desire soared.

The possibility of what that might mean was terrifying.

He closed his eyes. 'Say something.'

The seconds beat with his heart until she softly exhaled. 'I'm not certain what to say. My father, society, our positions at the store . . . all of those things are stacked against anything personal happening between us. Yet . . .'

He slowly opened his eyes and when he saw happiness in her gaze, relief swept through him squeezing hard inside his chest. 'I don't want you to think badly of me. Kissing women, my associate no less, is not something I do every day, but with you . . . you're intelligent and beautiful. Confident and kind. You care, Elizabeth, and all those things are becoming extremely hard for me to resist.'

'Then kiss me again. Here. Now. While we're alone.'

Despite the folly, Joseph pulled her into his arms and kissed her. She tasted of the sweetest honey, mixed with a dangerous fire that told him just how deeply her passion resided under her formal, businesslike veneer. Her waist fit like his gloves in his hands, her lips softer than duck down.

He drew his mouth from hers and kissed a trail along her jaw, and when she tipped her head back, he kissed her neck. 'Elizabeth.'

'Joseph.'

Her fingers scored through the hair at his collar, sending tremors of want and desire ripping through his body. He gripped her tighter, pulled her closer and their lips met once more. Tentatively, he eased his tongue to hers and she met his hunger. It had been years since he'd kissed a woman. Years since he'd thought of anything but his working future. What did this mean? Would their embrace cause the inevitable destruction of everything they'd worked so hard for?

The sharp slamming of a door, followed by rapid footsteps made them leap apart, his mouth tender from their passionate kisses and his erection straining. He looked to the department entrance. 'I thought we were alone.'

'We are.' Her eyes were dark with want, her beautiful mouth reddened. 'No one would've seen us.'

Fear gripped him, and he whirled away, ran his hand over his face. 'I can't lead you into deeper trouble with your father. I won't.'

She laid her hand on his arm, and the heat and tenderness of that solitary gesture melted a little more of the ice around his heart.

Her gaze was soft with understanding. 'Until very recently whatever I did, whatever I suggested, was of no importance to my father. I was dismissed. Ignored. Made to feel of little consequence or worth. Slowly, my father is accepting I am good at my work, a possibility for his successor, whether he wants to admit that or not. I am not someone to sit back and not take what she wants. So, from now on, I'm going to do whatever my head — my heart — tells me to do.'

Protectiveness rose fast and hot in his chest. In that moment, he would have given anything to grab Edward Pennington by the scruff of his neck and toss him into the River Avon. 'Please tell me you won't let anything he says affect you anymore.'

'I won't.' She laughed wryly. 'Because tonight, I feel stronger than I ever have before and that's because of you. I have no idea what the future holds, but I do know I become a better person, happier and more excited, when I'm *with* you. That has to count for something and, no matter my fears, I want to explore it.'

As pleased as he was by her words, apprehension and shame mixed inside him. 'I'm not the man you think I am. Maybe you are better off without me. Sometimes, when I think of Lillian's killer, I feel such venomous anger.'

'You have said nothing that has made me disbelieve how good a man you are. A loyal man. A man capable of unerring love.'

Words and confessions bit and burned his tongue.

She touched his hand, tears glinting in her eyes. 'You have no reason to think so little of yourself. My state of mind was determined by my father's words and actions, his treatment of my mother. Why not join me in this moment? This time, and be damned to everyone else?'

The vehemence in her words belied the tears in her eyes and Joseph's heart thudded painfully. He owed her his honesty. Only then would she understand.

Sliding his hand from hers, he walked to a small seating area at the corner of the department and sat, exhaustion laying heavy on his shoulders. Slowly, she approached and sat beside him.

When she reached for his hand, he didn't pull away but tightened his fingers around hers. 'Lillian was a kind and generous woman with room in her heart for me, my father and countless other people.' He met her sombre, sympathetic gaze. 'She was killed delivering food to the poor. Killed for the meagre contents in her basket and purse.

'The constables believe it could've been any of the poor and desperate people in town. Violence and despair is par for the course for these people.' He clenched his jaw. 'But one day, I'll find him.' He shook his head. 'You need to understand what Lillian's death has done to me. I failed to protect her. Failed to save her. I can't risk another love. I can't risk letting another woman down. I won't.'

She looked to their joined hands and Joseph stared at her profile. Would she consider him a cad now he'd kissed her lips, her neck, cherished the feel of her in his arms, only to turn away from her?

Slowly, she lifted her gaze. 'I understand wanting to protect yourself, to not risk any further hurt, but can either of us really live that way forever? I thought I could, but now I'm not certain I even want to.'

She'd echoed his thoughts and feelings so beautifully, Joseph leaned closer and put his mouth to hers, sliding his arms around her slender body. The meeting of their lips, the tentative touches of their tongues, ignited a rush of heat deep in his groin and he accepted it was inevitable he was falling in love again. His father's plea for him not to spend his life alone seeped into Joseph's mind . . . and a second later, so did Edward Pennington.

He eased back. 'There's more than our past hurts

standing between us. What of the years of hostility between our families?' He gave a wry smile. 'Hardly the foundations for a lasting romance.'

Defeat darkened her eyes and she eased from his arms, her gaze sliding gently over his face, before she stood and walked to the other side of the room. She plucked at a bolt of material atop the counter. 'If my father discovers anything more than professionalism between us, he'll do whatever it takes to remove you from my life. He must be kept in the dark or else your life will change for the worse. Even more than mine. He had no part in your coming to work here. Like you, I was afraid you might have been manipulated or exploited by him.' She inhaled a shaky breath. 'So that part, at least, I can lay to rest.'

'And everything else?'

'Is true. He had an affair with your aunt.'

Joseph stilled as the realisation he'd been holding on to a small hope that his father might have been mistaken about the affair was snuffed out. How could he and Elizabeth move forward with such an ugly past between them? 'Did he know she was with child?'

'No. And his shock was plain to see. My father wants nothing as badly as he wants a son and heir.'

'So, if he didn't cast my aunt Clara aside because of the baby, what happened? He must have done or said something for her to believe the only answer was to take her own life.'

'She mentioned marriage and my father would never divorce my mother. She also threatened to tell her about the affair, so he severed all contact. He loved your aunt, Joseph, but he ended their relationship as soon as he realised the depth of her feelings. I honestly believe he thought he was doing the right thing and the result was a tragedy. I'm so sorry your family suffered.'

Anger burned inside him. 'Did your father think Clara was dead?'

'No.'

'Then where did he think she had been all this time?'

'He thought she'd moved away. His shock and despair when I told him of her death was real, but, the longer we spoke, the more the confrontation grew between us until, once again, we separated on hostile terms.'

'I see.'

'But we can get past this, Joseph. I know we can. I will speak to him about your designs and ideas for the new line. Show him I refuse to let you go.'

Partially convinced there would not be a new line if the say-so came down to Edward Pennington, Joseph took a long breath and stood. 'I should get back to my father. Can I walk you home?'

'I'd like that. Let me get my purse and coat.'

His mind whirled with uncertainty as he waited, and when she came back to him, he resisted offering her his arm as though they were lovers. The slamming door earlier, and how they had so quickly leapt apart, highlighted the taboo foundation of their relationship. Could anything personal ever really happen between them?

They walked to the department entrance and Joseph exhaled a shaky breath. God only knew how the next few days would fare, but he would not walk away from Pennington's or Elizabeth.

But that didn't mean she wouldn't be forced to walk away from him soon enough.

28

Despite a week of barely speaking to her father at the store, strained dinners followed by silent and separate evenings, strength from Joseph's care for her made Elizabeth strong as she sat in front of her father in his office. She clasped her hands together as he looked back and forth over the pages of Joseph's sketchbook. Aveline sat straight-backed beside her.

The window was open to a warm, sunny day at the beginning of May and the promise of summer only enhanced Elizabeth's eagerness that the year might yet become what she hoped.

A resounding success. An exultant twelve months of achievement.

At last, her father raised his head and carefully laid Joseph's sketchbook on the desk. She wasn't surprised by the suspicion in his eyes as he studied her, and she stared back, her body rigid, determined that he speak first.

He leaned back and steepled his fingers under his chin. 'So, you present me with Mr Carter's ideas, but not the man himself. Why?'

Damn him. He knew exactly why. She cleared her throat. 'I wanted you to make a judgement on whether or not we go forward with the collection based on Mr Carter's designs, rather than who he is.'

'He has talent. I'll give you that.'

It was a small but significant victory and she fought to keep her expression impassive. 'If we were to advertise — '

'But, despite his talents, these designs are little more than provocation of women believing them equally as apt at business and work as men. Something I still find loathsome.'

She clasped her hands tighter. 'Whether you agree with the women's movement or not, Papa, it is happening. The anticipation as we grow ever closer to the next election is feverish. People are being swept up in what could be deemed a revolution. It would be a missed opportunity if we do not supply what these women need. We want Pennington's to be Bath's driving force in retail, do we not?'

'Yes, but to — '

'Then let us be just that. Instead of sitting on the side lines and ignoring public feeling and female progression, let Pennington's embrace it, encourage it and, in turn, become the store where this emerging group of men and women come to shop.'

He studied her with narrowed eyes. 'Fine, but you cannot expect me to put even more money into this venture through advertising.' Her father shook his head. 'Mr Carter has not done enough to convince me of such investment. His idea might well prove profitable, but, for now, my agreement for it to go ahead will have to suffice.'

Her heart leapt with satisfaction, and Elizabeth could not halt her smile. 'You agree to the new collection?'

'Reluctantly, but yes. If you wish to add some of your own income to advertising, that's entirely up to you, but it will not come from me.'

'Then, that's exactly what I'll do. The sales of both the ladies' and men's departments since Mr Carter came here will justify every penny.'

Elizabeth fought to keep her excitement and triumph under control. It filled her heart with joy to think what Joseph would say, of how happy he would be. A slow but assured change was occurring with her father and she would embrace it. She'd worked hard for it.

Aveline smiled. 'I think this is a wise decision, sir. Mr Carter and Miss Pennington will make a resounding success of it, I'm sure.'

'Hmm.'

Although, this latest agreement could easily stem from the guilt over Joseph's aunt rather than anything Elizabeth or Joseph might have presented to him, Elizabeth couldn't help hoping her father had room in his often cold heart to regret what had happened to Clara Carter.

She sat straighter in her seat. 'You have my word Mrs Woolden, Mr Carter and I will work closely together on this venture to ensure it's as successful as it can be.'

'Is your enthusiasm just about this collection? Or is this a chance to prove yourself the forward thinker you keep promising me you are?'

She knew he goaded her, but she refused to rise to the bait. Joseph was a valuable commodity to the business and her heart ached to think he would eventually leave, but, for now, she'd keep him with her for as long as possible.

Mrs Woolden coughed. 'Sir, if I may . . . .'

He flitted his gaze to Aveline and nodded.

'Just from overhearing the shop girls' conversations, it is clear to me that women are changing and growing, sir. We'd be foolish to fight back too harshly. As Mr Carter has only suggested a small batch of products

270

in the first instance, I think the financial risk is minimal.'

Elizabeth's heart swelled with gratitude to her deputy.

'Maybe.' Her father picked up the sketchbook and held it out to Elizabeth. 'You'll oversee the project and it will be as much of a test for you as it is for Mr Carter.'

Elizabeth stood. It was the most enthusiasm she could expect, and she couldn't wait to break the news to Joseph. 'Thank you, Papa. We won't let you down.'

'Good. But I wish to speak with you further on another matter entirely.' He looked at Aveline. 'Would you please excuse us, Mrs Woolden?'

'Of course, sir.'

Dread quashed Elizabeth's short-lived elation as Aveline left the office, softly closing the door behind her.

Immediately, her father stood and walked around to lean against his desk in front of Elizabeth.

Her heart beat hard, but she steadfastly kept her gaze on his. 'Is this about Clara?'

'Yes. Clara and you.'

Trepidation whispered through her. Had the real issues that smouldered between them recently finally come to the fore? If they had, she prayed her project with Joseph and its success would lead her father to accept the feud between their families could be left in the past.

She'd be a fool to believe his trust in her with the store had changed so quickly, but there was every possibility the news of Clara Carter's sad and untimely death had shifted something, however small, inside of him.

He crossed his arms. 'I agreed to your request to not approach Carter, not out of respect for your wishes, but because of my own fears.'

Elizabeth stilled. Never in a hundred years would she have believed her father feared anything. His gaze shadowed with what looked to be shame and her heart quickened.

'Ever since you delivered the devastating blow that Clara had been carrying my child, a deep sickness has laid heavy in my stomach. I am not, alas, the unfeeling man you see me as. Everything I do and say to you is for your own good and, sooner or later, you'll thank me for it.'

Irritation simmered deep inside her and she pursed her lips to stop her undoubtedly untimely retort.

'I do not understand why Clara didn't tell me about the baby. Maybe my words to her on that final day were too harsh, too cruelly delivered. I accept that I played a part in her death, as well as your mother's.'

Elizabeth could not find her tongue, her shock striking her mute.

He briefly closed his eyes, turning older in front of her as she fought to not weaken with premature sympathy. Her father was a man with a quick and fiery temper. A man she could not entirely trust. Yet, his expression seemed to show his deep shame.

She quickly looked past him towards the window lest she faltered further.

He cleared his throat, and when Elizabeth met his gaze, his eyes were shadowed with sadness. 'Two women. A child. Three deaths. Three stains of human blood on my hands. You were right, I'll never sleep peacefully again.'

Tears burned in Elizabeth's eyes as her father

272

returned behind his desk. He gripped the back of his chair, his knuckles strained to white. 'Neither your mother or Clara were you, my dear. Neither of them had your strength or willingness to do daily battle with me.'

A sudden anger gripped her over the needless loss of two women, one each loved by her and Joseph, and a babe not even born. 'So, you're sorry? I'm not certain what am I supposed to say in return, Papa. So much pain and loss has occurred at your hands.'

'And I will take that to my grave. It will burn in my heart until the day I die. That's why . . . ' He tipped his head back and stared toward the ornate ceiling. 'That's why . . . '

It was as though she watched a stranger. He was changed. Had his baby's passing been one death too many? Or had his heart always been Clara Carter's and when he thought her alive, he could live freely, but now she was dead.

'My only concern is you, Elizabeth. You and the man for whom you have clear feelings.'

She swallowed. She would not deny she felt more for Joseph than she had any man, but her father would not sully what had passed between her and Joseph with his fury and usually cold heart.

'I want you married to good stock.'

She lifted her chin. 'You want me married to Noel.'

'I did, but he is clearly too weak to fight for you. Too weak to appreciate the poise and strength of a woman who would support his every endeavour. He's a fool, just as I was. Your mother had once been as feisty and fiery as you, but I soon put paid to that.'

'Yes, you did, and you will not do the same to me. I will not be controlled. You will not send me spiralling into a darkened hole where I see no way out. That stops now, Papa. It stops today.'

He pulled out his chair and sat, his gaze steady on hers. 'I agree, which is why I have given you permission to go ahead with this project of Carter's. I'm giving you further reach within the store. I'm willing to show faith in you, even if yours in me has been destroyed.'

Trembling with shock and deep mistrust, Elizabeth stood. 'Thank you.'

He nodded. 'You may go.'

She turned and walked to his office door, closing it behind her. On unsteady legs, she walked to the lift and pressed the call button. She glanced toward her father's office door, waiting for victory to rise inside her. But only distrust remained.

Her father had said he was giving her further reach within the store. She couldn't help but think he'd just offered her the length of rope needed to hang herself.

A few minutes later, she exited the lift and headed for the ladies' department, desperate to be alone in her office where she might analyse what her father had said and what the change in him might mean for her, the store and even Joseph.

It was too soon for her to hope for more changes from her father, but the fact she now had Joseph's project to work on as they saw fit was enough for the time being.

The ladies' department was a bustling mania as she entered, customers and staff alike gathered around the counter and Esther Stanbury.

What on earth was happening?

Frowning, she strode forward. 'Esther? Mrs Woolden? Whatever is the matter?'

274

'Oh, Miss Pennington.' Aveline walked from the throng. 'It's the king.'

'The king?'

'He's dead, Elizabeth.' Esther shook a newspaper above the heads of the shop girls. 'After a sickness that barely lasted a few days. Bronchitis, they say. I can't quite believe it.'

Elizabeth stared. The king was dead? 'But that's impossible. Surely we would've been told if he was suffering a serious complaint.'

'It's here in black and white.' Esther shook her head, her cheeks flushed. 'The king is dead and now Prince George will take the crown. King-Emperor George the Fifth. Everything in this country will surely change now. The Prince of Wales is young, his wife beautiful and forthright. Who knows what the future will be.'

Elizabeth turned away and slowly walked into her office, closing the door behind her.

Yes, indeed. Who knew what the future would be?

29

As Joseph sat side by side with Elizabeth on the settee in her office, he could hardly believe what he was
hearing. 'He said yes? He wants us to go ahead with
the new line?'

Elizabeth's beautiful green eyes shone with satisfaction. 'Yes.'

Joseph stared at this stunning woman, the only
regret in his heart was to see just how much of her
happiness depended on her father's approval. 'You
look happy. It suits you.'

She faintly blushed as her smile faltered. 'I am, but
I'd be happier if I could believe my father's approval
wasn't laced in arsenic.'

'Arsenic?'

She sighed and leaned back. 'We also spoke about
your aunt and my mother. I saw genuine remorse in
his eyes, which, strangely enough, made me warier
than if he'd shown his usual defence. I'd like to think
my father meant it when he said he was giving me further reach in the store, but I wouldn't be surprised if
he has something underhand planned.' Her gaze softened, and she touched her hand lightly to his thigh.
'He guessed I feel something more than the professional respect for you. I didn't deny it.'

Joseph covered her hand with his. 'I spoke to my
father last night and told him how things were between
us, too. Did you mean it when you said you'd like to
meet him?'

'Of course.' Her eyes shadowed with sadness. 'I

want to tell him how sorry I am about your aunt.'

'If anyone should apologise, it should be your father.'

'I agree, and maybe one day he will, but, for now, do you think I could be enough?'

He stared at her, marvelling how much she had come to mean to him. That she was important enough that he'd admitted his care for her to his father. He had taken the news surprisingly well, considering Joseph's heart was fast becoming the possession of a Pennington.

Sighing, he lifted Elizabeth's fingers and pressed a kiss to her knuckles. 'You'll always be enough. More than enough. Why don't you come for tea this Saturday? Pa is always more comfortable at home.'

She smiled. 'I'd like that.'

'Good. My father is a level-headed man and knows his son far too well. He said he likes the change in me and if it has taken a Pennington to make me smile again, he wants to meet you for himself.'

'I'm glad. There was also something else my father, thankfully, yielded upon. He is no longer pushing me to accept a man I neither respect nor love.'

A jolt of jealousy shot through him. 'I didn't realise you were promised.'

'Promised?' She shook her head. 'I was never promised to Noel. My father now sees, as I've implied all along, Noel is not strong enough for me and never will be. Papa still wants me to marry well, but at least I've had a small victory as far as his choice is concerned.'

Loss dropped like lead into Joseph's gut. Edward Pennington would undoubtedly see Elizabeth betrothed to a man of status, wealth and property. What did he have but adequate savings, a small shop and its flat on the upper floors?

'Joseph?'

He blinked and slowly eased his hand from hers. 'Why are we pursuing our feelings if, in the end, your father will see us separated?'

'Separated?' Her eyes darkened with determination. 'That will only happen if we allow it. We just need to bide our time and not flaunt our feelings for one another in front of him or anyone else. This can work between us if we are patient.'

'Do you really believe your father will agree to me working here now he knows your feelings for me? At the moment, I am a supplier. An outsider. Can you imagine proposing to him that I work here permanently?'

'Maybe not yet. But who knows? If this show goes well and profits soar, he'll want someone who knows what they're doing working for us in order to get ahead of our competitors.'

Joseph lifted her plans from beside him on the settee. They worked phenomenally well together, but every time the personal mixed with the professional, inner demons circled his conscience and heart. He came here for *his* family, for Lillian.

'I've told you it is my wish to see less fortunate people being given the chance to work and better their prospects . . .'

'Yes?'

'If I was to consider closing Carter & Son and working permanently at Pennington's, would you support the idea of employing people the store has not previously given a chance?'

'Of course.' Her chest rose as she inhaled. 'My father will not be here forever, Joseph, and I'm working hard to do all I can to ensure the store is passed to me. When that day comes, I'll be free to employ whomever I want . . . regardless of their status or class.'

He studied her. Her expression glowed with conviction, her chin high. He nodded. 'Good, because that's what I owe to Lillian as well as continuing with her charity work. Of which, I have badly neglected since working here *and* at Carter & Son. I don't know how much longer I can go on juggling both. Something will need to change, and I'd like for that to be my working solely here. At Pennington's.'

The hope that lit in her eyes should have made him happy but doubt still whispered through him that their mutual dreams would never be possible while Edward Pennington remained in charge.

Joseph took a deep breath and forced a smile. 'Let's just concentrate on the show. Everything else can be discussed in due course.'

A flicker of disappointment showed in her eyes before she dropped her focus to the papers in his hands. 'Of course.'

'I should get back to the workroom.' He stood. 'I also need to speak with Miss Stanbury about the designs for the ladies' department and front window.'

'I spoke to her briefly first thing this morning and she's as excited about the prospect of promoting the show as we are of pulling it all together.'

'Good, then hopefully she already has some ideas.'

'If I know Esther at all, she would've been thinking of nothing else. I swear her brain works at a rate far superior to the rest of us. Why don't you find her now? She'll need time to delegate her workload. You'll most likely find her outside. She's working on the final touches to her latest window this morning and always likes to see it from the pedestrians' point of view.'

They lingered in front of one another and unspoken words danced on Joseph's tongue. Their kisses still hung in the air like a bittersweet moment never to be repeated. 'Elizabeth . . .'

'Work, Joseph. Let's just focus on that, for now.'

He nodded and walked to her office door. As he stepped into the corridor, bitter loss twisted inside him. He was falling for a woman way out of his league. His desires were beyond laughable. He wanted her. Wanted them to share in their work, aspirations and dreams. Yet, still, he couldn't move past the fact he didn't deserve personal happiness and that Edward Pennington would never believe him good enough for his daughter.

Burying his hapless thoughts for the time being, Joseph walked downstairs and made his way outside in the hope of finding Esther.

She stood on the pavement in the bright afternoon sun, waving towards the shop window. Joseph smiled to see her pretty face etched in concentration, or maybe frustration, as her hand gestures grew ever more impatient. He slowly approached.

'Miss Stanbury. Good morning.'

She turned, her cheeks flushed and her hazel eyes glinting with annoyance. A second passed before she blinked and smiled, her gaze instantly softening. 'Joseph. How are you?' She glanced towards the window and held up her palm, indicating her two female assistants inside pause in their positioning of a country-attired mannequin.

Facing him once more, she sighed and planted her hands on her hips. 'What can I do for you?'

He nodded towards the window. 'It looks grand.'

'Hmm. Maybe it will eventually, but not at the moment. Sometimes, I feel I must do everything myself to get it right first time. Anyway . . . ' She waved her hand. 'Time is pressing on.'

'Of course.' Suitably hurried, Joseph cleared his throat. 'I understand Elizabeth — Miss Pennington, spoke to you about the fashion show?'

'She did, and I can't wait to get started. I'll be done with this window this morning and can have my assistants start on a new project for Haberdashery while I work with you and Miss Pennington. I understand it's a matter of urgency?'

'It is. We can't afford to allow Mr Pennington time to change his mind.'

'Understood. He seems determined to reside in the dark ages from what I know of him.'

Joseph looked along the building to the biggest of Pennington's three picture windows, pride speeding his heart that, very soon, his hats, gloves, jackets and skirts would be on display in that very window. 'Your displays are phenomenal, Miss Stanbury. You're clearly far more creative as far as advertising is concerned than I am.'

'Thank you.'

'And you're inspired by this project?'

'Inspired? I'm passionate about the women's suffrage movement so happy Pennington's is encouraging women in their endeavours. I'm looking forward to getting started. I'm confident my staff will be equally as excited when I tell them the source of your inspiration.'

'Then I look forward to hearing your ideas.'

'My mind is full of ideas, as far as women's empowerment is concerned.' She faced the window once more. 'But for now, I'd better get back to work.'

Joseph wandered back into the store and headed downstairs to the workroom. Once the new window display was revealed, interest in the fashion show would gather momentum. He wanted the evening to sparkle. For every woman without an invitation to hanker after one for the next show. It was imperative his clothes and accessories became something that women would do everything in their power to own.

Elizabeth filtered into his mind once more. She was beautiful and inspiring and he wanted her, no matter what it might mean for them. His impatience to hold her in his arms grew stronger every day.

They were consenting adults. If they wanted to be together, no one else had a say. Elizabeth had to be around the age twenty-four or twenty-five, he twenty-seven. Any backlash from her father, or anyone else, he and Elizabeth would deal with it.

Yet, guilt that he might love again simmered painfully in his chest. Would Lillian really have wanted him, expected him, to fall in love again and so soon? He had to believe she would or else linger in this grey, dark place for the rest of his life.

Elizabeth was a precious jewel with a father who had the capability of stealing her glitter and making part of her sit in the shadows.

Joseph clenched his jaw.

He'd do everything in his power to make her believe how she would shine once she stepped out of her father's shadow and into the light. A light Joseph intended to empower her with.

30

Rare trepidation twisted in Joseph's stomach and he tightened his hand on Elizabeth's where it lay on his arm. 'Pa is one of the nicest blokes on the planet, but I still have no idea how this afternoon will turn out.'

She drew her gaze from the colourful gardens before Pulteney Bridge. 'Are you actually a little nervous, Joseph Carter?' She smiled, her eyes sparkling with amusement. 'There was a time when I believed nothing could ruffle your feathers. It pleases me to see it is only your father who can make you a little on edge.'

Joseph pulled back his shoulders and feigned an expression of nonchalance. 'No one, including my Pa, can put the wind up me.' He winked and slumped. 'Well, maybe he can a little.'

She laughed. 'Everything will be fine. You've told him I'm coming, and he didn't refuse the notion of us having tea together. That has to be a positive.'

'I agree, but . . . ' Joseph looked towards the bridge, its grey stone and imposing structure suddenly feeling less like the place that housed Carter & Son and more like a looming threat. 'That's not to say when he sees you, he might not doubt his decision for this afternoon's get-together.' He drew her to a stop, concern and love for her pulsing inside of him. 'No matter his reaction, no matter his words, I'll stand by you. I want you to know that.'

She glanced over his shoulder towards the bridge. 'You don't anticipate him turning violent upon sight of me, do you?'

Joseph laughed and stepped back, realising the intensity in his words and, most probably, his expression had frightened her. 'Pa is the least violent man you're ever likely to meet.' He brushed a curl from her cheek. 'But that doesn't mean his feelings towards your father don't twist and turn like a thunderstorm inside him. I want this feud between our families brought to an end as much as you, and if that means intercepting my father and calming his temper, I will.'

She inhaled a shaky breath and sighed. 'Well, let's just hope things go better than either of us fears.'

Taking her hand, he pressed a kiss to her gloved fingers, pleasure filling his heart that she wore the gloves that she'd tried on weeks before during their clandestine meeting in Pennington's workroom. He gently folded her hand beneath his arm and led her forwards.

The streets were busy with Saturday afternoon shoppers and carriages, horses, the occasional motor car and stall traders, as they walked ever closer to Joseph's home. Time and again, he waited for concern about what Elizabeth might think of his home, considering the magnificence of hers, but no such concern materialised. She was so far from a snob, a judge, that he instinctively knew she would barely look at his home. Today, her focus would be entirely on his father.

They walked a short distance along the bridge and Joseph released her to pull his key from his jacket pocket. He pushed it into the lock of Carter & Son, pleased his father had agreed that closing the shop for a single afternoon would not be the end of the world.

Not when the closure was for something as important as Elizabeth's visit.

Pushing open the door, Joseph waved her inside ahead of him.

The shop was in semi-darkness, the dark wood panelling and counters criss-crossed with lines of sunshine coming through the latticed windows. Joseph stood back as she wandered slowly round, her gaze darting over everything from the cubbyholes of material, to the single mannequin in the corner, to the big cash register on the counter.

A soft smile curved her lips as she faced him. 'Your shop is wonderful. So intimate and warm.'

Pride swelled inside him that she had been immediately immersed in the open and welcoming atmosphere of the shop each of the Carters had intended it to be. 'Thank you.'

'I completely understand your father's reservations about you coming to Pennington's. Shops like this, as beautiful as they are, will soon close. If not this year, then maybe next. That must be incredibly hard for him.' Sadness clouded her gaze. 'And if he blames me for that loss . . .'

Joseph stepped forward and cupped his hand to her cheek. 'It's no one's fault. Not yours. Not your father's. It's progression. Nothing more, nothing less. My father is starting to see that. No blame is on anyone, all right?'

She nodded, and Joseph placed his hand to the small of her back and led her towards the back stairs.

Walking ahead of her into the living room, Joseph hesitated on the threshold as he watched his father, unnoticed. He father placed a teapot in the centre of the small dining table and stood back, his hands on his ample hips, as though assessing the overall impression of the tea, sandwiches and sliced Victoria sponge he'd laid out.

Love for the man who'd raised him simmered deep in Joseph's chest. This afternoon was a big compromise for his father. A big step back that allowed his son to step forward.

Heading decisively into the room, Joseph cleared his throat. 'Pa? This is Miss Elizabeth Pennington.'

At first, Joseph thought his father hadn't heard him. He stood stock-still, his hands on his hips and his back turned. The seconds passed, before his father slowly swivelled around.

Relief swept through Joseph when his father's face broke with a smile, his hand outstretched. 'Miss Pennington, a pleasure.'

She stepped forward, her perfume infusing Joseph's nostrils as she brushed by him to clasp his father's hand. 'Mr Carter, the pleasure is mine. Thank you so much for welcoming me into your home.'

'Not at all. Not at all.' He dropped her hand. 'It's probably nowhere near as grand as anything you're used to, but it does us well enough. Eh, Joseph?'

'It certainly does.' Joseph stepped forward, his previous elation faltering at the undertone of defensiveness he caught in his father's voice. He pulled out a chair and nodded at Elizabeth. 'Why don't you take a seat?'

She hesitated, her smile a little too wide and her eyes cautious. Sitting down, she carefully removed her navy-blue hat and set it on the table, her auburn hair glinting in the sunlight from the window beside her. 'Thank you.'

Joseph took the seat next to her as his father lowered into the chair opposite. 'So . . .' He picked up the teapot. 'Here we are.'

286

The tinkling of the tea as it filled their cups was the only sound as Joseph struggled with what to do or say next. How did he start the conversation? Did they talk of their families? Their businesses? Elizabeth's father?

'Mr Carter?'

Joseph stilled as Elizabeth spoke.

Her face was sombre, her eyes dark with passion. 'I am so sorry for the pain my father has caused your family. When Joseph told me about your sister and the part my father played in her death, I was shocked, angry and aggrieved. I hope, someday, you'll be able to find it in your heart to forgive what happened, even if you can never forget. My father is a man who uses people, Mr Carter. Uses and discards them as though they are of no matter. He has tried time and again to discard me in much the same way.' She smiled softly, her gaze focused entirely on Joseph's father. 'But I will never ever give him the satisfaction of wavering, let alone crumbling. I am here today to offer my sincerest apologies and condolences. I assure you, I do not condone my father's actions and honestly hope we can do everything possible to build bridges between our families.'

Joseph flicked his gaze to his father. He bore the expression of a man torn. Torn between like and dislike. Adoration and contempt.

'Pa — '

'You know, Miss Pennington, you don't look at all like your father.'

Elizabeth laughed. 'No. Thankfully, I followed after my mother in both looks, temperament and patience. The only things I've inherited from my father are bullheadedness, determination and an ability to work ten-hour days. Thank the Lord.'

Joseph smiled, pride filling his chest. 'Amen to that.'

She met his smile and faced his father. 'I really am so very sorry, Mr Carter.'

His father studied her for a long moment before he nodded, his shoulders lowering. 'Then let us talk no more about it. Tell me, what are your intentions towards my son?'

'Intentions? Pa, for crying out loud.' Joseph looked between them. 'Elizabeth has no intentions past work and what we can achieve together. Intentions. What ever — '

'He has quite the hidden temper, does he not, Miss Pennington?' His father's eyes glistened with laughter. 'The boy needs to learn to understand when I jest and when I don't. Isn't that right?'

'It is.' She laughed and lifted her teacup. 'It is indeed.'

Joseph leaned back and shook his head as Elizabeth's gaze locked with his father's. Whether or not her apology was entirely accepted by his father, only time would tell, but it seemed, whether this was but a single time or the beginning of a hundred future visits, he suspected whenever Elizabeth and her father were together, Joseph would find himself a third wheel.

And that was something he wouldn't mind in the slightest.

31

Elizabeth took a deep breath as she stepped from the lift onto Pennington's fourth floor. A month of back-breaking work and organisation meant the live mannequin show would go ahead tonight. The anticipation had kept her awake half the night, but all traces of tiredness evaded her as her body pulsed with adrenaline.

She marched through the Butterfly's open, bevelled glass doors and into the restaurant. The flurry of activity and atmosphere of unrestrained excitement was intoxicating. She could not remember a time when her staff had looked so animated about their work, their faces alight with smiles.

Miss Stanbury and her team had excelled with the decor. The tables had been put into storage and chairs had been arranged in rows either side of a long wooden walkway. Careful not to favour one suffragist or suffragette organisation over another, Miss Stanbury had come up with the idea to combine all their colours, and gorgeous, pleated banners of purple, white, green, red and gold satin swathed the walls and covered the furniture.

The chairs had been sheathed with simple white sheets, tied at the back with gold taffeta bows. The sign at the end of the walkway, from where the models would emerge, read, 'Modern Clothes For Modern Women'. A simple and clear message without political connotation.

Everything looked perfect and striking enough to

289

ignite aspiration in even the most sceptical of women.

Walking into the fray, Elizabeth approached Esther as she helped a member of her team put a length of material over the foot of the walkway. She tapped her friend's shoulder. 'You've outdone yourself. Your team's work is truly outstanding.'

'Thank you.' Esther smiled, her eyes bright with clear pride as she brushed a stray blonde curl from her brow. 'I've thoroughly enjoyed every part of this project. Mr Carter obviously greatly respects women. He's a real credit to Pennington's.'

Satisfaction swept through Elizabeth as she thought of the lacklustre atmosphere her father often left on the female staff, compared to Joseph.

'He's a credit to everything.'

Esther raised her eyebrows, her gaze teasing. 'Hmm. I can see that. I don't think I've ever seen such a look of admiration on your face for any man. You really care for him, don't you?'

Heat warmed Elizabeth's cheeks and she looked to the far end of the room. 'He's changing me.'

'In a good way, too.'

Elizabeth faced her friend, anxiety fluttering in her stomach. 'My father has noticed my care for Joseph and I worry he'll destroy whatever might grow between us before it's even begun.'

Esther gently touched Elizabeth's arm, her brow furrowed. 'You mustn't let him. You deserve everything in this store, as well as a good man beside you. I really thought you'd never find someone you could trust in the way you clearly do Mr Carter. You must protect that. Men who give us confidence, who support our dreams and desires, are scarce. Don't let your father destroy what you've found.'

290

'And what of you? Aren't we equally guilty of pushing away any romantic interest in the name of self-protection. You have your secrets, too, Esther. I know you do.'

'Maybe I do, but those secrets don't stretch to me spending a life alone. Neither should yours. Whatever your father might have done in the past, or even now, don't let it ruin your chance for happiness.'

Esther squeezed Elizabeth's arm before walking away. Elizabeth looked around the room, her focus landing on George Weir, the head of the men's department. Although, he'd finally come on board with the show — albeit reluctantly — he remained her father's eyes and ears.

Tonight, had to be a success, or else she didn't doubt George would bask in telling her father of its failure. As for her father? Elizabeth glanced towards the restaurant doors, whether he would make an appearance was her guess as much as anyone else's.

She pulled back her shoulders. What did it matter what her father chose to do? The fifty specially selected guests, from the very wealthy to the fashion-loving friends and family of her staff, a wide selection of people, would be here to witness something innovative and exciting.

Fingers crossed, with added glowing reviews from the invited press in tomorrow's paper, the evening would draw to a perfect conclusion.

Her gaze settled on Joseph's back and her stomach gave a lurch of attraction. His jacket discarded, and his shirtsleeves rolled to the elbows, he worked side by side with the men employed to erect the walkway and wooden backboards. He embraced whatever task needed to be done, nothing beneath or above him. Elizabeth breathed deep. He was as like-minded and equally innovative as her. Surely, between them, they'd thwart any plans her father might have to sabotage the possible future they could have together.

She walked towards him. 'Mr Carter? Could you possibly spare a moment?'

He looked up from the wood he and Albert Griggs were slotting into place, Joseph's brilliant blue eyes hitching her heart. 'Miss Pennington.' He straightened and faced Albert. 'Are you all right to carry on here?'

Albert touched his hand to his brow in a salute and turned back to his work.

Joseph motioned for her to lead the way and they strolled to the side of the room. As they stared at the comings and goings, Elizabeth sighed. 'It looks better than anything I dared to imagine, yet I can't fight the feeling there may be trouble tonight. I haven't heard from my father if he'll be attending.' She faced him, nerves gripping her stomach. 'When he falls quiet like this, it usually indicates his simmering anger.'

He looked deep into her eyes, his expression determined and his eyes dark, making her feel stronger just for being beside him. 'He can't say or do anything to stop us being together. Is that what you're afraid of?'

She crossed her arms. 'Yes. Does that make me weak?'

'No. That makes you aware of who your father is. And I don't doubt your distrust of him has escalated now you know what he did to my family.'

Potential loss of Joseph once more seeped like ice-water through her veins. 'What if he comes after you, rather than me. What then?'

'What do you think he can say or do to me? He could terminate my contract, but if he orders me

292

away from you?' He lifted his fingers as if to cup her jaw before dropping his hand to his side. He glanced around them. 'That won't happen. No matter what he says. Why don't we talk to him? Tell him our relationship has grown past the professional.'

'Talk to him?' Elizabeth huffed a laugh and fought the tears pricking her eyes. 'There is no talking to my father, especially about my future.'

How could she tell Joseph how much control her father's opinion had on her? Despite Joseph's admiration for her, she sensed it would be her weakness to ultimately refrain from fully standing up to her father that would make Joseph eventually turn away.

She faced the walkway. 'I just want to give the best show Bath has ever seen and not have to think about my father.'

'I have too much care for you to allow him to jeopardise our working together. You *must* trust me.'

She opened her mouth to respond, but before she could form the words, Joseph strode away from her.

Hating that she'd allowed her father's absence to shake her enough that she'd doubted Joseph's care for her, Elizabeth stood a little taller.

Edward Pennington's days of affecting her in any way were over. She admired how deeply Joseph had loved Lillian. Loved that he was determined to see through his wife's hopes and dreams in the same way he seemed committed to Elizabeth's.

Joseph was the man she had been looking for and she loved him. Felt she'd always love him, no matter what her father might attempt to do to quash that love.

He could wield his power as much as he liked, Elizabeth was determined she and Joseph would ultimately triumph.

32

Joseph planted his hands on his hips and assessed the finished walkway and platform through narrowed eyes. Everything looked just as he, Elizabeth and Esther had envisioned.

He'd become embroiled in so much more at Pennington's than he'd intended. Over the heads of the guests waiting for the start of the show, Joseph stared at Elizabeth seated on the opposite side of the restaurant. She smiled and talked with Esther and Mrs Woolden, but he couldn't ignore the anguish Elizabeth clearly fought to hide. He longed to stand side by side with her in everything. Personal and professional.

Glancing towards the restaurant's doors for the twentieth time in as many minutes, Joseph clenched his teeth. Where was Pennington? Would he grace them with his presence? What did it say about the man if he could snub such an original sales strategy, one his daughter had brought to fruition, as it unfolded in his store? Joseph shook his head. It stank of little more than Pennington's arrogance and malevolence.

Tonight's show had been drawn from Joseph's ambition and imagination, made possible by a group of the most wonderful people he'd ever had the honour to work with. Yet, with his relationship with Elizabeth hidden and causing her so much apprehension, everything felt tainted. As though neither him, nor her, deserved tonight to be a success.

But what could he do? He could not confront

Pennington and cause her further distress. Look what Joseph's selfishness had meant for Lillian. She was dead. Pushed to walk into a dangerous situation alone because he'd been too wrapped up in his work to notice hers. Would he not be doing the same with Elizabeth if he forced her to speak about them to her father?

Joseph flinched as the four-piece band struck up the first note of the opening music. The chatter and laughter filling the room immediately subsided. Purposefully burying his growing love for Elizabeth, Joseph embraced the energy, sweat and occasional tears that had been spent over the last week as the staff battled to get this evening's show ready in time. He strode forward and took his seat behind Elizabeth.

As she stood and stepped onto the walkway, he stared at her burnished bronze hair and delectable figure. Swallowing hard, he sat straighter in his seat as his want of her burned through him.

'Good evening, ladies and gentlemen. My name is Elizabeth Pennington and I am the head of the ladies' department here at Pennington's. I'm thrilled to welcome you to this very special event in the store's magnificent Butterfly restaurant.

'We're delighted to see so many of you here and hope our new and exciting fashions and accessories catch your eye and imagination. We have skirts, blouses, jackets, hats and gloves to fit every budget. Your exclusive invitations mean you are the first to see the new collection designed by the extremely talented and successful glove maker, Mr Joseph Carter, and made with the devoted care and attention of our exemplary manufacturing team. Mr Carter, please stand.'

Surprised and exceedingly pleased that Elizabeth had chosen such a public event to introduce him, Joseph stood, pride filling his chest to see such joy and admiration in Elizabeth's eyes. He raised his hand to the applause and curious looks centred on him.

Elizabeth smiled and re-clasped her hands. 'Mr Carter's designs are aimed at dressing women both beautifully and practically for what promises to be a future of positive change and incredible opportunity. Without further ado, let the show begin.'

Applause erupted as the band played louder and faster, causing a wave of excitement to ripple through the room. The audience sat straighter in their seats, their eyes wide and eager as the first model strode confidently onto the walkway.

A second model, then a third, emerged from behind the boards. Resplendently cut jackets over long skirts, hemmed just above the ankle and teamed with elegantly buttoned leather boots, showcased grace and practicability. The skirts' waists were cinched tight with wide, leather belts, which meant less need for cumbersome corsets, but still created a feminine, hourglass silhouette. Bold greens and purples, worn with snow-white or soft gold blouses, stated a message of women united; of women not afraid to stand out in a crowd.

He turned his gaze to the shop girls who'd opted not to model but wanted to share their support for the show. Dressed in his designs, they walked amongst the rows of spectators offering glasses of champagne and canapés, a walking advertisement of just how easy it was to work and interact in these new, revolutionary outfits.

Satisfaction burned inside him as the show

progressed and the glasses of champagne gave way to questions and order sheets. Once the fashion parade was over, people left their seats to examine the clothes more closely and Joseph immediately sought Elizabeth. He spotted her talking avidly with three clearly upper-class ladies as she gestured towards the models and touched her hand to her own jacket and belt, all designed and made by Joseph's hands.

She looked up and their gazes locked.

His heart kicked. She looked happy . . . beautiful.

One of the shop girls approached her and he was about to turn away and make a circuit through the guests, when whatever the girl said to Elizabeth caused her smile to vanish and her eyes widen. She snapped her gaze to his as anguish, shock and — his heartbeat escalated — fear clouded her stunning eyes.

Joseph strode towards her, a dangerous protectiveness rising inside him. What had the girl said? It had to have been about Edward Pennington. Nobody else had the power to destroy Elizabeth's elation in such a way.

When he was beside her, he cupped Elizabeth's elbow and led her to the back of the room. 'What is it?'

She flitted her gaze to the restaurant entrance. 'He's here.'

'Your father?'

'Yes. This is what he does. He senses when I'm happy and then swoops in to put an end to it. I should've known he'd ruin this for us.' Tears glistened in her eyes, her cheeks flushed with agitation. 'We have to be prepared for whatever he might do.'

He clasped her hands, not caring who saw them. 'He can't ruin tonight. It's done. The orders are coming in. Your father gave you permission to oversee this project. You've done nothing wrong. The show is yours.'

Her shoulders relaxed a little. 'And yours.'

Before he could answer, she turned to the entrance and quickly snatched her hands from his. Joseph followed her gaze.

Edward Pennington stood between the newly erected curtains, his top hat clutched in one hand, a cane in the other. He stared at his daughter with malicious amusement.

Anger unfurled in Joseph's stomach as he eyed Edward Pennington, willing the man to look at him rather than Elizabeth. Come on, you bastard. Bully me, not her.

Pennington entered the restaurant, a much younger woman behind him. The press' lightbulbs flashed as he strolled slowly, like a king overseeing his realm. He roamed his gaze around the crowded room, the odd flash of surprise or disappointment showing in his expression as he took in the mix of class and age amongst the guests.

Joseph pulled back his shoulders and waited for Pennington's approach. Elizabeth stepped to the side, opening the space between them like a chasm as a photographer shot forward and took their picture, the flash momentarily blinding Joseph. Elizabeth's single action of moving away from him had sliced through his pride like a sharpened knife blade.

She continued to stare at her father. 'Let me deal with this alone.'

Joseph glanced at her profile and his irritation turned dangerous. 'No.'

She turned her angry glare to his. 'What?'

'No. Your days of being alone are over. You have me now.'

He faced Pennington, and when the man met his gaze and smiled, Joseph smiled straight back. Another flash lit the space and Joseph didn't doubt he and Pennington looked like two wolves braced to pounce.

* * *

Elizabeth fought to control the hateful, returning inadequacy her father always caused in her. She tilted her chin as he came to stand in front of her. 'Papa, I'm glad you could make an appearance. What do you think?'

Ignoring her, his steely gaze bored into Joseph's. 'We meet again, Mr Carter.'

Elizabeth stiffened. All the change and excitement she anticipated for the future teetered on a knife-edge now her father and Joseph stood face to face again.

Much to her relief and admiration, Joseph congenially put out his hand. 'Mr Pennington, a pleasure, sir.'

Her father's eyes darkened with distrust as he slowly took Joseph's hand. 'Elizabeth speaks very highly of you. I must say, it surprises me that a son of Robert Carter carries himself with such authority. Then again, I recall your mother cut quite an arresting figure.'

Elizabeth's breath lodged in her throat as second after excruciating second passed.

Joseph released her father's hand and smiled. 'She did, indeed. Together, my father and mother taught me self-respect as well as respect of others. Especially women . . . including my beloved aunt.'

Elizabeth closed her eyes against the flash of shock in her father's eyes. She hardly dared breathe, let alone move.

Her father coughed. 'Then clearly Robert took to fatherhood more than he did retail.'

Elizabeth snapped her eyes open. 'Papa,' she hissed, shooting a glance at his smiling companion. 'Now is hardly the time or place to have this discussion.'

She yearned to push her arm into Joseph's so they stood united against the man who had hurt his family so deeply. The tremors still lingered in Joseph's heart, and it was undeniable that they lingered in her father's too. Yet, what was she to do in that moment? If she antagonised her father, his anger would only escalate, his wrath becoming detrimental to the show and Joseph.

She forced a confident smile. 'The show is proving a success. If you look at these women's faces —'

'Oh, I can see their faces, Elizabeth. I see many, many faces of which I would not have expected in the store at all.'

Incensed, she lowered her voice and held her father's stare. 'You've no right to judge these women, any woman. Including me.'

'Half of them clearly cannot afford to shop in Pennington's.' He glanced over his shoulder. 'What was your intention by inviting them to this spectacle? To humiliate them? Shame them? Or maybe you'd consider yourself successful if you managed both?'

'I see no such thing on any faces. Everyone is having a marvellous time and making orders as they do. The staff have worked so hard to make tonight possible. The manufacturing staff worked day and night to —'

'And what is your opinion, Mr Carter?' He slid his gaze to Joseph. 'You hardly strike me as a man who loses his voice.'

Elizabeth turned. Joseph's gaze burned into her father's, their deep blue depths so volatile she struggled to refrain from stepping between them.

'The world is changing, sir. It would be profitable to the store to be ahead of the progression, rather than behind it.'

'And you believe you're the person to make that decision?'

Elizabeth glared. 'No, but I am.'

Her father's smile turned amused as he faced her. 'I might have said I'm willing to enhance your duties at the store, Elizabeth, and this evening might even prove a success, but that does not mean I'll stand for your aggression.'

Anger and humiliation swept through her as she glanced at his latest lover. How dare he undermine her in front of this woman and Joseph. 'How long is this battle to go on between us, Papa? Mr Carter, myself and the rest of Pennington's hard-working staff deserve the benefit of your undisguised doubt.' She narrowed her eyes, renewed strength pulsing through her. 'I refuse to act as an underling any longer. I'm trying so hard to prove my worth to you, but I want a life. *My* life. Not one ruled by you.'

'You need to watch your tongue, Elizabeth.'

She took a step closer and his companion immediately stepped back. 'If you think I'm going to wait while you find some way to punish me or Joseph for your mistakes, you can think again. Joseph working with me is the best thing to ever happen in my paternally controlled life and over my dead body will you

301

take him away from me.'

Her body trembled, and her blood thundered in her ears. Even as Joseph's arm circled her waist, she couldn't control her harried breathing.

Her father looked at Joseph's arm, rage flashing in his eyes and his cheeks darkening. He smiled maliciously at Joseph. 'Why don't you join me and Elizabeth for dinner with some associates tomorrow evening? I'm sure they'd be interested to hear about tonight and what you have in mind for the future. Elizabeth will remind you of our address. I will see you at seven sharp.'

'Very well.' Joseph's arm tightened around her waist. 'I look forward to it.'

With a lingering look at Joseph, her father turned to his ridiculously young companion. 'Come along, my dear. Let us find a nice restaurant for some dinner, shall we?'

Nausea rose in Elizabeth's throat as her father exited the room. Once he'd disappeared, she slumped against Joseph's arm. 'What have I done? He'll make me pay for my outburst and use you as a weapon. If we pursue our relationship, it will lead to heartbreak for us both. That much, at least, my father will ensure.'

'Then we'll do all we can to protect ourselves.' Desire burned in the dark depths of his eyes. 'You were astounding. I think it's time for me to find a little more courage and face my demons, too. I want you, Elizabeth. I want every part of you.'

33

As Joseph walked into the parlour above Carter & Son, his father stared out the window, his back rigid. He'd told Joseph all too clearly he didn't want him to attend the dinner with Edward Pennington that evening. Robert might have got along with Elizabeth better than Joseph could have hoped for, but his father's animosity towards Pennington would take longer to vanquish . . . a fact Joseph understood only too well.

Joseph coughed. 'So, how do I look?'

His father turned. 'Like a man who has no idea what he'll face tonight. Pennington's not a man to be taken lightly. He's a dangerous and insolvable puzzle . . . and nothing like his daughter.'

'I can take care of myself, Pa. I'll be careful not to provoke him. I'm going to this dinner because Pennington's invitation was a clear challenge and a way to rile Elizabeth.'

'Which means he's up to something. If his daughter means anything to you, anything at all, you'll go along with what Pennington asks of you until his requests become so absurd you have no choice but to refuse them. If you allow your pride to get in the way, it will lead to your ruin. Not his.' His father's brow furrowed, and he walked across the room, before sinking into an armchair in front of the fireplace.

Joseph crossed his arms. 'Having him know I care for his daughter doesn't bother me in the slightest. I won't let him hurt her anymore.'

'You won't have a choice.'

Joseph's heart beat faster with the fear that he might fail Elizabeth as he had Lillian. 'Granted, the man's a bully, but when he sees I could make his daughter happy, that I only want her happy, then surely — '

'What did he care of her happiness when she was a child? How do you know he cares for her happiness now? You told me of the pain in her eyes whenever her father's mentioned. The man's a narcissist and a controller. If he sees that she looks to you, rather than to him, he'll do all he can to get rid of you and bring her back in line.'

Fisting his hands, he stared at his father. Could his predictions be accurate? 'He's begun to extend her responsibilities at the store. Surely, that's a sign he is coming to trust and believe in her. She deserves a happy personal life as much as the next person. Elizabeth and I will face Pennington together, and maybe she'll realise she doesn't have to deal with him, or anything else, alone, ever again.'

'You more than care for her, don't you?'

Did he admit how quickly, how certainly, he'd fallen for Elizabeth? That from the moment he'd laid eyes on her, his heart had sunk with a terrifying certainty this woman would become a vital part of his life. Her luscious red hair and phenomenal green eyes had been what caught his attention, but as he spoke to her, his attraction had rapidly grown to be about her grace, intelligence, kind heart and intuition. She'd burrowed into his heart quickly and deeply.

He briefly closed his eyes against his father's intense scrutiny. 'Fine. I'm falling in love with her.'

'And against my better judgement, I'm happy for you. But that doesn't stop my worry for you

304

both. You're walking into a house owned by the man who happily cast aside your pregnant aunt. If I could — '

'You're wrong, Pa.'

Anger darkened his father's gaze. 'My sister's dead, isn't she?'

'He cast her aside, but he didn't do so happily, and he didn't know Aunt Clara carried his baby.' Joseph blew out a breath. 'As much as it pains me to give that man any credit, if Aunt Clara could've found the courage to tell Pennington about the baby, it might have led to a different outcome. Regardless of the child being illegitimate. He was, possibly still is, desperate for a son and male heir. Clara's pregnancy could've been the chance he so desperately wanted.'

His father's eyes were unreadable as he took a long breath. 'If that's true, it's not beyond the realms of possibility he still believes he needs a son to make his life complete. If you love this woman, Joseph, you must protect her. Her happiness must come above your own.'

Pain struck deep in Joseph's heart. 'Like Lillian's didn't, you mean?'

'I'm not saying that.'

'Then what are you saying?'

'I'm saying if, at any time, you suspect Elizabeth will be hurt in another of Pennington's egotistical games, you get her out of there. I promise you, she'll be welcome in this house.'

'Get Elizabeth out of where? His house? The store?' Anger swirled inside him. 'I saw the fear in her eyes when he invited me to dinner tonight. She thinks he'll drive me away. Make me turn my back on her.' He picked up his hat from the table and put it on. 'That won't happen. I've the chance to be happy again. To live again. And, if she wants me, I'll protect her for the rest of my life. This time I won't make a mess of the grace God has given me.'

'I'm glad to hear it.' A teasing light lit his father's blue eyes and a small smile played on his lips.

Joseph slumped his shoulders. 'This whole conversation was to provoke me, wasn't it?'

'Yes. I needed to see your passion. Needed to see what Miss Pennington means to you. Now I have, I know you and her will be just fine. Now, get out of here before you're late.'

Joseph stepped towards the door and then stopped. 'Don't wait up. I'll be all right.'

'Ah, I know, but I won't be here tonight. I'm going to visit your Ma's brother. Uncle Jack will no doubt want to put me up for the night.'

Pleased his father wouldn't be alone, Joseph walked to him and clasped his shoulders. 'Have a good time. I'll see you tomorrow.'

'That you will.'

Striding from the room, Joseph walked downstairs and into the street. He breathed in the cool night air to clear the anger from his heart and the tension from his body. Whatever Edward Pennington had in mind to happen tonight, Joseph would be ready.

★ ★ ★

Elizabeth walked into the drawing room and glanced at the table beneath the window filled with canapés and sweet treats, trays of champagne, brandy and cordial on each edge. She pressed her hand to the nerves in her stomach, wishing to be anywhere else but at home and waiting for Joseph to be in the same room as her father.

His cough sounded behind her and Elizabeth whipped her hand from her stomach and smiled. 'Papa, good evening.'

'Good evening, my dear.' He slowly appraised her from head to toe. 'You look quite lovely.'

'Thank you.' She'd chosen the white taffeta dress with a green sash with care, asking Beatrice, her lady's maid, to adorn her hair with emerald jewels and pearl-tipped pins. 'I wanted to look my best tonight.'

'For Mr Carter?' Her father shook his head. 'You are wasted on the man.'

'I disagree, Papa. He makes me a better person than I was before I met him.' She walked to the table and took a glass of champagne, bringing it to her lips for a fortifying sip. 'Brandy?'

'Please.' He took the glass she offered and wandered to the seats in front of the fire. 'Will you join me? I want to speak to you before our guests arrive.'

Trepidation rippled through her, but Elizabeth followed him to the fire.

Once they were seated opposite one another, her father studied her. 'I can't deny the change in you these past months, but that's not to say I wholly credit Carter with the improvements.'

'Nor would I expect you to. I think the improvements, as you put them, have been a big part of my own doing as well as Joseph's.'

'Hmm, maybe, but it's Carter I would like to speak of now.'

Elizabeth held her tongue. She could not afford to leap to Joseph's defence every time her father mentioned him. If she was to demonstrate her own will and ability, then her father needed to view Joseph as Elizabeth did. As an ally, a friend, a supporter . . . a lover. Rather than a man whose shoulders she rode upon.

Her father leaned back, sipped his brandy and held it on the chair's arm. He stared at her. 'You might not like what I'm about to say, but I intend sharing it, anyway. If Carter is to continue to work with us at the store, to come to spend more and more of his time there as his father edges towards retirement, you need to accept that Carter will always belong to me, not you.'

Elizabeth gripped her glass. 'Belong to you?'

'My staff, yourself included, are mine to do with as I will. Carter will not be any different. If, on the other hand, he was to leave the store, he would be a free man to do as he would.' His cold eyes bored into hers. 'Including pursuing you, as he seems most keen to do, and you seem most keen to encourage.'

'Is this a way of telling me that either Joseph leaves the store or leaves me?' Her anger rose. 'That he cannot have both?'

'Precisely. Business and pleasure do not mix, my dear. If you want to lower yourself to be associated with someone of Carter's status, I won't stop you. However, to fornicate under my roof will never happen.'

'Fornicate? Since when — '

'George Weir told me of your after-hours tête-à-tête with Carter at the store. What on earth was going through your head, I have no idea.'

Elizabeth glared. The night they decided to host the fashion show. Their kiss. The slamming door. So, it had been George Weir. Of course, he would have taken immense glee in sharing her and Joseph's private moment with her father.

She inhaled and slowly released her breath. 'I see. So, if Joseph wishes to court me, he loses his position at the store, despite the fact he is willing to consider closing his own business and give his loyalty to Pennington's. You hold no credit of him for that? You don't realise the sacrifice he's willing to make to be a part of our name? Our success?' She shook her head and smiled as her pride for Joseph and all he was willing to do to make their lives at the store wonderful burned deep inside her. 'Do you not see that you need me and Joseph at the store? That, together, we shine more than we ever have apart?'

'It doesn't matter to me what he does as long — '

'As you make us both as unhappy as possible.'

The door knocker reverberated through the house and Elizabeth stood.

'Perfect timing. Your commands must come to an end for now, Papa. We have guests arriving.'

Elizabeth strode to the door as Cole showed the first guests up the stairs to the drawing room.

By the time the eight men and two women who'd been invited prior to her father's impulsive invitation had been extended to include Joseph, had exchanged pleasantries, Elizabeth's cheeks ached from keeping her smile in place.

Nausea swirled with the wine in her stomach.

Usually she shone at these dinners, making easy conversation whilst learning more about what other stores and businesses around Bath were doing or planned to do. Tonight, her mind raced with little else than the fact she and Joseph were doomed. How could she be with him if it meant him not only giving up his own business, but finding himself without a position at Pennington's?

She had to give him up. She would have to surrender her personal happiness to ensure Joseph's ambitions.

She slowly exhaled in a bid to calm her insecurities, and approached their housemaid, who circled the room with a tray of filled wine glasses. Elizabeth replaced her empty glass with a new one, hating the slight tremor in her hand. 'Thank you, Molly.'

'You're welcome, miss.'

Elizabeth glanced at the wall clock. It neared ten past seven. Surely Joseph knew her nerves would be stretched to breaking?

Her father's laughter boomed across the room and Elizabeth struggled not to narrow her eyes as he shared a joke with an owner of one of the city's music halls.

She turned away and sipped her wine, forcing herself to move confidently around the room. Her self-confidence and happiness had grown so much since meeting Joseph. She needed to hold tightly to the way he made her feel for as long as possible.

And tonight, she would.

The drawing room door opened.

Joseph crossed the threshold and Elizabeth's heart stumbled.

He scanned the room, his alert blue gaze taking in each guest until at last his focus landed on her. He smiled softly, his gaze unwavering as he came towards her. Dressed in a black suit with a white wing-tipped shirt, bow tie and waistcoat, he had never looked more handsome. Her heart swelled with pride as she walked towards him. He stood a good half a foot taller than the men he passed and, one by one, they turned to look at the stranger who had entered the room.

Yet, Joseph looked only at her.

They came together, and her body instantly warmed in response to him. 'You're here.'

'I am.' His gaze wandered over her face to linger at her mouth. 'Apologies for my lateness. My father felt it necessary to voice his reservations about me coming tonight.'

Her happiness faltered even as her smile remained in place. 'He didn't want you to come?'

'No.' His gaze drifted over her neck, lower to her collarbones and lit with an undeniable hunger laced with tenderness. 'You look astounding. Truly.'

'Thank you. So do you.'

He took her hand and kissed it. When he raised his gaze to hers, the hunger was gone and instead, determination burned in his brilliant blue eyes. 'I won't let anything or anyone spoil what we are together. Do you trust me?'

Hope rose inside her and she nodded. Could he find a way for them to be together and also see through their ambitions? 'I do.'

She tried and failed to wipe her smile, tried and failed to step back from him as propriety demanded. Instead, she longed to kiss him. Everything would work out. It had to. She couldn't imagine going back to a life without Joseph being part of it.

Nor would she.

'Ah, Mr Carter. You're here at last.'

Elizabeth flinched as her father's voice resounded across the room. He strolled towards them, making everyone else turn in their direction. Her and Joseph's moment of shared intimacy shattered like a rock being thrown against glass.

311

Joseph stood back and dipped his head. 'Mr Pennington.'

Her father shifted his attention to Elizabeth and the unfathomable concern in his eyes hitched her heart. She'd expected malice, or at least, amusement. The look in her father's eyes was the opposite. He looked defeated. But why, when he'd so easily laid out his rules?

She frowned. 'Papa?'

He turned to Joseph. 'The fashion show was quite the success, Mr Carter. I have no option but to congratulate you . . . ' He looked at Elizabeth. 'Both of you.'

'Thank you, sir.'

Elizabeth stood stock-still, not trusting or believing in her father's sincerity. Had he seen something when Joseph looked at her? Could she hope that he'd witnessed their connection? Their love, and it had affected his so often hardened heart?

It would take so much more for her to hope that he began to see what an asset Joseph could be for the store . . . what an asset he could be for her.

'Elizabeth greatly admires your work, and after the success of the show, I took a closer look myself. You have talent, Carter.'

'Thank you, sir.'

Elizabeth stared agog at her father. It was as though he was metamorphosing right in front of her eyes. Was this change about Clara, Joseph's aunt? Or was it because he was humbled by Joseph's craftmanship? Whatever the cause of change in her father, Elizabeth was loath to even hope it might be about her and her achievements.

'Papa. Are you quite all right?' she asked, softly.

He stared at her, a slight flush at his cheeks. After a moment, he dropped his usually stiff shoulders and slowly smiled. 'You're concerned for me, my dear? This is quite novel.'

Her defences slipped into place. 'As is your behaviour towards Mr Carter.'

His gaze wandered over her face, his eyes giving away nothing of his thoughts. He faced Joseph. 'The show has convinced me that Elizabeth is right and you working together will be a great advantage for the store. My question to you, Mr Carter, is what of your own business? If I were to ask you to work permanently at Pennington's, would that not anger your father?'

There it was.

Elizabeth glared. 'Not here, Papa. Not now.'

'This is my home. If I choose to speak — '

'Why does it have to be this way?' She lowered her voice, her body trembling. 'Why try to provoke a scene in front of these people?'

'You are paranoid, Elizabeth. I merely wish to know how Mr — '

'What happens to Joseph's business is none of your concern. Only his and his father's. You drove Mama to take her own life through your ruthless ambition, pursuit of other women and drinking, but that's not enough for you. Still, you want to hurt more people.'

'Hurt people? What on earth — '

'Joseph scares you, is that it?' Although aware of their guests watching her, Elizabeth couldn't halt her tongue. Fear ran through her blood that somehow her father would dupe her into a false sense of security. He had to know it was Joseph she chose in that moment. Not him. 'Joseph is strong and intelligent.

313

Talented and kind. Attributes you have no understanding of, but why try to hurt him? Hurt his father?
Joseph doesn't belong to me, he's

his own man. So why — '

'Don't I?'

Elizabeth flinched, and her father stiffened as they
both stared at Joseph. Her heart picked up speed.
'Pardon?'

Joseph slowly lifted her hand to his mouth and ten-
derly kissed her knuckles, his gaze boring into hers
with staunch determination. 'I want to belong to you,
Elizabeth, but that can only happen if we keep the past
far away and start from now.' Still grasping her hand,
he turned to her father. 'We will leave, sir. Whether
or not I decide to work at Pennington's, I will not be
your puppet and nor will Elizabeth. We're striving to
make our own mark on the store. On each other. I
will look after her, sir. Of that, you can be certain.'

Elizabeth's heart beat faster as her father's glare
slowly softened with — dare she think it? — respect.
He pulled back his shoulders, his gaze on Joseph's. 'If
my daughter returns your feelings, Carter, you'll have
to convince her you are entirely hers and to hell with
what I, or society, might think. Is that something you
think yourself capable?'

Stepping away, Elizabeth pulled on Joseph's hand.
'He's capable of that and more.' She looked at Joseph.
'Let's go.'

'You and Mr Carter do not have my permission to
leave, Elizabeth.'

'We can do whatever we wish. I'm a grown woman.
It's just a shame it has taken finding Joseph for me to
understand that. Goodnight, Papa.'

Joseph dipped his head. 'I thank you for your invite

314

this evening, sir. Maybe we can get better acquainted another time.'

Her father narrowed his eyes. 'Oh, you can depend on it.'

With her father's glare burning into her back, Elizabeth walked hand in hand with Joseph through the crowd of gawping guests. As they walked from the house, pride swelled inside her. From this night forward, whatever happened, she was changed. Undoubtedly forever.

34

Joseph gripped Elizabeth's hand tighter as they quickly walked away from her home and along the street. People parted around them as though they knew of their new, unbreakable bond. The stars shone brighter, the street lamps and lit shop windows showering them with light. His heart was full of Elizabeth and nothing else.

She faced him, her eyes glittering with a mischief he hadn't seen before. 'Where shall we go? I feel so liberated. So free. We have to do something. Something reckless.'

He laughed. 'Reckless?'

'I want to keep this feeling inside me forever. We can't waste what we just did, Joseph. My father will know I am changed. He'll know nothing he can do will return me to the insecure, cautious and lonely daughter I was before I met you.'

Joseph roamed his gaze over her beautiful face and pulled her closer as the previous guilt for falling in love a second time slowly and entirely dissolved. Lillian would want him happy. Elizabeth embodied that happiness and he couldn't let her go. Not anymore. 'And I will never again be the man I was before I met you.'

He lowered his mouth to hers and poured all his love and admiration for her into his kiss. She grasped his biceps and deepened their kiss, her soft moans sending lust shuddering through his loins. He pulled her closer as though he might be deep inside her.

She sighed against his mouth before easing back. The fire in her eyes shot flames of need through him, her softly swollen lips urging him forwards again. He brushed his mouth across hers. 'You're so beautiful.'

'So are you.' She stared into his eyes. 'I want you, Joseph.'

Her meaning could not be misinterpreted, but he had to be certain. 'You want me?'

'Yes. I want you to make love to me. I want you to show me what it is to fully trust a man, have him touch me . . . love me. Even if just for tonight.'

His heart pounded, and he pulled her into his arms once more. 'It will never be for just one night. Never.' His kiss was fiercer than intended, but the yearning inside him was hot and dangerous. To have her beneath him and sighing with her pleasure was all he wanted. All he needed. He gripped her hand. 'We will go to my house. My father is away tonight.'

A flicker of hesitation flashed in her eyes before she nodded. 'Yes.'

'You are certain you want me?' Joseph softly caressed her cheek.

'With all my heart.'

They hurried through the streets until they were at his door leading to the living quarters above Carter & Son. He pushed the key into the lock and led her upstairs. She brushed past him into the living room. With her in his home, Joseph didn't want to imagine going back to a life without her being a part of it. He would do everything he could do ensure they were happy and bound together for the rest of their lives.

He walked to the drinks cabinet. 'Sherry?'

'Perfect.'

He poured their drinks, surreptitiously watching

her as she slowly walked the room. She studied the bookcases, gliding her hand over the back of the settee as she strolled to the fireplace. She briefly stared at the foliage on the hearth before turning.

Joseph hastily looked back to the drinks, finished pouring and picked up their glasses. 'Here.'

'Thank you.' She took the glass. 'Your home is lovely. It's you. The real you. Full of warmth and masculinity. Practical, but welcoming. Strong, yet . . . I'm not certain.' She smiled softly, taking a gentle sip of her drink 'It's just perfect.'

Joseph took a mouthful of brandy, impatience to hold her gripping him. He could wait no longer. Easing her glass from her hand, he put it on a side table with his own and faced her. Her eyes darkened with the desire that he didn't doubt was reflected in his own.

Taking her hand, he led her along the short corridor to his bedroom.

Nerves rippled through him and he gripped her fingers tighter. It had been so very long since he'd made love to a woman and yet he knew, with absolute conviction, that making love with Elizabeth would be the most natural, erotic union he'd experienced in years.

They stopped by his open bedroom door and Joseph cupped her jaw in his hands. 'If you don't want this — '

'I do.' She gripped his fingers. 'So much.'

He kissed her, his teeth gently grazing her bottom lip as they entered the room. Once inside, Joseph opened his eyes and she eased from his embrace. He had expected her to examine his bedroom as she had the living room, but her eyes remained on his as she stepped away and reached for the buttons at the front of her dress.

Joseph's heart pounded, his blood roaring with impatience and a deep, burning need to hold her, touch her . . .

Her dress crumpled to the floor and, with her gaze on his, she reached behind her to detach her bustle and corset. He pulled off his jacket and tossed it onto a nearby chair.

She stepped forward in her chemise, her breasts creamy-white beneath the thin material, her nipples dark.

His erection pulsed against the confines of his formal trousers and he snapped open the buttons. Pulling off his shirt, arousal trembled through him as her interest slipped to his chest, her eyes slightly widening as the tip of her tongue delicately wet her bottom lip. Toeing off his boots, Joseph discarded his socks and trousers and walked forwards.

Colour rushed into her cheeks as she stared at his erection.

Joseph, halted. 'Elizabeth, if you —'

She fell into his arms, her mouth urgently crushing his. Their tongues tangled as she scored her nails over his shoulders and into the hair at the nape of his neck. Blindly, he plucked at the pins in her hair, loosening the rich red strands until they fell almost to her waist. He screwed the thick, luscious tresses into his hands, revelling in their soft, heavy weight.

They parted, and she softly smiled, the heat in her eyes mesmerising. She took his hand and led him to the bed before releasing his fingers and pulling the chemise over her head.

Joseph's breath caught. He'd imagined her. Fantasised and thought of how she would look without clothes or adornment, but nothing could've prepared him for the sight of her naked perfection, but for the rubies and diamonds about her neck and ears.

She lay down on the bed, her hand raised to him. Joseph slid his fingers between hers and lay down beside her. He kissed each of her fingers, before trailing his hand over the smooth skin of her thigh and hip, the gentle curve of her waist. He brushed his thumb over the hard peak of her nipple and she sighed, relaxing into the mattress, her eyes drifting closed.

His hand trembled against her skin. She possessed a beauty he couldn't name; a powerful, eroticism that shot deep into his heart and loins. He gently kissed her and slipped his fingers between her thighs.

Her grip on his shoulder tightened as he rubbed her, one finger gently teasing her entrance. She exhaled against his lips, her fingers relaxing as she kissed him harder. Joseph eased a finger inside and her mouth dropped away from his, her eyes wide.

He smiled. 'Trust me.'

She nodded.

He kissed her jaw and neck, lower to her shoulder as he massaged her until she grew moist with wanting. Her gasps mixed with moans and Joseph pushed another finger gently inside. She was hot and tight, and his balls ached with need. His cock hard.

'Joseph, closer. I want you closer.' She moved slightly away from him, opening her legs. 'Please. Lie on me.'

He moved over her body, before taking her nipple in his mouth, sucking and teasing. She gripped her hands to his face and he lifted his eyes to hers.

'Now, Joseph. I want you.'

Her whispered words gave him all the belief he

needed that she wanted this, wanted to lay with him in the darkness and have him love her.

Slowly, inch by inch, he eased inside her. Her eyes were wide on his as he ensured her comfort and enjoyment. Her mouth dropped open and he pushed fully inside, a moment of resistance and then she was his, and he was hers.

She put her hands to his waist, lower to press at his buttocks, easing him deeper. Joseph thrust a little harder and then slowed again, waiting for her. Always, he would wait for her.

Over and over, they moved together as her confidence grew and she joined him in the slow, yet urgent pursuit of their pleasure.

Softly she groaned, her teeth biting into her bottom lip, her green gaze burning with the thrill of discovery and the power of uninhibited lust. And then, without warning, her tightening came.

She closed her eyes, her teeth gritted, and Joseph thrust again and again, her eyes snapping open as she convulsed around him, her brow furrowed and her expression still in pleasure.

Joseph pushed again and again and tipped all the way over. The waves of pleasure ripped through his body and he groaned aloud. 'You, Elizabeth.

Always, you.'

35

Elizabeth closed her office door behind her father and the euphoria of the last week spent working with Joseph, of being in his arms and exchanging stolen kisses vanished. Her tread was heavy on the plush cream carpet as she walked to her desk and sat, her hands trembling against the desktop.

Whether her father despised the deepening of hers and Joseph's relationship, or her barely contained happiness had been too much for him to witness, he had again reminded her that anything personal between her and Joseph would lead to his dismissal from the store.

Tears burned behind her eyes.

Ever since she and Joseph had made love, the risk that she could be with child terrified her. If she fell pregnant, what then? She would be ruined in society's eyes and abhorrent in her father's. And what of Joseph's reaction? He'd said he didn't believe he deserved a family. Would he cast her aside as her father had Clara Carter? Turn his back on her and declare the child not his?

She couldn't imagine Joseph ever being so cruel, but how well did she really know him?

The glint in her father's eyes and the challenge in his words meant that he would enjoy watching hers and Joseph's fledging relationship fail.

She picked up a pen and gripped it tightly.

It wasn't herself or Joseph she doubted. Her confidence in them both was strong. The weakness came from knowing she would never be able to fully trust her father. Too much hurt had been inflicted at his hands. Too many years of emotional abuse to her mother. Too much verbal condemnation and disparagement to his daughter.

This time, she was certain, it wouldn't be her who suffered from her father's malice, but Joseph.

She could not allow her father or anyone else to hurt the one man she had ever loved. Joseph had already suffered far too much at her family's doing.

Abruptly standing, she dropped the pen and marched to the door. She had to speak to him. Had to discuss with him the dread filling her that her father could eject Joseph from Pennington's and there would be little she could do to stop him. As much as Joseph was likely to tell her they could continue to see one another regardless of where he worked, she could not bear the thought of him giving up his dreams and seeing his products grace Pennington's windows.

Their work together had to take precedence over their love. Surely, after everything he had done and sacrificed to get to this stage in his life, he would understand they could not pursue a love affair whilst her father remained at the store.

Yanking open her office door, she strode into the ladies' department looking for Mrs Woolden to send a message to Joseph in the workroom.

She halted.

Joseph stood at the counter with Esther. Their heads bent close together over a large sketch sheet. Elizabeth's heart swelled with love for the man she'd found and was now forced to give up. Was she being weak by giving him up so easily? Her heart ached with the depth of her love for him, but she could not risk her father finding a way to destroy him. Whatever their separation, Joseph had changed her in so many fantastically beautiful ways, he would forever remain in her heart.

She cleared her throat and lifted her chin. 'Mr Carter? Might I speak with you alone for a moment?'

Both Joseph and Esther straightened and turned.

The moment Joseph's eyes met hers, Elizabeth's body betrayed her. Heat immediately whispered over her skin, as every memory of his touch and kisses flooded her senses. It was as though she had no control over her care for him, no control over her body's need of him. The fact she had gone years without a man's touch and now she'd found a man whose touch she wanted forever was so very cruel.

He said something quietly to Esther before stepping towards Elizabeth. She flicked her gaze to Esther who immediately smiled and crossed her arms, her eyes glinting with knowing.

Elizabeth abruptly turned, ashamed that her wanton desires were so clearly etched on her face. Joseph's steady footsteps sounded behind her as he followed her to the back of the department and her open office door.

The minute he closed the door, Elizabeth turned, clasping her hands tightly in front of her, lest she reach for him. 'We need to talk.'

His eyes were soft as he came closer. 'Talk? I don't need to talk to you. What I need —'

'Joseph.' She struck her palm in front of her. 'No.'

He halted, his smile dissolving, his outstretched hand dropping to his side. 'What is it? What's happened?'

She briefly closed her eyes and forced her rapidly

beating heart to calm. She had no idea how to tell him they could no longer be together. Even a clandestine affair would be discovered, considering the number of people and associates her father was acquainted with throughout the city.

If Joseph loved her as she did him, his heart would undoubtedly be as broken as hers within the next few minutes.

She sat in her chair and leaned her forearms on top of the desk, her fingers laced tightly together. She stared into his deep blue eyes, her heart aching with loss. 'Please. Will you sit?'

He walked to one of the visitors' chairs in front of her desk and sat, his gaze intently studying her and his strong jaw tight.

'My father has given me an ultimatum.'

'Which is?'

'You either remain at the store or you continue your personal relationship with me. He won't allow both.'

'He won't *allow* both?' He shook his head. 'Who does the bast — then I will leave. I'm not giving you up, Elizabeth. I won't.'

'And what if it comes that I am with child?' Her voice cracked. 'Would you find it easier to give me up then?'

'What?'

'I could be pregnant, Joseph. What then?'

'Then I'll be right beside you. Elizabeth . . . ' He smiled. 'I love you.'

Every instinct in her body screamed to touch him, but she resisted, not wanting to make their romantic separation any harder. 'You don't understand. If my father — '

'How does he think he can stop us from seeing

325

one another? Loving each other?' He glared. 'Do you think so little of me that I'm incapable of protecting myself? Protecting you?'

'My father will enjoy watching us become closer and, when he's ready, he'll do all he can to destroy that love. Destroy you. He won't care what it will do to me to have you go through that. He has history with your family, Joseph.' She stood and came around the desk. Leaning her bottom against it, she curved her fingers around the wood. 'He is ashamed of his treatment of your aunt but, instead of living with that shame, he chooses instead to prove you unworthy in some way. Try to show me that he was right to cast your aunt aside. You didn't see the malicious gleam in his eyes and the amusement on his lips when he spoke with me. He'll not stop until he has sullied our care for one another.'

'Fine. Then I'll leave. Today, if I have to.'

'Joseph, no. You don't want that and neither do I.'

'If my working here is what prevents us from being together, I'll seek work elsewhere.'

'You have to stay here. You have to let Pennington's provide the means to have the life, the success and enable you to do all the things you want to do for Lillian. Isn't that what you wanted from the start?'

'Yes, but now everything's changed.' He stood and took her hands, looked deep into her eyes. 'I love you. That's more important to me than anything.'

Tears burned, and she quickly blinked them away. 'You don't understand.'

'No, Elizabeth, I don't.' His voice was measured, his tone clipped. 'Why would you have me stay here, if in doing so, we have no personal relationship? I thought you loved me, too.'

'I do, but — '

'But nothing. I'll go.'

'If we end our personal relationship, my father's spiteful interest in you will disappear and leave only the profit you can make him. Joseph, please. My father could make you the star of Pennington's. You've barely scratched the surface of what you might do here. You're too important to me to let you walk away from what I'm certain is your destiny.'

He stared at her before abruptly dropping her hands. Pushing his hand into his hair, he gripped the dark strands. His eyes blazed with determination. 'You're right. I shouldn't leave. Not by his doing. But if I stay, I still want you, Elizabeth. Sooner or later, we'll be together. I am neither a coward nor a quitter. Your father can throw whatever he likes at me and I'll withstand it. What I can't withstand is losing you.'

Tears welled in her eyes and her heart splintered. She pushed away from the desk, desperate that he listened to her, that her father didn't come to cause him more pain than he already had. 'I'm sacrificing us so you can soar. Because of my love for you. Nothing else. My father is taking a month-long tour of Europe so, for a while at least, we can continue with your plans for the new collection, but once he returns — '

'He's going away for a whole month?' The anger seeped from his gaze and, instead, lit with triumph. 'Then we have four weeks to be together, to make love and plans.'

'Joseph, we can't. My heart won't bear it.' Sorrow pressed down on her. 'I wish there was another way, but to try to outmanoeuvre my father is futile. Lord knows, I've tried enough times before.'

She dropped her gaze to his mouth, yearning to kiss

him and have him take her in his arms. She could not. Would not.

'Then we'll worry about us later. When he returns. But for now, we cannot waste your ideas when such a fantastic opportunity to bring them to reality shows itself. Just as you don't wish for me to sacrifice my hard work, I don't want you to, either. Your father will be gone an entire month. We have to show him what you are capable of. You still have plans for the toy department as well as the ladies' and men's departments, do you not?'

'Yes, but — '

'Then why not take this time to concentrate on the toy department and allow me to ensure all is ready for the new collections?'

The excitement in his eyes swept over her on an irresistible wave. The way he looked at her, the way he spoke, filled her with a sense that she could do anything — be anyone. Not being with him would most likely hurt forever, but what he had done for her with his belief, respect and admiration would never fade from her heart.

He slipped his hands to her waist. 'We can take this time to see through a complete overhaul of the toy, ladies and men's departments with a view to extending the new look throughout the store when possible.'

She laughed. 'That will surely take longer than a month? You can't expect me just to announce an overhaul to the heads of the departments and have them agree to it.'

'Why not? Would they really question that you are not in charge when your father's away? Does he leave such a thing on paper?'

'Of course not, but — '

'You can do this, Elizabeth. You've been working on some quick and achievable changes that will make all the difference in bringing Pennington's into the new decade and onto the next. People will be astounded and excited.'

Despite her reservations, her stomach knotted with anticipation. She stared into his eyes, allowing the beauty and determination of his gaze to break through her sadness. She lifted her hands in surrender. 'And your new designs, the colours, the fabrics . . . could we do this? Really?'

'Yes.' He pressed a firm kiss to her lips. 'We can.'

He walked to the door, whistling as he opened it before disappearing into the department. Elizabeth stared after him, her smile faltering and her resentment towards her father growing. Whatever he'd said to Joseph's aunt had led to her feeling she had no other option but to end her life and that of her unborn child. Her mother, too had died because of his mistreatment. Any hope Elizabeth held that she and her father might one day reconcile had been utterly destroyed by that knowledge.

She would forever be on her guard with him.

Elizabeth glared ahead, hurt and resentment burning dangerously inside her.

If her father thought her hot-headed before, he had no idea what she was capable of now he'd done his best to strip her of a happiness — of a love and passion — like she'd never known or even dared to dream of.

He would not succeed.

36

Two weeks after the show, Edward Pennington was still away and the workroom was inundated with orders. Joseph and Elizabeth had worked tirelessly, along with the staff, to implement their ideas and changes, and time continued to pass quickly. Joseph looked at his watch, worried he might have to postpone this afternoon's scheduled meeting with Elizabeth. He swiped the perspiration from his brow with the back of his hand. Despite his satisfaction that the show was a resounding success, as the hours passed with his and his colleagues' fingers at the needles and scissors, the time ticked steadily away from getting Elizabeth's and his ideas for the store's overhaul fully into place.

He leaned back in his chair and stretched the kinks from his neck and shoulders. Having wanted to help with the workload, he'd taken his hands to the needle. Carter & Son had withdrawn the gloves from their shop and now only his father's remaining hats were left to be sold before they closed the shop's doors forever.

As much as Elizabeth feared he would lose his position at Pennington's now that Carter & Son planned to close, Joseph did not share her fears. He would find a way for them to be together and maintain his position at the store. Whether Edward Pennington could see it or not, Joseph had become important to the man's profit. For everything else, Pennington embodied, he was a businessman, first and foremost.

Joseph had to believe Elizabeth's father would come

to see firing Joseph would be a foolish and entirely emotionally-driven decision.

He glanced around the workroom. While he and his colleagues laboured on the show orders, Esther and her team worked on the decorations and new staff uniforms needed for the overhaul. With commission agreed for the production staff as well as paid over-time, the difference the extra money made to their lives was visible in everyone's attitude and output.

Momentary satisfaction unfurled inside him as the men at another table shared a joke, hands slapping hands and their grins infectious. It was a scene that would've been unimaginable a few months ago. The pressure on them had unequivocally increased, yet the morale in the room was at an all-time high.

He looked to Albert, whose head was bent over a pair of gloves, his brow furrowed in concentration. 'How are you doing, my friend?'

Albert looked up, his eyes rimmed red with exhaus-tion, but his smile wide. 'Not too bad. Tired, but happy. This speed of production will take some get-ting used to, but if Pennington's makes more money, they'll employ more people to get the job done.' Albert dabbed his face with a scrap of cloth. 'That can only be a good thing for us and our fellow man, right?'

Joseph nodded, hopeful he'd made at least a small step towards his goal of helping others. 'Right.'

God, he loved being at the store — he loved Eliz-abeth — he just prayed to God, she held onto what they had with the same conviction he would. They had to fight her father. They had to protect what they had above everything. He refused to believe her insistence they separate was what she truly felt in her heart.

Glancing at the wall clock, he pushed to his feet.

'Right, I'm off for a meeting with Miss Pennington. I'll see you later.'

He drew his sketchbook and some papers from beneath the table and strode from the room. The ladies' department buzzed with activity. If he was forced to leave Pennington's in order to be with Elizabeth, at least the changes he'd made here would leave an indelible mark. She would have that to remember him by, if nothing else.

'Mr Carter?'

He started and turned. 'Mrs Woolden. How are you?'

'Very well. I understand you have a meeting with Miss Pennington. If you'd like to follow me.'

He followed her to Elizabeth's closed office door and waited as Mrs Woolden knocked and poked her head around the doorway. 'Mr Carter for you, Elizabeth.'

'Lovely. Please show him in.'

Mrs Woolden flashed him a warm smile, her brown eyes kind. 'In you go.'

'Thank you.'

As he walked by her, she touched his arm and lowered her voice. 'I really hope you're thinking of renewing your contract with us when the time comes. You're needed here.' She tilted her head in Elizabeth's direction. 'By some more than others.'

Rare heat hit his cheeks when the older woman winked and ushered him inside the office, softly closing the door behind him. Despite his and Elizabeth's best efforts, at least one other person within Pennington's walls suspected their romance. Instead of the possibility worrying Joseph, it pleased him. After all, he'd have given a thousand guineas to be able to shout it from the rooftops.

Elizabeth was sat on the settee in the corner of her office, her gaze happy as she looked at him. 'Come and sit with me.'

He walked forward and fought the need to take her in his arms and, instead, sat beside her and slid his papers onto the low table in front of them.

She immediately picked up a sketch sheet from the table. 'Your colour choices for the overhaul are wonderful, Joseph. They represent style, optimism and hope. Swaths of gold and white, red and green. Everything will look stunning. If we combine these colours with new uniforms, using my idea of seasonal changes throughout the store, everything in Pennington's will look more luxurious, more aesthetically pleasing than ever before.'

Every part of him longed to hold her hand or stare into her eyes, but he refrained. Considering her assertion their romantic involvement had to end, any intimacy would only be more hurtful.

'But still I want more.' Her eyes glittered with excitement as she leaned over the arm of the settee and pulled up a sheaf of notes from the floor. 'Ever since the store opened, I've wanted to make Pennington's a legitimate place for women to feel liberated. To shop and enjoy each other's company without feeling improper or having to worry about gaining their father's or husband's approval. So, I think we should expand our services as well as the décor.' She passed him her notes. 'I've devised a way to make it perfectly acceptable for men to visit the ladies' department and vice versa.'

He raised his eyebrows. 'I'm not sure the good ladies and gents of Bath are quite ready for that.'

'How will we know unless we try? My ideas are simple. We expand our services to include repairs. Whether that be buttons being sewn back on, beads being restrung, or gloves being cleaned. We think of all the errands ladies send their maids out to do and give them a valid reason for doing them themselves. To be seen in Pennington's using our services will not be something to be frowned upon. Rather, it will be seen as the lady of the house relying on herself to get jobs done. How could having the mistresses stepping out to do some of the household chores possibly be viewed as anything but good?'

'And by visiting the store under the guise of house-wifely duties, they'd also have the opportunity to shop.'

'Exactly, and we promote the idea of ladies doing more for themselves through the window displays. Esther has already thought of some truly fantastic designs.'

'And what reason would men have to visit the ladies' department?'

'Gifts. We promote perfume, lingerie and jewellery. We make buying for their ladies a positive thing, a *fashionable* thing. Birthdays, anniversaries, Valentine's day. We could display the goods and clothes in seasons so there is a reason for a husband or lover to treat the woman in his life all year round. The same will apply to the toy department and their children.'

Joseph smiled. 'I like it. I like it a lot.'

'We'll give a firm message that women no longer need to be afraid to reach out and grab a slice of liberty.'

He put her notes on top of his on the table and, surrendering, Joseph looked into her eyes. 'And what about *your* liberty?'

She dropped her gaze to his mouth, her cheeks faintly colouring, before she abruptly stood. 'It's here. You brought it to me even if we can't share it. I'll not stand in my father's shadow any longer. I'm stronger and more capable than I've ever been before. I want *us* to make these changes and by the time my father returns, he'll be forced to realise how good a team we are. Your future at Pennington's will be secure and you can go on to do all you want to do.'

Joseph exhaled a heavy breath. 'All I want to do? Now there's a dream.'

'Isn't Pennington's the dream?' Elizabeth frowned. 'Working here and making a success of your gloves, and more, is what you want, isn't it?'

'Yes. That and my promise to Lillian. My plan was to give people who are struggling employment. I want to make enough money to continue Lillian's charity towards the desperate families by the river. I won't be happy until I've achieved that and Lillian's legacy lives on.'

Tears glistened in her eyes as she squeezed his hand. 'You're a wonderful man, Joseph. You'll make everything Lillian stood for continue.

We will. I promise.'

His heart swelled with love for her and, not caring about the consequences, Joseph reached for her.

She shot out her hand, halting him. 'No. I might be strong, but I'm not strong enough for you to touch me.'

'I think you're as strong as you need to be.'

'Joseph . . . '

The worry in her eyes settled his heart and mind and he eased back, raising his hands in surrender. 'I'll behave, but I want to be with you, Elizabeth. I think I always will.'

'Joseph . . .'

The pain in her eyes squeezed hard at his heart, but he had to endure, had to have her know what she meant to him. 'I'll wait however long I have to for you to come to me.'

'Until I've fully broken the chains my father has around me, we can't be together. Please, tell me you understand that.'

'I don't, but your tenacity only makes me love you more.' He dropped his hands. 'I'll wait.' He inhaled a shaky breath and released it. 'However long it takes.'

37

As Joseph looked around Pennington's ground floor, his pride rose. It had taken another two weeks of hard work, but the entrance foyer and the men's and ladies' departments looked as spectacular as he and Elizabeth had envisioned. Mirrors glistened, lights sparkled, and merchandise shone. It was a wonderland what he, Elizabeth, the upper management and almost every member of the staff had worked to achieve.

He took a deep breath. Of course, the risk remained that Edward Pennington would lose his mind when he saw the gargantuan changes — possibly firing Joseph *and* Elizabeth.

A risk they were both prepared to take.

The last month had tested every last ounce of Joseph's self-control. The strain of working with Elizabeth, while maintaining a distance, both emotionally and physically, had been close to unbearable. There had been a time when he'd endeavoured to put his professional life above all else. Now, he struggled to think past anything but Elizabeth and how much he wanted — needed — to be with her.

God only knew how much longer his restraint would last before he stepped over the mark and told her he was leaving. Leaving Pennington's so he could be with her.

Pulling his grandfather's watch from his pocket, Joseph glanced at the time. Fifteen minutes until they threw open the doors and allowed the steadily growing queue waiting outside in the warm June sunshine to enter. The three window displays, so fantastically and controversially designed by Esther Stanbury, had been revealed to the public a week before. The underlying nod to women's liberation and their new and deserved chance in the workplace, as well as the subtle suggestion that household shopping was the most fashionable pastime for women to be seen doing, had provoked chatter and whispering throughout the store for days.

Heels clicked against the marbled floor and Joseph turned, his heart giving a sharp kick.

Dressed in a beautifully cut, ivory skirt and jacket, with fine gold thread weaved in pinstripes through the fabric, Elizabeth looked astounding as she led Pennington's staff towards him. Her red hair shone beneath the overhead chandeliers, her pretty face lit with pride. Regret clawed through him that she wasn't his to hold, kiss and touch, but he'd never give up hope of their reunion.

She stopped in front of him and smiled. 'Mr Carter? May I present Pennington's staff.'

The young men and women came forward and lined up in a row.

Joseph smiled. Each member of staff, all bar George Weir who seemed intent on believing Edward Pennington's way of doing things was eternally the right way, smiled at him, their eyes bright with anticipation for what would surely be a momentous day. The atmosphere amongst the workers while Elizabeth had been in charge had improved so much, in the shop girls especially, as they adopted a more relaxed way of working and walking about the store.

It was clear a heavy and threatening cloud had dispersed with Edward Pennington's absence.

The new security men who would wander the store wore dark green suits with gold braided epaulettes and matching buttons. The shop girls long, pale yellow skirts were cinched tight at the waist and complemented with simply embroidered, white blouses. Their hair was swept up and decorated with a single butter-yellow feather. The staff of the men's department looked approachable and fashionable in the latest cut of suit, taupe in colour, with a pristine white shirt beneath and matching taupe tie. This was Pennington's summer uniform. Come Autumn, it would change again and so forth with each season.

The new, fashionably updated uniforms had been produced in store by a small, dedicated team in the workroom and they'd truly outdone themselves. The modern cut and style propelled Pennington's forward as the height of fashion. More informal than the previous uniforms, they made the staff look less intimidating and far more approachable. No matter the customers' class or status.

The sight of them was arresting, but none as arresting as Elizabeth, who beamed at her staff, satisfaction alight in her beautiful eyes and lightly flushed cheeks.

'Ladies and gentlemen.' She opened her arms. 'I've never been so proud of you as I have these last few, hectic weeks. Opening day has arrived and I expect the store will be fit to bursting from the moment we open the doors. Remember, I have invited several members of the press and their photographers to walk freely around the store taking pictures and talking to you and the customers. Robert Sharp is one such reporter and, as you most likely know, he does not refrain with his opinions. Let's ensure they're glowing. Are we all ready?'

Applause erupted, arms waved, and faces lit with smiles.

She laughed and faced Joseph. 'Ready?'

He stared at her beauty, his heart swelling and his libido stirring. Never before had he felt such pride. When he had started work here, he would never have imagined Elizabeth displaying such authority. Her lifted chin and shining eyes were a testament to her strength and ambition.

God, he wanted her so badly. 'Absolutely.'

Her gaze lingered on his, darkening with hunger and understanding. She quickly looked to Mrs Woolden who stood at the head of the staff line. 'It's approaching nine. If you would stand by the doors, Mrs Woolden?' She faced Joseph. 'Would you use your considerable charm to entice the lady shoppers to the second floor?'

He smiled. 'Consider it done.'

Her gaze lingered on his again, before she turned to her staff. 'Into position, everyone, and good luck.'

A low hum of excited chatter, clicking heels and camaraderie filled the mammoth foyer as the staff dispersed to their various stations. Joseph winked at Elizabeth and when she mouthed, 'I love you,' his heart soared.

Her eyes widened before she abruptly turned, her expression all-business again as though she'd momentarily forgotten herself.

Inwardly smiling, Joseph forced his gaze away from the woman he swore he would love until the end of time, and turned to welcome the deluge of men and women who swarmed through the store's open doors. Exclamations and gasps filled the foyer, women and men hurrying and shouldering their way deeper

340

inside. Joseph barely contained his laughter to see the sea of faces displaying such unabashed curiosity.

He strode forward. 'Ladies, the transformation continues in the ladies' department on the second floor. The new clothing and accessories collections can be found on display for your viewing and exploration. Feel free to ask the shop girls if you wish to try on any piece from our new ready-to-wear collection, personally designed by myself. Alternatively, indulge in our bespoke clothing, which can be made to order. Enjoy.'

As the crowds continued to come, Joseph sneaked peeks around the vast space, keeping an uncontrollable watch on Elizabeth. She shone like a beacon amongst the shoppers. Her face, a delight of smiles and shining eyes. God, how he ached to love her, to hold her in his arms.

Would Edward Pennington's far-reaching shadow forever darken Elizabeth's desires? Joseph's father had warned him Edward Pennington would show his hand upon his return from Europe, which could be any day now. Yet, Joseph's fear of Elizabeth's father was non-existent, and now she'd mouthed she loved him, he had to take action.

Upon Pennington's return, Joseph would speak with him. Make him understand his and Elizabeth's feelings for one another were never likely to diminish. After all, what could one man really do?

38

Elizabeth held her office door open as the handsome journalist, Robert Sharp, whose stellar wit and astute reporting was synonymous with his name, left her office. 'I trust you have enjoyed your day at Pennington's?'

'I have, Miss Pennington. Very much so.' He donned his hat and offered his hand. 'My feelings and findings will be duly printed in tomorrow's *Post*.'

'I very much look forward to reading it. Have a lovely evening.'

'Same to you. Goodbye.'

Elizabeth stared after him as Robert walked to the lift where Henry stood waiting. She nodded at Henry, inhaled a deep breath and turned back into her office.

Walking to her office window, she stared at the darkening street below. The day had been an enormous success, which meant the foreboding tip-tapping up her spine could only be caused by the trepidation of what would be printed about Pennington's in tomorrow's newspapers.

Her father was still away in Europe, the cash desk and order books had thrived all day. She studied the slowly quietening city below. It was a night to celebrate and there was only one man with whom she wanted to share their triumph.

No matter how hard she tried to harden her heart to Joseph and all that he meant to her, she could not resist sharing her jubilation with him. Which was why they had to make it that they continued to work

342

together. Their success today had been testament to what they could achieve professionally, if not personally.

But, in a single moment of absolute insanity, she'd mouthed that she loved him.

She briefly closed her eyes and wrapped her arms tightly around her as though erecting a protective barrier around her pathetic heart. Just for tonight she would sit with him in a darkened corner in the Cavendish club and pretend she was free to be with him. To look into his eyes and share a drink like so many other lovers were liberated to do.

As long as she didn't touch him, everything would be perfectly fine.

Taking a strengthening breath, Elizabeth walked through the ladies' department, flicking off the remaining lights and emerging into the marbled corridor. She lightly ran her hand over the grand staircase banister as she slowly descended. The passion between her and Joseph still simmered dangerously inside her, their kisses and lovemaking neither forgotten nor exhausted, despite her trying so hard to draw a line through their relationship for Joseph's sake.

Even the fear of pregnancy and the ruin of her reputation mattered less and less the longer she was intimately separated from him. He loved her. If she learned she was with child and told him, she had no doubt he'd move heaven and earth to be with her. Maybe even elope with her if that was what it took for them to marry.

She feared she'd never tire of wanting his lips upon hers. His firm, muscled body against her, making love to her until she burst with sensations that had been unknown to her just a few weeks before.

Annoyed with her stubborn and pitiful yearnings, Elizabeth shook her head and lifted her chin. She had to be stronger than this. Joseph would expect no less of her.

She descended past each floor, the store slipping into further darkness as each department head checked their department and closed for the evening. Elizabeth swept her gaze over the counters and displays, fighting the trepidation of her father's eventual reaction. Deep in her heart, she believed he would submit and tell her of a job well done. How could he not when he'd further extended her responsibilities, the day had gone so magnificently, and the chatter had been so rife?

Tomorrow would prove equally as profitable. As would the day after that and so on.

It neared seven and disappointment threatened as Joseph's handsome face still remained undiscovered to her. Surely, he hadn't left without speaking with her? His expression had been a picture of delight the entire day as walked among the men and women customers. He had to be equally as thrilled by their success as her.

She spotted Mrs Woolden talking with the head of Haberdashery and wandered closer, purposefully arranging her expression into one of happiness rather than the sadness curling around her heart. 'Aveline? Might I have a word?'

The older woman turned. 'Of course.' She looked back to the Haberdashery head. 'We'll see about those changes in the morning. Have a good evening.' Aveline faced Elizabeth and smiled. 'So, how are you feeling?'

'Amazing. Astounding. Every positive way possible.'

Elizabeth forced a smile, cursing the heaviness in her chest. 'Wasn't today fantastic?'

'It was.'

Elizabeth looked around the large space hoping to see a flash of dark hair, a pair of startling blue eyes . . .

'He's gone, Miss Pennington.'

Elizabeth snapped her gaze to Aveline. 'Pardon?'

'I'm sorry, but Mr Carter left over an hour ago. Many of the staff have gone for drinks or something to eat together, but Joseph left alone.'

Hurt slashed through her body as Elizabeth struggled to maintain a nonchalant expression. Joseph had gone home early? On today, of all days?

Elizabeth swallowed and waved her hand dismissively. 'It's of no matter. I'll speak with him in the morning.'

'We could go out for a drink or something to eat if you like.' Aveline's gaze softened. 'I've no plans.'

Guilt pressed down on Elizabeth. Normally, she'd love to share a quiet drink or two with Aveline, but tonight she could think only of Joseph. 'No, it would be better for me to go home. I'm expecting my father to return any day now. It would be sensible for me to make sure everything is ready. After all, none of us have any idea how he'll react once he sees the changes to the store. I suspect I'll need every ounce of energy to face him.'

Aveline looked to the floor, her cheeks colouring.

Elizabeth frowned. 'Aveline?'

She lifted her gaze. 'Your father's already back.'

Shock rippled through Elizabeth, her heart quickening. 'When? Did he come into the store?' Her hand turned clammy around her purse. 'But I would've seen him.'

'I don't think he did. I overheard George Weir saying to a member of staff that news of your changes reached Mr Pennington as soon as he entered Bath and he chose to — '

'Stay away.' Elizabeth shock gave way to anger. 'He's biding his time. Looking for the best way to humiliate me. Disparage the changes. Damn him.'

She darted her gaze around the darkened atrium, its absent glitter and glamour reflecting the returning shadows that lingered over her.

Fury burned behind her chest and Elizabeth blinked. 'Are you happy to ensure everyone has gone and lock up for the night?'

Concern shadowed her deputy's eyes. 'Of course, but — '

'Excellent. Goodnight.'

Elizabeth struggled to walk rather than run. Trembling under the weight of her trepidation, she headed towards the back entrance of the store as images of Joseph flitted in her mind. Where on earth was he?

But what did she expect? She'd cut their relationship short. What did it matter that his caresses and kisses still burned like brands on her skin? Why would he want her solitary company, rather than seek enjoyment with someone free to be with him?

The horrible depth of her self-involvement through their time together caused her selfish heart to ache with his absence. She only had herself to blame that he left without her this evening. Her ingrained suspicion, distrust and resentment of her father had tainted anything beautiful she and Joseph might have had.

Her mind whirled with what to do next as she rounded into the small corridor leading to the exit, her head low as she bumped straight into Esther. Elizabeth pressed her hand to her chest. 'Goodness. You gave me a fright.'

'And you almost gave me a heart attack. What are you still doing here?'

'I wanted a moment alone to take in the day.'

'Oh, I understand perfectly.' Esther's hazel eyes lit with pride. 'Wasn't it wonderful? Did you ever imagine such excitement? Women and men almost lost their minds over the decorations, clothes and accessories. Pennington's has truly become the store you and Joseph envisaged.'

Esther's gaze softened as she squeezed Elizabeth's hand. 'I think you've found something very special in Mr Carter. Very special indeed. Don't you?'

'Maybe,' Sorrow curled around Elizabeth's heart as she blinked back the tears pricking her eyes. 'But there's nothing personal between Joseph and me. Not anymore.'

'So you say, but I see the way you look at him and he you.' Esther gently touched Elizabeth's arm, her gaze sympathetic. 'Don't throw that away, Elizabeth. It would be sacrilegious.'

Suddenly the thought of going home was the worst possible scenario with which to end such a momentous day and Elizabeth slipped her hand into the crook of her friend's elbow. 'How about you join me for a drink? Or will you abandon me too?'

'Who's abandoned you?'

'Mr Carter. And no, don't look like that. The fact he has is entirely my fault. Joseph is innocent in everything that has happened between us.' She tugged Esther towards the door. 'Come on. The Cavendish is calling.'

347

They walked outside, and the lightly falling rain did nothing to lift the sinking of Elizabeth's heart that Joseph wasn't with her tonight.

39

Joseph stared at the front of Edward Pennington's house. The building was a grand town house, yellow-stoned and sash-windowed, situated on the most prestigious street in Bath. Yet, despite the uniformity of its neighbours, a person could sense something different about the Pennington house. The front door was painted black, the brass knocker an exotic bird rather than the customary lion. Joseph smirked. Well, at least Pennington seemed to know he was more peacock than king of the jungle.

Glancing towards the drawn drapes at the window, Joseph hoped he was admitted without preamble because there was little chance of him leaving. As soon as he heard the whispers that Elizabeth's father had returned, Joseph had left the store and come straight to Pennington's home, no longer willing to keep his feelings and his determination to be with Elizabeth from her father. He might have given Elizabeth a seemingly stringent ultimatum, but Pennington hadn't had the guts to do the same to Joseph

He lifted the knocker and stood respectfully back, his shoulders squared.

The sound echoed inside before the door slowly opened. The butler stood to attention. 'Good evening. How may I help you?'

Joseph dipped his head. 'Good evening. I wonder if I might speak with Mr Pennington?'

'Mr Pennington is at dinner, sir. Might I suggest you return in the morning?'

'I'm afraid I need to speak with him this evening.'

The butler's amicable expression hardened. 'I'm sorry, but Mr Pennington had just returned from an extended trip overseas. He does not wish to receive visitors this evening. If I take your name, I can tell him —'

'My name is Joseph Carter. I assure you Mr Pennington is unlikely to turn me away when he knows I'm on his doorstep.'

The butler glared before he stepped back. 'Wait here.'

The door closed.

Turning his back, Joseph contemplated the beautiful, affluent surroundings of Royal Crescent. If anyone doubted Pennington's wealth before learning of his address, they certainly wouldn't thereafter. The outskirts of the park glistened and glittered beneath the lamplight, the early evening dew playing like crystals upon the grass. Dusk had fallen suddenly tonight, indicating imminent rainfall.

Joseph lifted his gaze to the sky. Rain or not, he wouldn't leave without speaking with Pennington. Elizabeth meant too much to him and he could not walk away from her without trying a final time for them to be together. Tonight, he would make his intentions towards her clear to Pennington. Joseph wanted her hand and he wanted her father to accept her skills and talents. He would not leave this house with anything less.

The door opened behind him and Joseph turned.

The butler waved him inside. 'Mr Pennington has asked that you join him in the drawing room.'

Joseph stepped inside. 'Thank you.'

'Can I take your coat and hat, sir?'

Joseph passed over his coat and hat. 'Shall I go up?'

'Indeed, sir.'

'Thank you.'

Joseph walked upstairs and entered the drawing room.

'Mr Carter. This is a surprise.'

Pennington's voice reverberated from the wing chair in front of the fireplace.

'Thank you for agreeing to see me, sir.' Joseph walked around the chair and stood in front of Elizabeth's father. 'I trust your trip was successful?'

Pennington narrowed his eyes and slid his gaze over Joseph from head to toe. 'Help yourself to a drink from the bureau and join me by the fire. I must say, I'm deeply disappointed my daughter isn't with you.' He gave an inelegant, disapproving sniff. 'I imagined the pair of you joined at the hip during my absence.'

Joseph strolled to the bureau and tipped an inch of brandy into a snifter. Stoppering the decanter, he took a sip before returning to the seat beside Pennington. 'I've no idea where Elizabeth is this evening. I wanted to speak with you alone. Give you the opportunity to respond to what I have to say without Elizabeth present.'

Pennington smiled, his gaze steady. 'Well, that is interesting. I thought she might have foolishly sent you in her place to tell me why my store has been turned into a circus. I've been away for four weeks and in that time half of Bath is talking about the transformation of my store. A transformation for which I did not give my permission.'

'True, but you entrusted Elizabeth with running the store in your absence.'

'I did.' Pennington took a sip of his drink. 'It might

be her tenacity to prove herself worthy at the store has begun to take effect. I can't deny a few of her recent changes have impressed me. But . . . ' his gaze hardened, 'it also seems since your arrival, the girl is making other, more personal and, in my opinion, detrimental decisions.'

'With respect, sir, since knowing Elizabeth, she seems happier, more excited about her work and keen to try new ideas and innovations. Not just her own, but mine and those of many of the other staff, too. She's told me footfall and sales are up. Not to mention the increase in morale and production output. I see no cause for your continuing doubt of her. Unless, of course, your doubt has everything to do with my personal relationship with your daughter, rather than the professional.'

Pennington narrowed his eyes. 'You'd be wise to tread carefully, Mr Carter. I may be aging more quickly than I'd like, thinking of lessening my time at the store, but my decisions will not be affected by how my lovesick daughter feels about you. I don't trust that you hold my store, or my daughter, with the best of intentions.'

'Then I'm glad I'm here. I want you to know exactly how much both Elizabeth and the store mean to me. I love your daughter, Mr Pennington. I love her more than anyone or anything. I walked into Pennington's all those months ago expecting nothing more than the chance to have my designs brought in front of a wider audience. Neither Elizabeth or myself could have predicted our love for one another.'

'And where does your passion for Pennington's leave Carter & Son?' He shook his head, his eyes gleaming with malicious satisfaction. 'Where does your love for my daughter leave your father? Do you plan to abandon him?'

'Of course not.'

'Then what happens next?'

Joseph gripped his glass. 'My father has decided to retire. He deserves to live the rest of his life at leisure and in ways that please him. If I was to remain at Pennington's, I would do all I can to make it flourish and close my own business. I have no family other than my father. I have no heirs. Pennington's could easily become my new focus.'

Pennington carefully watched him over the rim of his glass. Joseph returned his stare, unable to decipher the look in Pennington's eyes. He would like to ascertain interest, but it would be folly to assume any positive consideration.

Joseph cleared his throat. 'I think your misperceptions of me and my feelings for Elizabeth are founded in you knowing I'm extremely ambitious and have a hunger to make money.'

Pennington lowered his glass, his eyebrows raised. 'Are they misperceptions? Have I got you so very wrong, Carter?'

'You have, sir. I have money of my own and shares in my business, the rest of which will eventually become entirely mine. I want to earn more money in order to open opportunities to others.'

'What others?'

'Those willing to work hard. Those who are desperate to make more of their lives for themselves and their loved ones.'

'You speak of the poor.' Pennington laughed. 'Is your charity supposed to impress me? Your father's little shop is supposed to fill me with confidence it isn't Elizabeth's inheritance that has you so desperate to seduce her into loving you?'

'What you choose to believe is up to you. I don't need Elizabeth's money and never will. I may be ambitious, but I want Elizabeth as my wife more. I want to walk, work and laugh beside her every day. Elizabeth and I are far from adolescents, sir. We do not need your permission to be together. To love one another. All I ask — '

'She's my daughter, Carter. Mine.' Pennington's eyes flashed with a dangerous fire, his cheeks mottling with patches of angry redness. 'For years, I've hankered for a son, but not anymore. Now, I know — '

'Your daughter is enough.' Satisfaction eased Joseph's frustration. 'You now know Elizabeth is equally as capable of running your empire as any son you might have sired or any man you might employ. Am I right?'

Pennington stared and Joseph held himself rigid, waiting for whatever came next.

Pennington exhaled and slowly pushed his glass onto a mahogany side table. 'I think it's time for you to leave, Mr Carter.' His voice was quiet, his gaze once again unreadable. 'I will speak privately with Elizabeth tomorrow. What I have decided to do next with the store, with Elizabeth, has absolutely nothing to do with you.'

Joseph put down his glass and slowly stood. 'I love her, sir.'

'So you say, but first I need to make my own investigations, because if I discover you have an agenda that doesn't involve the care of her heart . . . ' His jaw tightened. 'If I believe that she might well choose you over the good of the store, I will have no choice but to cut her out completely.'

Joseph stilled. 'What?'

Pennington slowly smiled. 'You heard me.'

Fury pulsed in Joseph's ears as he curled his hands into fists. 'She loves the store. It's her life. Pennington's has nothing to do with her and me being together.'

'It has everything to do with you if you marry her, you fool. So, if you really, truly, love my daughter, you'll walk away from her.'

Sickness rolled through Joseph on a nauseating wave. He could never have her. The store was meant to become Elizabeth's. It was what she had worked for her entire life. Hadn't she told him as much? He would never make her choose between Pennington's and him.

He dipped his head and squeezed his eyes shut before slowly opening them. He lifted his gaze to Pennington's and held out his hand. 'Elizabeth's happiness will always be my priority. She deserves for the store to be hers. I'll step away.'

Pennington narrowed his eyes, his gaze boring relentlessly into Joseph's. Finally, he clasped Joseph's hand. 'Maybe there is something of a gentleman in you, after all.'

Joseph shook Pennington's hand and left the room. He took his coat and hat from the butler and departed, his heart broken but his conscience whole.

But be damned if he would not speak with Elizabeth one last time.

40

Elizabeth leaned against Esther as they emerged from The Cavendish Club.

'I do believe you to be a little intoxicated.' Esther laughed and firmly cupped Elizabeth's elbow, pulling her up straight. 'Can you imagine what Mr Pennington would say if he could see us now.'

'So, what if he does? We've had a fabulous night celebrating the store's success.'

They both laughed, and Elizabeth snaked her hand into the crook of Esther's elbow.

'We're going to be rather worse for wear in the morning.'

'We are . . . let's hire a carriage. It's starting to rain.'

The paving slabs beneath Elizabeth's feet swayed back and forth and the lights from the hotel across the road flickered incessantly as Esther hailed an approaching carriage.

Tears burned behind Elizabeth's eyes and she angrily swiped away evidence of her weakness. It was her father's and Joseph's fault that she'd drank far too many glasses of over-priced champagne. Esther was a real friend to accompany her in Elizabeth's bout of self-destruction, but she certainly didn't deserve Esther's generous sympathy. It was Elizabeth's inability to stand up to her father, to feel truly deserving of such a wonderful, kind and inspiring man as Joseph, that had brought her to this sorry state.

The hired carriage pulled to a stop at the kerb and she and Esther climbed unsteadily inside. The

356

carriage drew away, jostling and bumping through the city towards her father's house. Smiling softly, Elizabeth brought to mind every blessing she had in her life: the store, Esther, Mrs Woolden, her staff . . .

A tear escaped from beneath her closed lids. Would she ever manage to hold on to anything other than the professional? Would she never have a chance of love, happiness, a marital home and children? Things she desperately wanted but kept secretly locked in her heart for fear it would weaken her hold on the store.

'My goodness, Elizabeth. You have company.'

Esther's voice and her prod to Elizabeth's upper arm jolted her fully awake as they pulled to a stop outside her house. 'What do you mean? It's after midnight.'

Her friend nodded towards the window.

She followed Esther's gaze and froze.

Joseph.

Elizabeth swallowed against the sudden dryness in her throat.

Esther squeezed Elizabeth's fingers. 'Tell me what to do. Shall I send him on his way? You can wait in the cab while I speak with him.'

'No, no, I'll be quite all right.' She dragged her focus from Joseph's intense gaze, her heart racing. What was he doing here? Why now, when she was too inebriated to refuse him, to stand her ground and make him leave. She grasped the door handle. 'You go home. I'll be quite all right.'

'Are you sure?'

'Of course. Is there a man on the planet I can't manage?'

'Before Mr Carter, I would have said no, but now . . . '

Elizabeth pushed open the door and Joseph immediately stepped forward and handed her from the
carriage. They faced each other, their hands joined as
the cab slowly moved along the street.

Gathering her senses, Elizabeth eased her hand
from Joseph's and fumbled in her purse for her key.
'What are you doing here? Do you know how late it
is?'

'I do.'

Where was her key? Of all the times to lose the
blessed thing. She briefly closed her eyes before forcing her gaze to Joseph's. 'What do you want? Why are
you here now, of all the times you could've been?'

'I don't understand.'

She glared, traitorous tears burning behind her eyes.
'I looked for you. At the store. I thought, I thought
you might want to celebrate with me. Just be with me
because . . . because . . . Oh, damnation.' Her tears
spilled. 'I have no right to say these things to you, but
tonight . . . ' She swiped at her cheeks. 'Just tonight I
would have liked to have celebrated with you.'

'We need to talk.'

His sombre tone and the distant look in his eyes
was too much to bear. She dragged her gaze from his
strong jaw and she looked to her bag, finally locating
her key and whipping it out in triumph. 'I must go in
before I'm soaked. Goodnight.'

'Elizabeth . . . .'

'I can't speak with you now. It's too late. Too late
for everything.'

She stepped towards the house and he grasped her
elbow. 'I've spoken with your father.'

Her stomach knotted as the air left her lungs.
'When?'

358

'This evening.'

'Oh, Joseph. Why would you do such a thing?'

His jaw tightened. 'Because I love you and want to be with you. I thought I could reason with the man, but —'

'Reason with him?' Hysteria bubbled up and lodged like glass in her throat. 'My goodness, you really haven't listened or understood anything I've told you of him, have you?'

He glanced towards her front door. 'Please, Elizabeth, stay out here and talk with me. Listen to me.'

Elizabeth stared. To stay with him was as dangerous and tempting as inviting him into her home. She lingered over her study of his wonderful mouth. 'Fine. We'll talk. I can't refuse you anything, no matter how damaging that might be to either of us.'

* * *

Joseph led Elizabeth from the Royal Crescent and along a cobbled path into the park. The rain had ceased, and he laid his coat down on a bench for her. She sat and pulled her purse into her lap, her focus on the full, leafy trees ahead of them.

He sat and leaned forward, dropping his clasped hands between his knees to stem the nervous energy rippling through him. Now he was with her, he had no idea what to say or do to take the sadness from her beautiful green eyes or return the colour to her pale face, shining almost pearlescent beneath the street lamp beside them.

He blew out a soft breath. 'I had to see your father, Elizabeth. I had no choice.'

She turned, tears glinting in her eyes. 'Why?'

He took her hand, relieved when she did not immediately snatch it away but instead wrapped her fingers firmly around his. He pulled back his shoulders. 'I said I'd wait for you. Do whatever I had to for us to one day be together, but I can't wait. Time is too precious to wait for the things that make us happy, that bring us joy. We should grab them at the first opportunity. For me, those things come from being with you. I visited your father in the hope of making him understand that.'

'But he would never understand anything remotely connected to affection. The man thrives on control and his own pleasure. He didn't care for my mother's feelings and he doesn't care for mine. Why on earth would he care for yours?' Tears glazed her eyes once more. 'You will have made things infinitely worse for both of us.'

Indecision battled inside him. He could walk away, or he could fight for this beautiful, intelligent and sensual woman. Not for himself, but for her. She needed to see how deserving she was of the love and cherishing he would bestow on her for the rest of his God-given life. He tightened his grip on her hand. 'Maybe I have made things worse, but for you, I suspect I've made them better.'

'What do you mean?'

'Your father damn near admitted you're as capable as any son he might have had of running the store. For all his stand-offishness and judgement, he's come to trust you with Pennington's.'

Her gaze darted over his face, uncertainty creasing her brow. She eased her hand from his and stood. Taking a few stiff steps along the path, she stared into the dark distance.

Joseph's heart beat fast. Couldn't she see how wonderful she was? That Edward Pennington no longer controlled her, but needed her?

She whirled round. 'So, what was the outcome of your discussion with my father? Did he order you from the house? Embrace you as his future son-in-law?' She swiped at her cheek. 'Your optimism inspires me, Joseph, but my goodness, how easily it blinds you.'

Frustration rose, and he joined her at the path's edge. 'The outcome was that he rejected my love of you. Rejected that I'm sufficiently solvent in my own right and do not want or need your money. He rejected that I wish to marry you —'

'Marry me?' She stilled, her eyes wide. 'You actually told him you wish to marry me?'

'Of course.' Gently, he touched his finger to her chin, raising it so she looked directly at him. 'Why wouldn't I? I want to marry you so much. But even that was not enough to prevent your father from threatening to completely disinherit you unless I disappeared.'

Her gaze immediately hardened. 'He said that?'

'Yes.' He slipped his finger from her chin. 'And that's the last thing I want, so I'll leave the store.' He forced a small smile. 'Please, don't look at me like that. You know, sooner or later, Carter designs will be known throughout Bath, maybe throughout England.' He winked. 'I'll make it so.'

She didn't smile or even blush under his flirtation. Instead, she stepped back and crossed her arms. 'And you think I care more about my inheritance than you?'

'Elizabeth —'

'Before you, the store meant everything to me, but not anymore. You're right. My father needs me, not

361

the other way around. I broke from you, from us, for fear he would manipulate and play with you. But now I understand that you are not my mother. You scare him, Joseph.' She gripped his hand. 'Together, we absolutely terrify him. If he wants to cut me out, disinherit me, let him. We can start somewhere else. Together.'

Love for this amazing woman pulsed hard in his heart. 'Elizabeth, I can't let you — '

'Stop.' She pressed her finger to his lips, her eyes full of passion and love. 'No man will ever *let* me do anything ever again. It's you I want, Joseph, and with our love strong and safe inside us, we can travel the world. Go wherever we want and start something new. Something of our very own.'

He gripped her waist, hope bubbling inside him when, only hours before, he'd began to fear he'd lost her forever. 'That's truly what you want? You would walk away from everything for me?'

'Isn't that what you were willing to do for me?'

'Yes, but . . . '

She laughed softly. 'Then that's what we will do. We'll walk away together.'

Lifting onto her toes, she kissed him, and Joseph pulled her hard to his chest and returned her kiss with every ounce of the love and passion burning inside him. Her fingers gripped his arms and she pulled him closer, kissing him deeper.

She smiled. 'It's our time now.'

He nodded. This was it. Come what may, he would never consider being away from Elizabeth Pennington ever again.

41

Elizabeth stared around Pennington's bustling, gloriously lit foyer, her heart filled with pride. In the week since Joseph's confrontation with her father, he had chosen to stay away from the store and the house.

During a brief conversation, he'd told her his retirement was imminent and he'd met someone aboard the liner he'd taken to tour Europe.

A woman, judging by her father's unusual reticence, who had quickly come to mean more to him than his habitual passing fancies. In a strange way, Elizabeth was happy for him. She hoped this new emotion she suspected in him, would go some way to her father understanding her love for Joseph.

When she'd told him as much, he hadn't laughed at her, as she'd expected. Instead, he'd studied her for a long moment, before turning and retiring to his study. The contemplation in his eyes had confused her and when she'd knocked on his closed door to speak with him further, he'd demanded she leave him alone.

Which was what she had done ever since.

If he did not care for the safety of her heart, then he could no longer name himself as her father. She and Joseph had plans of their own. Plans in which her father had no place.

Whenever she and Joseph had stolen time together, they had embraced and kissed frantically, and then lovingly, as though they did all they could to purge themselves of her father and everything his threats had jeopardised between them.

363

When the day came that she walked away from the store, she would do so with her head held high and her arm in Joseph's. The man with whom she wanted to spend the rest of her life. His soon-to-be wife.

She glanced at her left hand, at his mother's diamond engagement ring, which he'd surprised her with that very morning. Her heart stumbled. She had never been so happy.

Taking a deep breath, she continued her walk through the store's aisles, all too aware her father could appear at any time. She did not doubt he would make his returning presence known with as much fanfare as possible.

She nodded and smiled at the shop girls standing or serving behind their counters, enjoying their smiles and shiny, happy eyes. Their pretty expressions were devoid of the wariness and tension that had been so prevalent whenever her father walked his rounds. The newly installed security men touched their hats or dipped their heads to her and, best of all, the customers were far too busy shopping to notice her. Just as they should be. When she and Joseph left Bath, they could at least take pride in what they had achieved in these past months.

A hand at her elbow halted her and Elizabeth turned.

'Joseph . . .' Her smile faltered. His face was stony, his beautiful blue eyes dark with concern. She frowned. 'What is it?'

'Your father has just walked into the store.'

Her gaze shot along the aisle towards the front doors. 'He's here?'

'Yes.'

She smoothed her hands over her jacket and pulled

364

back her shoulders. 'Fine. Then let us greet him.'

'He's not alone.'

'Who is with him?'

'A woman. An older woman.'

'An older woman?' Elizabeth frowned. 'It could be his sister. My Aunt Margaret.'

Joseph shook his head. 'I wouldn't have thought so judging by the way he's looking at her.'

Elizabeth stared along the aisle again. So, her suspicions her father had met someone special were correct. Had he brought this woman here to meet his daughter?

She exhaled a shaky breath. 'Then let us say hello.'

They strode into the foyer.

Her father stood on the centre P imbedded in the marble floor. The elegant, beautifully dressed woman stood with her arm on her father's, her silver-grey hair stylish, coiffed beneath a wide-brimmed hat. Her gentle gaze perused her surroundings, a soft, appreciative smile playing at her mouth. The calm serenity emanating from her, inexplicably eased the tension in Elizabeth's shoulders.

Joseph's voice was soft and laced with a smile at her ear. 'Shall we say hello?'

'Oh, yes. I think absolutely we should.' She walked forward. 'Good morning, Papa.'

Her father's gaze snapped to hers, his expression immediately hardening. 'Elizabeth, my dear.' He looked to Joseph, his gaze unreadable. 'Mr Carter.'

'Sir.'

Elizabeth stepped closer and held out her hand to his companion. 'Elizabeth Pennington. It's nice to meet you, Mrs . . .'

She eased her hand from Edward's arm and took

365

Elizabeth's hand. 'Heimann. Annabelle Heimann. The store is just wonderful.'

'Thank you.'

She smiled and turned to Elizabeth's father. 'Might I not look around while I'm here?'

With his gaze locked on Elizabeth's, her father nodded. 'Of course. I'll join you as soon as I can.'

Annabelle Heimann nodded at Elizabeth and Joseph, her eyes kind. 'It was lovely to meet you both. I look forward to seeing you again soon.'

Elizabeth nodded and smiled, before Annabelle wandered away. She faced her father and forced a lightness into her voice 'Mrs Heimann seems exceptionally nice, Papa.'

'She is.' His gaze lingered at Mrs Heimann's retreating back before he met Elizabeth's gaze. 'I've made a decision I'd like to share with you.'

Unease whispered through her. 'A decision?'

'Indeed. You see, despite Mr Carter coming to see me, I had already decided my time at the store was over. The only decision left to make was who would succeed me.' He looked between her and Joseph, his gaze steady. 'I am now ready to tell you the outcome of my thinking. Shall we go to my office?'

'Of course.' Her heart picked up speed and she turned to Joseph. 'I'll come and find you shortly.'

'I think it best Mr Carter join us, Elizabeth. This concerns him, too.'

Her father walked away, leaving her and Joseph staring after him.

Elizabeth slowly exhaled. 'Whatever he's about to say will be something unexpected. Something neither of us will immediately fathom nor understand. We need to be prepared for anything.'

'I am. Are you?'

She looked into his eyes, fell into the honesty and love that resided so deeply and so honourably for her and only her. She smiled softly. 'Yes. Yes, I am.'

His gaze lingered on her lips as if he meant to kiss her, before he looked in the direction of the lift. 'Then let us not keep ourselves in suspense.'

They travelled to the fifth floor in silence. The atmosphere crackled and burned with tension as Elizabeth considered and discarded every possible scenario that could be about to unfold. To do so was a waste of time. Her father sang to his own tune, nobody else's.

The lift doors opened, and she and Joseph exchanged a single, encouraging glance before she walked ahead of him into her father's office.

He stood at the window behind his desk, looking down at the street. His shoulders were rigid, his back straight.

Joseph closed the door and her father turned.

His expression was one that Elizabeth hadn't seen for many, many years. His eyes, locked on hers, were shadowed with regret, remorse . . . apology. Her stomach knotted with trepidation so much deeper than if she'd seen spite and anger in his eyes.

He blinked, and his expression hardened once more as he waved her and Joseph to the visitors' chairs. 'Sit. Both of you.'

The urge to refuse his demand bit at Elizabeth's tongue and she turned to Joseph. He gave an almost imperceptible shake of his head. She exhaled. He was right. To retaliate now would only risk turning what she hoped would be an amicable separation from her father into a volatile one. No part of her wanted to come to hating him and he her. For now, at least, their relationship held a trace of civility.

He paced back and forth behind his desk, his hands clutched behind his back. He halted, his gaze firmly on Joseph. 'Am I to truly to believe you love my daughter, Carter? That your adulation of her has nothing to do with the millions of pounds she'll inherit upon my death?'

'Yes, sir. I love your daughter more than I ever could any amount of money. I want to marry her and love her for the rest of my life.'

'You told me you'd be willing to walk away rather than have me disinherit her, yet here you still are. Why should I believe anything you say?'

Elizabeth inched forwards in her seat, her body rigid with tension. 'Joseph is only here because I asked him to stay. If you want him gone, then I shall go too. We won't be separated. Not ever.'

Her father held her gaze and Elizabeth recognised rare hesitation in his expression as he mulled over hers and Joseph's words.

She slumped her shoulders. 'Papa, when Joseph walked into the store, I immediately saw something different in him. Something new and exciting. Before long, my intuition was proven right. Joseph and I are not a threat to you, or the store, and now I can't imagine working without him beside me.' She looked to Joseph and grasped his hand. He winked, giving her silent encouragement to say everything in her heart. 'But more than that, I love him. Deeply. I am happier, feel more alive . . . ' She swallowed as her heart raced with the need for her father to truly hear her. 'He's made me feel validated and valued for the first time in my life. He sees me, Papa. He sees who I am and loves me for my faults as well as my strengths. I've never had anyone accept me the way Joseph has, including you . . . especially you. I won't be without him.'

Her father's eyes softened unexpectedly. He cleared his throat and blinked. Elizabeth stilled. Were tears glazing her father's eyes?

She faced Joseph, who continued to study her father, his brow furrowed and his body tense, as though, like her, he waited for the real Edward Pennington to emerge.

Slowly, her father walked around the desk and gestured with a flip of his hands for Elizabeth to stand, his palms outstretched toward her. Uncertainty rippled through her as she stood and cautiously slid her hands into her father's.

He halted and stared at her fingers.

Snapping his gaze to hers, her father tightened his grip. 'You are engaged?'

She swallowed. 'We are.'

He looked at the ring again, then at Joseph, a muscle twitching in his jaw. 'You assumed this without my permission?'

Joseph pulled back his shoulders, his eyes burning with determination. 'I love her, sir.'

Her father faced Elizabeth and softly studied her before inhaling a heavy breath. 'I'm old, Elizabeth. I was old from the moment your mother took her life and I was to blame.' He turned his gaze to Joseph. 'I'm so sorry for what I did to your aunt, Carter. If I would've known . . .' He shook his head and looked at Elizabeth once more. 'I watched you grow under the hands and love of your mother and governess, I trained and coaxed you to think of nothing else but Pennington's and then expected you to marry a man of my choosing. I was wrong.'

Elizabeth stared at him, her shock halting any words. Was he ill? She swallowed. 'Papa . . . '

He turned to Joseph. 'I intend paying a difficult visit to your father, Carter. The time has come that I attempt to atone for the pain I've caused your family and give the next generation the opportunity to work together for a better, happier and more profitable future.' He faced Elizabeth. 'I knew you were lost to me from the first time I saw you look at Carter at the drinks party.' He smiled softly. 'The store rightfully belongs to you, my dear. I am just sorry it has taken me so long to realise it.'

Tears burned, and Elizabeth blinked them back, dread whispering around her heart. 'Are you ill, Papa?'

He laughed. 'No, my dear, I'm not ill.' He looked past her to Joseph. 'Mr Carter?'

Joseph stood and tugged down his jacket. 'Yes, sir.'

Elizabeth tensed, her mind racing with what this change in her father meant.

He released one of her hands and clasped Joseph's elbow, his other hand still firmly holding Elizabeth's. 'I'm leaving you the store, Elizabeth. From this day forward, it will be yours to do with as you will. I'm giving you . . . ' He looked to Joseph. 'Both of you, the reins. I just hope that neither of you lives to regret it. You have my blessing.'

He dropped his hands and with a final, long look into her eyes, her father turned and left the office.

Elizabeth stared after him, her body trembling. 'Did he just . . . '

Joseph moved silently behind her and wrapped his arms around her waist. 'Yes, I believe he did.'

She rested her back against his chest, her whole body softening as years of tension seemed to slip away. 'But I don't understand. After all this time, he's giving me the store?'

'It's yours, Elizabeth.' Joseph whispered against her ear. 'Your father believes in you as we believe in us.'

She nodded, her tears blurring the corridor through the open door. She turned in Joseph's arms. 'I love you so much.'

'I love you too.'

She laughed and swiped at her cheek. 'We can finally let the real Pennington's Department Store open its doors. Everything will be all right. We'll be together, Joseph. In everything.'

'We will. Always.'

Elizabeth kissed him and pushed her father far from her mind, at least, for now. The store was hers. Was Joseph's. She could not wait to see what that would mean and what events would unfold from here on in.

But, more than that, Joseph was finally hers. For-ever.

Acknowledgements

To say the journey from writing *A Shop Girl in Bath* to its acceptance by Aria, has been a long one is an understatement. There are so many people who have encouraged and supported me along the way, but I want to give special thanks to my critique partners, Jessica Gilmore, AJ Nuest and Sharon Struth whose comments and feedback were invaluable.

Also, a very, very special thank you to my fabulous editor, Caroline Ridding, who saw the potential in the Pennington's series and whose enthusiasm might even surpass my own! And finally, to my copy editor, Jade Craddock, who I believe, has made *A Shop Girl in Bath* the very best it can be.

We do hope that you have enjoyed
reading this large print book.

Did you know that all of our titles
are available for purchase?

We publish a wide range of high
quality large print books including:
Romances, Mysteries, Classics
General Fiction
Non Fiction and Westerns

Special interest titles available in
large print are:
The Little Oxford Dictionary
Music Book, Song Book
Hymn Book, Service Book

Also available from us courtesy of
Oxford University Press:
Young Readers' Dictionary
(large print edition)
Young Readers' Thesaurus
(large print edition)

For further information or a free
brochure, please contact us at:
Ulverscroft Large Print Books Ltd.,
The Green, Bradgate Road, Anstey,
Leicester, LE7 7FU, England.
Tel: (00 44) **0116 236 4325**
Fax: (00 44) **0116 234 0205**

Other titles published by Ulverscroft:

A WIDOW'S VOW

Rachel Brimble

1851. After her husband saved her from a life of prostitution, Louisa Hill was briefly happy as a housewife in Bristol. But then, her husband is found dead. Left with no means of income, Louisa knows she has nothing to turn to but her old way of life. But this time, she'll do it on her own terms. Enlisting the help of Jacob Jackson to watch over the house, Louisa is about to embark on a life she never envisaged.

GIN PALACE GIRL

Gracie Hart

After being orphaned as a child, Mary is taken in by her mother's friend — and ex-prostitute — Nell. But when Nell dies her step-father takes too much of an interest in Mary and she is forced to leave home, landing a job as a barmaid. Mary thinks she's landed on her feet. More so when she catches the eye of William Winn, the charming owner of a glamorous new hotel. Will she ever be good enough for a man like William?

THE MOTHER'S DAY CLUB

Rosie Hendry

Norfolk, 1939. The residents of Great Plumstead agree to open up their homes to evacuees from London. Pregnant Marianne is determined to make a fresh start for herself. Local lady Thea opens up her beautiful home, Rookery House, to the evacuee mothers. The ladies of Great Plumstead are fighting their own battles on the Home Front — but can the community come together in a time of need to protect their own?